MERCILESS

A Born Assassin, Book 1

JACQUELINE PAWL

ALSO BY JACQUELINE PAWL

Defying Vesuvius

A BORN ASSASSIN SERIES

Helpless (prequel novella)

Nameless (prequel novella)

Merciless

Heartless

Ruthless

Fearless

Limitless

Copyright © 2021 by Jacqueline Pawl

All rights reserved.

No part of this book may be reproduced in any form or by any electronic or mechanical means, including information storage and retrieval systems. without written permission from the author, except for the use of brief quotations in a book review.

1

An arrow whistled through the air, its razor-sharp point flying straight toward Mercy's face.

Thunk!

Sharp pain burst through Mercy's ear as the arrow buried itself in the aged wooden wall against which she stood. She released a long, slow breath. A twist of the breeze, a slight shift of the fingers was all it had taken to bury the obsidian tip in the old shed, rather than Mercy's skull. A warm drop of blood welled where the jagged teeth had cut her skin, and it trailed slowly down the soft flesh of her ear.

"Almost got your pointy little ear, elf," Lylia said, sauntering forward to examine her shot. Mercy scowled up at the apprentice as she pulled the arrow from the wall, sending another fat droplet of blood down Mercy's ear. Lylia smiled coldly. "But we wouldn't want to do that, now, would we? Lose those ears and you might forget you're no better than dirt."

She feigned a yawn. "Do you intend to talk me to death? Because if so, I'll gladly save us both the trouble and end the misery of being in your company. Just give me your dagger."

Lylia glared down at her, toying with the fletching of the

arrow. She was a strange sort of beautiful—perfect to the point of flaw, her delicate features cold and unnatural. Despite their varied backgrounds, all the Daughters of the Guild shared a similar look, a beautiful ferocity, but none were as striking as Lylia. Her long hair was a bright auburn woven through with deep red, her eyes an icy blue. "Mercy, you're *so* funny."

"Well, it's good to know those born bereft of a sense of humor are still capable of recognizing it in others. Here I thought you were hopeless."

"Trade places!" Mistress Trytain shouted from somewhere to her right.

Mercy strode to the mark on the forest floor, beside which her smaller and less ornate bow was resting against the trunk of a tree. It was nowhere near as flashy as Lylia's bow, but it did the job. All around them, arrows thudded into the walls of the dilapidated old shack, and Mistress Trytain's snapped corrections rang out across the small clearing.

Lylia leaned against the wall, her arms crossed loosely over her chest. "You really think you can beat that shot? You're good, but you're not that good."

At the next mark, Faye glanced over. Although she was eighteen, six months older than Mercy, her porcelain skin and large hazel eyes gave her a deceptive air of youthfulness, of innocence. She shot Mercy a wicked grin and mouthed, *Show her just how wrong she is.*

A matching smile tugging at her lips, Mercy nocked an arrow and lifted the bow. She took a moment to gauge the wind's speed and direction, then pulled the string taut. It naturally slid into place between the calluses on her fingers, formed through years of archery training, and she felt the bow quiver with barely restrained power.

She closed her eyes—and released.

Crack!

Someone let out a gasp, and for a moment, the forest was deathly silent. Mercy opened her eyes. Lylia was standing against the wall, her arms limp at her sides. Her head was bent at an awkward angle.

No—not bent.

Pinned.

The arrow was a millimeter from Lylia's face, the tiny braid she wore above her ear caught in the teeth of the arrowhead. Mistress Trytain approached from farther down the line and examined the shot. When she pulled it from the wall, a few strands of Lylia's hair floated away on the breeze. The rest of the apprentices wandered over, gaping. Mercy's chest swelled with pride at the mix of awe, envy, and fear she saw on their faces. *You told me I was nothing for so long—that I don't deserve my place here. Do you still believe that?*

"Now seems as good a time as any to end today's lesson," Trytain said, arrow clasped in her hand. "Remember, one millimeter can be the difference between life and death, and between failing and fulfilling your contracts. In a real fight, your blood will be pumping so hard you won't be able to hear anything else. Your hands will shake and you will be jittery with adrenaline. Never flinch. You must learn to control your reflexes, or they'll betray you when you need them most."

A wave of murmured agreement rose from the apprentices. Their tutor nodded a dismissal, and girls in groups of twos and threes began gathering their supplies and walking back toward the castle. Trytain was one of a handful of instructors in the Guild, former Daughters who were fortunate enough to grow too old to continue working assassination contracts. She taught fighting and weaponry to the apprentices—girls ranging from six to eighteen who had found a home in the Guild. Most had made their way to the Guild after a family tragedy. Some had come searching for a new beginning. Others had been abducted by Daughters instructed to find new 'recruits.'

Regardless of their background, all had some idea of what the outside world was like.

All except Mercy.

She slung her bow over her shoulder and paused at the edge of the forest path, waiting for Faye to finish gathering her arrows. Lylia's ice-blue eyes flashed with annoyance as she passed. "You may be skilled with a bow, knife-ear, but that's never going to make you one of us," she hissed. "Elves were only meant to be two things in this world: slaves and savages."

Mercy's fingers twitched reflexively for the bow slung over her shoulder as Lylia strode away, laughing. If Mother Illynor didn't have a rule against killing other members of the Guild, Lylia wouldn't have lasted a week here.

"What in the Creator's name is wrong with her?" Faye spat as she jogged over.

"She's jealous." As much as Lylia hated her, she knew—*all* the apprentices knew, even if they refused to admit it—that Mercy was the most skilled among them.

Faye shook her head, falling silent as they started toward the castle. As they walked, Mercy tilted her head back and stared up at the familiar canopy of leaves, a sea of fire over her head. Kismoro Keep sat in the center of the Forest of Flames, nestled among tall redwoods that burned with leaves in every shade of red, orange, and gold imaginable.

Mercy looked at her friend sidelong. "Is it true that some trees are green?"

"Most are." Faye knew better than to laugh at Mercy's ignorance of the outside world. "They're green like grass, except when autumn comes, the leaves turn red and orange— like these—and fall. They crunch underfoot and dance on the breeze and scrape against the stone in the streets. When spring comes, the trees begin again, with flowers and little green buds. It's breathtaking."

"It sounds pointless. Why not keep their leaves year-round, like these?"

"The *why* is not important. Because they do. Because the Creator willed it to be so—"

Mercy groaned. "The Creator. How can you believe so wholeheartedly in the existence of something for which you have no proof?"

Faye rolled her eyes. "Some*one*. It's called faith for a reason."

"I call it foolishness."

"You do not believe in anything you cannot kill with your sword."

"Practicality."

Faye snorted. "Whatever you say."

They continued on in silence, listening to birds sing and tiny creatures scamper in the underbrush, until the trees suddenly parted. The Keep rose high before them. Ivy and moss covered its ancient ramparts, which had begun to crumble after thousands of years of existence. Mother Illynor had never bothered to have the walls repaired; the Guild had no enemies from which to defend itself and, even if it did, the forest was far too thick for any army to maneuver easily. A tall iron gate hung over the entrance to the courtyard, permanently open since most of the chain suspending it was more rust than metal.

Mistress Trytain was waiting for them by the gate, her usual sour expression firmly in place. "Clean yourselves up before coming down to dinner. The armorers have arrived."

A flash of excitement shot through Mercy. "Already? I thought they were coming next week."

"They must have made good time. Now, shoo. Change

your clothes and, for the Creator's sake, brush your hair for once. I won't have the Strykers thinking we take in strays."

"Yes, Mistress."

Mistress Trytain looked them over, frowning, then strode across the courtyard and into the Keep, her cloak swishing behind her. Mercy turned to Faye and found her friend grinning broadly, excitement sparkling in her eyes.

If the Strykers were here, it only meant one thing:

By the end of the week, one apprentice would become an Assassin.

2

In her bedroom, Mercy ran a comb through her thick hair, growling when the teeth caught on a tangle. The window's closed shutters blocked out most of the light, but she didn't care. Even if her room were furnished with a mirror, she wouldn't have used it. She knew what she'd find. She wasn't ugly...just plain, with dark eyes and unruly black hair that preferred to knot rather than curl. Yet somehow, it never managed to hide the telltale points of her ears.

"Creator's ass!" Mercy snarled when the comb tore at yet another knot. She tossed it aside and tied her hair into a bun at the nape of her neck, huffing with frustration when three strands immediately sprang out and fell into her face. She contemplated cutting them off for a moment too long before shaking her head.

The Strykers awaited.

She didn't bother to change her tunic; the one she was wearing was clean enough, and the three others hanging in her wardrobe were scratchy and threadbare after years of scrubbing on a metal washboard. Nothing in the Guild was wasted; when a Daughter was killed, her belongings were scavenged, sorted, and distributed among those remaining. As the sole elven apprentice, Mercy was allotted the worst of the lot. The knees of her riding pants had patches sewn over patches, and her cracked leather boots bore the imprints of someone else's feet—but thankfully, she'd only have to put up with them for a little while longer. Soon, she'd leave the Keep for her first assassination contract, and Mother Illynor always gave the Daughters a cut of the job's pay. She'd be able to purchase all the luxuries she could afford.

Mercy left her room in the apprentices' wing and descended the spiral staircase, emerging on the main floor of the castle. The hallway was dimly illuminated by torches, the faint scent of smoke mingling with the divine aroma wafting from the dining hall—roasted meat, hearty stew, baked vegetables. The cooks had clearly outdone themselves.

When she cracked open the door to the dining hall, the chatter of voices and the clinking of cutlery on plates swept over her. Two long tables spanned the length of the room—one for the Assassins who had already sworn their vows, and one for the apprentices. Mistress Trytain and the other tutors were flitting about, snapping orders to servants and arguing amongst themselves about the plating of food and other mundanities. At the moment, there were fewer than thirty Assassins, apprentices, and tutors living in the Keep, in addition to a fleet of slaves, stablehands, cooks, and maids.

Right now, every person's attention was focused on the four men lounging on the cushions in front of the head table.

The Strykers were laughing and conversing jovially with the young women hanging around them, lapping up every word they deigned to utter. The youngest, Oren—a skinny, mousy little man—had lost weight since he was last here, Mercy noted. His cheeks were pockmarked and sallow from a recent illness, and his chest rattled with a cough when he laughed. Even so, Cianna knelt on the floor at his side and blushed every time he looked at her, and Lahrenn giggled at something he said. The sight filled Mercy with equal parts mirth and disappointment that her fellow Guildmembers would so easily forget themselves in the presence of men.

To their left, Faye was seated on a cushion beside a handsome blond man named Nerran, each clutching a goblet of wine. He said something that made her eyes light up. When she threw her head back and laughed, he took the opportunity to shift closer and rest a hand on her thigh. Her lips curled into a flirty smile before her gaze landed on Mercy, still standing just beyond the threshold. She waved Mercy over, giggling when Nerran leaned over to nuzzle her neck.

"Mercy! You remember Nerran, don't you?" she asked when Mercy drew near enough to hear them over the chatter.

"Of course. How could I forget?" Last spring, Nerran had spent the entire night flirting with all the apprentices, including Mercy, but she had the grace not to mention it now. After all the wine he'd consumed, he probably didn't even remember it. "How have your travels been?"

He shrugged, looking slightly annoyed at the interruption, but he was either too polite to say anything or wise enough to know better than to offend a member of the Guild. "Traveling with the Strykers keeps me busy, as always, but it's good pay for an honest day's work."

"They're planning to sail to Feyndara after the Trial," Faye said. "How exciting is that?"

"Feyndara? What's it like?" Mercy asked, unable to hide her curiosity. "Is it true that elves rule there?"

"It is. Not only is it ruled by elves, but it's rumored the royal family is planning another attack on the Cirisor Islands. A bunch of damned fools they are." Nerran laughed humorlessly, draining the last of his wine. "They've been trying to claim the Islands for generations, but all they've managed to do is get more soldiers killed on both sides. Well, not killed—the soldiers *vanished*."

Mercy glanced over and met Faye's confused look. "Vanished?"

"You didn't know? Well, I suppose you wouldn't, living so far from the rest of the kingdom." He leaned forward and dropped his voice to a whisper, his eyes alight with the charisma of a natural storyteller. "Nearly two decades ago, in the last bout of the Cirisian Wars, a group of Feyndaran soldiers lured our men into a trap. We don't know who won the resulting battle because every single soul—*fifty men*—disappeared. There one day, gone the next."

"No bodies?" Mercy asked, intrigued.

"Not a one."

"How many times are you going to tell this story, man?" Hewlin, the leader of the Strykers, said. He reached over to ruffle Nerran's hair. "Last week it was only forty men."

Nerran dodged a teasing punch from Faye. "Liar!"

He caught her wrists, grinning. "Believe me or don't, the moral's the same. Whatever riches the sovereigns think those islands hold, I say leave it to the Cirisians. The Feyndaran queen is in love with a fantasy, and our own dear king is simply mad."

"Be glad he's not around to hear you call him that," Hewlin warned, "or he'd relieve you of your head."

"I'm not afraid of him."

"Oh, no? Let's see if you say the same next time we're in the capital."

Mercy left them to their friendly bickering, her attention snagging on the woman who had just entered the room. The headmistress of the Guild wore a high-necked black blouse under a gleaming silver breastplate, looking like a warrior from the ancient tales of the Year of One Night. Her head was bald save for two rows of short horns that started at her temples and met in a V at the nape of her neck. As she walked, her reptilian scales glittered green and gold under the flickering light of the wrought iron chandeliers.

Mother Illynor turned as Mercy approached, her slitted pupils wide. "Mercy. How are you enjoying the evening?"

"It's fine. Mother, the Trial—"

The Guildmother's expression changed immediately. "We have discussed this before. *At length*."

"You're going to announce the girls who are competing tonight, are you not? The girls who will fight to become Assassins? Allow me to try. I'm ready—"

"Mercy—"

"I'm the best," she insisted, desperation causing her voice to rise. She had trained all her life for the chance to prove her worth to the other members of the Guild. After all the torment and mocking she'd endured at the apprentices' hands, hadn't she earned the right to at least *try?* "You've seen me in training—you know I'm right. Ask Mistress Trytain. Today, at archery practice—"

"That's *enough*, Mercy!" Illynor's face was pinched, annoyed. "I do not doubt your ability, nor do I doubt your dedication. It gives me no pleasure to deny you this, but you know our rule: you must be eighteen to compete in the Trial. You can compete next year."

"Two months, Mother! You would have me wait until next year's Trial because I was born two months too late? I could spend that time serving you!" When a few apprentices looked over from their table, Mercy sucked in a breath and forced herself to lower her voice. "You say the others are ready. Lylia and Faye have been here for ten years. Cianna has been here for seven and Xiomar, five. I have been here for *seventeen years*. You shoved a sword into my hands the day I learned to walk."

"Don't be melodramatic. You shame yourself."

Mercy opened her mouth to retort, but faltered when her gaze landed on a stranger lingering in the doorway, amusement on his face. Surprise rippled through her. Five Strykers had come, then, although she didn't know this one. She scowled, turning her attention back to Illynor. "You raised me to fight for the Guild. That is what I intend to do."

Mercy brushed past Mother Illynor, shooting a dirty look at the man who had been eavesdropping on their conversation as she passed. A cool breeze wrapped around her as she stepped out onto the balcony overlooking the courtyard. The springtime cold had not yet given way to summer, and the crisp wind shot straight through the thin fabric of her tunic. She glanced back at the grand dining hall and watched the flames in the hearth dance. She'd go back inside, but not until the flush of anger had left her skin.

How could Mother Illynor, knowing Mercy as well as she did, deny her the chance to finally serve the Guild? How could she keep Mercy from the only thing she had ever wanted? Every spring's-end for as long as she could remember, the arrival of the Strykers signified the start of a competition to determine that year's Daughter; a week of hard training, the Trial, and the swearing of the Guild's sacred oath by the victor.

This year, I will become a Daughter, she vowed. *No matter what Illynor says.*

Footsteps sounded behind her, too heavy to be one of the girls. The intruder took a deep breath and Mercy rolled her eyes. Most people, even when trying to be silent, had noise-making habits of which they weren't even aware . It was what made them such easy targets.

"Out with it," Mercy said after a few seconds.

"Forgive me, I could not help but overhear your conversation—"

"You could have, but you listened anyway." She turned

around. Sure enough, the young man who had been watching her was standing there, his hands tucked into his pockets. He was only a few years older than she, perhaps twenty or twenty-one. A few strands of his brown hair had fallen from the ponytail at the nape of his neck, softening his otherwise severe features. The jacket he wore was simple but finely made, loose around the collar and fitted through the torso—a capital city fashion. "What do you want?"

"Must I want something? Perhaps I came out for a bit of fresh air."

"Everyone wants something. The only question is how far they'll go to get it."

The stranger moved to her side and rested his elbows on the railing. "I want to help you."

She shook her head. "The only help I need is not something you can provide."

"You want to fight in the Trial. Maybe I could make that happen."

Her gaze dipped to the dagger sheathed at his hip, the ornate hand guard sculpted with whorls of shining steel. It was Stryker-made; flawless. Each newly-sworn Daughter received a Stryker-made weapon after swearing her vows, as unique as the assassin wielding it. He noticed her staring and pulled the weapon out, offering it to her hilt-first. "Try it."

Her fingers curled around the grip, and she examined the dagger, admiring the razor-sharp edge and perfect balance.

"Show me your skills," the stranger said softly, encouragingly.

Mercy lunged, slashing out in a wide arc. He jumped back and blocked her next swing with his forearm, letting out a startled laugh. She whirled, the blade whistling as it cleaved the air, and struck again and again until he was pinned between her and the railing, the tip of the knife an inch from his neck.

"I'm impressed," he said, not looking the least bit intimidated by the blade at his throat. In fact, he was beaming at her. "You've been well taught. I'll help you win the Trial."

Mercy stepped back. "There is nothing you could do or say that would make Mother Illynor change her mind. I've tried."

"I'm sure I could think of something," he said as he tugged the dagger out of her hand, returning it to the sheath at his side. "My name is Calum Vanos."

"Mercy."

His lips twitched, fighting back a smile. "Strange name for an assassin."

Mercy shrugged. "The Guildmother has a fondness for irony. If I had a name before I came here, I don't remember it. This one serves its purpose well enough."

Behind them, a chorus of cheers erupted from the dining hall. Calum glanced at the double doors. "What's going on in there?"

"Mother Illynor is announcing the names of the girls who will be competing in the Trial."

"Well, we shouldn't miss that." He started toward the doors, then paused when he realized Mercy wasn't following. "Don't you wish to hear?"

She shook her head, turning back to look out over the courtyard. "I already know. It's Faye, Lylia, Cianna, and Xiomar." *And me,* she thought, *but how?* As confident as Calum appeared in his ability to help her, she was certain he wouldn't achieve anything. Mother Illynor was not one to be tested, and she wouldn't be kind if she discovered Calum meddling with her sacred Trial.

Calum regarded her sympathetically.

"I don't want your pity," Mercy growled.

At once, his expression shifted, and he returned to her

side. "Then perhaps you can answer something for me, seeing as I am new to the Strykers. Why do you call her 'Mother?'"

"Most of us come here as children. The Guild is the only family we know, and we make it official when we swear our vows and forsake our family name."

"And Illynor is the head of the Guild, a Qadar from Gyr'malr?"

Mercy nodded. "She's been here from the beginning, hundreds of years ago. She and her sister were exiled from their country, so they created the Guild, taking odd jobs until they built up the reputation we have today."

"Mercy! There you are, love."

They turned as a very flushed and *very* drunk Faye pranced through the door. Her long blue-black hair was free of its usual braid, falling in a tumble of loose waves to her waist. She stumbled over to Mercy and wrapped an arm around Mercy's shoulders, her breath scented with the sour tang of wine. "Did you hear? I'm going to be in the Trial!"

"Yes. You've known you'd be competing all year."

"We should celebrate!" She did a double-take, belatedly noticing Calum standing beside them. "You can come, too!"

"Oh, I think you've done enough celebrating tonight. We have training tomorrow morning, remember?" Mercy said, slipping an arm around her friend's waist when she swayed dangerously close to the balcony railing. "Come on, I'll help you to bed."

Faye slurred an objection, but Mercy ignored her and guided her toward the dining hall's double doors. Calum lingered at the railing, an amused grin on his lips. "Consider my offer," he called as they stepped into the dining hall.

3

Breakfast the next morning was a quiet affair. Most of the girls and Strykers were nursing various degrees of hangover from the previous night's celebration, and yet the energy in the air was almost palpable. In a few minutes, Mother Illynor would announce the form in which the Trial would take place: archery, hand-to-hand combat, tracking, hunting—all skills necessary for an Assassin. Despite still feeling jaded by Mother Illynor's refusal to include her in the Trial, Mercy couldn't wait to hear.

The door at the end of the hall flew open, and all eyes rose to see Calum sauntering in with a broad grin, seeming to revel in the attention. He walked down the long central aisle, nodded a good morning to Mother Illynor and the tutors, and plunked down on the bench next to Mercy. She frowned.

"Careful, love, or your face might get stuck that way." He reached for a roll and took a bite, grinning slyly at her.

"Don't call me that."

"I like calling you that."

"Okay," Mercy said, turning to face him. "I'll rephrase that. Call me that again and I'll gut you. Understood?"

Calum nodded, although the teasing glint in his eyes didn't fade. He glanced at Faye, who was sitting across from him. "Is she always this moody?"

"No," Mercy said.

"Yes," Faye responded at the same time. When Mercy glared at her, she smiled. "Careful. You heard what the man said."

"You have training today?" Calum mumbled around a mouthful of bread, turning back to her.

"Of course."

"Come visit me when you're finished. You know the way to the forge?" When Mercy nodded, his grin grew. "Excellent. Don't keep me waiting too long."

"Vanos," said a deep voice.

Calum swallowed and looked up as Hewlin's hand dropped onto his shoulder. Instantly, his expression shifted into respectful admiration of the older man. "You came up with something?" Calum asked, and Hewlin nodded. Behind him, the rest of the Strykers had begun filing out of the room.

"We should go now so we can make sure it's finished in time for the Trial. Sorry to drag you away from your friends."

Calum started to rise, but Mercy caught his arm. "What is it?"

He bent down and whispered, "Later, you'll see. I promise. Right now, I must go help." He straightened, and his voice returned to normal as he swiped another roll. "Don't forget to visit me later, love."

Mercy turned to smack his arm, but he had already darted out of reach, chuckling. "He's an idiot," she muttered as she turned back to the plate before her. Faye merely raised a brow.

A few minutes later, Mother Illynor's chair screeched against the floor as she stood, surveying the gathered Daughters and apprentices. "Faye, Lylia, Cianna, Xiomar. The four of you have completed your training, and by the end of this week, one of you will become a Daughter." Her gaze flitted to each girl in turn. "The Guild demands a price: your loyalty, your strength, your blood, and your life. Will you give these and more to serve alongside your Sisters?"

"We will," they said in unison.

"And you, dear Daughters," she said, focusing on the other table. "I have found these girls to be ready and worthy of swearing the Guild's vow. Upon the completion of the Trial, will you accept the victor and welcome her into our family?"

"We will," they responded.

"The Trial is the final test each apprentice must pass before swearing her oath. It will test not only your physical strength, but your mental and emotional strength, as well. This year's Trial is…close-range combat."

Mercy grinned. Combat-related Trials were one of the favorites in the castle. The only rule was that a competitor could come as close to killing her opponents as possible without stopping their hearts.

"In accordance with tradition, the victor, upon swearing her vow, shall receive a weapon crafted by the master blacksmiths of the Strykers, some of the finest weapon-makers and armorers in the world."

Faye reached across the table and seized Mercy's hand. "I've heard their blades cut through a man's armor like he's wearing nothing at all."

"It's true," Threnn, an eleven-year-old apprentice, interjected from a few seats down. "I've seen it."

"Oh, yeah? Where?"

Threnn opened her mouth, then closed it, pouting. "I've seen it," she repeated, and Faye laughed.

"Never you mind. It's a fine prize. I wonder what it will be? A sword or dagger? A crossbow, maybe?"

Mercy shrugged. As Faye turned to speak with the girl

beside her, Mercy stared up at Mother Illynor, who had taken her seat and resumed eating. Sensing someone's gaze on her, she glanced up. Mercy tensed, waiting for the Guildmother's eyes to find her. They did—then they passed over her as if she were made of nothing more than air.

Mercy glared at the uneaten food on her plate, her appetite gone. After seventeen years of dedicated training, only two months separated her from her rightful place in the Guild.

She refused to wait for next year.

As the Daughters left to complete their chores and the slaves cleared the table of the breakfast scraps, Mistress Trytain gathered the apprentices for training in the courtyard. She gestured for Lahrenn to step forward, and the second she did, Trytain lunged, feigning a punch to the girl's right. When Lahrenn moved to block, Trytain dipped and struck her unguarded side. Then she hooked her foot around the girl's ankle, sending her sprawling, gasping for breath. Somewhere down the line of apprentices, Lylia snickered.

Trytain straightened, not even winded. "Find a partner and practice sparring. Do not expect your adversary to fight honorably. When you are on a contract, the fight is not over until you or your opponent is dead. You must do whatever is necessary to survive."

"Come on, lazy," Faye singsonged, dragging Lahrenn to her feet. The girl made a noise of protest, but her lips spread into a grin as she and Faye faced off. Mercy felt a flash of envy as she watched them. She'd never had Faye's charm, her easy smile. After a lifetime dedicated to learning to kill for coin, there were few facets of her that weren't sharp as a dagger.

Mercy turned just as Lylia's fist swung toward her face.

She raised an arm instinctively to block it, ducking low and slamming her other fist into Lylia's abdomen. Lylia ducked under Mercy's next swing, landing two quick jabs to Mercy's ribs. Pain flared in her side, still sore from the last time they'd sparred. Lylia had managed to knock Mercy to the ground and land a hard kick there. Mercy grimaced and took a step back, falling into a defensive position. Lylia smiled.

The monster of a girl *smiled*.

The sight made Mercy's blood boil. She'd never been well liked among the apprentices—they'd all teased her for her elven blood and pointed ears—but Lylia had despised her from the moment they'd met. Rumor had it she'd gotten a perverse sense of pleasure from terrorizing her wealthy father's slaves before coming to the Guild. Predictably, being bested by Mercy in training had done *wonders* for their relationship.

Lylia advanced, cocking her fist to strike Mercy's face. At the last moment, Mercy twisted and caught her arm, wrenching it behind Lylia's back so hard she let out a yelp. She struggled, but Mercy kicked the back of her leg, sending her to her knees, and wrapped her arm around Lylia's throat.

"Not bad for an elf, huh?" Mercy asked as the girl gasped for breath. Lylia drove her elbow into Mercy's stomach, and she grunted, but didn't loosen her hold. "Yield."

In response, Lylia reached up and raked her fingernails across Mercy's face.

Mercy recoiled as blood welled from the cuts. "Yield, Lylia. Give up. ...No? I'm happy to keep going after all the shit you put me through," she spat. "Cutting me, threatening me, trying to poison me. For years—"

"*Mercy!*" Mistress Trytain snarled, in a tone that made it clear she'd called her name several times already. Two strong hands clamped around Mercy's arms and dragged her backward. Trytain shoved her against the Keep's stone wall, her face a mask of fury. "I said," she seethed, positioning herself between them, "that's *enough*."

Only then did Mercy realize that everyone else had stopped fighting and were currently gaping at her—except this time, they were watching with horror, not awe. Lylia was gasping, slumped on all fours as she sucked in breath after pained breath.

"You," she rasped, lifting her head to glare daggers at Mercy. Bruises had already begun to form around her neck. "I will *kill* you." She struggled to her feet and shoved Lahrenn aside when the girl reached out to steady her. "Get away from me."

Faye moved to Mercy's side and placed a hand on her shoulder. The adrenaline of the fight faded as Lylia stormed into the castle, slamming the door behind her. Mercy scowled and rubbed her ribs where she'd been hit. She wouldn't have killed Lylia, even though she hated the girl.

"Now," Trytain said with a sharp clap, startling the other apprentices. "The show's over. Get back to work."

Little Threnn ran into the courtyard and planted herself before Mistress Trytain. "Mistress Sorin is in need of assistance. She asked for Mercy."

Mercy turned to leave, but Trytain caught her arm. "Watch yourself, girl. We spar, but we don't try to kill our own."

She bit her tongue, holding in the retort that sprang to her lips. *She didn't yield. And* you *told us not to fight honorably!* Instead, Mercy nodded, backing away. When the tutor turned back to watch the girls train, she pivoted on her heel and escaped to the safety of the castle.

"Mistress Sorin?" Mercy called as she rapped on the ancient wooden door of the infirmary. "You sent for me?"

The door swung open and a woman filled its frame, her pinched face relaxing when she saw Mercy. "Follow me."

An earthy, herbal scent filled her nose when she stepped into the room. Cabinets teeming with jars of herbs and bottles of salves lined every wall, and four cots were crammed against the fall wall of the room. A young girl lay on the closest one, curled in a tight ball.

"Her name is Arabelle," Sorin said, shuffling through papers on the desk. She opened a thick leather-bound book and flipped through until she came to a drawing of a seven-petaled flower, pink with stripes of white in the center. "Ever seen that?"

Mercy leaned over the healer's shoulder to read the label scrawled above the image. "Lusus blossoms. No, I don't think so."

"I'd be surprised if you had. They're not indigenous here; they thrive in the warmth of the north. So, the question is how little Arabelle managed to stuff her pockets and eat enough to paralyze a full-grown Qadari warrior." She gestured to a pile of crushed blooms on the bedside table, her nose wrinkling in distaste.

"She found them here? Did one of the Daughters bring them back from a contract?"

"I don't know; she was unconscious when Amir brought her here. He's the one who found her."

Mercy sat on the edge of Arabelle's bed. Although the apprentice was only covered in a thin sheet, her cheeks were flushed, and a sheen of sweat glistened on her forehead. Mercy pressed the back of her hand to the girl's forehead. "She's running a dangerously high fever."

"A side effect of the poison, I'm afraid. I've managed to counteract the toxin, but I don't know how long she'll be able to hold the medicine down. That's why I need you to help me make more." Sorin crossed the room and grabbed a mortar and pestle, which she passed to Mercy, before digging through the cabinets and returning with a small collection of ingredients: a jar of Nightwing berries, a bundle of Claudia's Song leaves, and dried Benza root. "Mash those into a paste, please."

Mercy mixed the amounts Mistress Sorin instructed as the healer bustled around the room. Most of Sorin's time was spent in the infirmary, but she sometimes ventured out to instruct the apprentices in poisoning and general healing. Mercy had a natural talent for herbalism, Sorin had claimed when she decided Mercy would one day succeed her as the Guild's healer. Whether she truly believed that or had simply taken pity on the child the apprentices had always picked on remained to be answered. Either way, she'd taken Mercy under her wing and had been helping her develop her skills over the years. This was hardly the first time Mercy had been pulled out of training to assist in the infirmary.

"You should be glad the girl's asleep," Sorin said, "or she'd bolt the second she saw your face. How'd you manage this?" Her fingers lightly brushed the scratches on Mercy's cheek.

She grimaced. Lylia had deserved the turn the sparring session had taken, but she didn't doubt the girl would strike back twice as hard. "It's nothing. I'm fine. Worry about Arabelle."

"I worry about all of you here. Do not act like you are worth less than anyone else."

"I'm not. I'm acting like *poisoning* is more serious than a few scratches."

Sorin shot her a knowing look. "Mercy..."

She sighed. "Lylia."

"Of course." Sorin shook her head, a shadow passing across her face. "I know Illynor has a rule against killing one another, but I'm not going to apologize for praying that girl meets some unfortunate accident on her first contract."

Mercy smiled to herself, continuing to mix the medicine. Affection for the healer rose within her. Sorin cared for all the apprentices here, but she'd chosen Mercy to be her assistant out of everyone in the castle. She was the only one who had never treated Mercy differently because of her blood. Sorin was the closest thing Mercy had to a mother.

With a few more pounds of the pestle, the deep red berries mashed into a bright purple juice, which thickened with the addition of the root and leaves. "Nightwing for pain," Mercy began, "Claudia's Song as a muscle relaxant—but what does Benza root do?"

"It counteracts the poison. Lusus blossoms are very dangerous. They take their time to kill you. It targets the blood first, so it can spread through the entire body rapidly. Within minutes, the victim will complain of a pounding headache and suffer weakening of the muscles and loss of coordination. Complete paralysis follows thereafter as the muscles and organs begin to shut down."

"You consider that slow?"

"No, the worst part comes after. The victim will remain paralyzed as the toxin seeps into the brain tissue and nervous system—if he's lucky, he'll die in a matter of hours. Most people last a few days, sometimes a week or more." Mistress Sorin frowned as she brushed a strand of Arabelle's hair back, cupping her cheek the way a mother would her child. "The poison kills in the worst way possible. Can you imagine being a slave in your own body, unable to move, unable to do anything but wait for the agony to be over? It's not a death I'd wish on anyone, contract or no. Luckily, the poison had not taken hold of her completely. With enough rest and medicine, she'll be up and moving again within the week."

Sorin stood and wiped her hands on her dress. In the

blink of an eye, her expression returned to a carefully-crafted mask of neutrality—her healer's face, Mercy called it. "Hand me the mixture and that dropper there," Sorin said, pointing to the desk. Jars clinked against each other as she searched through a chest and emerged with a small bottle in hand. "A little bit of milk to soothe the throat and help the medicine down. Now hold her mouth open."

Mercy parted Arabelle's lips while Mistress Sorin filled the dropped with milk, then squeezed out the contents into the back of the girl's throat. She then dropped a spoonful of the paste into Arabelle's mouth. The healer looked up and caught Mercy's doubtful expression. "The medicine looks awful and tastes worse. Trust me, this is the easiest way to administer it."

They held their breath, waiting for some response.

Arabelle's eyelids fluttered, then she jerked upright and vomited on the floor.

Sorin didn't bat an eye. She handed the girl a bucket, which Arabelle clutched to her chest as she blinked up at Mercy dazedly. Mercy attempted a reassuring smile but didn't fail to notice the way the girl shrank away, huddling into Sorin's arms. She didn't know the apprentice, but clearly the apprentice knew her. It seemed her reputation preceded her. As Sorin had said, the scratches on her cheek didn't help.

"Unfortunately, Benza root also acts as an emetic in some people," Mistress Sorin sighed. "She's going to need another dose. You remember the quantities?"

Mercy nodded and returned to the mortar and pestle, pouring in each ingredient as Sorin had instructed.

"Good, good," Sorin said distractedly. When Mercy glanced over, she pointed to a jar on a nearby shelf. "Winter's Lace can also be used as a substitute when Benza root is not readily available, but it's not as effective at neutralizing the poison—it requires twice the quantity."

"...Why are you telling me this? Are you leaving?"

"I have to go to Ellesmere for some supplies, and I want you to take over the infirmary while I'm gone." Arabelle began retching again, and Sorin rubbed her back with a hand. After the vomiting gave way to rasping, dry coughs, Sorin eased the girl back onto the pillow and pressed a cloth to her forehead. "I want you to take care of her. I trust in your judgment and skill."

"But the training—"

"Another Daughter can watch over her while you're out with Trytain—just make sure she knows what to do if Arabelle needs another dose."

Mercy's gaze slid to the blossoms, fierce protectiveness sweeping over her. She had no great affection for the apprentices her age, but Arabelle was young, and she'd done nothing to deserve this. "I'm not entirely convinced the timing of her poisoning was an accident. The Guild has no shortage of enemies. Do you think one of the Strykers brought the blossoms? Could someone have planned to slip the poison to a Daughter?"

"Hewlin and the others have been coming here for many years. If one of them wished to harm an Assassin, he would have done it already, and he would have paid for it with his life. That new Stryker—Calum, is it?—is a stranger to us, but he didn't strike me as a fool." Sorin returned the cloth to the bedside table and moved to Mercy's side, lowering her voice as Arabelle began to snore softly. "As you said, the blossoms could have belonged to one of the Daughters. Aelis and Tanni were in the north recently. It's possible one of them brought some back. Whatever it is, keep an eye out for more. We don't need anyone else falling ill."

"I will, Mistress Sorin."

"Thank you. Now, let's give her the next dose. Be ready with the bucket."

4

Hours later, Mercy stumbled up the stairs to the apprentices' wing, the scent of Arabelle's vomit stinging her nose. It had taken four doses before the girl had managed to stomach the cure, and Mercy's hand ached from working the heavy mortar and pestle for so long. Right now, all she wanted was to collapse into bed.

She entered her room and moved to the window, letting the breeze sweeping in through the open shutters chase away the stench of vomit clinging to her skin and clothes.

Something shifted in her periphery, and she stiffened.

Lylia.

Her hand slowly drifted to the small dagger tucked into her waistband, hidden by the drape of her tunic. She carried it everywhere. She held her breath, pretending to stare out at the night as she listened to the intruder approach, just a whisper of leather boots on the stone floor. Her fingers closed around the grip of the dagger and she whirled, the blade flashing.

"Creator's sake, Mercy, it's me!" Calum yelped, jumping back.

"Calum!" Mercy tossed the dagger on her bed and punched his arm, annoyance flaring. "You ass. I could have killed you. Why were you trying to sneak up on me?"

"I was waiting to find out why you didn't meet me in the forge like I asked you to. When you didn't seem to notice me, I decided to see if the rumors about the Daughters' legendary skills are true." He shot a wary look at her dagger. "Apparently they are. I'll watch out for that one next time."

"There won't *be* a next time." Mercy sank onto the edge of her bed and began unlacing her boots. *Sure, Sorin. He's not a fool at all.*

"What happened to your face?"

She glanced up at him. "Nothing."

"It doesn't look like nothing." He reached out as if to trace the lines of the scratches, but she recoiled before he could make contact. Clearing his throat awkwardly, he stepped back and shoved his hands into his pockets. "Why didn't you come to the forge?"

Mercy cringed. After everything that had happened today, she'd completely forgotten to visit him in the smithy. "I was busy. I'm here now," she said as one of her boots thumped to the floor. "We could go down there."

He rolled his eyes. "Not now. Hewlin locks up the smithy at night—says he doesn't want anyone to steal the weapon."

"Is that what you wanted to show me? The prize for the Trial?"

"That, and something else. Illynor has something special planned, something no one is supposed to know about until the night before the competition."

She pulled off her other boot. "But you're going to show me. Why?"

"Because I think you're going to win."

"I *will* win. I just need to figure out how to convince Mother Illynor to allow me to compete."

He spread his hands. "Hello? Did you forget the offer this wonderful, handsome, generous man gave you last night?"

"I think you missed an adjective or two there. Infuriating. Arrogant, perhaps. Why do you want to help me?"

"I told you, I think you can win."

"No." Mercy shook her head. "You stated an opinion. Why are you, Calum Vanos, interested in helping some random apprentice? I'm not even a *kind* apprentice. What's in it for you?"

"Yesterday you said everybody wants something, right?" he asked, and Mercy nodded. "Well, this is going to help me get what I want."

Mercy waited for an explanation, but he provided none.

"Come to the smithy tomorrow while everyone is eating dinner—I'll wait for you there. Find a reason to come down. Tell them you find me irresistible and incredibly charming, and then you won't even have to lie." He grinned at her, then turned on his heel and walked out of the room. "Goodnight, love," he called as he stepped over the threshold and closed the door behind him.

The next day, Mercy descended the stairs to the smithy, a plate of food in one hand. The armorers' workroom was deep below the castle, and the warmth from the forge steadily intensified the further Mercy went, as did the scents of leather and sweat. She knocked on the heavy door at the end of the hall, and Calum opened it a few seconds later, a blast of heat slapping her across the face.

He grimaced, pushing sweat-slick hair off his brow. "I know—building a forge underground wasn't the architect's best idea. Sorry about the heat." He stepped aside and Mercy followed him into the room, surveying the expensive tools and scrap metal lying around. A stand of weapons stood against the far wall, and the beauty of the blades left her speechless.

She tore her gaze from the swords and extended the plate —heaped with fruit, roasted vegetables, and wild game—to Calum. "Here."

"Put it there, I want to show you something first." Calum led her over to one of the workstations, where a notebook lay open. He tapped the page, looking proud. "This is the weapon we're crafting."

The drawing depicted a double-sided dagger. The grip was wide enough to be used with two hands or one, and the note scrawled along the bottom of the page said it would twist apart at the center to create twin blades. "Wow," Mercy breathed. "This is amazing. I've never seen anything like it."

"Hewlin designed it. You saw how excited he was yesterday. Come here, that's not the only thing I wanted to show you." He gestured for her to follow him toward the opposite wall, this one hidden behind an old, stained curtain. "Mother Illynor's trick," he announced as he pulled it down.

Mercy gasped. Four mannequins were clad in identical suits of armor, differing only in color: black, gold, silver, and bronze. The shining metal was smooth, simply designed, elegant. A wicked grin spread across Mercy's lips. "Close-range combat...wearing armor."

She should've guessed it. Combat in armor was one of the hardest Trials, and a favorite among the Daughters. It was unlikely they'd have to fight in full armor as an assassin, but it served to prove their prowess in battle. Piercing the gaps between the thick steel plates was challenging for the most seasoned of Daughters. It was exactly the type of challenge Mother Illynor would issue; if her apprentices were skilled enough to disable an opponent in full armor, they were more than ready to swear the Guild's vow.

"Look at the visor," Calum said, holding up a gleaming helmet. "As long as it doesn't get knocked off in the fight, it'll hide your face."

Dangerous, dangerous hope bloomed within Mercy for the first time since she had spoken to Mother Illynor. "No one will know it's me until after I win."

"Exactly. The armor was made for humans, so it'll be a little big, but I can pad the inside so it'll fit better."

He grinned at her, and excitement fluttered in her stomach. After so many years of training, she was finally going to become who she was meant to be. "Thank you," she said, meaning it wholeheartedly. She couldn't keep the smile from her face.

"You're welcome."

Mercy turned and headed for the stairs, needing to work off the sudden burst of energy within her.

"Aren't you hungry?" Calum called after her.

She paused, her foot on the first stair. When she looked back, he raised a brow and held up the plate.

"Let's go for a ride."

Half an hour later, Mercy and Calum were riding on horseback along the bank of the Alynthi River, just within the tree line.

"This is incredible," Calum said, staring up at the canopy of leaves over their heads. The rushing rapids of the river hummed in the background, and—aside from Mercy's murmured directions—the two of them had enjoyed a comfortable silence until now.

"I'm sure you've seen better in your travels with the Strykers."

"Not really." He shrugged. "I only joined last summer, and

I've never been outside of Beltharos. Hadn't even been *around* Beltharos much until a few years ago."

"You lived in the capital, didn't you?"

"You could tell by my clothes, I bet."

"And your manner of speaking. You were tutored as a child, I'm guessing." She lifted her chin and peered down her nose at him. "I suppose you think that makes you clever."

"You're trusting me to help you win the Trial. You'd better hope I'm as clever as I think I am," he responded. "My father worked in the castle, but he died when I was very young. Still, his connections allowed me to be tutored by some of Sandori's finest. What about you? I heard you've been here all your life. How did that happen?"

"It's not an interesting story."

"No? Well, we can make up a better one then." He grinned, tapping his chin in feigned thoughtfulness. "Let's see... You're the bastard child of King Ghyslain and Feyndaran Queen Cerelia, hidden away in the forest where no one can discover your true lineage." He bowed theatrically, dipping forward as gracefully as he could manage while sitting in a saddle. "Your power could topple kingdoms, Your Highness."

Mercy spurred her horse forward, smirking despite herself. Damn it—he *was* charming. "That's quite the tale."

"I can do you one better. Hmmm... Your father was the leader of an elven resistance group in the capital, your mother a noble lady in the Sapphire Quarter. They fell in love and fled to the forest to raise their child in peace."

"Yes, that's exactly it."

Calum clicked his tongue to his horse, and his leg brushed Mercy's as he pulled ahead. "Won't you tell me the truth? What's there to hide? It's the past. Who cares?"

"*You* seem to care a lot."

"I'm curious. It's one of my few character flaws."

Mercy sighed. "One of the Daughters, Llorin, was working on a contract in Sandori. Her target was some nobleman who worked closely with the king. She tracked him to his estate and murdered him in his study, but one of his slaves discovered her standing over the body. That slave was my father. She was going to kill him—the Guild doesn't leave witnesses—but he offered me in exchange for his life. Llorin accepted. She brought me here, and my father fled the capital that night. I was one week old."

"He just handed you over?"

"Yes."

"And your mother?"

"I assume she went with him. Or she's dead."

"Don't you ever wonder about them?"

"Why would I?"

"Because they're your parents!" Calum gaped at her, dumbfounded.

"And?"

"*And?* You don't care about them at all?"

"Care about the people who abandoned me? I was brought here at one week old because my father decided his life was worth more than mine. For all he knows, the Daughters killed me or enslaved me the moment I arrived," Mercy said. "He made his choice. The Guild is my home—the only one I've ever known. It's where I'm meant to be. I would pledge myself in Illynor's service this minute if I could."

Calum slowed his horse. "Let's stop here," he said, already dismounting. He sat down against the trunk of a tree and gestured for Mercy to do the same, pulling out the bundle he'd made of the food she had brought him. He extended it to her. "Have some."

Mercy sank down beside him and stretched her legs out in front of her. She accepted a roll and left the rest to him; he was probably starving. The Strykers worked hard from dawn to dusk every day, either traveling, forging weapons, or selling their wares in markets across Beltharos and abroad. Any food that had not been dried or jarred was a delicacy to those who spent their lives on the road.

"Will you tell me about the Strykers?" she asked, unable to deny her curiosity.

Calum snorted. "You've been here a long time. You probably know more about them than I do."

"Probably," she conceded, "but everything I know came from books. Being a member is different."

"I suppose you're right. Let's see... We're an ancient order of blacksmiths created by the late King Alyxander to service the crown and provide weapons and armor to the Beltharan army. For three hundred years, the Strykers worked in the Sandori royal smithies, mastering the techniques of our warrior ancestors," Calum said, smiling wistfully.

"Then came Auric."

He nodded. "The Strykers were allowed to carry out private orders, as well. However, Auric wasn't satisfied selling swords to stuffy, overfed nobles who were content hanging their blades over the mantles in their salons, nor did he enjoy fitting the scarcely-trained farm boys who had been conscripted into the king's army with weapons they would only mishandle or lose on the battlefield. The art of crafting armor and weapons had been lost over the years, and he wished to return to the techniques of the ancient masters: the spears and crossbows of Rivosa, the poisoned daggers and traps of Feyndara, the mauls and cudgels of Gyr'malr—"

"—so he left, along with most of his brethren," Mercy cut in. "Alyxander begged them to stay, promised a mightier smithy with forges to craft the fiercest blades known to man. He promised them riches beyond their dreams."

"But they stayed true to their craft instead of their purses," Calum finished, grinning. "You know your history. I'll admit, I'm impressed."

"Seventeen years in the Guild provides a lot of time for reading."

Calum pulled out his dagger and twirled it in his palm, watching the fading sunlight reflect off the blade. "When the Strykers left, they split into smaller bands to travel more easily, and that's what we've been doing since. There must be...I don't know, fifty of us around the world."

"It's amazing. No wonder Illynor continues to welcome you all here. No one in the world crafts anything as wonderfully as you do."

Calum's gaze lifted to hers, but he didn't say anything. He just sat there, searching her face.

Her smile dropped. "What?"

He leaned his head back, staring straight up at the canopy of red-gold leaves and the sunset beyond. "Faye told me about how the others treat you. And when I handed you my dagger the other night, I saw the scars hidden under your sleeves." He reached over and pulled her sleeve down a couple inches, exposing pale, puckered skin. "After all that, why are you so desperate to win the Trial? Why not leave?"

"The simple answer? Mother Illynor wouldn't let me. She has invested seventeen years into training me."

"And the complicated answer?"

Mercy frowned. "Because it wouldn't change anything if I left. They'd think I was a coward, and if any other elves came to the Guild, they'd treat them the exact same way." She tugged her sleeve up, hiding the scars, and wrapped her arms around herself. "After I win the Trial and complete my contract, they'll see that they were wrong about me. I was meant to be an assassin. I'll have these scars for the rest of my life. They might as well mean something."

He nodded slowly, thoughtfully, then nudged her foot

with his. He jerked his chin to the bundle of food. "Help me finish this, won't you? It'll be dark soon, and they'll wonder where we've sneaked off to."

They ate in silence. Once they finished, Calum stood and extended a hand to help Mercy up. They walked their horses to the river to drink, then mounted them there, riding side-by-side to the Keep at an easy pace. The stars had just begun to twinkle overhead when they entered the courtyard and dismounted beside the stable.

"We should meet tomorrow to discuss the Trial," Calum said as they began unsaddling their horses.

"I can't—training at dawn and work in the infirmary all afternoon and evening."

"You can't escape for one moment?"

Mercy shook her head as she led her stallion into his stall. "Don't worry. The others don't want to admit it, but I am ready for this Trial. I *will* win."

"Of that, I have no doubt, *love*," he said with a teasing wink. Mercy pushed him away with a sound of disgust.

"Good *night*," she called as she walked out of the stable.

"Creator bless your sleep with good dreams."

She snorted. "I was raised in a house of assassins. My bedtime stories alone would send your god running."

5

Irella, the stablewoman and groundskeeper, started when Trytain, Mercy, and the other apprentices approached the stables the next morning. "Didn't think you were coming today," she said, glancing over from where she was tending to a tall mare. "I haven't finished brushing all the horses, and a few of them need new—"

Trytain cut her off with a wave of her hand. "They'll be fine." She entered the stable and returned with a bow and quiver slung over her shoulder. She plucked out an arrow and pursed her lips, weighing it in her hand. The apprentices watched as she twirled it between her fingers then—in the blink of an eye—nocked and aimed it straight at Mercy's heart.

"We're going to play a game," she announced.

"Mistress Trytain!" Irella cried.

A corner of Trytain's mouth twitched upward as she lowered the bow. "You have ten minutes to ride to the Alynthi River without being struck by one of my arrows. Ride fast, ride hard, and—by the Creator—*do not* ride in a straight line. I expect you to saddle your horse and be out of my sight in two minutes."

The girls scattered instantly, no one bothering to mention the obvious:

It was impossible.

In the chaos, Faye shoved Cianna out of the way and seized the reins of the horse the other girl had begun to saddle. She swung herself up and dug her heels into the horse's sides, taking off at a gallop. Cianna uttered a curse and bolted to the next stall. Mercy ran to her horse's stall, relieved to find that no one had taken him yet, although no one in her right mind would dare. Blackfoot was an enormous stallion, gray-haired with black feathering around his hooves; he was mean, ornery, and stubborn—which meant they got along splendidly.

In her haste, someone had stolen the saddle Mercy always used. She huffed, resolving to ride bareback. There wasn't time to find another saddle. Outside, Trytain counted aloud with an unnerving amount of glee. Although the arrows in this special quiver had been dulled to a blunt tip, they still left bruises that ached for weeks, if they didn't break the skin outright. Mercy reached for the bridle and tightened the straps, her brows furrowed in concentration. An arrow thudded into the wall above her head. Blackfoot's eyes widened and he jerked out of her reach, stamping his foot in indignation.

Trytain was standing in the doorway of the stable. She nocked another arrow. Mercy ducked as it sailed over her head and cracked against the wall, sending splinters of wood flying.

"Not in here, you barbarian!" Irella shouted. "For the Creator's sake, destroy the forest, not my stables!"

Mercy leapt to her feet, clutching Blackfoot's reins with

white knuckles as she ran out of the stable and across the courtyard. When they were far enough away, Mercy swung herself onto Blackfoot's back, and they sped into the forest as Trytain called, "Time's up!"

Mercy was not the only one in the forest, although it felt like that at first.

The woods were strangely quiet, the creatures that usually scampered in the underbrush scared away by the horses that had already bolted past. For a moment, the only sound was the wind whooshing by Mercy's ears, plastering her clothes to her body and sending her hair streaming behind her.

A second later, the forest was deafening.

Seven other girls riding seven other horses surrounded her, galloping so fast they flickered between the tree trunks like phantoms. Hooves pounded against the hard ground, echoing like trees falling in a storm, and branches whipped at Mercy's face. Blackfoot snorted with exertion, twigs snapping under his hooves. Every so often, an apprentice yelped when an arrow found its mark.

Mistress Trytain had a horse.

It was loud, heavy, and fast, and Mercy caught glimpses of it in her periphery. Sometimes, Trytain changed course and targeted someone else. Other times, Mercy was peppered with wooden needles when an arrow embedded itself in the trunk of the nearest tree, barely missing her.

She leaned close to Blackfoot and knotted a hand in his mane, her grip on him threatening to give way with every sudden turn and jolt on the hard, uneven ground. She could feel each powerful pump of his legs as she fought to remain on his sleek back.

Mercy jerked the reins to the side, and Blackfoot pivoted so quickly she was almost thrown off then and there. Blackfoot leapt over a fallen branch, and Mercy's head snapped back as his hooves reconnected with the earth. Mistress Trytain was behind her but losing ground with every missed arrow she was forced to retrieve. The split in the forest was just ahead, Mercy knew, and she would have to decide whether to go right—to the bank of the river, as Trytain had commanded—or left, to the waterfall.

Trytain's horse was a shadow, weaving between tree trunks with the ease of a fish in water. Mistress Trytain herself was having a harder time—she had never been a natural rider; the bouncing of the horse and the dazzling colors of the leaves were making it difficult for her to aim. Frustration was getting the better of her. She growled when yet another arrow missed, and slowed her horse to retrieve it. The other girls thundered ahead of Mercy, and she spurred Blackfoot faster, jerking the reins at the split in the forest.

Left.

The hill's incline was gentle at first, hardly noticeable, but it sharply increased until Blackfoot was snorting with the effort, quickly falling out of a full gallop. The trees here were thicker, the branches wild and low-hanging. Blackfoot's hooves trampled the underbrush, but thankfully, they were the only ones Mercy could hear. She smiled triumphantly; Trytain thought she had gone right, like all the other girls— like she was supposed to.

The forest was so thick here that light barely penetrated the canopy. Just when it seemed to be the thickest, it broke, and Mercy and Blackfoot were thrust into the open air. Thirty feet ahead, the ground dropped off in a cliff, and Dead Man's Waterfall joined the Alynthi River a hundred feet below.

Mercy patted Blackfoot's neck as he slowed to a stop.

After she slid off his back, he snorted and moved to the water's edge to drink. His body shone in the sunlight, slick with sweat. Mercy sat at the edge of the cliff, her feet dangling in the open air as she stared down at the forest spreading out before her.

A sea of red and gold swept outward for miles, the Alynthi River carving a jagged blue scar through the trees. It was said the river ran all the way to the ocean, but Mercy didn't know if that was true; she had never seen it. She couldn't imagine so much water in one place.

A figure emerged from the tree line below. It was too far to tell for sure, but the girl appeared to be Faye. There was something distinct about the way she moved, a natural grace as she dismounted and led her horse to the bank of the river. Minutes later, one, two, three more girls joined her, until all seven had made it out of the forest. Some of them waded carefully into the water, nursing the wounds left by Trytain's arrows.

Blackfoot neighed, and a second later, something hard flew into Mercy's back. She let out a yelp of surprise and turned to glare at Trytain, who was striding out of the tree line with her bow in hand.

"You didn't go to the river."

"No, I didn't." Mercy rubbed her back where the arrow had struck her spine, feeling the hard bump already forming under her skin. At least there was no blood. She picked up the arrow and tossed it aside, where it clattered in the dirt at Trytain's feet. "You always tell us not to do what our pursuers expect."

"After the stunt you pulled with Lylia, I wanted to test your ability to follow orders. You think I care about the rest of them? They *always* follow orders—every one of them, except for you." Trytain moved to Mercy's side, staring over the lip of the cliff with her arms crossed over her chest.

"Mistress—"

"You think the Guild wants Daughters who disregard our orders and do what they please? Do you think this will convince Illynor to give you a spot in the Trial?" Trytain's eyes narrowed, and Mercy shrank away from her tutor's withering gaze. "You are not clever; you are not special. You are one of hundreds of apprentices who have lived in this castle and, next year, you will swear your vows and become a Daughter. You will be a great Assassin—you're too skilled not to be—but you're a fool if you think it's going to bring you honor or glory or whatever it is you seek. It certainly won't win you the affection of Illynor or the other girls here."

"I don't care about their *affection*," Mercy spat, trying not to show how much the words wounded her. "I have always known my place in the Guild."

"*Elves* have no place in the Guild."

Mercy scowled at the toes of her boots as they dangled in the air, droplets of water beading up on the leather from the waterfall's spray.

"Would you care to hear a story?" Trytain asked.

Mercy hesitated, then nodded. She'd learned long ago that it was best to go along with whatever the tutors asked. Below, the apprentices began gathering near the tree line, peering into the forest with confusion at their tutor's absence.

"I remember every detail of the day Llorin brought you here," Trytain said. "You were this ugly, wrinkly little thing with a sharp face and pointy ears too big for your body. When you reached out and wrapped the ends of Llorin's hair in your fist at dinner that night, Illynor smiled and said you'd make a fine Assassin one day. After the meal, I spoke with Illynor and begged her to reconsider taking you in." Her lip curled in distaste. "The Guild had always trained the most beautiful, cunning, deadly *human* Assassins, and she was willing to throw all those years of tradition away for a sickly elven baby whose own parents didn't want her!

"Of course, she said if the Guild can be run by someone who isn't human, why can't we train someone who's not human? Why don't you have the same right as anyone else to become an Assassin? I laughed at her, yelled at her, threatened to leave, but she refused to reconsider. I thought if I could make her see... Elves are good for nothing but slaves. That's what the Creator made you to be—servants for his favored Creations. You're abominations, remnants of a traitorous Old God." Her eyes were distant, lost in the memory of that night. "I knew Illynor would turn the Guild into a laughingstock. That night, I snuck into the infirmary where you slept and stole you from your crib. I wrapped you in a blanket and shoved a cloth in your mouth so you couldn't make noise and wake the others.

"I walked all the way to this river—just down there." She nodded to the girls below. "I knelt on the bank and stared at your face, let the moonlight shine on you and tried to see what they saw. Where was the beauty, the grace, the power they all saw in you? What had you done, a week-old babe, to captivate them so? I searched and searched, but I never found it. All I saw were those damned *ears*. So, I wrapped you in that blanket and lowered you into the river, waiting until the cloth became heavy with water, and let you go."

Mercy's eyes widened in horror. Trytain had tried to *kill* her?

"I was ready to watch you sink under the waves, watch your body be slowly pulled under, and to face the consequences of my actions. But the sounds you made," she said, "the sounds you made were so raw, so incredibly *human*." Her voice dropped to a hoarse whisper. "It's my one regret."

Mercy gaped at Trytain, too shocked to be angry. "How

can you say that? I work as hard as any of them. I work *twice* as hard—"

"Sure, you work twice as hard and will reap half the benefits. That's how it works here—that's how it works everywhere." She shook her head. "I want you to understand that my regret isn't that I tried to drown you. It's that I failed. Because you, Mercy," she said over her shoulder as she retreated into the tree line, her bow swinging from one hand, "you will be the ruination of the Guild."

Mercy sat there for a long time, watching as Trytain appeared at the bank below and escorted the rest of the apprentices back to the castle. Faye faltered at the edge of the forest, clearly torn between waiting for Mercy and following the others, then reluctantly spurred her horse forward. Following orders. Blackfoot wandered around the clearing and nudged Mercy with his velvet-soft nose a few times. When she failed to acknowledge him, he huffed and moved into the shade to graze on the underbrush.

Mercy stared down at her fingers, unsure how to process the revelation that had been dumped into her lap, thrust into her hands, shoved down her throat.

As ruthless as the Assassins could be, she hadn't realized a grown woman could see a newborn child and decide she must die. Trytain had felt qualified to weigh the value of a life that hadn't yet had the chance to be lived. Murdering a Daughter was an insult of the highest degree to the Guild, and Trytain had been willing to accept the consequences until her humanity had kicked in.

And she *regretted it*.

Mercy stood and wiped off the dirt clinging to her legs. *This changes nothing*. She would do what she had always done:

survive. She would take their hatred and craft it into her armor, because whether they would admit it or not, she would become the best Assassin the Guild had ever trained.

You will be the ruination of the Guild.

So be it.

❦ 6 ❦

Mistress Sorin had already left for Ellesmere by the time Mercy entered the infirmary that afternoon. Noting that Arabelle was still asleep, she sprang into action. Jars clinked against one another as she shuffled through them, pausing only long enough to glance at the handwritten labels before shoving them aside. She searched through the clutter on the table, the bottles on the shelves, and the clusters of herbs drying in the corner to no avail. She sighed, frustrated, and slammed her fist on the desk.

There was a *clink*, followed by the sound of something glass rolling over the stone floor.

Mercy dropped to her knees and groped blindly across the dusty floor, squinting against the darkness. Her fingers closed around a cold glass jar, and she leaned back on her heels, grinning.

The label was distorted, partially covered by the thick white paste that had adhered it to the underside of the table, but the pink-and-white flowers inside were unmistakable.

Lusus blossoms.

"Mercy? What are you doing down there?"

She jumped, banging her head on the underside of the table. Uttering an oath, she tucked the jar into the leg of her boot and crawled out from under the desk. Arabelle was sitting upright in her bed, clutching her blanket as she regarded Mercy with curious eyes.

"Catching a rat."

"A rat!" Arabelle squeaked, drawing her knees in close. "Where?"

Mercy waved a hand in the general direction of the desk. "Don't worry about it. How do you feel?"

"...Not worse."

"We're almost out of Benza root, so I'll have to go dig some up later. Lucky for you, we have enough for one more batch." She moved to the cabinet and pulled out the mortar and pestle, then gathered the various ingredients from the rack along the wall.

Arabelle was quiet while Mercy worked, and when she finished, she sat on the edge of the cot. "Allow me to give you a little tip for the future," Mercy whispered, a conspiratorial grin tugging at her lips. "You find something you're not familiar with? Make someone else try it first. If she lives, it's safe. If not, she's a fool for trusting you."

Arabelle smiled.

"So, medicine now or later?" Mercy asked, holding up the mortar and pestle.

She considered. "Later."

"Okay." She set them on the bedside table. "Tell me, where did you find those flowers you ate?"

"In one of the Strykers' bags. Elia said they carry weapons more glorious than anything we have here, and I wanted to see them. All we found were the flowers, though."

"So you decided to have a snack instead?"

Arabelle shrugged, lifting her chin as if daring Mercy to

chastise her. She'd never been very good around children, but she was starting to like this one.

Mercy leaned forward. "Whose bag was it?"

"OREN!"

Mercy barged into the smithy and grabbed the lapels of Oren's jacket. The other Strykers stopped their work and stared open-mouthed as she pinned Oren against the wall, her fists at his pale throat. He struggled against her grasp, his fingers scrabbling to free himself. His eyes grew large as saucers.

"Who did you intend to poison?" she spat, her face contorted in rage. "Hm? Did you think you would get away with it? In the *Guild?*"

"I didn't—"

"A little girl nearly died because of you!" she snarled. "Don't lie to me! I know you brought it here. Who is your target? What, were you planning to get revenge for some murdered family member or something? Are you that *stupid?*"

"Mercy," Calum warned, prying them apart. "Let go of him."

She lunged for Oren, but Calum caught her before she could grab him again. Oren shrank away. She whirled on Calum, eyes blazing. "Those flowers came from the north. The capital. Only five strangers have been there recently, and they're all standing in this room."

"But I didn't— It's medicine!" Oren cried, trembling.

"It's *poison!*"

Calum dragged her away, positioning himself between Mercy and Oren. "Mercy, calm down."

"Get out of my way, Calum. He tried to hurt one of my own. Let me deal with him." She tried to step around him, but he blocked her path. She glared at him, her hands clenching into fists. "I'm not joking."

"Neither am I." He leaned in close, anger simmering in his eyes. "Take a deep breath and calm down, or our deal is off."

She forced herself to take a deep breath, then another. "Happy?"

Calum scowled at her. "Oren didn't bring the flowers to hurt anyone. He has seizures."

The objection on the tip of Mercy's tongue died. "...What?"

The other Strykers glanced away and resumed their work, all except Calum and Oren. The latter slumped against the wall, pale and shaking. Mercy studied him over Calum's shoulder.

"Yes, he has seizures. He has had them since he was born. Lusus blossoms, when brewed in a tea, ease them."

Heat crept up Mercy's neck, but she clenched her fists tighter, willing the blush not to spread to her face. Perhaps it was true. Most likely it was true—and a fairly new treatment, judging by Oren's sallow skin and recent weight loss. Still, Arabelle had managed to stumble upon them, and had almost died because of it.

She turned to Oren. "You should keep them better hidden. If I hear of another apprentice finding them—"

"You won't." Oren's head bobbed up and down. "I promise."

"Good."

Calum looked at her and raised a brow expectantly.

"And...I'm sorry," she added, then bolted out of the smithy, mortified and ashamed.

Mercy avoided everyone for the next couple days, filling her time by holing up in the infirmary with Arabelle and planning her strategy for the Trial. On Illynor's orders, each participant would be armed with a dagger and wearing full armor, but would be carrying nothing else. That meant no one would expect what Mercy had up her sleeve. Calum had decided that Xiomar's armor would fit her best out of the four sets, and had Mercy try it on in secret so he could make any necessary adjustments. He'd also shown her the most vulnerable points, places where she could slip a blade between the chinks in the metal.

As infuriating as he sometimes could be, it felt good to have someone on her side.

On the second day, Arabelle returned to her own room, having recovered enough from the poison to continue her training. Before she left, the little girl had gotten a kick out of Mercy's story of barging into the smithy and threatening Oren. Mercy didn't have much aptitude or affection for children—she'd never known what to do with them, and for some Creator-forsaken reason, their hands were always sticky—but she had to admit that the infirmary felt bleaker without Arabelle.

Now, she searched the infirmary shelves for Oil of Ienna. Once she'd located it, she rolled the jar between her fingers, admiring the way the gold liquid shimmered under the light. The description from Mistress Sorin's textbook surfaced in her mind; she'd read it so many times over the past few days, she had memorized it: *Oil of Ienna: relieves headaches, migraines, and shortness of breath. May also be used to cure insomnia—causes drowsiness; best taken thirty minutes before resting.*

Mercy turned as the door swung open. Mother Illynor entered the room, her scaly forehead creased in concern. "I had assumed you would be training, not cooped up in here," the Guildmother said. "Do you not feel well?"

"I'm fine," she responded, setting the bottle of Ienna oil on the desk. "Just came to make sure we have enough bandages for the Trial, which we do. I've also double-checked the inventory. We're well stocked for the fight."

"I didn't inquire about the bandages. I asked about you. You've been sulking."

"I have not," Mercy objected, although this, too, was part of the plan she and Calum had concocted. *Don't let them see you preparing,* Calum had said. *Pout, like you're angry Illynor won't let you fight.*

No great challenge there, she had responded. It still irked her to no end that Illynor had refused her a proper place in the Trial. Instead of scheming and sneaking about all hours of the night, she should be celebrating with the other apprentices, preparing for what would be the greatest day of her life.

"The Trial is important to you. It's important to all of us, but so is tradition. So are rules. So is obedience."

"Tell me what to do to change your mind," Mercy responded, a note of pleading slipping into her voice. It wasn't entirely feigned. "Tell me what to do, and I'll do it." As Illynor turned to leave, Mercy caught a handful of her cloak and hung onto it. "*Please.*"

The Guildmother peeled her hand away. "There is nothing you can do but wait."

7

Later, Calum peered over her shoulder as Mercy knelt in front of the pot hanging over the infirmary's hearth, boiling Lusus blossoms in water. "If this works," he said, "you're a genius."

"I need to achieve the right toxicity for it to work as a contact poison. Too weak and it will take too long to be effective. I'll dip my dagger in it, and just a scratch will down the victim in a matter of minutes."

"That also means if you accidentally cut yourself or get a drop of that poison in an open wound, you're as good as dead."

"Why do you think you're here? Make sure that doesn't happen. Besides, we have plenty of herbs for the antidote. I wrote down the recipe, so anyone can make it." She removed the pot from the fire, taking care not to burn her hands, and poured the contents into a stone bowl. As it cooled, the poison formed a dark film over the surface of the water. "Hand me that, won't you?"

Calum passed her the dagger, and the metal hissed when

she slid it into the poison. Little bubbles formed along the blade. "You're ready for tomorrow?"

"Of course."

"I heard from a servant that there's a special contract in Mother Illynor's room. It bears the royal seal. I think she's going to give it to the winner of the Trial."

She turned to him, surprised. "The royal seal? What use would the king have for the Guild? He has an army at his beck and call."

He lifted a shoulder in a shrug. "I don't know who the target is, but it makes sense to use an Assassin if he's high-profile. King Ghyslain would want someone no one could trace back to him, and a Daughter could slip in and out without being noticed."

"Okay, but why not give the contract to an older Daughter, someone with more experience?"

He raised a brow. "Are you saying you would turn it down if you won? That you're unqualified?"

"No," she said quickly, and he chuckled.

"There you go." The smile dropped from his face. He settled on the edge of the nearest cot, resting his elbows on his knees as he studied her. "Whatever this contract is, it's going to be dangerous. You'll be risking your life. I thought you should know about it before going into the Trial. Consider if this is something you want to do."

"Of course I'll do it," she scoffed. "I'm the best one for the job."

"I thought you'd say that." He stood and offered Mercy his arm, once again wearing his usual charming, crooked grin. "Since that will take a while"—he nodded to the dagger —"shall we go to dinner?"

She passed him the bottle of Ienna oil, which he tucked in the pocket of his jacket. "We shall."

If the night the Strykers arrived had been a party, tonight was a festival. The tables were piled high with food and laden with goblets and half-empty bottles of wine. The Daughters' chatter echoed off the high ceiling as the girls wandered from conversation to conversation. A couple of Daughters were playing a pair of ancient-looking lutes they had found in the castle's storage, filling the hall with a lively—if somewhat off-key—melody.

Across the room, Calum stood with a group of Daughters, listening as Nerran and Amir shared tales of their travels. Mercy watched from the doorway as Calum leaned down and murmured something in Xiomar's ear—something that made her face flush immediately. He slung an arm around her shoulders, his eyes alight and a smile on his face, and she melted into him.

Faye was sitting on a bench, talking to Oren. When Mercy sat down beside her, he flinched and stammered an excuse, nearly knocking over his goblet in his haste to leave.

"What was that?" Faye asked, lifting a brow.

"A couple days ago I accused him of trying to murder one of the apprentices. As one does when hosting esteemed guests."

Faye's eyes widened. "You didn't!"

She nodded.

"Oh, if he didn't have to change his trousers after that, poor, sweet Oren. He looks like he's seen a ghost."

"Just me."

"Well, that's infinitely more terrifying," Faye chuckled.

At the front of the room, Mother Illynor rose from her place at the head table, and all eyes turned to her. "Tomorrow morning, we shall meet in the courtyard to witness the Guild's three hundredth Trial. To commemorate the anniversary, the Strykers have created a special challenge for the participants. Hewlin, will you do the honor?"

He crossed the room and disappeared through the doorway. A moment later, he returned, followed by four servants, each one wheeling a mannequin bearing the armor of a participant. The name of the wearer was scrawled across a piece of parchment hanging from the neck: black for Lylia, gold for Faye, silver for Xiomar, and bronze for Cianna.

"She expects us to fight in *those?*" Faye whispered.

"The apprentices will be fighting in full armor," Mother Illynor announced. "It is a challenge that befits a Daughter of the highest degree—the one who shall carry this weapon upon winning."

She extended a hand, and Oren strode into the center of the room, a bundle of cloth in his arms. When he stopped, the fabric fell away to reveal a gleaming double-sided dagger. He held the grip in two hands and spun the dagger like a staff, the razor-sharp blades flashing as they cleaved the air. It was even more glorious than it had appeared in the drawing. The blades curved on each end, giving the entire weapon an *S* shape, and the hand guards were sculpted like interlocking branches, a nod to the forest where the Guild made its home.

Oren's awkwardness faded as he spun the dagger, his entire being moving with the graceful slashes and arcs of the weapon. In the blink of an eye, he twisted the center of the grip apart, and the simple-looking ring of silver became the pommels of two separate daggers.

Mercy tore her eyes from the amazing sight, and her gaze landed on Calum, who was taking full advantage of everyone's distraction. While Xiomar watched Oren in rapt attention, Calum broke the wax seal of the bottle of Ienna oil and dumped the contents into Xiomar's drink, forgotten on the table behind her. He tucked the empty bottle into his pocket, then leaned forward and nuzzled Xiomar's neck, making her giggle. He handed her the goblet and she took a sip, laughing when Calum kissed a droplet that escaped from the corner of her mouth. His free hand slipped around her waist and pulled her close.

Oren lunged forward one last time, twisting the daggers back into one, and bowed to Mother Illynor. She nodded and he hurried to the corner of the room, grateful to be out of the spotlight. Wild applause followed him and a blush colored his ears bright red.

"I am going to win that weapon," Faye breathed, a thought Mercy couldn't help but second. *I am going to win that weapon.*

"So, friends, enjoy the feast while the night is young," Mother Illynor said. "Lylia, Faye, Xiomar, and Cianna—take care to remember every moment of this night. For one of you, it will be your last as an apprentice." She raised her glass once more, and took her seat as the conversations swelled around her.

"Can you believe it, Mercy?" Faye asked, practically dancing with excitement.

"Can you believe it, Mercy? *Can you?*" a cruel voice mocked.

Lylia's beautiful face was sour as she stalked up to where Mercy and Faye sat. She was clad in all black, her eyes ringed with a haze of kohl smudged in striking contrast to the icy blue of her irises. An inky bruise peeked out above the neck of her tunic.

Faye sighed, but Mercy noticed her friend's grip on her goblet tighten almost imperceptibly.

"What do you want, Lylia?" Mercy asked.

"Nothing from you, knife-ear." Lylia's eyes narrowed and she cocked her head, studying Faye with cruel delight. "My business here concerns your friend." She leaned forward and wrapped an arm around Faye's tense shoulders, then jerked her chin toward where Cianna was sitting a little way down the table. "Since *this one* couldn't find the pointy end of a sword if it ran her through, and *this one*"—pointing to Xiomar—"is too focused on the first man to show interest in her to think twice about accepting that third glass of wine, I bet you're thinking your chances of winning are pretty good, aren't you?"

She waited until Faye nodded to continue.

"I wanted to stop by and tell you how foolish you are to think that. Because, you see," Lylia said, her voice dropping to a purr, "I remember all the times you interrupted our fun to help your pet here." She caught Mercy's chin and tilted it upward, smiling patronizingly. "You know the ones I'm talking about: when we thew her stuff into the river, when we burned her clothes in the hearth, when we hid poison ivy in her mattress... Tomorrow, you're going to regret ruining our games."

She strode away, laughing. Faye bristled. "The one rule—the *one* rule—of the Trial is that we can't kill. I'd almost like to throw all this away for the chance to wipe the smirk off that psychopath's face."

"We're assassins, Faye," Mercy said. "We're all psychopaths."

"I'm not joking, and you shouldn't be, either. You're the one she has been terrorizing all these years—you heard her! She doesn't just hate you. She does all this because she *can*—because no one will stop her." Faye slammed her goblet down on the table, sloshing wine over the rim and earning a few curious glances from the girls around them. "Why doesn't this bother you? I know you; you should be fuming!"

Mercy waved a hand dismissively, even though she knew her friend was right. "She's just saying it to distract you. See? It's working. Focus on the Trial—you can take all of your anger out on her then."

Mercy didn't say the real reason why she wasn't worried about Lylia: while Lylia had been busy intimidating Faye, Mercy had watched over her shoulder as Calum, an arm around Xiomar's shoulders, had led her out of the dining hall. To any onlookers, it would have appeared that they were seeking somewhere more private. In reality, Calum had just cleared the last obstacle barring her way into the fight tomorrow morning. A dose as large as he had given her would knock Xiomar out long enough for Mercy to take her place in the Trial.

Come dawn, she would no longer be an apprentice.

8

Mercy stood in the hall just inside the castle, a time-warped wooden door the only thing between her and the courtyard where the Trial was about to begin. Her stolen silver armor was on; last night, Calum had delivered it to her room after Xiomar fell unconscious. The helmet's visor obscured her vision somewhat, but it hid her face well. She had braided her hair and pinned it back so none of her telltale curls would pop out during the fight. The armor, although heavy, fit snugly to her body after Calum's adjustments. Strapped to her hip was a simple seven-inch-long dagger.

I am invincible, she thought, fighting to keep her excitement in check.

"Time to go," Mistress Trytain said, setting a hand on Mercy's shoulder and propelling her toward the door. Panic shot through Mercy, but she tried not to let her feet drag as she walked forward. She hadn't seen Calum since last night.

He was going to be too late.

The iron knuckles around Mercy's fingers flexed and

curled around the handle of the door. She was about to pull it open when a voice down the hall cried out, "Wait!"

She and Trytain turned as Calum flew around the corner, frantic and unkempt, his jacket and shirt open to his bare torso. He sighed when he saw her, his face breaking into a beaming smile. "I wanted to wish you luck. I thought I'd missed you."

Mercy squealed and ran to him. He caught her in his arms and spun her so his back blocked Trytain's line of sight. "Not quite," she murmured. Calum lifted the visor of her helmet and pulled her into a desperate kiss. His arm went around her waist and tugged her close. Mercy slid her hands along his hips, his skin warm under her palms.

"That's quite enough!" Trytain huffed, pulling at Calum's jacket. Mercy backed away in time for the visor to fall over her face. Even though Calum couldn't see it, she grinned.

"Fine, fine! I'm leaving!" Calum backed away, holding his hands up in surrender. "I'll see you later, Xiomar."

"Come now, you've wasted enough time already." Trytain clamped a hand around Mercy's wrist, dragging her toward the door. "We'll discuss this later," she called to Calum.

Mercy glanced back to see him slowly and theatrically buttoning his shirt. A spot of silver flashed from inside his jacket and he whistled three short, sharp bursts—their signal. The feeling of invincibility swelled again as she and Trytain emerged in the courtyard. Calum's kiss had distracted the tutor long enough for him to switch out the plain dagger Trytain had given her that morning with the poisoned one they had prepared the day before, which Calum had kept hidden in his room.

Mistress Trytain nudged Mercy forward. A wide circle had been drawn in the center of the yard, and people pushed in on every side, craning their necks to see over the heads in front of them.

"They're here!" someone shouted.

The crowd split before her, and she took her place on one side of the circle.

Mother Illynor was seated atop a large platform overlooking the ring, a dark silhouette against the gray of the predawn sky. Mistress Trytain claimed the seat to Illynor's right; the other tutors were scattered among the crowd of Daughters, apprentices, servants, and Strykers. In her peripheral vision, Mercy spotted Calum working his way to the front, his eyes trained on her. A mischievous grin was already tugging at his lips.

Each participant stood on an opposite side of the circle: Lylia across from Mercy, Faye on her right and Cianna on her left. Mercy couldn't see their faces, but the color of their armor helped the fighters and the onlookers keep track of each girl. Cianna was standing tall, staring straight ahead. Faye cracked her knuckles, bouncing on her toes with excitement. Lylia's dagger was already unsheathed; a flick of her wrist sent it flipping end over end through the air.

Mercy's heart began to pound. This was it—the moment she'd waited seventeen years for.

Mother Illynor nodded, signaling the start of the Trial. As Faye lunged toward Cianna, Lylia charged straight for Mercy. She slashed out with her dagger and Mercy knocked the blow aside, aiming for the soft, unprotected flesh of Lylia's underarm, as Calum had shown her. Before the blow could land, Lylia ducked and struck again. Her blade grated against the steel of Mercy's breastplate.

At first, it was all Mercy could do to block each attack as it came. Lylia wanted this victory almost as much as Mercy did; her every movement was laced with hunger, with the need to prove herself. A twist of Lylia's wrist sent Mercy's poisoned dagger flying from her grasp. She dove for it, but

Lylia grabbed the back of her breastplate and flipped her over before her fingers could close around the grip.

Lylia straddled her hips, grabbing the straps of her breastplate and pulling her almost upright before slamming her back to the ground. Mercy's neck snapped back and she gritted her teeth, prying at Lylia's grip on her. The wretched girl was enjoying this far too much. Mercy's free hand grasped only grass and dirt as she fumbled blindly for the poisoned blade.

Her fingers closed around the leather grip just as the weight was lifted off her.

"Oof," Lylia groaned as Faye dragged her off, a bloody dagger in her hand. Mercy scrambled to her feet and glanced about the ring. Cianna was nowhere to be seen, but she didn't have time to wonder what Faye had done to her. She tightened her grip on her dagger and leapt into the fray.

Faye whirled, slashing at a vulnerable part of Mercy's arm. Mercy backed away, feigning intimidation. The poisoned blade was not meant for her.

When Faye lunged again, Mercy flipped her dagger and slammed the pommel down on her helmet. Faye swayed, dazed not from pain, but from the loud, jarring noise so close to her ears. Lylia seized the opportunity and tackled her, landing on her torso with her full body weight.

Something crunched.

The crowd, which had been buzzing with whispers, went silent.

Faye's breastplate was dented, caved in and crumpled under Lylia's knees. Her eyes fluttered shut as she shuddered once, then went still.

An inhuman roar of rage escaped Mercy's lips. Lylia didn't even have time to glance back before Mercy was on top of her, knocking her sideways off Faye's limp body. They rolled twice in the dirt, scrabbling for a hold, kicking and punching and slashing with their daggers.

Then Lylia yelped.

Mercy's blade was buried in her thigh.

She howled and yanked the weapon out, bright red blood painting the black of her armor. She threw the dagger to the side, out of the ring, and climbed on top of Mercy, pinning her legs beneath her. Again, she lifted Mercy up and slammed her to the ground, sending shooting stars through Mercy's vision.

This time, though, the impact knocked off her helmet.

Lylia froze and lifted her visor, her eyes wide with shock.

Up on the platform, Mother Illynor jumped to her feet. Trytain leaned forward in her chair, her mouth agape.

"Mercy," Lylia hissed.

Mercy blinked up at her and smiled. "Hello."

Her hair had sprung free of its braid. It stuck to her face in sweaty tendrils, and her cheeks were flushed bright pink. Her smug grin faded when she realized Lylia's blade was hovering over her eye.

Lylia was going to kill her.

Judging by the outraged shouts from Illynor and the crowd, they weren't going to stop her.

The point of the dagger began to approach her eye, then stopped. Lylia straightened, her face slackening with shock and confusion when the blade slipped out of her hand, nicking Mercy's cheekbone as it fell.

"What—did you do to me?" she spat, her eyes widening with fear as the poison took hold. "You are...an abomination," she forced out. Her lids fluttered shut and she shuddered, then slumped face first onto the grass.

Mercy snatched up the dagger Lylia had dropped and pushed to her feet, choking on a laugh as utter chaos erupted around her.

Everyone was yelling over one another, their enraged voices blending into a cacophony. Mother Illynor and Hewlin stood at the edge of the platform, attempting to calm their fury, as Trytain leapt into the ring. She checked Lylia's neck for a pulse, then ordered Amir and Nerran to carry Lylia to the infirmary. On Mercy's left, Faye's pale lips parted to let out a low moan. Mercy sighed with relief. Her friend wasn't dead; only unconscious.

As Mother Illynor and the tutors attempted to reestablish order, Mercy stood in the center of it all, the eye of the storm, grinning like a madwoman.

She won.

She won the Trial.

Mercy pushed through the crowd and grabbed Lahrenn by the arm. "Lylia will be fine as long as the antidote is administered quickly. I wrote out the recipe, and all the ingredients are sitting on the desk in the infirmary. Start making it."

Lahrenn nodded, her chin bobbing up and down, but didn't move.

"Now!" Mercy growled, and Lahrenn yelped, bolting into the castle. Mercy followed at a leisurely pace, heading up the spiral staircase when she came to the fork in the hallway. From the apprentices' wing, the shouts and cries from the courtyard were muffled by the thick stone walls, but they were still audible.

She gasped as exhaustion unlike anything she had ever felt settled deep within her bones.

Her iron knuckles clattered to the ground. The metal plates around her forearms followed, then she removed the cuisse and chain from her right leg. Another ten steps down the hallway and the left leg followed. Her bedroom door was within sight. She closed it behind her and sagged against it as she undid the straps holding her breastplate closed. She slipped the metal over her head and tossed it to the opposite side of the room.

A relieved, hysterical laugh bubbled up inside her.

She won the Trial.

9

An earthquake beat against her door.
It sounded like a thousand fists. Looked like it, too, from the way the warped old wood shuddered under the force of the Daughters' blows. The Assassins and apprentices had gathered in the hall, and they demanded blood.

Mercy sat against the wall in the back of her tiny room, her legs stretched out before her, her hands folded in her lap. A warm breeze swept in through the open window above her head. After removing the rest of her armor, she had changed into a clean tunic and simple pants. She had washed her hair with water from the ewer in the corner of her room, and her curls now hung in loose tendrils around her face.

She was calm.

She had known the rules of the Trial, and still, she broke them. There would be consequences. She'd have to pay for cheating the competition, and she would. Mother Illynor would make her pay a thousand times over for disobeying her orders, but the Guildmother wouldn't kill her. She wouldn't kill the greatest apprentice the Guild had ever trained.

Mercy was not sorry for what she'd done.

The Guild was her life. She hadn't chosen it, hadn't *wanted* it for years. But when she stopped fighting it, stopped resisting all the ways the tutors were trying to change her, to harden her, she realized she *enjoyed* it. All the bullying, all the mockery, all the quips about pointy ears and the girl whose own parents had cast her out—they didn't matter in a fight. Mercy had not chosen this life, but she had accepted it.

She would be hated for serving the Guild—by the Daughters who would see every success as a personal slight, by the families whose father, mother, or child she would slay.

She would be hated.

And she would love every minute of it.

10

Eventually, the pounding on her door stopped.

The sun had set by the time Mercy finally rose. The moon, which should have hung bright and full in the sky, was obscured by clouds, cloaking her bedroom in darkness. She didn't bother to light a candle as she crossed the room and opened the door wide enough to peer into the hall. It was dark and empty. At this hour, the others had either gone to bed or were drinking in the dining hall. Luckily, Mercy's destination was in the opposite direction.

She tucked the dagger she'd stolen from Lylia into the waistband of her pants, adjusting her tunic so the folds of fabric hid the weapon's bulk, as she crept toward the stairwell. She ascended the spiral staircase, lightly trailing her fingers over the stone wall, and soon the clash of angry voices drifted to her.

"Can't be allow to stay—"

"—*did* complete the Trial—"

"—cheating! It was an insult to the Guild!"

Mercy stepped onto the landing. At the end of the hall,

the door to Mother Illynor's room was ajar, a sliver of light bleeding out into the corridor.

"We'll have a riot on our hands if we let her live."

"Enough," Mother Illynor said, and the bickering voices immediately fell silent. "Mercy did complete the Trial, but she broke one of our most important rules, and that is not an issue taken lightly. I will consider what you all have said, and—"

A hand knotted in Mercy's hair and yanked her head backward. Another leveled the edge of a blade at her throat.

"Make a sound," Lylia breathed, "and I will have you gutted like a fish before they make it through that door. Nod so I know you understand."

Mercy obeyed, silently cursing herself for being too absorbed in the tutors' conversation to pay attention to her surroundings. Her fingers twitched reflexively toward the dagger concealed in her waistband. The poison had only been in Lylia's system for an hour at the most, but it had to have some latent effects. She would be sluggish, weaker than usual. Considering Lylia was one of the most skilled apprentices in the Guild, that didn't mean much, but it still gave Mercy a slight advantage.

Just as Mercy thought it, Lylia reached down and grabbed the concealed dagger. "Don't think I didn't notice you steal that." She set the weapon on the floor and kicked it well out of reach, then pricked Mercy's neck with the point of her blade. "Now walk."

Mercy glanced at Illynor's door. If she and the tutors heard the sounds of a struggle, they would no doubt come out to investigate, but Mercy wasn't certain they would stop Lylia. Killing another member of the Guild was a crime punishable by death, but she had cheated the Trial. Half the tutors were already advocating for her execution. If Lylia killed Mercy, she would be applauded. She would be celebrated. If Mercy killed Lylia, it would seal her fate. She wouldn't live long enough to see the dawn.

She slowly descended the stairs, the dagger still pressed to her throat, and followed Lylia's murmured directions. She had to bide her time, wait for the perfect opportunity to strike. One wrong move, and Lylia would slit her throat.

"Just down the hall—through there," Lylia whispered when they emerged on the main floor. With her free hand, she pointed to a narrow archway, and they began to climb the staircase just beyond. The landing ended at a half-rotted door. The bottom had been chewed away by tiny teeth, and piles of rodent droppings were scattered about the floor. "Open it," Lylia hissed.

Mercy tried the handle, but it turned a quarter of the way, then stopped. Locked. After another prod from Lylia's dagger, she leaned her shoulder into the door, planting her feet on the uneven stone tiles, and shoved with all her weight. The lock snapped with a sharp *crack!* and the door flew open.

A gust of wind slapped Mercy in the face.

They were standing on the battlements.

Lylia shoved her, hard, and Mercy's stomach dropped as she pitched toward the edge. Like a cat toying with its prey, Lylia grabbed the back of her tunic and pulled her backward just before she would've fallen into the courtyard several stories below.

"You have humiliated me for the last time, Mercy," she snarled. "This Trial was supposed to be *mine*—not yours, and certainly not your pathetic friend's. All these years, everything you've ever done has been to undermine me. When I'm finished with you, the tutors won't be able to recognize your body."

"*Undermine you?* From the moment you met me, you've made it your mission to ruin my life," Mercy responded with a sharp laugh, trying not to let her fear show. She eyed the jagged edges of the battlements, just a mere foot away on either side. The bricks were ancient and worn, slick with moss, and many of them looked like they'd crumble at a mere touch. One careless step could send them both to their deaths.

Lylia set a heavy hand on Mercy's shoulder and pushed her toward the middle of the wall, directly above the gate. Without a word, she nudged Mercy forward until the toes of her boots hung over the edge, nothing but empty air before her. "Look down," Lylia whispered. "Can you imagine yourself lying there on the cold, hard ground? Broken, bloodied, pitiful Mercy."

Mercy could hear the smile in her voice. Lylia's free hand was splayed on the center of her back, providing a steady pressure. She wasn't pushing—not yet.

"The walls are high, but they're not high enough to kill you outright. I imagine you'd break some pretty significant bones. How long do you think you'll last, lying there, before the agony becomes too much to bear? I bet after a few hours, you'll be begging me to put you out of your misery. Can you see it?" she asked, the words full of venom. "Lying in a pool of your own blood, feeling it grow colder and colder around you, tasting the dirt in your mouthful of broken teeth."

Despite her resolve, Mercy's knees began to quake. All that stood between her and a slow, agonizing death was one push.

"I would savor hearing you beg," Lylia purred.

She swallowed tightly, her eyes trained on the grass far below, the vivid green rendered nearly black in the midnight darkness. "I would never."

The pressure on her back intensified, until—

Something clicked.

"Let go of her."

In one dizzying instant, she was yanked away from the

edge. Lylia's arm snaked around Mercy's throat, tightening, choking. Calum stood fifteen feet away, a crossbow trained on Lylia—and on Mercy, caught between them. Calum stalked closer, pausing when Lylia tightened her hold on Mercy, cutting off her air supply entirely. Mercy sputtered, clawing at Lylia's bare arm.

"This is not your business," Lylia spat. "Go inside and forget what you've seen."

Calum's body was tense, his finger resting on the trigger. "I assure you it *is* my business. Should any harm come to her, I will show you just how serious I am."

Lylia's grip didn't waver, but Mercy felt her hesitate. Her lungs were gasping, igniting, failing. Stars danced in her vision.

"A demonstration, then?" Calum asked, his voice betraying no emotion.

Mercy's eyes widened. The crossbow was still aimed straight at her. *No!*

The string released, and a bolt whizzed through the air. Mercy watched in terror, then disappointment, as it sailed past, thudding against stone somewhere behind them.

He'd missed.

And yet, Lylia sucked in a breath and released Mercy, who crumpled to her knees, gasping as she sucked in the cold night air. Without so much as a glance in her direction, Calum strode past her and muttered something to Lylia in a low voice. A second later, Lylia's running footsteps sounded past Mercy, then the door to the castle slammed shut.

Mercy pressed her forehead to the cool, rough stone, her heart pounding. She choked on a breath, wincing. Two arms encircled her gently, but alarms bells were still clanging in her head, mingling with the rush of her pulse in her ears. She elbowed Calum and scuttled a few feet away, then glanced over the edge of the ramparts and thought better of it.

Strong hands clasped hers, and she stilled.

"You're okay, love," Calum whispered. He knelt in front of her, his earnest gaze searching her face. "You're safe."

Mercy pulled her hands away and rose, mortified by her fear. Her knees were trembling, but she chose to pretend they weren't. "You should be asleep by now, like the others."

"We're lucky that I'm not."

"Thank you," she whispered, tugging at the hem of her tunic. Calum nodded gravely.

He stepped around her and picked up the crossbow as if it were made of nothing but air, which—given the Strykers' skill—hardly seemed impossible.

"What did you hit?" Mercy asked, turning. She found the answer when her eyes landed on a crossbow bolt embedded in the wall of the stone watchtower several yards behind her, at exactly the height of Lylia's head. The bolt was buried up to the fletching, a spider web of cracks blossoming across the brick. It wouldn't have merely killed Lylia. It would have shattered her skull. "Oh."

He nodded. "Usually a demonstration is enough to scare people away."

Mercy tugged on the bolt. Except for freeing a chunk of pulverized stone from the wall, it didn't budge. "You're not getting this back anytime soon."

"I can make more." She heard soft footsteps behind her, and she turned back to find him gazing down at her. "I did not kill her, Mercy, but make no mistake," he said, "if she ever comes for you again, I promise I will not hesitate to drive a bolt through her skill—or anyone's, for that matter."

"Why do you care? Why are you so insistent on helping me?"

Calum stared at her for a few long moments, his lips a tight line. Instead of answering, he said, "You should leave."

"Leave?"

"I remember what you said about proving them wrong about elven assassins, but no one needs to explain to me the severity of cheating the Trial. I know"—he held up a hand when Mercy opened her mouth to object—"that I pushed you to do it. I thought that when they saw the way you fight —the way you *really* fight, like you have everything to lose— Mother Illynor would change her mind. She hasn't. I don't know if she will. Leave, Mercy. Pack your things, grab the daggers you won, and run." He closed the distance between them and pressed a heavy iron key into her palm. "I stole this key for the smithy from Hewlin. Take the daggers, mount your horse, and ride north."

Mercy shoved the key back. "I won't."

"Why not?"

"I made my choice. I will not run and hide like a coward."

"You may not survive the night."

Mercy gestured to the shallow cuts Lylia had left in her neck. "You think I don't realize that?"

Calum tugged at his hair and began to pace. "Then *why*, Mercy? Do you have a death wish?"

"The Guild is all I have! It's all I am!" Mercy lowered her voice to a whisper, casting a glance at the castle. "I will either be a Daughter or dead. I refuse to be no one." Before he could argue again, she pivoted on her heel and marched toward the door to the Keep.

"Mercy?" he called.

She stopped, but didn't turn back.

"You were extraordinary today."

Pride swelled in her chest, and she laughed, ignoring the soreness of her throat. She squared her shoulders and grinned to herself as she strode across the battlements and into the castle.

11

The next morning, two Daughters arrived to escort Mercy to her execution.

When Tanni and Sienna barged into her room an hour before dawn, they had found her standing in the center of her room, meeting them with a leveled gaze and no expression on her face. They hadn't said a word as they took in the shadows under her eyes, the fresh scabs dotting her neck, and the dark bruises coiled around her throat. They had merely searched her for weapons and bound her wrists behind her back with a length of thick rope.

Now, Tanni opened the Keep's main door and pushed Mercy into the courtyard. The sun had already begun to rise, tingeing the eastern sky a pale, rosy pink. Mother Illynor and Mistress Trytain were standing under the gate, exactly where Mercy's body would have lain had Calum not intervened last night. Mercy shivered at the memory and searched the crowd for Lylia. She spotted the girl's flaming auburn hair near the front of the group. Lylia looked every bit as exhausted as she should after having been poisoned, but she wouldn't have missed Mercy's execution for the world.

Faye was nowhere in sight.

"Is Faye alive?" Mercy whispered to Sienna. The memory of her friend lying unconscious in the grass, her chest plate crumpled, haunted her. No one had bothered to tell her how Faye had fared after the Trial.

The Daughter ignored her and shoved her forward.

Everyone in the Guild had formed a half-circle around Mother Illynor. Tanni and Sienna pushed through the crowd, but the people quickly parted of their own volition, drawing back from Mercy as if she were diseased. As they approached the Guildmother, someone's foot snaked out and hooked Mercy's ankle, sending her stumbling forward. A giggle erupted from the crowd. Mercy set her jaw and glared straight ahead, her cheeks flushing with anger.

"Mercy," Mother Illynor said, her cool, rasping voice filling the courtyard, "you disobeyed my direct orders. You drugged one of your Sisters, poisoned another, and cheated your way into the Trial, our most sacred tradition. Turn to face the family you betrayed, and kneel."

"I. Betrayed. No one."

"Kneel."

Awkward and off-balance, Mercy knelt, to snickers from the crowd. The Strykers were scattered throughout, but Calum was not among them. Perhaps he couldn't face her death, knowing he'd had a hand in the outcome of the Trial.

"Master Hewlin," Illynor called.

Hewlin nodded to Oren, who approached Mother Illynor with the double-sided dagger in his hands—the dagger Mercy had earned. Sunlight glinted off the twin blades as he passed it to Mother Illynor. Mercy closed her eyes and hung her head, every muscle in her body tense. Mother Illynor stood behind her, out of sight, but Mercy could tell when she aimed the blade at her neck by the collective intake of breath from the crowd.

She bit back a terrified cry as the dagger whistled through the air.

But instead of severing her head from her shoulders, the blade sliced through the binding around her wrists. The rope hit the ground with a soft *whump*. Mercy's arms fell limply to her sides; her face went slack with shock and relief.

"Rise," Illynor commanded.

Mercy did as instructed, her knees wobbling, and Mother Illynor placed the double-sided dagger in Mercy's hands. Confused whispers spread throughout the crowd.

"Everything you did proves your dedication to the Guid. You emerged victorious from the Trial, so tradition will be honored. Kneel once more—as an apprentice, not a prisoner—so you may take your vows." Mercy gaped at her, disbelief etched across her features, until Illynor leaned in and whispered, "*Kneel.*"

Mercy sank to one knee, twisted the daggers apart, and held the blade of the one in her right hand before her face. Her forehead brushed the cool metal. When Mother Illynor placed her hand atop Mercy's head, she began to recite the vow she knew by heart:

"On this day, before the rising of the sun,
I pledge myself to the Guild.
My mind, my body, my sword, my dying breath is yours to take,
from this moment to my last.
I shall have no family but my Sisters, shall serve none other than my Mother.
From this moment forward,
I am your Daughter."

No one heard the last line. The Assassins and apprentices were raging; they felt cheated out of the blood they had expected Mother Illynor to spill. Their shouts reached a cacophony, drowning out Illynor's attempts to calm them, and—for the first time—a flicker of fear crossed the Guildmother's face. She removed her hand from Mercy's head, and Mercy jumped to her feet.

The sunlight broke over the trees, shining with such brilliance it momentarily blinded Mercy. She held her hand over her eyes as the crowd stilled.

Mother Illynor jumped at their distraction. "The Great Creator, with his all-seeing eye, shines his light on Mercy. He has accepted her vow."

"None of you may lay a hand on her," Trytain added, somewhat grudgingly, "unless in retribution for the breaking of her oath."

"Come, dear." Mother Illynor slipped an arm around Mercy's shoulders and guided her forward. As before, the onlookers parted as they neared, watching with barely concealed outrage. "This is only the beginning of your journey."

Half an hour later, still not quite believing her luck, Mercy sat on the plush couch in Mother Illynor's room—the same room in which the tutors had debated whether to kill her only a few hours earlier. Her newly-won daggers lay on the cushion beside her, back in one piece. The beauty of the weapon struck Mercy anew as she admired the craftsmanship. The grip was smooth brown leather, and the hand guards had been inlaid with tiny orange and red crystals, the same shades as the leaves of the Forest of Flames. She wondered if Calum had had any input on the design; it seemed like the kind of absurdly sentimental thing he would do.

As if Mercy could ever forget the place she called home.

Mother Illynor strode out of her dressing chamber. She

had taken off her thick fur cloak and was clad in a long-sleeved shirt and riding pants. The crackling fire in the hearth provided more than enough heat for her cold-blooded, reptilian body. She settled into a high-backed chair across from Mercy.

"I have a contract for you—one of the utmost importance. Usually, I prefer to give a new Daughter a few days to recuperate from the Trial and prepare herself before sending her out, but I thought it best with your...*extenuating circumstances*"—she fixed Mercy with a pointed look—"that you leave right away. Aelis and the Strykers will escort you to Ellesmere, where Sorin is now. She will accompany you to Myrellis Castle, in the capital."

Calum was right about the contract. "The castle? Who is my target, the king?"

"Close," she said. "His son."

12

"The prince? You want me to assassinate the prince? Isn't that treason?"

"The Guild does not owe allegiance to the royal family of Beltharos. We offer a service to those who have the coin to pay for it." Illynor crossed her arms. "Do you consider yourself a subject of King Ghyslain?"

"No."

"Good. The king is a man, Mercy. Prince Tamriel is a man. Royal blood or no, it spills just as easily," Illynor said. She stood and moved to one of the bookshelves lining the room, plucking a heavy leather tome from the shelf. "Before you leave, you must know that the tension between humans and elves in the capital has reached an all-time high for the first time since Liselle Mari's death nearly eighteen years ago. Do you remember learning about her in your lessons?"

Mercy shrugged. "A little."

Mother Illynor flipped through the pages until she landed on the one she wanted, then she handed the book to Mercy. There were no words on the page, just a drawing—an image so grotesque it turned Mercy's stomach.

An elven woman was chained by each limb to the front gate of Myrellis Castle. Her head had lolled forward so all that was visible was the crown of her head and the dirty tendrils of hair hanging down onto her chest. She was completely naked, her skin coated in dirt and grime. Her throat had been cut so wide and so deeply that the slice was still visible despite her head hanging forward, the wound a gaping chasm, and dry rivulets of blood trailed down her breasts. Only her stomach was clean, pale skin peeking through the dirt as if someone had wiped her down with a filthy rag. Carved in shaky, blood-clotted lines across her tender skin were the words: *Temptation of the king.*

"Horrible, isn't it?" Illynor said. "Liselle was the king's mistress. She was Queen Elisora's slave and was serving as her handmaid when she met Ghyslain. After the king and queen were married, she was given her own quarters in the castle. While the queen was bedridden with pregnancy complications a few years later, Liselle began to appear in public with the king and preach freedom for the elven slaves, even going so far as sitting on Elisora's throne during court."

"And she was killed for it?"

Illynor nodded. "The nobles hated her. It was inappropriate for an elf to have as much power as the king had given her. So when the king was pulled to the queen's side during the birth of Prince Tamriel—the birth that killed her—the nobles ambushed Liselle and murdered her. They strung her up like that to send a message to the king." She leaned forward and met Mercy's eyes. "Please be careful in the capital, my dear."

"I will." Mercy shut the book, grabbed her double-sided dagger, and stood. "When do I leave?"

"In one hour."

Faye's bedroom door was ajar when Mercy arrived.

"Hello?" she called softly as she stepped inside. She was shocked to find Faye awake and sitting upright in bed. She wasn't wearing a shirt; her torso was bound with layers upon layers of bandages, and the edge of a dark purple bruise stained her upper ribcage. Just looking at it made Mercy sick.

Beautiful, kind Faye.

Beautiful, kind Faye, who was glaring at Mercy like she desired nothing more than to rip her apart piece by piece.

"Come to gloat over your victory?" she snarled. "What is *wrong* with you? You know how much this meant to me. You know how long I have waited for this opportunity, and still, you took it for yourself."

"You know how important the Trial is to me—"

"You don't think it was important to me? You're not special, Mercy!" Faye seethed. "You didn't want to become a Daughter any more than the rest of us. You weren't meant for this. You're a mistake—your own parents didn't want you!"

Mercy flinched, and guilt flitted across Faye's face, but she quickly blinked it away. Mercy could have turned around and walked away—Faye wouldn't have been able to follow her—but she forced herself to stand there and listen. She deserved her friend's loathing. She deserved the insults. Faye would never forgive her, and she knew it. If that was the price of becoming a Daughter, of finally having the chance to prove her worth to the girls who had tormented her all her life, she would pay it.

But that didn't make it hurt any less.

"I have never asked you for anything. I stuck up for you when the other girls teased you. I helped you fight them when you were too scared to do it on your own—don't pretend that you weren't. But now that you're all grown up, what do you do in return? You take away the one thing that means the most to me. You couldn't wait one year to fight in your own Trial, so you had to ruin mine. You saw what you wanted and you took it without any regard for anyone else. What about me? I can't train with broken ribs. Do you even care?" She paused, trembling with anger, then scoffed. "Of course you don't. You didn't choose this life. I did— I *want* this."

Mercy was quiet for a few moments. "You're right," she finally said. "I didn't choose this life, but this is the life I have. If you were meant to win the Trial, you would have done it whether I was competing or not."

Faye recoiled as if Mercy had slapped her. "How dare you? Get out! Leave for your contract and don't come back."

Mercy turned to leave, and something shattered above her head. She ducked as shards of porcelain landed in her hair, pieces of the plate Faye had thrown tinkling to the floor. She shook her head and brushed the shards off her clothes, then left the room without another word.

Goodbye, Faye, she thought, Faye's sobs trailing her down the hall. *I'm not sorry for what I did, but I'm sorry that I hurt you.*

Aelis and the Strykers had already saddled their horses by the time Mercy passed through the main doors of the Keep, a small bundle of clothes in her arms and her daggers sheathed at her hips. A cart laden with the Strykers' tools was strapped to Amir's horse. Calum tossed something inside before meeting Mercy in the center of the courtyard, leading Blackfoot and his horse, both saddled.

He offered her Blackfoot's reins. "For you, Daughter."

Despite her tumultuous emotions, Mercy smiled. She shoved her clothes into one of the saddlebags, along with a small coin pouch that Mother Illynor had given her, then climbed onto Blackfoot's saddle. He chuffed and stamped a hoof into the ground, sensing her excitement. She had never been beyond the tree line before, and she couldn't wait to see the world beyond the Forest of Flames.

"Be safe, my child," Mother Illynor called, striding over. "Be strong, be swift, be *ruthless*, and never forget your vows."

"I won't."

"Master Hewlin, shall we not meet again until next spring's-end?"

"Afraid so. Our journey takes us east, across the sea." He dipped his head in respect, and Illynor did the same.

"Creator ease your path."

"He'd better," Amir called. "This one gets seasick taking a bath." He elbowed Calum teasingly, and Calum muttered something crude under his breath, just loud enough for all to hear. Oren burst into laughter. Hewlin pretended not to have heard.

"May he guide us all," he said with an expression of weary affection for the younger men. "Come, all, let's be off."

Mother Illynor stepped back as Hewlin mounted his horse and spurred it to the front of their small group. Oren and Amir took up their places behind him, and Aelis and Nerran followed, already deep in conversation. Calum joined Mercy at the rear.

"Ready to become the greatest Assassin in history?" he asked with a wink.

As the trees began to close in around them, Mercy couldn't help but glance back. The castle stood tall and stoic, as it had for thousands of years. A backlit figure stood atop the battlements, directly above Mother Illynor's head. Although she couldn't make out the woman's face, Mercy knew Lylia was watching, cursing her for her victory.

She turned forward in her saddle and did not look back again.

Four hours passed with little change.

The trees shimmered red, gold, and orange, thousands of narrow redwood trunks punctuating the landscape as far as Mercy could see. They rode as the sun passed directly overhead, then began its western descent. The Strykers joked amongst themselves, every so often letting out peals of laughter that rippled out across the forest. Aside from Calum, they didn't pay Mercy much attention, but it wasn't out of malice. This band of Strykers had been making this journey for years, each spring escorting another newly-sworn Daughter out of the forest. Mercy was just another name on that list.

In the meantime, Mercy considered her contract. She trusted Mistress Sorin to find a way to get her into the capital, if not directly into Myrellis Castle, but how she killed the prince would be entirely up to her.

Poison? There were plenty of medicinal herbs that could be deadly with the right dose—or the *wrong* dose, Mercy supposed, depending on whether one was the *poisoner* or the *poisoned*. Provided she could sneak into the kitchen, it would be easy to slip the poison into the prince's food or drink, but that was assuming the prince didn't have a food taster. If he did, it would be difficult—nearly impossible—to sneak it into his food without being discovered.

Blades? She had her daggers, large enough to be lethal and small enough to be hidden in the folds of the absurd fashions worn in Sandori. The problem was the blood. Mercy would have to kill Prince Tamriel somewhere private, somewhere the royal guards wouldn't stumble upon them, and she would have to bring a change of clothes. It wasn't the most convenient option, but it would certainly be effective.

She didn't notice they had stopped until Blackfoot nearly collided with Nerran's horse.

"Mercy," Calum said softly, his smile crinkling the corners of his eyes. "Look."

She followed his gaze and—

"*Oh*."

The edge of the Forest of Flames lay straight ahead, no more than ten feet away. The trees were more spread out here than by the Keep, the leaves a pale yellow-green, the underbrush long but sparse. Green grass and a clear blue sky were visible beyond the redwood trunks.

"Lead the way, Mercy," Hewlin said, his eyes sparkling.

She slid off Blackfoot's saddle and took his reins in her hand, unable to keep the awe from her face as she approached the forest's edge. Her stallion's hooves clomped softly on the moist grass as he trailed behind her, his warm breath tickling her arm. This. *This* was the moment she had fought so hard for. Aelis and the Strykers parted before her.

Ten feet, then eight, then six.

Calum beamed at her as she passed.

Three, two, one.

And she was out.

13

There was so much *space*.

Wide-open prairies sprawled around them, long grass and vibrant wildflowers swaying gently in the languid breeze. The path they were following widened, then became a dirt road, marred with imprints of horseshoes and wagon wheels. They rode side-by-side here, Hewlin once again in the lead, and Calum to Mercy's right. Every so often, he dipped his head and chuckled softly at the look of wonder on Mercy's face as she took in the world she'd only read about in books, only imagined through Faye's stories. She had known what to expect, of course, but the images her mind had conjured paled in comparison to reality.

"The Forest of Flames covers the southern edge of the agricultural sector," Calum explained as they rode. The landscape gradually changed, the prairies giving way to fields overflowing with lush vegetation. "Sandori is straight north, at the place where the mining, fishing, and agricultural sectors meet. The city is backed by Lake Myrella, which connects all the major rivers in the country; anything bought in Sandori can be shipped anywhere in Beltharos."

"Did you know the lake is named after the first king?" Nerran cut in. "Centuries ago, Colm Myrellis settled there with his family and created a shipping company on the bank of the lake. Once he'd made enough money, he built a dam on the junction of Lake Myrella and the Alynthi River, which enabled him to charge the hell out of his competitors' ships and allowed his own to transport goods tax-free...but that's neither here nor there. His family grew incredibly rich from the profits, the dam kept the city from flooding during the springtime storms, and his eldest son eventually became the first king of Beltharos."

"Smart-ass," Oren called from the front of the group. "You trying to impress someone?"

"Not you, that's for sure," Nerran retorted, eyeing Aelis.

"Lay a hand on me and that'll be the last time you *have* hands." The Daughter reached for the dagger at her hip, her lips curling into a wicked grin.

"Promises, promises. My charm simply needs time to take full effect."

"Please. You'd have better luck getting ass from *that* ass over there." Amir pointed to the field on their right, where a donkey stood in its pen, blinking at them blearily.

"Do you think I'd still have to buy it dinner first?"

Mercy snorted. "Depends. How much do you enjoy eating hay?"

"Well I'll be damned—"

"She speaks!"

"Silence wasn't one of your vows, huh? We thought they had added something new." Amir elbowed her jovially.

"We had a bet going to see how long it would take you to say more than two words to someone other than Puppy-Dog-Eyes here," Nerran said, nodding to Calum. "Oren, you owe me six aurums, and don't you dare try to weasel your way out of paying like you did in that tavern back in Xilor."

Around and around their banter went, so quickly Mercy couldn't keep track of who said what. Even Hewlin joined in, spinning tales of his early days in the Strykers. Calum, being the newest addition to the group, seemed to be the butt of most of the jokes, but he accepted the teasing with a grin and several clever wisecracks of his own.

Once the sun sank below the horizon, Hewlin stopped their small party to make camp for the night. Amir unstrapped his horse from the cart, clambered up, and tossed each of the Strykers a bedroll.

Aelis rapped on the side of the cart. "Have any extras? Illynor rushed our departure so much I didn't have a chance to grab one," she said, shooting a dark look at Mercy, who had packed no bedroll of her own, either.

"You can sleep here, my darling," Nerran called, patting the ground beside him.

She sneered. "I'd rather my ass be covered in Fieldings' Blisters than spend one night next to you."

"Just as well, then," Oren said cheerfully. "Lie with him for a night, and you'll find something equally repulsive growing down there soon enough."

Nerran threw his shoe at Oren, who caught it and made a rude gesture with his free hand. "I'll show you repulsive," Nerran said, feigning a lunge at Oren.

Hewlin stepped between them. "Alright, alright, that's enough. You're not five years old anymore, as much as you may act like it." Without waiting for a response, he sat down on his bedroll, facing the road. "Get some sleep now—we've another day's ride to Ellesmere. Amir, you're next watch. I'll wake you in two hours."

Behind him, Nerran made a face at Oren, who threw the man's shoe back.

"I said *sleep*," Hewlin said without looking back at them.

The shock of a cold wind woke Mercy late in the night, shooting through the thin fabric of her worn tunic. Although summer was fast approaching, the nights were still chilly, and Hewlin had argued against building a fire in case bandits or highwaymen were to see it. Mercy shivered on the hard ground. Her fingers, wrapped around her sheathed daggers, were freezing, and she slipped them into her sleeves. Back at the Keep, her departure had been so rushed she hadn't had time to grab so much as a cloak. She gritted her teeth and drew her knees in close. In only a few hours, they would rise with the dawn and start riding once more. She only had to make it a little while longer.

Something crunched softly in the dirt a few feet away. Although it was probably one of the Strykers shifting in his sleep, Mercy stiffened. After seventeen years in the ancient stone Keep, it was unsettling sleeping with nothing but a thin canopy of leaves over her head.

Someone draped something heavy across her body—a blanket made of scratchy, but warm wool. She lifted her head and blinked up at the silhouette standing over her, stars gleaming in his hair.

"Rest now, love," Calum whispered, and walked away.

Mercy closed her eyes and tugged the blanket closer, the residual heat of Calum's body lulling her into a deep, dreamless sleep.

A weight crunched down on her fingers.

Mercy spat an oath at the sudden pain. Her eyes flew open to bright sunlight, blinding her, and she scrambled for her daggers.

They weren't there.

A man's face, rough with stubble, appeared before her. Before she could react, he grasped Mercy's wrist and dragged her to her feet. She drew back a fist to strike him, but Calum's voice stilled her before she could swing.

"Mercy! Don't!"

Across the small camp they'd made, Aelis and the Strykers stood in a line beside the road, facing down the wrong side of Calum's crossbow. The man holding the weapon grinned with wicked glee, his finger curled around the trigger. He was short, stocky, and had a face like leather that had been left in the sun far too long. Two more ragged-looking strangers were rifling through the Strykers' cart. The horses were a short distance away, tethered to a tree.

"Find anything good?" Crossbow Man called, aiming at Aelis and the Strykers in turn. The Daughter's face was purple with rage. Mercy wasn't entirely sure whether Aelis was more angry about the bandits or the rude awakening.

"Plenty," one responded, lifting a gleaming dagger.

"After we sell 'em, we'll have enough coin to feed us for months," the other added, flashing a gap-toothed grin.

"Coin will be the least of your concerns when I get my hands on you," Aelis snarled.

Calum's eyes met Mercy's, and he offered the slightest shake of his head. His gaze shot to the tip of the crossbow bolt, currently aimed straight at Hewlin's heart. The meaning was clear enough: *Don't do anything that will get them killed.*

"And how about your purses?" the man with the crossbow asked Hewlin. "By the looks of you, you're well enough off yourselves. Traveling with as many fancy weapons as you've got, you've gotta be a rich lot."

Hewlin set his jaw. "Are you sure you want to do this, friend?"

"Quite sure. Hand your coin purses over, along with any

other valuables you're carrying." Crossbow Man grinned, revealing two broken front teeth. "Make this nice and easy, and we'll be on our way before you know it."

"I think I'll keep this trinket for myself," the bandit holding Mercy said. He held up the double-sided dagger in his other hand, admiring the way the orange and red gemstones of the hand guards sparkled in the early morning sunlight. He looked down at Mercy. "It's prettier than you are, but I like a little fight in a woman." He yanked her closer, watching the Strykers' faces for a reaction. "And who does this belong to? She a slave, or just some elven whore you picked up on the road?"

Calum's expression turned murderous.

The man laughed, catching Calum's glare. "O-ho! We have a winner. And you know what? Because you were so honest, I won't kill her. Yet. Not before I take her myself."

Mercy scoffed. "You can try."

Oren fainted.

Crossbow Man jumped back as Oren began convulsing in the dirt, saliva foaming at the corners of his mouth. Even the men pawing through the cart stopped to watch, their eyes wide. "What's wrong with 'im?" one asked.

Mercy elbowed the man holding her in the stomach. He grunted, his grip on her wrist slackening enough for her to slip free. She snatched her twin daggers back as he doubled over, gasping for breath, and plunged the blades deep into his back. Hot, sticky blood gushed over her hands.

"Pointy-eared bitch," he groaned as he staggered, then fell to his knees.

"Nice to make your acquaintance," Mercy hissed as he died. She spun, bloody daggers raised, to find Aelis and the Strykers making quick work of the other bandits. Oren was still convulsing on the ground, caught in the seizure, and—knowing she could do nothing to help him—Mercy ran past him to slash the throat of one of the thieves, freeing Amir from the scuffle. She jerked her head to Oren. "Go—help him!"

Hewlin, Nerran, and Aelis easily dispatched the other man, leaving Calum alone with Crossbow Man—although now the crossbow was back in its owner's hands.

The bandit held up his hands in surrender, stumbling backward. Calum matched every step. "Whoa, there, friend. How about we call it a draw, hm? Didn't mean nothing personal by it, we just—"

A bolt through the skull cut off his words.

Calum lowered the crossbow and placed the toe of his boot on the man's forehead. With a sickening sucking noise, he pulled the bolt from the man's head, the shaft coated in blood and gore. He looked down his nose at the corpse. "No, nothing personal."

They gathered around Oren, whose convulsions had slowed, but not stopped completely.

"He hasn't been taking his medication?" Hewlin said sharply, more an accusation than a question.

Amir's gaze cut toward Mercy. "He ran out at the Keep. He was hoping he'd be able to manage until he could buy more in Ellesmere."

Mercy said nothing, but she didn't fail to notice the guilty look Calum shot her before turning his attention back to Oren. "He'll be fine," Calum said. "He'll just need some time to rest before we set out. In the meantime, we'll clean up this mess and fix something to eat. Mercy, Aelis, why don't you go wash the blood off your clothes? There's a stream about a half mile west of here where you can wash up and change."

Mercy and Aelis nodded. They each grabbed a change of clothes from their packs and left the Strykers behind to tend to Oren, picking their way around the bandits' corpses.

14

Ellesmere was huge.

There were so many buildings—short and squat and built haphazardly atop one another, as if the layout of the city had been decided on the roll of a die. By the time they arrived at the hub of the agricultural sector, the sun was little more than a sliver on the western horizon, yet people still bustled along the narrow, twisting roads. Mercy watched them with interest. Unlike the Daughters, who shared a savage, lethal grace, these people were tall and brawny, with sun-tanned skin and muscles built from lives spent tending crops or livestock. Every so often, Mercy's eyes landed on an elf or two amidst the crowd, their pristine white sashes stark against their plain tunics and trousers. She'd never seen one of the sashes in person before—there was no reason for the elves in the Keep to wear them—but she knew what they were: marks of slavery. By law, every slave in Beltharos had to wear one.

Calum slowed his horse, falling back to ride beside her. "So...we should talk," he said, watching an elven slave follow a human family, lugging a basket of fruits and vegetables down the street.

"About?"

"Sending you to the capital is a death sentence. I grew up there—I saw firsthand how cruel humans can be to innocent elves, and you're far from innocent. If the nobles discover that you were sent by the Guild..." He shook his head. "Tensions between humans and elves have been high since Liselle's death. Plenty of people in the capital have lost loved ones to the Guild over the years, and they have old scores to settle. I shudder to imagine what they'll do if they catch you."

Mercy frowned. "You're the one who offered to help me compete in the Trial. You knew I would receive a contract if I won. Why are you so afraid now?"

"I... Look, I know you're a skilled fighter and you can take care of yourself, but after seeing the way the bandits treated you this morning—calling you a whore, threatening to...hurt you—I just want you to be careful. Don't underestimate the nobles."

"I'm sure I can handle a bunch of perfumed lords and ladies."

Calum shot her a pointed look. "Lylia nearly had you in a puddle in the courtyard yesterday. How well do you think you'd fare against a mob?"

Mercy faltered. "Alright, you've made your point. Any advice?"

"Just some things you should be aware of. You know the king met Liselle while she was serving as a slave and handmaid to Elisora Zendais, his queen. Ghyslain claimed to love Elisora, but it was no secret that his heart belonged to Liselle. She had the king at her beck and call. When the queen was bedridden while pregnant with Prince Tamriel, Liselle began appearing in public at the king's side. When there was a slave uprising in the slums, it was she who addressed and appeased the rioters on the king's behalf, promising to abolish slavery and grant them equal rights to humans."

"And the nobles had her murdered for it. I've learned all this before."

Calum rolled his eyes. "Let me finish. Even before her death, elves and humans alike called for a revolt against the crown. The humans claimed the king was mad for giving so much power to an elf, and the elves wanted him to pay for the injustices suffered by the slaves. Even now, Ghyslain's position is a precarious one. His courtiers vie for power behind his back, waiting for the day his madness claims him entirely, and they're not kind to outsiders. You'll be in the thick of the court. Watch yourself."

"Thank you," she said. "But...why do you care so much? Why do you bother to help me? I'm just a stranger you met a few days ago."

He laughed. "A stranger? You're so much more to me than that, love."

Before she could ask his meaning, he spurred his horse and joined Hewlin and Aelis at the front of the group. Mercy frowned at his back, then turned her attention back to the people walking past, mulling over what he'd said. A small group of slaves lingered on the street corner, speaking in hushed voices. Every woman's hair was braided back or pinned into severe buns, and the men's hair had been shorn close to the scalp, leaving their pointed ears on full display. A few of them regarded Mercy with curiosity. Others narrowed their eyes at her lack of a sash, envy evident in the bitter twist of their lips. Mercy's stomach tightened, and the image of Liselle's lifeless and defiled body strung across the castle gates filled her mind. Liselle had done nothing but try and secure freedom for the elves, and that was how the courtiers had repaid her efforts.

I shudder to imagine what they'll do if they catch you.

She pushed Liselle and the slaves from her mind as they cut through a small market. As much as she pitied them—as abhorrent as she found slavery—she could do nothing to help these people. She was an Assassin, nothing more.

They followed the twisting roads until they arrived at Pearl's End Inn & Tavern. The wide, cozy-looking building dominated the block, its walls crafted of dark wood and stone bricks. A chimney stuck out from the roof, churning out a steady stream of smoke. Mother Illynor paid the owners of the tavern to ship supplies down the Alynthi River to the Keep.

Sorin was already waiting for them outside, drumming her fingers on the side of the carriage which was to transport them to Sandori. The healer's jaw dropped when she saw Mercy. "What are you doing here? Don't tell me you—"

"—won the Trial?" Nerran finished for her. "Yeah. Didn't see that coming."

Calum winked at Mercy.

Sorin raised her brows. "Illynor changed her mind about letting you compete?"

"...Not quite," Mercy said. "I'm sure you'll hear all about it when you return to the Keep."

They dismounted, and Aelis took Mercy by the arm, dragging her over to where the tavern's sign hung over the sidewalk. "Look here," she said, pointing up at the lettering. "Do you see that mark in the corner of the sign? The dark patch in the woodgrain?"

Mercy nodded. About a quarter of the way down, there was a faint teardrop-shaped shadow, light enough for a layman to mistake it as the natural texture of the wood. It was too perfect, though. Too symmetrical. "The mark of the Guild."

"Anyone who works with Illynor is going to have that mark on his sign. Go inside, flash the owner this coin"—she pressed a circle of metal into Mercy's hand—"and he'll get you anything you need."

The coin was real gold, chipped around the edges from age and wear, and bore no marks save for the single teardrop at its center. "You won't need it?"

"There are plenty more at the Keep. Go on, now. Daylight is fading. I'll spend the night here and head back with Blackfoot tomorrow."

Mercy nodded and returned to Blackfoot's side, running her fingers through his coarse mane and down his neck. He turned to nuzzle her with his velvet-soft nose. "I'll see you soon, my friend," she breathed.

"Time for us to be off, too," Amir said. "Can't say I envy your job, Mercy, but if anyone's fit for this task, it's you."

"Try not to get yourself killed," Nerran interjected, and Oren elbowed him. "What?"

Calum dismounted and followed her to the carriage, extending a hand to help her climb inside. "Remember what I said. Don't draw any undue attention to yourself, and you'll be fine."

"I'll be careful. Thank you for everything, Calum."

"You'll do great, love."

Mercy swung around and punched his arm. "Don't call me that."

He offered her a crooked grin. "See you next spring?"

"I can't wait."

"Alright, let's go before you get all sappy and shit," Nerran called.

Calum returned to his horse and waved to her once before following the others down the street and around the corner. Sorin bade farewell to Aelis, then climbed into the carriage and settled onto the bench opposite Mercy. "Ready to go?"

Mercy watched through the carriage's narrow window as Aelis led Blackfoot to the tavern's stable, then turned to face the healer. She reached into her pocket and closed her fingers around the Guild token, the metal cool against her skin. "Absolutely."

For a while, they rode in silence, Mercy staring out the window at the darkening countryside while Sorin pondered how she was going to sneak Mercy into the castle. If Faye or Lylia had been the victor of the Trial, the matter would have been simple. Either of them could have blended seamlessly among the nobles and courtiers, but Mercy's elven blood complicated things. Sorin had first suggested that she disguise herself as one of the castle slaves, but had dismissed the idea almost immediately. The castle and its grounds were enormous; there was no guarantee Mercy would ever have contact with the prince.

That, Sorin had said, *and you're far too stubborn to take orders from anyone.*

What? That doesn't sound like me at all, Mercy had responded with an innocent look.

"You're going to impersonate a royal," the healer finally said. "When we reach the next town, we'll send a letter to the castle that Lady Marieve Aasa of Feyndara will be attending the upcoming Solari celebration. Queen Cerelia is the only member of the royal family to visit Sandori since she ascended the throne, so no one should realize you're not Marieve. You've kept up on your lessons, haven't you? What do you remember about Feyndara?"

"Enough to get by, I think. Beltharos and Feyndara have had almost no contact in decades, save for the battles in the Cirisor Islands. No one's going to know if I make a small mistake."

Sorin nodded. "Even so, study their family tree and

history while you're in the capital. Elvira, the young woman who will act as your handmaid, can help you. You must be able to answer any question without hesitation. A contract of this importance isn't one where you can simply slip in and out. It could take weeks for you to find an opportunity to strike."

"And you expect me to...what? Sip tea and attend balls while I'm waiting? You want me to bat my lashes at Prince Tamriel and swoon like all the other lovesick young noblewomen?"

Sorin's lips twitched into a ghost of a smile. "Don't forget to blush and giggle at everything he says."

"When we get to the capital, remind me to practice fainting gracefully onto a divan."

"Will do." The humor faded from Sorin's face. "Your instincts are correct, though. The prince will turn eighteen in little over two weeks from now, and he will be eligible to ascend the throne that night. Now, his father will never abdicate, but even so, the nobles have begun pressuring Tamriel to find the woman who will become the next queen. That's where you come in. Use the pretext of a marriage alliance to get close to him."

Mercy nodded. They lapsed into silence once again, until she asked, "Sorin, who paid to have Prince Tamriel killed?"

"You can guess who. You know Illynor's rule."

"...The king?"

"Only a royal can buy a contract on another royal. If the commoners had their way, there would be no royals left to rule."

"It makes sense. If the court is pressuring Ghyslain to abdicate, why not have his sole heir murdered? Remove the threat to his power. If the king is truly as unstable as people claim, it's not hard to believe he would go to such lengths to secure his place on the throne."

"Fathers have done far worse to their sons for far less," Sorin agreed. "Stay alert when you're in the capital, Mercy. The court is a nest of vipers. Just fulfill your contract and get out. If you somehow get trapped in the city, play along with anything the courtiers demand, and don't give the guards any reason to suspect you. Some will point the finger at you, the granddaughter of a foreign queen, for Tamriel's murder, but you must not give an inch. Cry if you must—"

"I don't cry."

"—but do not breathe a word of the Guild to anyone except Elvira. Remember your vow. No matter the circumstances, no matter what you must do to return to us, you belong to the Guild until your last breath."

15

The entire ride, Mercy couldn't stop looking out the window.

The plains surrounding Ellesmere gradually gave way to rolling hills, each meadow and valley a sea of vibrant wildflowers. Quaint one-room cottages dotted the landscape, surrounded by flocks of sheep or goats grazing in the fields. They rode through town after town, some no more than a tavern and a half-dozen buildings, others large enough to rival Ellesmere.

Four days after leaving Pearl's End, the gray stain of Sandori appeared on the horizon.

Against the cloudless blue sky and sea of long, swaying grass, the capital rose from the ground like a wound. A wall nearly twice the height of Kismoro Keep's encircled the city, blocking all but Myrellis Castle and the Church spires from view. Narrow wood-framed houses and cramped tenements spilled across the land outside the city limits. Everything was made of drab gray stone—so different from the vibrant golds and reds of the Forest of Flames, the verdant rolling hills of the agricultural sector.

"We'll be coming up on the southern gate shortly," Sorin said. "From there, it's a short ride to the house where you'll be living. I'll stay with you for a day to make sure you have everything you need, but then you're on your own. Creator knows I can't be away from the infirmary too long. While you're here, try to make some allies, but be careful who you take into your confidence. A man with a sharp tongue is often more dangerous than a man with a sharp sword."

Soon enough, the carriage joined a line of carts and carriages waiting to enter the city, and it wasn't long before they were rolling down one of Sandori's main avenues, the wheels clattering and jouncing on the ancient cobbles.

As they passed, Sorin pointed out the window to a wide-open square laden with merchant stalls. "That's Myrellis Plaza. Middle-class. Most of the people here are artisans, craftsmen, shopkeepers. The castle and Sapphire Quarter are to the north, and Beggars' End is to the west—home to cripples, slaves, and, of course, beggars."

"Where will I be staying?"

"The Guild owns a manor called Blackbriar in the Sapphire Quarter—a base of operations, one might say. Elvira will accompany you to the castle. She knows what we do here in the Guild, but don't involve her in anything too serious. She can be...flighty."

Mercy nodded, too absorbed in the sights outside to heed what the healer said. Sandori dwarfed Ellesmere by a factor of ten; houses upon houses upon houses, stores and stalls jammed onto every block. It was a marvel of engineering. Many of these buildings dated well over a thousand years back, Mercy knew, having been constructed when Beltharos was nothing more than a cluster of warring city-states.

Finally, they rolled to a stop in front of Blackbriar. The white limestone manor stood three stories tall, with a small patch of manicured grass between the house and the street, and bright, sweet-scented flowers blooming in the window boxes. Unlike many of the houses they had passed, Blackbriar had the luxury of glass windowpanes, which had been flung open to allow the early summer breeze to sweep through. Flourishes of gold and silver paint coiled around the windows and door frame. Despite all its grandeur, it was one of the most modest estates on the street.

Elvira greeted them at the door. She was a skinny, quiet girl, perhaps ten years Mercy's senior. Sorin was right—*flighty* was the perfect word to describe her. During their introductions, her hands did not stop moving once; she fidgeted with the hem of her shirt, the thin silver band on her ring finger, the strand of hair that had fallen from her bun. She led them on a quick tour of the house, somehow finding a piece of furniture to straighten in every room. It exhausted Mercy just to watch her. When they reached the second floor, Emryn and Quinn—the carriage drivers—immediately excused themselves to the guest rooms, grumbling under their breaths about the breakneck pace Sorin had set for their journey. The healer clicked her tongue reproachfully but permitted them to leave.

Once they'd left, Elvira turned to Sorin. "You'll be taking your usual room, Mistress?"

"Yes, just for tonight."

"Then I will prepare a meal while you two get settled. Mercy, the third floor is yours to use as you see fit. There is a bedroom, bath chamber, and a fully-stocked wardrobe. Should you need anything else, please let me know."

The elf descended the stairs to the first floor, and as soon as she was out of earshot, Mercy glanced at Sorin. As kind as the woman was, Elvira seemed timid as a mouse, which concerned Mercy for what they would face in the mad king's court. If the nobles were as cutthroat as Calum and Sorin had claimed, she would need someone reliable to watch her back. "Can we trust her?" she asked softly. "If anyone discovers my true identity, they'll question her—try to make her betray everything she knows about the Guild. She doesn't exactly seem fit for interrogation."

"She won't talk. She's well aware of the risks of helping us, and she's been doing it for a long time. Remember that as an elf, the danger she faces in the king's court is no less than your own. Do not underestimate her."

Her fears somewhat assuaged, Mercy nodded and started up the stairs to the third floor. Sorin fell into step behind her. "Now, let's go over what we discussed earlier," the healer said. "Don't hesitate. Family history."

Mercy sighed. They'd gone over this at least a half-dozen times during the journey from Ellesmere. She was more likely to forget her own name than any of the facts Sorin had made her recite. "My grandparents are Queen Cerelia and Prince-Consort Dion. They have three children: the heir Nymh, General Cadriel—my father—and Lord Justus. Cadriel sent me to live with my uncle Justus and cousin Alistair when I was four so he could attend to his military duties. My mother was a soldier named Ayven. She died protecting Nymh from an attack on the royal family when I was a child. I have no memory of her."

"And your childhood?"

"Spent almost exclusively in Castle Rising, tutored alongside Alistair. Lord Justus is guardian of the Cirisor Islands, and he uses his personal army to defend the archipelago from Beltharan attacks. My father visits when he has time, but he is often occupied with business in Rhys, the capital."

"Good." When they reached the landing, Sorin stepped in front of her, her face softening. "You'll do well, Mercy, I know you will. The king is holding court tomorrow, where you will have your first glimpse of the prince. Be patient, bide your time, and you'll find an opportunity to complete your contract soon enough. By the month's end, you'll be back home, one contract under your belt."

Mercy grinned wickedly, a flutter of excitement filling her. She would be the Daughter who killed a prince.

16

"This isn't going to work," Elvira said the next morning, lips pursed and brows furrowed. She crossed her arms and stared into the open wardrobe in Mercy's bedroom, full to bursting with extravagant silks and lightweight chiffons. Behind her, Mercy stood in nothing but her underclothes, frowning.

"You've had others from Kismoro Keep here," she pointed out. "How did you hide their scars?"

"Creative draping." Elvira grabbed a gown and held it up to Mercy contemplatively, then tossed it onto the steadily-growing pile on the bed. "None of the others had so many."

Mercy crossed her arms, imitating Elvira's earlier stance. An uneven crosshatch of pale, puckered skin trailed across her forearms and over her shoulders, stray scars peeking out below her collarbone and above her hip. Her thumb absently brushed the long, jagged scar that ran along the inside of her left arm. Once, years ago, Mistress Trytain had carved her flesh open and forced her to sew the wound closed. It was a lesson all apprentices endured, yet none of the other girls had been cut so deeply. Even now, the thick scar pulled tight whenever she straightened her arm.

"They weren't too friendly with the only elven apprentice, huh?" Elvira asked as she held up another gown. "Your scars don't befit a royal. They're going to give away your identity."

"Well, if you can't dress me in Beltharan fashion, why not Feyndaran?"

Her eyes brightened, the tension on her face melting. "I don't know much about the fashion beyond the Abraxas Sea, but neither does anyone in the court. None of them have ever been to Feyndara. Give me a minute—I'm sure I can find something."

Elvira ran down the stairs and returned moments later, a triumphant smile on her face. "These will work. One of the other Daughters left them behind." She helped Mercy into a pair of wide-legged silk pants and tied the wide sash at the waistband into a bow at the small of her back. A black military-style jacket followed. It was fitted, tailored perfectly, with a floral pattern embroidered in gold thread along the hem. The shoulders were topped with gold chain epaulets that gleamed in the sunlight streaming in through the open window.

"Perfect," Elvira murmured as she slid gold flats onto Mercy's feet. Once she was finished, she stepped behind Mercy and swiftly ran her fingers through Mercy's wild curls, then twisted them into a loose bun at the nape of her neck. She pinned it in place with a fan-shaped comb, then stepped back to admire her work. A grin spread across her lips. "Lady Marieve, you're ready for the court."

Myrellis Castle sat on a hill overlooking the city, surrounded by a massive stone wall with an iron gate that stretched three times Mercy's height. When she saw it, the image of Liselle's corpse—her head lolling forward, dried blood trailing from the gashes in her stomach—filled Mercy's mind. A chill ran down her spine as she and Elvira passed through the gate and into the castle grounds. Despite her confidence in her skills, she couldn't deny the flicker of unease that passed through her at the memory of what the nobles had done to the king's mistress. Liselle had been the most powerful elf in all Beltharos, and even Ghyslain hadn't been able to protect her.

Her fingers twitched, itching for her daggers. Against her better judgment, she had left them at Blackbriar at Elvira's insistence. Today, her only task was to observe. The quiet elf led her down the long gravel carriageway toward the castle, her loosely-draped linen gown revealing her slender, feminine form. The severe white sash marking her as a slave was stark against the soft folds of her dress. Mercy spied several more men and women in similar garb following their masters into the castle.

Between the gate and the main doors spanned hundreds of yards of lush gardens. Gravel walkways wound lazily around carefully pruned hedges and rows of vibrant flowers, whose honeyed scent hung heavily in the air. At the end of the carriageway, a flight of gleaming stairs rose up to meet the ornately crafted doors of the castle, red wood wrought with whorls of iron. The castle itself was a mass of soaring towers, stained glass windows, and rambling corridors. The gilded roofs of the towers shimmered with flecks of onyx and obsidian.

Mercy tried not to gawk at the grandeur as she and Elvira climbed the steps, surrounded by members of the royal court. The current led them into the great hall, past countless royal guards whose uniforms proudly bore the Myrellis family crest. She admired the gleaming swords sheathed at their sides and wished for the hundredth time that she had brought her daggers. She felt naked without them.

Hundreds of well-groomed and over-perfumed noblemen and women surrounded them, slaves, courtiers, and royal advisors among the masses. Beyond two thick pillars, the hall narrowed. Portraits of past Myrellis rulers lined the walls, their faces grim and regal. Mercy slowed as they approached a bare patch of wall. A portrait of King Ghyslain should have hung there, but instead, the placard read: *King Ghyslain Myrellis and —————, expecting the arrival of the prince.* The second name had been scratched out so many times it was illegible, but there was no doubt who had stood in the painting with the mad king:

The last member of the now-obsolete Zendais family, the late Queen Elisora.

Mercy and Elvira followed the current through a set of double doors, and the throne room spread out before them. None of the courtiers paid them any heed as the sea of people split, forming a long walkway from the entrance to the raised dais at the far end of the room, atop which the throne sat. Behind it, a wall of windows provided a magnificent view of the rocky shore and choppy gray waves of Lake Myrella.

A door on one side of the dais opened, and a complement of royal guards stepped through, dressed in full armor with blades sheathed at their hips. They broke off in twos, taking up positions on the edge of the crowd all down the length of the aisle. The Master of the Guard entered next. He stood taller than every man in the room, his face sour and scarred, and his nose had been broken so many times it was hardly recognizable. He stood beside the throne with both hands resting on the pommel of his sword, his beady black eyes scanning the crowd.

Finally, the king made his entrance.

He was not at all what Mercy had been expecting. After

hearing so many stories of the grief-stricken widower, the unstable monarch on the verge of losing his throne, she had expected him to be a wretched shell of a man. She had imagined him hobbling down the aisle muttering nonsense under his breath, his fine clothes hanging off a decrepit frame mangled by years of anguish and sorrow. And—even though Liselle had only died seventeen years ago—Mercy had always pictured him old.

The king strode down the aisle, his black shirt draped loosely across his torso. A dark purple cloak trimmed in gold thread hung from his broad shoulders, clasped at the neck with an onyx brooch. His wavy black hair was combed into a ponytail at the nape of his neck, a gold diadem encrusted with sapphires and rubies nestled among his loose curls. Although he must have been in his mid-forties, the years had been kind to him.

Once he had taken his seat on the throne, the guards closed all the doors, and a flash of surprise jolted through Mercy. *The prince isn't coming?* She nudged Elvira, who glanced over and shrugged, frowning.

Ghyslain nodded, and a man stepped forward with a guard at his side. He was a commoner, his clothes much more akin to Mercy's usual threadbare tunic and pants than the luxurious robes and gowns surrounding him, and he wrung his hat nervously between his hands. Even so, he drew himself to his full height when the king's gaze landed on him.

"Your Majesty, I've come to ask for an edict requiring an increase in pay for factory workers. And...and an investigation into the owners of several factories across the city."

Derogatory snickers erupted across the room. The king lifted a hand and the courtiers quieted, but the whispers did not cease.

"Why should I grant such a request?"

"The wages we earn aren't enough to feed one person,

let alone a whole family. Most men in the factories earn six aurums a week. We have families to support, and the wives make hardly enough at the market stalls to buy fruit for breakfast. By your own law, Your Majesty, business owners are required to increase their workers' pay every two years. My salary has not changed in six years, and my complaints —along with those of the other workers—have gone ignored."

A courtier stepped forward, staring down his nose at the man. "If you don't like your pay, leave the city. There's plenty of work in the mines in Blackhills. Instituting a city-wide wage increase will undoubtedly bankrupt countless businesses."

"I don't want to cause any trouble," the man said, turning back to the king. "We just want what we are owed. I didn't come forward sooner because everyone who does ends up replaced. The boss will let us work and forget about us, but the moment there is a complaint, he replaces us with elves from Beggars' End. They'll work eighteen hours a day for two aurums a week."

"Employees earn their pay based on the quality of their work, and if they are unsatisfied, there are many far needier who would happily accept the opportunities others take for granted." The courtier offered Ghyslain a simpering smile. "Your Majesty, there is simply no need to change a system that has worked for years."

The commoner glared at him with unabashed hatred, cheeks flushed with anger. He balled up the hat he'd been wringing as if he wished to throw it at the courtier—or shove it down his throat.

The king leaned forward and rested an elbow on the arm of his throne. "Is it true my laws have been disobeyed, Seren Pierce?"

"Of course not, Your Majesty."

"Then why hasn't this man been properly paid in six years?"

The smile dropped a fraction. "I...don't know."

"You had better find out. Your position in this court depends on it," the king said. "Starting today, Seren, you will personally meet with the owner of every major business within the city walls and ensure that every worker is being paid what he is owed. When you are finished, you will do the same with every minor business."

Seren Pierce set his jaw, glared at the commoner, then turned on his heel and walked out of the room. A guard moved to follow him, but Ghyslain halted him with a wave of his hand. "Let him go. He is no doubt keen to return to his king's good graces." He turned to the worker. "What is your name?"

"R-Raidon, Your Majesty."

"Treasurer Evander, escort Raidon to the great hall and make sure he is paid every aurum he is owed. And—how many children do you have?"

"Four. And another on the way."

"Give him some extra for the children. I trust this is satisfactory?" he asked.

Raidon beamed, looking close to tears. "Better than I could have hoped, Your Majesty. My children will go to bed tonight with full stomachs. Thank you."

"You are welcome." Ghyslain nodded to Evander, who bowed and led the man out of the room. Just before the doors swung shut behind them, Raidon jumped up and whooped, pumping a fist in the air. Ghyslain smiled, but it only lasted a second. "The nest issue?" he asked the Master of the Guard.

The court continued in the same manner for the next three hours; a matter was brought before Ghyslain, a noble or advisor argued, and Ghyslain passed a judgment. Mercy half-listened as the king settled a property dispute, dispatched guards to shut down a growing crime ring in Beggars' End, and discussed a proposal to allow the mining of the Howling Mountains. She was growing bored and impatient, and her legs ached from standing in one place for so long. She should have been hunting down the prince, not stuck here in the throne room, useless.

"The Howling Mountains have been off-limits for nearly two hundred years, since His Majesty's great-great-grandfather made a treaty with the Rennox," Elvira whispered, mistaking Mercy's disinterest for confusion. "The Rennox attacked every scouting party the crown sent there, thinking the humans were trying to steal their precious eudorite. By the time the king finally convinced them to parlay, fifty soldiers had been lost to the Rennox."

"No one has seen a Rennox in over a generation," the advisor in favor of the proposal said. "They used to trade with some of the northern mining cities, but one year, they simply stopped. We've found no evidence of their continued existence; they might have gone into hiding or been wiped out by disease. Whatever the cause, we cannot ignore this opportunity."

"They wouldn't have gone into hiding over nothing," the other advisor shot back. "We have no idea what deadly creatures lurk in those mountains. We should not endeavor to find out."

"Perhaps they left. Perhaps they decided to stop trading with us. Whatever the reason, we would be remiss to leave those mountains sitting there, abandoned. They're a part of our country—we should know more about them."

The doors at the back of the throne room banged open. Four guards entered the room, with a fifth dragging a hissing, spitting woman behind him. Her hair was a tangled mess, clenched in the fist of the guard and stuck to the angry tears streaming down her face. Several noblewomen gasped. The two warring advisors shrank into the crowd, mouths agape in surprise and disgust.

As the guard shoved the woman to her knees at the foot of the dais, one more figure darkened the doorway. He strode confidently into the throne room, ignoring the curses the woman hurled at him. The silver pommel of the sword on his belt flashed as he walked.

Mercy pushed her way through the throngs of people before her until she stood on the edge of the crowd, right beside the aisle. The young man's dark eyes met hers, and Prince Tamriel smiled.

❧ 17 ☙

His gaze rested on her for a moment, tracing a line from her eyes to the points of her ears before dropping to her chest, searching for the sash that wasn't there. He could just as well have been staring at her breasts, Mercy mused, although it wasn't likely he would be impressed. There were plenty of young noblewomen here with twice her curves, and their sheer gowns left little to the imagination.

The prince turned away, climbed the steps of the platform, and took his place beside his father's throne. Aside from the age difference, he was nearly identical to the king—they shared the same wavy hair, olive complexion, and dark eyes. He was clad in a slate gray breastplate, black cloak, pants, and leather boots. At least two women near Mercy swooned.

The woman before the throne staggered to her feet, her skirt in tatters. She shoved the hair out of her face and glared up at the royals, her hands clenched into fists.

One of the guards said, "We caught her sneaking runaway slaves out of Beggars' End, Your Majesty." Another guard dumped the contents of a canvas bag onto the floor, spilling exotic coins and scraps of parchment. "We estimate she has led over thirty slaves to freedom thus far. The elves call her Hero. She refused to give her real name."

Prince Tamriel crossed his arms as King Ghyslain leaned forward, studying the woman through narrowed eyes. "You are aware it is against the law to aid or orchestrate the escape of a runaway slave, I am sure," he said. "Do you deny this allegation?"

She said nothing, merely lifted her chin in defiance. The throne room, which had previously been abuzz with whispers, was quiet enough to hear a pin drop.

"Have you anything to say in your defense?" Ghyslain asked.

"Nothing that will not fall on deaf ears," Hero retorted.

A shadow passed across Tamriel's face. "You should speak to your king with more respect."

"A king who profits off the work of those he has enslaved is no king of mine."

"That's enough," Ghyslain snapped. He looked to one of the guards. "You found her in Beggars' End?"

"Just outside, Your Majesty. With the aid of an unknown accomplice, she had created a tunnel through the wall that allowed passage in and out of the city. My men are filling it as we speak. The six elves she had been helping were captured and punished accordingly."

"And who is this mystery accomplice?" Ghyslain asked Hero. "Name him or her, and your punishment shall be less severe."

She said nothing.

He sighed. "Fine. If you insist on keeping your silence, allow me to make it a little easier for you. I won't have your poisonous views spreading to the rest of the city." He flicked a hand to the guards. "Take her to the dungeon and cut out her tongue. Throw her back in Beggars' End when you are finished."

"Yes, Your Majesty."

The guards grasped Hero by the arms, intending to escort her out, but she remained immobile, glaring at the king. "Move," one growled through his teeth. Whispers rose throughout the court. Prince Tamriel studied her with curiosity.

"Fool woman. What is she doing?" Elvira murmured.

One of the guards pulled his crossbow and swung it low. The butt cracked against the back of Hero's knee, sending her crumpling to the floor, pain contorting her face. "I said," the guard hissed, "*move.*" He raised the crossbow to swing again, and someone in the crowd cried out as it began its descent.

"Is this what Liselle would have wanted?" Hero snarled, silencing the room with the name. Several nobles looked more insulted than if she had uttered a curse. Pain and anger flashed through Ghyslain's eyes.

"Bitch," the guard spat, swinging the crossbow. It struck her shoulder and a sickening crunch echoed across the room, coupled with Hero's cry of agony. Bile rose in Mercy's throat.

"Get her out of my sight," Ghyslain ordered.

The guards hauled her out of the room, her shouts and curses fading down the corridor. Tamriel turned away as the doors swung shut behind them, while Ghyslain smoothed the folds of his shirt and took a breath before speaking.

"That will be all for today. Master Oliver, I'd like a word."

He left the room without another look at the court or his son, the Master of the Guard close on his heels. A weight seemed to lift off the shoulders of everyone in the room when he disappeared into the corridor—Prince Tamriel included. His tight expression softened, some of the tension in his stance easing. He descended the steps of the dais and was immediately pulled into conversation with two young, pretty noblewomen.

"Introduce me to the prince," Mercy said to Elvira.

Elvira took her hand and began wading through the crowd, closer and closer to the dais. Some of the nobles were making their way toward the doors, but many remained in the throne room, discussing the events of the past few hours. Mercy caught snippets of conversation as they wove between groups of people.

"—spilled it all down her lap and ruined a perfectly good gown—"

"—threw an extravagant party last week. He even had pastries decorated with real gold—and all that to try and hide the fact that his family's bankrupt."

"—fit to wear the crown? Nearly two decades later, he still bolts at the mere mention of her."

That piqued Mercy's interest. Part of her wanted to stop Elvira and eavesdrop, discover more about the king and Liselle. Was what the nobles said true? Did Ghyslain still carry so much guilt and grief over Liselle's death that he could not bear even the thought of her? Mercy found the thought absurd. She couldn't imagine belonging so completely to someone else. Love was nothing but a weakness. Llorin, the woman who had brought Mercy to the Guild, had lost her life because of it.

Elvira dropped Mercy's hand suddenly, startling her out of her thoughts. The elf planted herself between the two noblewomen speaking to the prince and stared at him expectantly, her hands clasped in front of her. Strangely, as shy as she'd been yesterday, she appeared wholly in her element among the nobility.

Tamriel paused mid-sentence and turned to Elvira with a puzzled expression, taking in the white sash across her chest. "Yes?" he asked, raising a brow.

Elvira smiled and stepped aside. "May I present to Your Highness the Lady Marieve Aasa of Castle Rising, granddaughter of the queen of Feyndara."

Surprise flashed across Tamriel's face as Mercy dropped into a curtsy. "It's a pleasure to meet you, Lady Marieve," he said. "Forgive my surprise—we received the letter announcing your impending arrival, but considering the tension between our countries, we dared not believe it was true. Welcome to Sandori, my lady."

"The pleasure is all mine, Your Highness." As she straightened, she eyed the smooth metal of his breastplate. Less than an inch of steel protected his heart. *I should've brought my daggers,* she thought sullenly.

The blonde at the prince's side smiled. "You've come to attend His Highness's eighteenth birthday celebration, then?"

"I would be remiss not to attend the festivities, I should think," she said. "But my main reason for this journey is to discuss the matter of the Cirisor Islands with the king. There have been three hundred years of fighting over the territory—there is no need for further bloodshed. Hopefully, this visit will be the first step to sowing peace between our countries."

Mercy mentally catalogued every chink in the prince's armor as she spoke. His breastplate was thick and finely made, but the rest of his body was vulnerable, swathed in fine fabric that would split like tissue before her daggers. He had certainly studied swordplay, and was excellent at it—that was evident in his strong, muscular build. If it came to a fight between them, she would have to rely on speed rather than strength to beat him, particularly because he stood almost a head and a half taller than she.

The brunette on Tamriel's other side nodded. "Both sides have lost many men for a foolish cause. The Islands belonged first to Beltharos. They should have stayed that way."

"I'm sure we'll be able to find an agreement that suits

both Beltharos and Feyndara," Tamriel said, giving the brunette a warning look. "Pardon my manners, Lady Marieve. This is Serenna Elise"—he nodded to the blonde—"and Serenna Emrie, daughters of two of my father's advisors."

Elise smiled conspiratorially. "You may have seen my father earlier. He was the one who stormed out with smoke pouring from his ears."

"The seren is a loyal—if stubborn—man," Emrie said, brown curls bouncing as she nodded. "Sandori must seem very different from your home, does it not?"

Play the part you've been given, Mercy thought, *and play it well.* "Yes, it is strange. I don't know how hundreds of thousands of people fit comfortably inside the city walls." It was true: growing up in the Keep, she'd never been able to imagine a city bustling with so many people. Thinking of the houses crammed on top of one another made Mercy's breath catch with claustrophobia. She longed for the wilderness of the Forest of Flames. "Feyndara is covered in forests, so there aren't many stone cities like this. Rhys—the capital—is the exception, of course—"

She was spared having to elaborate by Master Oliver's sudden appearance behind the prince. "The king wishes to speak with you, Your Highness."

"Is it important?"

"He would speak with you now, Your Highness."

Tamriel sighed. "Very well." He bade farewell to Emrie and Elise, who seemed to inflate with the attention, then turned to Mercy. "I hope we speak again soon, Lady Marieve. In the meantime, I will ask my father about granting you a private audience. Enjoy your time in Sandori."

"Thank you, Your Highness."

Once the prince had left, Mercy turned to Emrie and Elise. "You two are serennas? I'm not familiar with that title."

"To the crown, it's more an obligation than an honor. Our

fathers are lesser advisors, which means we're little more than glorified servants," Elise joked. "Most of our days consist of taking notes, delivering letters, duties of the sort."

"It's terribly boring, but we know everything about the inner circle—all the gossip, all the rivalries." Emrie's voice dropped to a whisper, a mischievous grin spreading across her lips. "We know secrets that would send half of these men running home to their wives, and the other half hiding from them for fear of a lashing."

As the girl spoke, Mercy's gaze wandered to the doors through which the prince had left. Forget staying in the capital for weeks; this could be her chance. Most of the royal guards would be surrounding Ghyslain's chambers, where he and Tamriel would likely be meeting, but if Mercy could sneak into the prince's chambers... Well, his soldiers couldn't possibly guard him every second.

Sensing her thoughts, Elvira caught Mercy's eye and raised a brow in question. She nodded, and Elvira turned on her heel, weaving through the throngs of people. She stopped beside the doorway and said something to a slave before leaving the room.

"What is your opinion of the prince?" Mercy asked the serennas. "Have you known him long?"

"All our lives."

"We were all much closer when we were children," Elise said. "He may seem a little stiff and aloof at first, but he's a good man. Court life has been hard on him. My father told me Tamriel used to sneak out of his bedroom in the middle of the night and curl up on one of the library's couches with a book and a candle. It drove the guards mad trying to find him in all the library's nooks and crannies." She grinned. "By the time they did, he'd have fallen asleep with the book clutched to his chest and the candle sitting a few feet away on the floor, almost burned down to nothing. My father said it was a miracle he never burned down the library."

Mercy smiled. "A miracle, indeed." Out of the corner of her eye, she saw Elvira reenter the throne room. The elf paused in the doorway and waved Mercy over. Her face had gone white as a sheet. "If you'll excuse me, I must be on my way."

"Of course. Will you be attending the Solari celebration in three days, my lady?"

"Yes, I'll be here," she said as Elvira gave a second, more insistent wave. Mercy dipped her head in respect to the serennas and hurried over to the doors, ignoring the faces the courtiers made when they noticed her elven ears. When she reached Elvira, she took the woman by the arm and led her into the hall, where they would have a modicum of privacy. "What in the world is wrong?"

"I followed the prince, and— It would be easier to show you. Come." Elvira pulled out of Mercy's grasp and jogged down the hall, her dress fluttering behind her. They quickly made their way through the great hall and down several twisting corridors. Occasionally, they passed slaves carrying platters of drinks or sheaves of parchment, but no one stopped them as they walked through a stone archway and down a flight of stairs.

Down?

"They're in the dungeon," Elvira whispered, sensing her thoughts. "Stay quiet."

Below the main floor, the stone walls were thick, the air earthy and moist. Torches lined the walls in even intervals, the flames dancing and crackling. They stopped before a fork in the corridor.

"Left or right?" Mercy whispered.

Before Elvira could respond, an agonized wail shattered the silence, echoing and distorting as it bounced through the stone corridor. A gasp of pain cut off the cry, and the resulting quiet made the hairs on the back of Mercy's neck stand on end. Beside her, Elvira began to tremble.

"There are guards nearby," Elvira breathed, peering down one of the hallways. "This way."

She led Mercy down the left hall and paused before a door so old the wood had turned the same color as the stone bricks surrounding it. The second another wail filled the hall, she pushed the door open, the creaking hinges drowned out by the scream, and gestured for Mercy to follow her inside.

They stood in an abandoned supply closet, rotting crates and dusty pallets stacked against one wall. The room was so small that—standing shoulder to shoulder—there was hardly any room for them to maneuver without toppling a pile and alerting the guards to their presence.

"Look."

Elvira pointed to a broken brick near Mercy's hip. She knelt to examine it and realized that some of the pulverized stone had been chipped away to form a makeshift peephole into the neighboring room. In the flickering light from within, she could make out the silhouette of man, but could see no higher than his hip. He circled a mound of dirty cloth, and when he struck it with the toe of his boot, there was a sharp, pained intake of breath, followed by a moan.

Hero.

Clutching her stomach with one arm, Hero rose to her knees and spat grimy hair from her mouth. Her other arm hung limply at her side, her broken shoulder swollen to twice its normal size. "You cannot hide from this forever. You cannot turn everything she did into nothing." She grimaced, but her words came out evenly, laced with disgust. "You are a wretched, pitiful excuse of a—"

Her head snapped to the side, the imprint of Master Oliver's hand blazing red on her cheek. "You'd better watch your mouth," he growled. "Remember who you address next time you speak, or your tongue won't be the only thing we take."

"Do you remember her?" Hero looked past the Master of the Guard, glaring at someone outside of Mercy's range of vision. The king was there, she realized belatedly. "Do you remember the way the nobles strung her up on the gate like some criminal? Almost eighteen years later, you still dance like a puppet for the court's amusement and run and hide whenever someone mentions your dearly departed—"

Oliver seized her arm and wrenched it upward. She screamed through her teeth as her broken bones ground against each other, somehow managing to stay conscious despite her obvious agony.

"Sweet Creator," Elvira groaned.

Mercy glanced behind her to find Elvira crouched on the floor, shaking. Her hands covered her ears, yet from a glimpse at her pale face, it was clear they did nothing to block out the sounds of Hero's suffering.

"Go upstairs," Mercy whispered. "Go back to Blackbriar. I'm fine on my own."

She shook her head, her eyes squeezed shut.

Another scream erupted from the other room. Hero's arms had been tied behind her back, and Master Oliver pulled her tongue forward with a pair of tongs. He lifted a red-hot dagger, the handle wrapped in thick cloth. Hero's eyes widened. With Master Oliver holding her still, all she could do was watch as the glowing blade drew closer to her tongue.

"Wait," Ghyslain said suddenly. "Tamriel will do it."

Oliver faltered. "Your Majesty?"

"Father?" Tamriel's voice came out pinched, tight with apprehension and surprise.

"You heard me, Oliver. Hand over the dagger." After a beat of silence, Ghyslain roared, "Hand him the dagger!"

Through the tiny hole, Mercy watched as the prince crossed the room and stopped at Oliver's side. He didn't take the knife. Hero knelt on the floor before him, her eyes wide and terrified.

"Take the dagger, Tamriel," his father said quietly. "Oliver, the knife."

At last, Master Oliver passed over the dagger and tongs. Tamriel's hand shook as he held the dagger over her tongue, the blade still glowing brightly. After a moment's hesitation, he sliced through it in one swift motion, and the sound of sizzling meat filled the room. Hero let out a bloodcurdling scream that chilled Mercy to the bone.

Tamriel tossed the tongs and the severed tongue aside as Hero swayed and collapsed, her eyes rolling back into her head. Mercy couldn't see his face, but she heard the disgust and hatred in his voice when he turned to his father and spat, "I will never forgive you for this," before storming out of the room.

18

Elvira was still trembling when they returned to Blackbriar. The second they stepped into the foyer, she excused herself and retreated to her bedroom, closing the door behind her.

Mercy tugged her hair out of its bun and moved into the study, dropping onto the settee by the window. She wished she could forget the cruelty she had witnessed in the castle. Sentencing a woman to elinguation, allowing the guards to beat her, and forcing his son to carry out the punishment? All for helping a few dozen slaves escape their masters—and this from Ghyslain, who had loved an elf enough to allow her to sit on the throne beside him. After Tamriel stormed out of the room, Ghyslain had run after him, calling his son's name, and Master Oliver had merely sighed before gathering Hero in his arms and carrying her into the hall.

This changes nothing, she told herself, trying to ignore the weight in the pit of her stomach. Calum and Sorin had warned her how dangerous the court was, and nothing would stand between her and the completion of her contract.

Yet as she rose and climbed the stairs to her room, she

could not help but think of the story Elise had told her of the boy who had snuck out of his bedroom every night to lose himself in one of the library's books. What must it have been like to grow up the son of the mad king, with nothing but his father's grief and madness to color his days? What must it have been like to attend court with the very people who had killed Liselle and now clamored to usurp Ghyslain's throne?

Mercy banished the thoughts from her mind. She would not pity him. He was her mark, and nothing more.

Elvira barely spoke the next morning, breaking her silence only to ask Mercy to pass the plate of fruit during breakfast. Mercy could tell by the shadows under the woman's eyes that the memory of what they had witnessed the day before still haunted her. She couldn't blame Elvira; even after everything Mercy had endured in her Guild training, Hero's screams had plagued her sleep. She had tossed and turned all night before finally giving up and throwing off the covers sometime around dawn.

After cleaning up breakfast, Elvira helped Mercy into a floor-length silk skirt and a long-sleeved tunic of emerald crepe. She fluttered around Mercy, biting her lip in concentration as she straightened the skirt's hem and fixed her hair.

"I want to explore the castle on my own today—get a better look around," Mercy finally said, eager to break the uncomfortable silence that had settled over them. "After everything that happened yesterday...are you alright?"

Elvira's cheeks reddened, and she turned back to close the wardrobe doors. "Fine. It's just that...my husband, he's a slave in the castle. Seeing what the king and his guards did to that woman who helped the slaves got to me. We always talk about running, finding freedom, but we live in dangerous times."

"That slave you spoke to in the throne room yesterday. Is he your husband?"

She shook her head. "Bron is only a friend. My husband is not often permitted to leave the kitchens, so Bron acts as our messenger." Pain and sorrow filled her voice. "My husband has been a slave in Myrellis Castle for twenty years. He was eight when he was taken from an orphanage in Beggars' End and brought to the castle. We met fifteen years ago, during the last Solari celebration, and we were married in secret only two weeks later."

Mercy's brows rose. "Two weeks? Truly?"

"I knew the moment I met him that I would marry him." Elvira smiled wistfully as she turned back, a necklace of silver and raw emeralds dangling between her hands. Mercy swept up her hair as Elvira clasped it around her neck. "The night my mistress passed, Kier and I snuck out of the castle, intending to flee to the Howling Mountains and then make our way east to the Islands. We stole a boat and were a couple hundred yards off the shore of Lake Myrella when the guards caught up to us.

"Sorin was a Daughter then, and was inside the castle when the guards brought us in. She killed them and saved our lives. The Guild had recently lost an important contact in the capital, and they needed someone to take care of Blackbriar and assist any Daughter who came to Sandori. Sorin promised no one else would find out about Kier's escape attempt if I agreed to work at Blackbriar, so I did."

"So are you a slave or an employee?"

"A bit of both, I suppose. I'm here alone most of the time, and Mother Illynor makes sure I have enough money to live comfortably. The slave sash just makes it easier to move around unnoticed. It can be lonely, but this way I'm close to

Kier," she said. "Mother Illynor has agreed to release me from my contract after fifteen years of service, but I don't want to wait. The tension between humans and elves only worsens every year. I can't watch my husband live in chains any longer." Her gaze cut toward Mercy, and her eyes narrowed, clearly weighing whether it was worth it to trust Mercy. Eventually, she said, "One day, Kier and I are going to make it all the way to the Islands, where we will finally be free, where we will finally be able to speak without having to sneak around. Please don't speak of this to the Guildmother. I've given her years of loyal service, but I can't do it any longer."

Mercy considered it for a moment, torn between her loyalty to the Guild and Elvira's story, then nodded. "Just help me complete my contract. Whatever you do after that is no business of mine."

Elvira sagged with relief. Mother Illynor would be furious with her if she ever learned that Mercy knew of the elven woman's plans, but that wouldn't happen; Elvira and her husband would be long gone before news of their disappearance reached the Keep. They could easily find a replacement to tend to Blackbriar.

"Take your daggers with you to the castle from now on," Elvira said as she left the room. "Nowhere in Sandori is safe for an elf on her own."

Never in her life had Mercy been more grateful for a pair of shoes than she was for the ones on her feet. They were black silk flats decorated with silver tassels and embroidery, the delicate filigree glittering with flecks of crystal, and were worth more than anything Mercy had ever owned, including her Stryker-made daggers. They were ridiculous. Beautiful, but ridiculous.

They were also completely silent as Mercy stalked through the halls of Myrellis Castle.

Without Elvira as her guide, Mercy wandered through the high-ceiling corridors with one destination in mind: Tamriel's private chambers. She had already discovered the kitchen and larders, storerooms, and pantries, as well as the main dining hall, multiple studies, and several unused apartments. Many of the bedrooms she had passed were furnished with nothing but a few pieces of furniture covered in dust cloths—memories of the years when the castle had bustled with foreign dignitaries, diplomats, and visiting royals. Now, they were home only to ghosts of the past. They would make excellent hiding places for the prince's body.

The castle was surprisingly empty; the only people Mercy encountered were those who lived or worked there. It seemed the rumors of the king's madness had long since scared away visitors. The slaves didn't so much as glance at her as they scurried about their chores. The guards who roamed the halls eyed her suspiciously but, seeing as 'Lady Marieve' had come in peace to speak with the king, they had no reason to keep her from exploring.

Finally, she thought as she turned a corner and found four guards standing watch over a door at the end of the corridor. *Tamriel's chambers.* She feigned interest in a painting on the wall as she studied the men in her periphery, taking stock of their arms and armor. Each wore plate mail and had a sword sheathed at his hip. Mercy could take on one of two of them at a time, but not four. If she wanted to kill Tamriel in his room, she would have to find a way to sneak in, or have him dismiss his guards.

Mistress Sorin's voice echoed in her mind: *Use the pretext of a marriage alliance to get close to him.* Mercy smiled. She had never been romantically interested in any of the Strykers, but she had watched enough Daughters and apprentices flirt with them to know what young men liked to hear. She doubted Tamriel would be any different.

She chuckled quietly to herself as she turned and walked back the way she had come. *Maybe I* really *should have practiced batting my lashes and fainting onto a divan.*

A strangled cry froze Mercy at the top of the stairs. She glanced down the empty hallway behind her, ears straining for another sob, or perhaps the bark of a guard's command, but nothing came.

She crept to the nearest set of double doors and rested her hands on the smooth wood, listening for any movement from within. The sob had come from inside, she was sure of it. After a beat of silence, she reached for one of the handles.

Something shattered against the opposite side of the door. Mercy jumped back, startled, then eased the door open just enough to peer inside.

King Ghyslain stood in the center of his study, his back to her. Without warning, he whirled toward the desk, wrapped his fingers around the neck of a vase, and hurled it into the fireplace. Shards of porcelain went flying. The logs crackled and sent a shower of sparks into the air. Ghyslain threw another, staggering from the momentum. At first, Mercy thought the king was drunk, but then she noticed the tears streaming down his cheeks.

He fell to his knees with a choked moan and buried his face in his hands. "*Go away,*" he breathed in a ragged voice.

Mercy looked down the hall again, sure a guard was going to show up any second, but there was not even a slave in sight. Was she the only one who had heard the commotion? Or was everyone in the castle so accustomed to the king's fits of madness that they had learned to ignore him?

Inside the study, Ghyslain lifted his head and stared at the blackening pieces of porcelain littering the fireplace. His dark eyes shone with the reflection of the flames.

"You have no hold over me. You have no right to torment me like this. Leave now!" The king's gaze moved to the space above the fire, tracking someone Mercy couldn't see. A chill ran down her spine.

The king scrambled backward until his back hit the desk. "You know I had to punish her. If I do anything to help the slaves, the nobles will take my throne and my head, and Tam will be next. I refuse to lose anyone else I love, Liselle!"

Mercy started. Hero was right: he was still haunted by the memory of his long-dead lover.

Inside the room, Ghyslain tugged at his hair in agitation. "The throne is mine. There is too much at stake. The Zendais boy has been stirring up sympathy for his family, and with Tamriel's eighteenth birthday coming up, I must have as much support from the nobles as possible. My son must never take the throne.

"Creator's grace," he gasped, visibly shaking. His eyes lifted to the air before him, and a sad, tortured smile spread across his face. "Why did they have to take you from me, Liselle?"

Ghyslain extended a trembling hand as if to caress Liselle's face, but he stopped himself short. His arm fell to his side as a new wave of tears rose.

Mercy quietly shut the door and hurried back to the stairs, unsettled by what she'd seen. The man in that room was not the king who had held court just one day prior—he was nothing but a mangled, grieving shell.

19
TAMRIEL

Tamriel ran his hands down his face, muttering softly to himself as he paced the hall outside one of the castle's many meeting rooms, the voices of his father's council members ringing in his ears. He had spent the entire morning in meetings, half-listening as the advisors discussed tax changes, street repairs, and other trivialities that neither concerned nor interested him, yet—for some reason—required his approval. They were the sort of duties his father had always assigned him, intended to give the illusion of him having some power in the kingdom. Tamriel wasn't sure who the charade was meant to fool: him, or the subjects.

Today, however, his distraction had not been due to boredom, but to the screams that still reverberated in his mind.

He couldn't forget the way Hero's shoulder had crunched when the guard's crossbow struck her, how her agonized screams had sounded more animal than human. He couldn't forget the defiance burning in her eyes as she stared down the king and taunted him with the memory of Liselle. He couldn't forget the feeling of the dagger in his hand, the blade glowing red-hot, and he would never, *ever* forget the look on Hero's face as he cut out her tongue.

Yet through it all, she had not given him up. She had not exposed their secret.

His stomach roiled, bile rising in his throat. Tamriel stopped in the middle of the hall and rubbed his eyes with the heels of his palms, sucking in deep breaths until the feeling passed. Damn his father. Damn the nobles. If yesterday was any indication of what he would one day face as king, his father could keep the Creator-forsaken throne. Right now, there was nothing he desired more than to board a ship and leave Beltharos far behind.

He turned on his heel and strode down the corridor, nervous energy leaving him restless. With no destination in mind, he wandered toward the great hall, hoping—for once—for some courtier to have arrived or some problem to have arisen that demanded his attention; anything to keep his mind off what he had done.

Tamriel rounded a corner and halted abruptly, blinking with surprise. Halfway down the hall, the Feyndaran royal he had met at court was examining a large oil painting hanging on the wall. *Lady Marieve.* While most of the castle was open to the public, he had not expected to see her again so soon—and certainly not without a guard or handmaid to accompany her.

"Do you like art, Lady Marieve?" he asked as he approached.

"I do, although I find my education on the subject somewhat lacking." She nodded to the painting, a rendering of a small western town Tamriel had never particularly liked. The painting, not the town, that was—although, judging from the expressions on the people's faces, they weren't too happy to be mining coal day in and day out.

He stopped beside her and studied the painting. "This

one is priceless—an original Faramond from almost four hundred years ago," he said, reciting a lesson from a tutor whose name he had long since forgotten. "It's supposed to depict the rise of the mining industry in Ospia. The artist used only shades of brown, black, and white in an attempt to highlight the industrialization of the town."

"Seems to me the only thing he managed to highlight was the fact that this painting is hideous."

He burst out laughing, taking by surprise at her blunt response. "I'm sorry—I feel the same. I've never liked Faramond's work."

The corner of her mouth twitched upward. "So was everything you said just meant to impress me?"

"That depends. Did it work?"

Marieve studied him from head to toe, her attention snagging on the royal crest embroidered on his tunic, just above his heart. "Our countries have been at war for generations, Your Highness," she finally said, "but you have treated me with more kindness than I had expected to find in my enemy's land, and for that, I am grateful. Perhaps one day, we could even be friends."

As she spoke, Tamriel couldn't help staring at the points of her ears. They just barely peeked through her intricately-braided hair, which was such a rich shade of black it was almost blue. Until yesterday, he had never met a member of the Feyndaran royal family. Queen Cerelia had broken all ties between the two countries when she ascended the throne over fifty years ago. Only the Strykers and a select few merchants were allowed on Feyndaran soil.

"Perhaps we could," he agreed, although the odds of that seemed slim considering the history between their countries. Still, he could make an effort to get to know her in the hopes that it would ease negotiations. "I seem to recall our last conversation being interrupted, my lady. What is Feyndara like? If you don't mind my asking."

"It's not terribly different from here. Because of the forests, the cities are farther apart and traveling can sometimes be difficult, but the land is beautiful. I believe the main difference is that in my country, elves are not considered property."

A challenge slid into her voice, and Tamriel frowned. He knew exactly what his father would want him to say, and although the words tasted bitter on his tongue, he forced them out: "Slavery, while unpleasant, has existed within this country for centuries. Entire cities owe their existence to the labor of slaves. Despite what you may think, there are laws in place to protect elves from abusive masters." Hero's face flashed in his mind, but he shoved the image—and accompanying wave of guilt—away. "The stories you hear of cruel masters are just that—stories. No decent man would mistreat his investments."

"*Investments?*" Her expression soured. "Losing a sock is unpleasant, Your Highness. Having one's freedom stripped, living one's life in chains..." She shook her head. "I would not wish that fate on my worst enemy."

Nor would I, he thought, wishing he could tell her the truth of his sympathy for the elves. Yesterday, Hero had remained silent, had lost her tongue, to keep the court from learning that Tamriel was her partner in sneaking runaway slaves out of the city. The cutthroat nobles would've had his head on a spike if they knew where his true loyalties lay. His already low mood sank at the thought.

I should have saved Hero. I should have tried harder to keep the guards from finding her.

But there had been nothing he could do. They had already found all the evidence they needed to arrest her.

"Are you alright, Your Highness?" Lady Marieve asked. As

she searched his face, he realized she had the most unusual eyes—brown with rings of gold around the pupils, like there was a spark inside her fighting to be released. Unlike the courtiers' daughters he had grown up with, she did not attempt any sort of flattery when she spoke to him, did not bat her lashes or blush and offer meaningless praise. She spoke directly, bluntly. It was refreshing.

"I'm fine." He smoothed his shirt self-consciously. He was well aware that he looked like he had been dragged through hell and back; he had tossed and turned all night, and the two hours of sleep he eventually found had offered only a short reprieve from his guilt and shame.

This is not the behavior of a prince, his father's voice whispered in his ear, ever critical.

Tamriel straightened and shot Marieve a tight smile. "If you'll pardon me, I must speak with my father about the preparations for Solari. Once the arrangements are made, you should expect an invitation to begin negotiations shortly."

Something flickered across Marieve's face at the mention of the king, but it disappeared before Tamriel could identify it. She curtsied. "Thank you, Your Highness."

"My pleasure." He bade her farewell and hurried down the hall, but turned back when he reached the corner. "Feel free to take look around the gallery on the second floor, as well. You might find a painting you hate more than Faramond's."

Tamriel's steps leadened as he neared his father's study. Muffled sobbing bled out through the closed double doors. He entered without knocking and frowned down at his father, who sat slumped on the floor in front of his desk. Broken pieces of pottery littered the floor in and around the fireplace. The sight made Tamriel's blood boil.

"How could you do that to me, Father?" he exploded. "How could you force me to harm that woman?"

"*I* did not force you to do anything. You know the laws." Ghyslain stood and moved behind his desk, shuffling absently through some papers. He didn't meet Tamriel's eyes as he said, "It is high time you faced the consequences of your actions."

"What are you talking about?"

His father shot him a knowing look. "You can drop the act, Tam. Save it for the nobility."

Tamriel set his jaw. "What act?"

"Don't play the fool with me. You should count yourself lucky Hero didn't name you as her partner before the court, or they'd have your body strung up on the castle gate like Li—" He choked on the name and shook his head. "What do you think the nobles will do to you if they find out you've been helping slaves escape?"

Tamriel looked away, saying nothing.

Ghyslain opened a drawer and pulled out a piece of parchment, examining the neat boxes drawn across the front and back. "I had Master Oliver gather the guard schedules from the past month. It's subtle, but the gaps are there, just wide enough for you to slip out of the castle late at night, and sneak back in before everyone wakes, all without being seen by a single soul. After I found that, I had him fetch *all* the recent guard schedules. It looks like you've been working with Hero for almost two years, Tam." He returned the paper to its drawer. "Who else knows?"

"...Just Master Oliver," Tamriel finally admitted.

His father didn't yell. He didn't shout or call for the guards. He merely dropped into his desk chair, rubbing his temples with his fingers. "You can't do this, Tamriel. I know how much you ache for the elves—by the Creator, you know how much *I* ache for them—but you cannot do this." Ghyslain's voice was soft—so soft and so, so sad. "I wish I could help you—I really do—but we're two people against a country of slaveowners.

"Hero will be returned to Beggars' End in a matter of days, once Alyss has finished tending her wounds. Do not seek her out." Ghyslain rounded the desk and stopped before Tamriel. "Oh, my son," he sighed. "I wish you never had to hurt that woman. Ever since I discovered that you were her partner, I prayed every day that you would come to your senses. You're too stubborn for your own good, just like your mother."

Tamriel stiffened. They never talked about his mother. *Never.* "It wasn't her you were hallucinating today, was it?" he asked, glancing at the broken pottery scattered across the floor. Over the years, he had grown used to his father's fits of madness: broken pottery and overturned furniture accompanied Liselle's appearances, while tears and agonized wails accompanied his mother's. For the majority of his childhood, his sullen, brooding father's outbursts had terrified him. Now, they were routine.

Ghyslain scowled. "I do not hallucinate."

"Sure, you don't." Before his father could object, he pushed on: "I ran into Lady Marieve on my way here. You must speak to her soon. It is in our countries' best interests to settle the matter of the Cirisor Islands as soon as possible."

"You're right. I shall have an invitation sent to her immediately." Ghyslain stood and left the room without another look at Tamriel, his son—as always—forgotten the moment he was out of the king's sight.

Tamriel sat in one of the leather armchairs and closed his eyes, trying to ward away the beginning of a headache. At some point, he fell into a light and uneasy sleep. The surprised gasp of a maid woke him.

"So sorry, Your Highness!" she said, scrambling to close the door behind her. "I didn't mean to disturb you."

"It's no problem. I should be leaving anyway." He stood and rubbed the back of his neck with a hand. When he saw the broom and dust pan in the maid's hand, he crossed the room and reached for it. "Allow me."

"Oh, no, Your Highness, I couldn't. It's alright—" she stammered, eyeing the mess around the fireplace. The king's tantrums were never a secret among the castle staff; the destruction was always carefully—and quietly—disposed of within an hour.

"Please." He smiled at her and reached again for the broom. "I'll clean it."

"Thank you, Your Highness." She handed it to him and left the room.

He placed the pan on the floor and held it steady with one foot as he swept. The fire had dimmed to embers, and he cleaned as many shards of porcelain out of the ashes as possible, not caring that the soot turned his fingers black.

20

"Leaving already?" someone called to Mercy from across the garden. She turned to find Serenna Elise running toward her, the skirt of her pale blue gown clutched in one fist. Elise halted a few paces from her, her cheeks flushed. "If my father had seen me run like that, he'd have died of mortification. He says it's not ladylike."

"I won't say a word," Mercy promised. "What can I do for you, Serenna?"

"Actually, it's what *I* can do for *you*. I thought you might like to take a walk around the city. It's a lovely day, and there is so much to see around Sandori. Come, this way."

Without waiting for a response, Elise slipped her arm through Mercy's and led her through the castle gate. From there, they could see all the way down the gently sloping main road to the tall, ancient walls that surrounded the city. A break in the peaked rooftops offered a glimpse into Myrellis Plaza; vendors and merchants sat on colorful blankets or leaned against tables laden with bits and baubles.

"How long has your father served the king?" Mercy asked as they continued through the Sapphire Quarter. Large, extravagant mansions with bright flowers bursting from the window boxes surrounded them. She inhaled deeply as a warm breeze wrapped around them, scented with the aroma of the sugary-sweet delicacies from a bakery on the corner. In another life, perhaps, she would have liked to live here. It didn't have the wild beauty of the Forest of Flames, but there was something fascinating about living in a city of this size, of being one person in a sea of thousands.

"Twenty, twenty-five years now, I think. My family didn't always hold the serenship. My grandmother, grandfather, and father all served King Alaric and Queen Guinevere, His Majesty's late parents. My father was named seren when I was young, which made us official members of the court almost overnight." Elise's full lips spread into a nostalgic smile, and her blue eyes sparkled. "I loved our new lives. We were suddenly invited to a dozen parties a month, each one grander than the last. I felt like a princess. I felt...well, a bit like you must every day."

"That must've been wonderful," Mercy said, imagining the way Elise would react knowing that the lady whose arm she held was really an Assassin of the Guild, with nothing but a couple daggers and a handful of aurums to her name.

"Yes, but unfortunately, we all must grow up eventually. Parties became less about entertainment and more about schmoozing those of higher rank. Banquets gave way to duties. Times changed, and people changed. Look here." She stopped abruptly and pointed to a dilapidated mansion halfway down the block. Its windows were cracked and boarded up, the small front lawn overgrown and untended. "His Majesty gave Queen Elisora that house shortly after they were betrothed. Her family had a mansion further east, but the king wanted her to be able to visit the castle whenever she desired."

"Visit the castle? Or visit him?"

"Ha. I suppose that was the real reason, yes. You've heard the story of how they met in King Alaric's court, have you not? How their betrothal was arranged by their fathers?"

Mercy nodded. She didn't know the specifics of the story, but most royal marriages were arranged.

"A nice tale, I'll admit, but a lie. Ghyslain and Elisora had known each other since childhood. He was smitten with her—always had been. They were best friends. Supposedly, he begged his father to approve the match, despite the Zendais family not holding a noble title. It was highly scandalous for him not to have married a daughter of one of the old families."

"I thought he only cared for Liselle."

Elise cast one last glance at the house before continuing down the road. Mercy fell into step beside her. "People can say what they like, but I believe he loved each of them. It's rumored that after Elisora died, her belongings were moved out of the castle and thrown in that house to collect dust because Ghyslain couldn't bear to see it. No one has touched it since, but he refuses to allow the council to sell any of it."

Mercy remembered the empty space where the portrait of the king and queen had hung outside the throne room, Elisora's name scratched off the placard so many times it was illegible. "What about Tamriel? Didn't the king save anything of hers for their son?"

"I don't think so. After her death, the king refused to set foot in their chambers. Every night, he wandered the halls, forcing himself to stay awake until he passed out from exhaustion. He seemed to think if he didn't face her death, it hadn't truly happened."

Mercy cocked her head, intrigued by how much the serenna was revealing. Eager to learn more about the prince she was to kill, she said, "I've heard many rumors about the king, but few about his son. How do you think he will rule?"

"His Highness has been taught well by his tutors, and the nobility respect him. Whatever agreement is made between Feyndara and Beltharos, he will honor until his last breath. Prince Tamriel may be a little serious at times, but I have no doubt that when the day comes, he will be the king Beltharos needs."

Mercy nodded. "I pray he will."

An aged, ivy-covered arch marked the change from the Sapphire Quarter to the market district. The houses turned tall and lean, crammed beside one another with nothing but a few inches between the limestone bricks. They leaned forward into the street so their tiled roofs created a sort of canopy, a reprieve from the sun for pedestrians on the road below. When the wind calmed, the houses in the distance appeared to dance, waves of heat blurring their white façades.

As they wandered into Myrellis Plaza, Elise held tightly to Mercy's arm, clearly concerned about being separated in the sea of merchants and shoppers. Her worry, however, was unnecessary. The crowds parted for them when they spotted Mercy's and Elise's fine clothing. A few paused to gawk at Mercy's pointed ears, but they quickly hurried on when she scowled at them, narrowing her eyes.

"You are brave to venture into Sandori without guards, my lady." Although Elise's voice was nonchalant, she studied Mercy sidelong. No doubt her father had instructed her to keep an eye on the strange Feyndaran royal. "I'm surprised Queen Cerelia allowed you to come all this way without a company of soldiers at your back."

Your plan isn't entirely foolproof, Sorin, Mercy thought. *What royal visits a foreign country without her own complement of guards?* "I came to negotiate for peace. Arriving with a fleet of soldiers is hardly the way to earn His Majesty's trust, don't you think? This is a gesture of faith and goodwill," Mercy said. Just in case the nobles got any ideas, she added, "Either way, I can handle a weapon."

"Really? You were given lessons?"

"I have an older cousin, Alistair, who taught me to fight." She lifted her chin and grinned. "I beat him frequently."

Elise laughed. "You must teach me sometime. Some of the noblemen can be quite insistent, given a little wine. One mistakes an innocent comment for flirting, and the next thing you know, he's dragged you into one of the spare bedrooms and is pulling at your clothes, all...*hands*." She shuddered.

They continued past the square and into the cluster of trading company warehouses crammed along the banks of the Alynthi River. When the dam was built, Elise explained as they walked, Colm Myrellis quickly grew rich from the levies he charged on rival traders' ships, and used the money to rig the dam to provide power to the factories. He helped to unite the warring city-states, and upon his deathbed, his son was made the first king of Beltharos.

"The Myrellis bloodline has been royalty since," Elise continued. "Not always without challenge, but they've managed to keep a tight rein on their power. Say, have you plans for tonight?" She spun to face Mercy, stopping them in the middle of the sidewalk with the abrupt change of subject.

"No," Mercy said hesitantly.

"Wonderful. You shall come to my house for dinner. My father is having some of his colleagues over for a pre-Solari feast. You're going to come, and I'll explain the meaning of the holiday to you."

"I— Very well." Dining with nobles and listening to their incessant chatter was likely to drive Mercy insane, but perhaps she could glean some information that would help her complete her contract.

Elise beamed at her. "Then I will have the servants prepare an extra seat at the table. You'll love it. My father brags that Liri is the best cook in Sandori. First, I want to introduce you to someone."

She led Mercy down a series of side streets. There were more workers here than anywhere else, stout, red-faced men carrying crates and boxes toward the river, where the tall masts of ships moved steadily southward. They turned a corner, and Elise stopped in her tracks when she saw the dock.

"Where is Atlas?" she asked a guard overseeing the loading of a shipment.

"Elise? Didn't think I'd be seeing you around for a while," he said. "Positions changed. Atlas was assigned to Beggars' End. He didn't tell you?"

She paled. "When did this happen?"

"Two weeks ago. He really didn't tell you?"

Elise glanced at Mercy, then back to the guard. "If this is about—"

"I don't know what it's about. The order came direct from Leitha Cain and Master Oliver. He's in Aldrich's Square, last I heard."

"Okay. Okay." She pivoted on her heel and walked away at a clipped pace. "It's my brother," she murmured when Mercy caught up. "The idiot. Allow me to walk you to the castle, my lady, or to your home. I'll speak with my brother afterward. I'll see you tonight, correct? Just tell me where you're staying and I'll have an invitation with the details sent right away."

"Let me accompany you to Beggars' End," Mercy said. She'd heard mention here and there of the problems plaguing Beggars' End, and she was curious to see what was happening in the slums. "You're upset, and I'm not leaving you to go there alone."

"No, it's highly improper. You don't need to see Beggars' End. My family's problems are our responsibility."

"I want to help," Mercy insisted. "Please, Elise. It's no trouble."

"I... Fine." Elise nodded, some of the color returning to her cheeks. "Let's go, then."

21

They smelled Beggars' End before they saw it. The stench flooded over the stone wall that enclosed the slum, a rank combination of sewage, rotting food, and unwashed bodies. The wall was shorter and more haphazardly constructed than those surrounding the city, and in some places, the stone bricks had been broken or removed. At each archway, a wrought-iron gate stood open, a padlock hanging open from a link in the metal. What occasion the king might have for locking people inside Beggars' End was left to the imagination.

The first person to notice them was a young boy with lank black hair hanging in his face. He was crouching in the street beside three other children, all of whom watched Mercy and Elise pass with expressions of distrust and wariness, bordering on hostility. They reminded Mercy of a pack of hungry, feral dogs she had spotted on the ride to Ellesmere. The children were too skinny, their once-round cheeks sunken and hollow. Mercy didn't fail to notice the way the eldest reached over and closed his small fingers around a sharp-looking rock. Without a word, she grasped Elise's arm and steered her well away from the urchins.

The serenna let out a sharp breath as they turned the corner. "I hate it here," she mumbled, her voice trembling slightly. "Oh, thank the Creator. There he is." She pointed to a building that looked like an old storage facility, its windows broken and boarded. A man in full armor stood near the doorway, his arms folded across his chest. Elise broke into a run.

"Elise, what—" The rest of his sentence was lost as she tackled him in a hug. His eyes widened in surprise, then his arms closed tighter around her, and he smiled. "It's good to see you, sister."

"You hadn't expected to see me so soon," she said as she pulled out of his embrace. "Atlas, why didn't you tell me you'd been transferred to this horrible place?"

Atlas's eyes slid to Mercy. "Ah—who is it you've brought?"

"Atlas, meet Lady Marieve Aasa of Feyndara."

"Aasa? You mean you're..."

"Feyndaran."

"Royalty," Elise said at the same time.

"Well. Welcome to Beltharos, my lady. I'm sorry you have to see this side of the city, but I applaud your choice of companions. Of course, speaking as her brother, I must admit that I'm biased." He turned to Elise, whose scowl had not softened. "I didn't tell you about my reassignment because I didn't know about it until the day it went into effect. Even if I had been able to tell you, do you really think Father would have let me near you?"

"There are plenty of times Father isn't around. You... You should try to speak with him, Atlas."

Shadows passed through the guard's eyes. "He has made his opinion of me abundantly clear."

They locked gazes then, and it struck Mercy how dissimilar they looked. While Elise's face was feminine and soft, Atlas's was long and lean, with high cheekbones and a hint of stubble along his jaw. His brows and short, cropped hair were several shades darker than Elise's white-blonde locks.

Elise relented first, her shoulders slumping in defeat. "Fine. But this doesn't mean I approve. I want us to be a family again."

"This is not a discussion to be having now, especially in front of our current company." He turned to Mercy. "I thought Feyndarans wanted nothing to do with Beltharos. Does that mean you're here about the Islands?"

"How did you know?"

"There's no other reason why Her Majesty would allow her granddaughter to journey here. In all honesty, I hope the king gives you the land. I've seen enough friends march off to fight and not return to know these ceaseless wars are not worth the cost."

Before Mercy could respond, Elise gripped her brother's arm tightly. "Atlas, what is this place?" she asked, her voice strangely high-pitched.

She was staring down the length of the building, where two elderly men had just stepped through a low doorway. One had frizzy white hair stuck out like a mane, and the other was bent into a hunchback, his head and neck jutting forward at a painful-looking angle. His hooked nose and wrinkled neck made him look like a vulture. The two men carried something wrapped in a stained sheet between them.

"*Leave.*"

The word was little more than a whisper, a hiss on the breeze. At first, Mercy wasn't sure whether she had imagined it. Then, out of the corner of her eye, she saw Atlas place a hand on the grip of his sword. Elise was still looking in the direction of the old men, and Atlas took a protective step toward her.

"Sister," he said, his voice laced with caution. "I have told you before not to come here."

Steel glided against leather as he pulled the sword from its sheath. Before Mercy's mind registered the movement, her daggers were in her hands. She ignored Elise's surprised gasp as she turned to face the threat.

It was the children.

Not only the children they had seen before, but at least a dozen more, as well as parents, siblings, elves, beggars, cripples. They surrounded Mercy, Elise, and Atlas, each holding a hefty brick in one hand, poised to throw. They must have pulled the stones from the wall, Mercy realized, noting that many of them were large enough to fracture a skull.

"Leave."

A four-year-old girl hissed it first. Brown hair hung in tangles around her heart-shaped face, and her skin was coated in a layer of grime. Her startlingly bright green eyes narrowed and her upper lip curled, revealing a flash of tiny, crooked teeth.

"*Leave. Leave. Leave.*"

The others joined in one at a time, until the words blended into a buzz. Their voices were scratchy and dry as old parchment, each one a rasp. They must have been two or three dozen strong, but Mercy couldn't look away from the little girl. Her cold, ruthless heart ached for the starving child.

"Enough." Atlas's voice cleaved through the whispers. "Drop your weapons and leave. They are nothing to you."

"*We* are nothing to *them*," someone spat.

"Go home."

Elise drew closer to Mercy. "Marieve. A body. That's— Th-That's a body."

A body?

Mercy followed Elise's gaze to the two old men down the

street, who were still struggling to carry the bundle stretched between them. Something white stuck out from under the sheet.

Oh.

The hand bobbed with every step, pale fingers grasping at empty air. A sliver of the person's wrist was visible through the folds in the fabric, a red rash flaming brightly on the bloodless, pallid skin.

Thunk.

Atlas grunted—more with surprise than pain—as a broken brick thudded against his armor and skittered harmlessly to the ground. He scowled and pushed Mercy and Elise behind him.

"Keep them out of our land." An elf with a voice like sandpaper stepped forward, his eyes narrowed. He spat at Atlas's feet, then stooped to reclaim the brick he'd thrown. "We don't want them here."

"What you want is no concern of mine, Ketojan, and I advise you to consider your next move carefully." Atlas lifted the point of his sword to Ketojan's throat. The elf smirked, his brown eyes peering out from under a shock of choppy white hair. Behind him, the crowd shifted from one foot to another, ready and eager to spill blood.

"Get them out of here and we'll go," Ketojan finally said. At this, the beggars simultaneously stepped back, and most dropped their bricks. Their hostile expressions didn't change, but they seemed to respect him.

"You are in no position to make demands, friend." Atlas's eyes flashed with warning, his sword's blade glinting in the sunlight.

The elf held Atlas's gaze for a long time, then without a word, he turned and walked away. The crowd followed him, and once they were out of hearing range, Atlas released a breath and sheathed his sword. Mercy did not do the same with her daggers.

"You must leave now, before he changes his mind."

"Atlas, what is happening here? Why are you here with these people? Come with us, won't you? *Please!*" Elise was near hysterics, her eyes wide as saucers. "Tell me *something!* Do the nobles know it's so awful here?"

Her brother gripped her shoulders, his face tight with anger and stress. "Don't you think all the nobles know what it's like here? Do you think they care about these people? They know, Elise, and they do nothing about it." He released her and ran a weary hand down his face, his anger fading to weariness. Little bruises the shape of his fingertips bloomed on Elise's bare arms.

She shook her head. "You are far too kind for a place like this, brother."

Atlas looked at Mercy. "I appreciate you accompanying my sister here, but you never should have come. It's not safe. You must leave now." He scanned the alleys around them. "They won't leave you alone for long—Ketojan doesn't have as much power among his people as he thinks. I'll see you to the gate to make sure you aren't followed."

They returned the way they'd come, a heavy, anxious silence settling over them, and arrived at the gate several minutes later. Elise hugged her brother once more. "Thank you, Atlas. Promise me you'll be careful."

"Aren't I always?"

She rolled her eyes, a smile tugging at her lips. "Then try not to do anything stupid, at the very least. And *write me.*"

He nodded, laughing. "It was a pleasure to meet you, my lady," he said to Mercy, "even if it was not under ideal circumstances. I wish you luck on the negotiations with the king. Creator knows you're going to need it."

22

Neither Mercy nor Elise spoke much on the walk back from Beggars' End, which was why when Mercy knocked on the front door of Elise's house two hours later, the girl's warm smile surprised her more than her uncharacteristic silence had.

"Come in, come in," Elise said, her family's slave hovering behind her.

Seren Pierce's home was slightly smaller than Blackbriar, but it was steeped in more finery than Mercy had ever seen—even more than the castle. Aelyn, the slave, led them down the hall, past vivid oil paintings, colorful tapestries, and several marble sculptures. Archways covered with curtains of sheer chiffon offered glimpses into a sitting room, a library, and—finally—the dining room. Inside, Seren Pierce and two other men were clustered around one end of the long rectangular table that dominated the room, bent over a map of the city. They spoke in low voices, and none of them seemed to notice Mercy and Elise's arrival.

"That's Landers Nadra," Elise whispered, nodding to the middle-aged man standing beside her father. Unlike the seren,

Landers was portly and round, his fine velvets straining over his midsection. Landers pointed to a building on the map with a heavily-jeweled finger. "The bald one is Cassius Bacha. He—" She paused. "Do you know much about noble titles in Beltharos?"

Mercy lifted a shoulder in a shrug. "A little."

"They follow titles from the old tongue, which is why they can sound strange when we use them today. The hierarchy is easy to understand, though, even for commoners. They're alphabetical." She nodded to Cassius, who was studying the map, his scalp shining in the light streaming through the windows. "Bacha is the second highest rank, which means he's the one lesser lords have to charm to get what they want."

"Must be nice for your father to have one of the most powerful men in Sandori as a friend."

"Ha. They only agree when it's within their best interests to do so—otherwise they hardly speak to each other. Cassius resents the new nobility. You noticed my father's title is Seren Pierce, and not Pierce Seren?" she asked. "My family name is LeClair. Titles are taken as surnames after serving the crown for thirty years—a test of loyalty, one might say."

"I see. What are they discussing?"

"Plans to fortify the city walls. Cassius Bacha showed up here late last night in nothing but his dressing robe, claiming that the city is going to be attacked. He saw it in a dream, he said. Don't look at me like that. Cassius's family has the Sight," she said, as if that explained everything. Before Mercy could inquire further, she continued: "They've been discussing it for hours, and aren't likely to stop anytime soon."

"I'm glad you all enjoyed the gallery." A woman's voice floated to them from down the hall. "My husband has an eye for art, doesn't he?"

There was a murmur of assent as a party of five entered the room, led by a voluptuous blonde draped in layers of peach-colored silk. She kissed Elise on the cheek, causing her to blush. "And my daughter has quite the hand for it, doesn't she?"

"Mother! We have guests!"

"Hush, darling. Lady Nadra was just remarking how talented you are. Am I not allowed to be proud of my daughter?"

"Your calligraphy is exquisite," Lady Nadra said. She was the polar opposite of her husband: willowy and tall, with sparkling green eyes and an easy smile. She clapped her hands delightedly, the gemstones in her rings sparkling. "If only my two had half your talent!"

"Thank you, Marlena," Elise said, looking somewhat uncomfortable with the praise. "Now may I, ah, present our special guest for the evening—"

"Lady Marieve," Seren Pierce interrupted.

They all turned. At the table, the three men were staring straight at Mercy, the documents abandoned. Seren Pierce crossed his arms and continued, "Granddaughter of the queen of Feyndara, if I'm not mistaken."

Mercy lifted her chin. "That's correct."

"I'm afraid I've not had the chance to formally welcome you. How do you find Beltharos?"

"It's lovely, as is your home, Seren."

"And you're here for the Islands, surely," he said, brushing aside the compliment. "May I ask, do you truly believe the king will give it to you after all these years of fighting?"

I hope it never gets to the point that I have to pretend to negotiate in the first place. "I don't think it will be that simple, but any step toward peace is better than our current position, wouldn't you agree?"

"Wisely said, my lady," Landers Nadra agreed.

"Oh! Where are my manners?" his wife exclaimed. "The twins, Leon and Maisie." She gestured to the young man and woman at her side. The twins were only a few years older than Mercy, and clearly took after their maternal family; Maisie had the same lithe build and chestnut hair as her mother, and Leon's slightly slanted eyes were markedly different from his father's hooded lids.

"Welcome to the capital, my lady," Maisie said. "I hope you enjoy your time here."

"Should you have need of anything, do not hesitate to ask," Leon added.

"And this is Lady Murray Bacha," Elise said, gesturing to an old woman with long white hair. "She is Cassius's wife, and an ambassador to the crown. She recently returned from a trip to Rivosa."

"It's a beautiful country. Quite a shame we don't have more western influence here. Did you know they once served chocolate-covered rosebuds with edible gold pearls?" Murray's smile widened, the wrinkled around her eyes crinkling. She moved to her husband's side and laid a loving hand on his arm, then smiled at Landers. "Your countrymen know how to put on a show, my friend."

"You should have gone during Iarra. The servants set up tables and tables of delicacies across the length of the ballroom, imported from all around the world for one massive feast."

Murray clapped a hand to her heart in delight.

"Nerida," Seren Pierce called, smiling at his wife. Liri, the cook, stood beside him. He gestured to the table. "Dinner is ready. Shall we be seated?"

"Of course, my dear. Make yourselves comfortable, everyone."

As Elise led her around the table, Mercy watched Seren

Pierce hand the map and documents to Aelyn. "Take these upstairs," he murmured, and she nodded and hurried away.

Pierce sat at the head of the table, Nerida at his right and Elise at his left. Leon pulled out the seat beside her, but Elise shooed his hand off under the guise of brushing away dust. "Sit here, Marieve," she said, smiling sweetly. She patted the seat, and Mercy offered Leon an apologetic look before accepting the chair. He dipped his head in respect and claimed the seat to her right.

As Liri carried in platter after platter of food, Elise leaned over and whispered, "My parents have arranged a marriage between Leon and me. While I do not dislike the man, I have no interest in conversing with him for the duration of this meal, let alone being married to him for the rest of my life."

"*Elise*," her father warned in a low voice. Nerida pretended not to notice.

"You have my gratitude for taking that seat," Elise continued, unabated.

"Well, this looks absolutely delicious, my dear," Marlena Nadra cooed, eyeing a platter of rabbit slathered in butter and herbs. "Your cook is so talented, I'm afraid I've been ruined for most everything else. Tell me, where did you buy her?"

Nerida seemed to inflate with the praise. "In Cariza a few years ago. I managed to steal her away from my cousin's estate after she passed, with only a minor fee at the city gates for owning a Rivosi slave over a Beltharan one."

"Are the advisors still telling themselves the tax will work? Who in their right minds would buy a slave from Beggars' End when there is such better stock across the border? Can you imagine bringing one into your home? You'd get fleas just looking at it." Murray shuddered. "Something needs to be done about that Creator-forsaken place."

"They should be carted off to the mines in the west," Landers grumbled. "There is no better place for them. Why the guards allow them to plague the city is beyond me. I say let the able-bodied ones work the mines, and when that damned underground air rots their lungs, there will be plenty more to replace them. That's one thing you can always count on."

Murmurs of agreement rose around the table. Elise scowled at the bowl of soup in front of her, no doubt thinking of Atlas and the things they had seen earlier that day.

"If it's such a problem, why doesn't anyone do anything about it?" Mercy asked. She didn't expect anything to come of interjecting, but the real Lady Marieve would have been horrified by this discussion, and she needed to appear interested in the kingdom's politics. Feyndara had outlawed slavery decades ago. "Factories and warehouses always need workers, and it wouldn't be difficult to train them to work the ships for the trading companies."

"Would you trust thousands of aurums' worth of inventory to a bunch of beggars and thieves?" Landers scoffed. "We don't offer them help because they don't *want* it. The last person to try and change their fortune lost her life because of it." Mercy noted that he avoided saying Liselle's name, but there was no mistaking about whom he was talking.

"No one has tried since? Surely people can't be happy with the way things are."

"No, but the people of Beggars' End are too stubborn to accept aid, and they see any outsider as a threat."

"Last year, they scared off a group of priestesses who had come to offer food and medicine to the sick. The poor girls returned hours later wearing tatters, and supposedly their nightmares were so terrible their screams kept everyone in their quarters awake for a month," Leon supplied.

Maisie nodded. "I was friends with one of them. She transferred to Blackhills shortly after—said she couldn't stand to live in the same city as that scum. She didn't feel safe anymore."

"Marieve is right," Elise said in a low voice.

All eyes turned to her. Her silver spoon was clenched in one hand so tightly her knuckles were white. Her lips pressed into a thin line, and she glared at each person in turn. She saved her father for last.

"Marieve is right," she repeated. "You should be doing something about that place, Father. You should be trying to fix it. Do you know Atlas is there? Do you even care?"

A muscle worked in the seren's jaw. "Now is not the time to discuss this, child."

"Do not call me that."

"Perhaps you should take a walk to calm yourself. Wouldn't you agree, Nerida?"

Elise's mother didn't respond, her face flushed with embarrassment.

"He's trying to help them! He's trying to gain your approval! If what he did with Julien gets out, the soldiers will just as likely kill him as the *scum* will. Or does that not bother you at all?"

"Elise—"

"That would get rid of the problem, wouldn't it? You can go on pretending you'd only had the one child, the good child—"

Seren Pierce's face was hard as stone. "It's looking less and less like that by the second."

"Darling," her mother interrupted, but they ignored her.

"He's trying to win your *favor*, Father! Can't you see? He's trying to make you *proud!*" Elise jumped up, sending her goblet of wine flying. Her mother shrieked as the dark wine pooled on the ivory silk tablecloth. "I should have told him that's not possible."

"That's quite enough!" Pierce stood, as well, his face

splotchy and red, his voice trembling with anger. His expression was cruel and sharp. For the first time, Elise shrank away—but only for a second.

"Atlas deserves better than you for a father," she spat.

"Elise!" Nerida exclaimed. "You will not speak to your father that way—not in private, and certainly not in front of our guests!"

Elise glowered at her parents for a long, charged moment. Finally, she snapped, "I need some fresh air."

She shoved her chair into the table and leaned down to whisper, "Forgive me," into Mercy's ear. Then she stormed out of the room.

After a few minutes of uncomfortable silence—punctuated by the scraping of silverware and the occasional request to pass a platter—conversation returned to the table, although the topic of Beggars' End was steadfastly avoided. Leon and Maisie were kind enough to engage Mercy in small talk, and she fielded questions about Feyndara with polite—if somewhat ambiguous—answers.

In turn, Leon and Maisie explained the traditions behind the Solari festival, of which she had heard, but never witnessed. Solari was mostly a holiday for the upper class, who could afford the fine gowns and lavish celebrations befitting such a special and holy day.

"The simplest explanation is that it occurs every ten years, but it's not alway exact. It depends on the location of the sun and moon, and sometimes doesn't occur at all," Maisie explained. "Sometimes generations pass without a Solari, and that's when we know something terrible is about to happen. The Creator foresees it and sends us a sign."

"That's the superstition, anyway," Leon said.

"*Anyway*," she continued, elbowing her brother, "when there finally is a Solari, it's said to be a blessed year."

"The last one was about fifteen years ago," Seren Pierce

said, having regained his earlier composure. "It was wonderful. There was partying in the streets all day, and the celebration itself went on for a week. I heard the Church was overflowing."

"What are the rumors this year?" Marlena leaned forward and propped her chin on her hand, eyes twinkling. "Shall our king lead us to glory in the war for Cirisor? Will peace finally be restored? Or will Prince Tamriel ascend the throne, do you think?"

Murray snorted, and Mercy had to fight a smile. *He won't ascend the throne if I have anything to say about it.*

"Perhaps it is something to do with your arrival, my dear." Nerida smiled at Mercy. "You're the first royal Feyndaran to visit Beltharos in generations. Maybe you'll be the one to break the animosity between our countries."

Mercy lifted her glass of wine in a toast, smiling to herself. "I hope so."

23

"Elise? Are you up here?" Mercy called as she climbed the stairs. Seren Pierce and his guests were still downstairs, dining, chatting, and pretending Elise's outburst hadn't occurred. Elise hadn't yet returned to the dining room, so Mercy had offered to comfort the girl in private, an excuse that would give her the opportunity to study the documents Pierce and the others had been pouring over not two hours earlier. Perhaps one of them contained information that would help her complete her contract.

She stepped onto the landing and peered down the length of the hall. Six rooms branched off of it, the archways draped in lightweight curtains that fluttered in the gentle breeze from the open windows. All were dark except for the one at the opposite end of the hall; soft candlelight cast the room in weak, flickering light.

"Elise?" Mercy said again, hoping she still had some time before the seren's daughter would return. When no answer came, she tiptoed down the hall and stepped into the lit room. A candle burned in a short, plain candelabrum atop the fireplace's mantle, and Mercy grabbed it before approaching the massive desk.

The city map sat on its surface, the dark lines of ink faded where well-worn creases divided the yellowed parchment into quarters. Dashes marked the boundaries of each neighborhood—the Sapphire Quarter, shipping and market districts, Guinevere's Square—and the lake stretched from the rocky shore behind the castle to the top of the page. Someone—likely Cassius—had circled the places along the city walls where repairs were in order.

Mercy's gaze caught on a patch of darkness along the western edge, and she moved the candelabrum closer, being careful not to drip wax onto the map.

The entirety of Beggars' End was covered in blood red ink.

Not only the walls, but every house, street, well, and abandoned factory was red. Her eyes automatically found the warehouse where she had met Atlas, unsure whether it was a trick of the light that the building seemed darker than the rest. Mercy frowned, unease settling in her stomach. She imagined Cassius waking from his nightmare and filling in the map with shaky hands, hastily marking the places where the strength of the walls was compromised. What had he seen in his dreams that terrified him so?

A stack of papers sat beside the map. Mercy set down the candelabrum and shuffled through them quickly, searching for anything of note. Most of the pages were covered in drawings, measurements, and other things of little import—financial reports, shipping orders, a calendar—but the last one was different. Cassius had drawn a plant.

The bulb was the size of Mercy's fist, covered in thick, upward-pointing scales, with four wide leaves sprouting from its base. Beside the picture, Cassius had scrawled the word *Niamh*.

"What the—"

"Elise? Lady Marieve?" Nerida called, her footsteps tapping up the stairs.

Mercy returned the papers to their places, praying Seren Pierce had not paid too much attention to their order, then set the candelabrum on the mantle and hurried out of the room.

The footsteps drew nearer, higher on the stairs. Her heart pounding, Mercy peered through the curtains of the nearby rooms and ducked into the gallery. Inside, no candles burned, but enough moonlight streamed through the window to illuminate the framed canvases covering every wall. She sank onto the edge of the divan in the center of the room, fanning her skirt around her legs, just before Nerida passed by the open archway.

"Ah, there you are," Nerida sighed, spotting Mercy out of the corner of her eye. She parted the curtain with one hand and leaned against the frame of the archway. "Elise isn't here, is she?"

"No."

"Don't worry about her—she's likely out on a walk, collecting her thoughts. She doesn't have a stomach for confrontation. Never has." Her smile faltered, and her gaze slanted to the side. "My lady, I shudder to imagine what you must think of us after our boorish behavior tonight."

"No, I understand," Mercy said, rising. "There's no need—"

"Please—" Nerida blurted. "Allow me to apologize on behalf of my family and me. Tensions have...run high for us lately, and it has been especially hard on Elise. My husband and son had a falling out recently and, um, haven't spoken much since."

"I...don't suppose this has something to do with Julien?"

Mercy asked, remembering the name from Elise's outburst earlier.

Nerida looked at her sharply, color blooming on her powdered cheeks. "What they were doing was unnatural. I tried to convince him to break it off, but..." She trailed off and shook her head. "One of his commanders found them together. It was humiliating. It's a miracle Atlas wasn't thrown out of the guard entirely."

"I won't tell a soul." Mercy stepped forward and took one of Nerida's hands in her own. She needed friends in the mad king's court, and while Seren Pierce didn't seem to like her much, it wouldn't hurt to ingratiate herself with his wife and daughter. "I am your guest tonight; you need not apologize to me. Thank you for your hospitality."

Elise's mother let out a choked laugh. "The entertainment was quite something, wasn't it?"

"That it was," she responded with a smile. Then she turned back toward the gallery. "I hope you don't mind that I found my way in here. After Marlena said how much she admired your gallery, I wanted to take a look."

"Of course not." Nerida swept past Mercy and crossed the room, pausing before a portrait of a white-haired lady in a blooming garden. "My father made this painting of my grandmother a few years before her death. We had never been close, but he loved Elise more than anything in the world. He and Elise used to sit on the floor of his studio and paint for hours." She let out a soft, wistful laugh. "Elise tried to teach me once, you know. She said I couldn't paint worse if I were holding the brush between my toes. Compared to hers, it certainly looked that way."

"She's that good?"

"Decide for yourself." She gestured to the opposite wall, which was adorned with so many paintings barely an inch of the limestone was visible between the gilded frames. The smallest ones had clearly been crafted by a child's hand; the colors bled together and the paper was wrinkled from too much paint. Further down the wall, the lines became sharper, surer, the colors more vivid. Many were landscapes—the view of the city unfolding from the top of the castle's steps, the rocky shore of Lake Myrella, the sun rising over the city walls.

"Wow," Mercy breathed. "These are amazing."

In the largest painting, a merchant knelt beside his wagon, its broken wheel resting on the street beside him. He was wiping his forehead with one arm and smiling at a boy crouching beside him, offering a handful of coin. A shock of brown hair hung over the boy's brow, obscuring all but his crooked smile and the sharp line of his jaw. He was upper class, finely dressed, but the hem of his pants was scuffed with dirt and his sleeves were bunched up around his elbows. A sense of familiarity nagged at Mercy. A quick count revealed the boy in four other paintings.

"Who is that?" she asked, pointing.

"That boy? A childhood crush of Elise's." Nerida glanced out the window and started. "Oh! Look how dark it is! I'm sorry, I completely lost track of time. We should head downstairs and finish dessert. I'll send Pierce to look for Elise, and I'm sure Leon won't mind escorting you home."

"Oh, that's not necessary—"

"I insist. What sort of host would I be to leave you to wander home in the dark in a foreign city? Come, come. I can practically hear my husband begging me to rescue him. He's not one for dinner parties, I'm afraid."

Nerida moved to the archway and held the curtain back for Mercy. Just before she slipped through, she glanced back at the painting of the young boy and couldn't shake the feeling she had seen him before.

"Thank you, Leon. Goodnight."

Mercy closed Blackbriar's front door, leaned against it, and sighed. Mere seconds later, Elvira scuttled into the hallway, her hair tied in an unkempt braid, and pulled Mercy forward by the elbow. Without a word, the elf deposited her on the divan in the study and perched beside her.

"The king sent a message earlier. He and the prince would like to have you for a private audience at noon tomorrow. I will accompany you to the castle, but likely will not be permitted to attend the meeting," she said. "Be careful what you say around them. The king can be quite, well, *touchy* about certain topics, as you have seen. And the prince may act polite, but royalty or no, you're still an elf. Growing up in the aftermath of Liselle's murder, hearing the rumors that his father favored Liselle over the queen, could not have instilled in him a great sympathy for our kind."

Elvira moved to the bookshelf and skimmed the spines of several books before plucking one out and handing it to Mercy. It was no more than fifty pages in all, the cover two thick sheets of waxed parchment. Twine looped through the spine to bind it together.

"Here. It's hardly comprehensive, but I started writing things down a few years ago. Notes. Rumors going around, city changes, information from my husband and the other slaves—anything that seemed important. You should study it," she said. "At your meeting tomorrow, you can't speak specifically or convincingly about Feyndaran politics, so it would be wise to talk about the effects of the war here. Try to persuade him by showing him how the end of the war can benefit *him*, not some foreign queen. Worst case scenario, you come one step closer to completing your contract. Best case scenario, you play a part in ending the Cirisian Wars."

"Assuming the prince doesn't immediately suspect something and have me imprisoned. It's not his father I need to convince—Ghyslain is the one who hired me. Besides, it's just a ruse to get closer to the prince. I don't actually care about the politics."

Elvira nodded. "It's late, and you should read some tonight. If there's nothing more you need from me, I'll take my leave."

"Sure. I'll stay down here, so you can leave the candles burning."

Elvira left without another word. As Mercy flipped through the pages, skimming the small book's contents, a flash of red ink caught her eye. "Elvira, wait. What's this?"

"Hm?" She poked her head into the room. Mercy held up the book for her to see, and she took a few steps forward, squinting her tired eyes. "Oh, that's Fieldings' Blisters. It's a fairly common disease found among the lower class—it looks like a rash or sunburn, and sometimes causes fluid-filled blisters. Why do you ask?"

"I saw a body in Beggars' End today with the same rash."

"You went to Beggars' End?"

"Briefly. It was interesting, to say the least. The rash looked like this." Mercy tapped the drawing—a man's torso inflamed with stripes of bright red skin and shiny welts. She'd seen mention of Fieldings' Blisters in some of Mistress Sorin's texts, but she had never heard of a case being fatal. "Is it lethal?"

"Not as far as I know. It targets the skin and can leave nasty scars if the blisters pop, but that's as bad as it gets. I'll keep an ear out for any news."

"Thank you, Elvira."

The elf dipped her head in respect and took her leave, and Mercy turned back to the book, frowning down at the drawing of the torso infected with Fieldings' Blisters. The ink with which the angry red rash and blisters had been drawn was the same shade of blood red that Cassius Bacha had painted across the entirety of Beggars' End.

24

"Enough pleasantries. You want us to give you the Islands."

"I want an end to the fighting, same as you, Your Majesty," Mercy corrected.

King Ghyslain leaned forward over his desk, a wholly different man than the one she had watched cower and sob not twenty-four hours before. The shattered remains of the porcelain vase he'd broken had been swept up and discarded, and a cheery fire now crackled in the hearth behind her. The desktop was bare save for a pitcher of wine and three goblets, all untouched.

Ghyslain folded his hands and studied her. "And what do you propose, exactly? Neither of us is willing to surrender, so you must forgive me if I do not see how this conflict can be resolved peacefully."

"There must be a way. Both of our countries are pouring money into a war with no end in sight—money that would be better spent on our citizens," Mercy said, remembering Elvira's advice from the night before. She leaned forward and propped her elbows on the arms of her chair, mirroring Ghyslain's position. "There is no need for us to lose more soldiers to ceaseless fighting. A compromise between our countries will save countless lives."

"Still, I have yet to hear a viable solution. So, I ask again, do you have a plan? Because if not, we will have to cut this meeting short, my lady. I'm afraid I have other matters to attend." Ghyslain stood and gestured to the doors.

Mercy glanced at Tamriel. The prince was leaning against the windowsill, his arms crossed over his chest. He wasn't wearing armor today, instead clad only in a simple—yet finely crafted—tunic and pants. He hadn't said a word to Mercy or his father since he had walked in, but he'd listened to their discussion with interest, a thoughtful expression on his face. His cold, quiet demeanor surprised her after the way he had smiled and joked with her the day before. Perhaps this meeting had reminded him of who Lady Marieve really was to him—not a friend, but an ambassador of their kingdom's greatest enemy.

For her part, Mercy had done her best to mount a convincing case on behalf of the Feyndarans. She and Ghyslain had played their parts, debating the topic of the Cirisian Wars with as much conviction and begrudging civility as one would expect between the Beltharan king and Queen Cerelia's granddaughter. Ghyslain had not once hinted that he knew of Mercy's true identity.

"Let the Islands become an independent country," Mercy blurted, desperate for an excuse to prolong her time with the prince.

"*What?*" Tamriel sputtered. He gaped at her as if she'd suggested he run naked through the streets. "You think we would consider giving the Islands up after so many decades of war?"

"If you want to stop losing men and equipment, yes."

Ghyslain sank into his chair. "You know we cannot agree

to this. If Feyndara wins the war, you may do what you wish with the territory, but I will not withdraw my forces. Who is to say the queen won't seize the territory the second my men leave?"

"*She* is our guarantee, I believe," Tamriel interjected, nodding to Mercy. "Would Queen Cerelia have sent her unaccompanied to an enemy kingdom if she weren't serious about her offer? Anything could have happened to Lady Marieve here; we could have decided to hold her hostage until Her Majesty agreed to surrender the land."

"Careful, Your Highness," Mercy warned, her expression darkening. "I do not take kindly to threats."

"Simply making a point, my lady." Tamriel turned to the king. "Perhaps you should consider her offer, Father."

"If not this, Her Majesty would take into careful consideration any compromise you extended," Mercy added, nodding. She knew no such offer would come. Both countries had invested too much money and lost too many soldiers to give in so easily. "All we want is peace."

Ghyslain rose, and this time, Mercy followed suit. She'd done her duty and played her part. "I cannot promise anything will come of this, but I will bring the offer to my council." He crossed the room and held one of the doors open for her. "Tamriel will see you out."

Tamriel pushed away from the windowsill and slipped past her into the hallway. He didn't look at his father once. "Shall we?" he said, already moving toward the stairs.

Mercy paused on the threshold and looked up at the king. Ghyslain's eyes remained trained on his son as he slowly nodded once. She returned the nod and stepped into the hall, and the king shut the door behind her without a word.

25
TAMRIEL

"Take a walk with me," Lady Marieve said as they descended the stairs, drawing Tamriel's thoughts away from the negotiations he'd just witnessed. He paused halfway down the staircase, and she stopped beside him, gazing up with an expectant look in her eyes. "Serenna Elise was kind enough to give me a tour of the city yesterday, but I have yet to see the castle grounds."

"I wish I could, but I'm very busy." He continued down the stairs, pretending not to see the hurt and surprise flash across her face. She was only a temporary guest here, he reminded himself, and she had only come to do Queen Cerelia's bidding. Her grandmother's stubborn and selfish need to claim the Cirisian Islands had cost his country countless lives. Besides, he was in no mood to humor her today. The shadow of his father's fit yesterday still hung over him, plaguing his thoughts, his dreams.

"Too busy to show me around your home? Not even for half an hour? Fifteen minutes?" Marieve snagged his arm and, when he slowed, slipped her hand into the crook of his elbow. He tried not to appear shocked by her audacity. "Is that any way to treat a guest? There's so much anger and animosity between our lands." Her sharp, piercing eyes met his, twinkling with mischief and something more. "Perhaps you and I could do something to fix that."

Tamriel knew where this conversation was heading. He'd seen that look on too many noblewomen in his father's court. He swiftly stepped out of her grasp. "Marriage is out of the question."

She laughed. "Prince Tamriel, we've only just met. I think we should exchange more than pleasantries before we exchange vows."

"Your grandmother must have suggested a match between us. I assume that's the real reason she sent you here."

"Perhaps, but don't mistake my motivations for those of my grandmother, or those of your father's council members. What I said in your father's study is true. I seek only to end the needless loss of lives, both on your side and mine," she said. "One day you will be king, and your soldiers' deaths will be on your hands. It could help to have a friend in Feyndara."

He relaxed. All his life, the council members had tried to arrange marriages for him, and he had refused them all. His father's grief-stricken madness was evidence enough of how dangerous love was, and he had no intention of falling prey to it, as well. Yet Marieve was right—she *was* a guest, and he'd been wrong to direct his anger at his father at her. "Very well," he said, offering Marieve his arm. "Fifteen minutes."

She grinned as he led her through the great hall and out the massive front doors of the castle. They paused at the top of the stairs to watch slaves walk the narrow paths of the hedge mazes on either side of the gravel carriageway, tossing handfuls of silver and gold tinsel over the leaves. The strands danced in the breeze, shimmering under the bright sunlight. A young elven boy ran through the maze on their right, chasing pieces of tinsel that had flown free, and his peals of laughter echoed off the castle's stone walls.

"This is for the Solari festival, isn't it?" Marieve asked as they continued onto the castle grounds. "I've never had a chance to attend one, so I have no idea what to expect. Do you remember the last one?"

"Not much of it, to be honest. I was just shy of three when the last one occurred. In fact, all I remember from that day are the clothes. I hated them."

Her mouth parted in disbelief. "The *clothes?*"

Tamriel nodded. "My servants learned that day not to dress a toddler in the finest velvets in Beltharos. They had wrangled me into this thick black coat—a *coat* in summer!— with these tiny silver buttons all the way from my navel to my chin. *For appearance's sake,* they said." He offered her a sly grin as they rounded the side of the castle, the lake's waves sparkling in the distance. "How do you think I appeared to my father when Master Oliver dumped me in front of all the nobility, crying and soaking wet after I'd decided to take a swim in the lake to cool off?"

"You didn't!"

His grin widened. "You should have seen my father's expression at watching his son be led through the throne room by the scruff of his neck, wet boots squelching with every step. His jaw just about dropped to the floor."

Marieve laughed. "I'm sure it was a sight to see."

"Oh, undoubtedly. Hopefully I'll be better behaved this time around, but I can't make any promises."

"Creator, I'll be sure to attend the celebration, then."

When they rounded the last tower and arrived at the rear of the castle, Marieve stopped, her eyes widening in awe. The wide expanse of Lake Myrella stretched out before them, its gray-blue water spanning for miles in every direction. Boulders twice as tall as a man rose from the lake's depths. The white-capped waves sent up spray every time they crashed against the rocks.

Entranced, Marieve dropped Tamriel's arm and walked toward the water's edge, pausing to slip off her flats when the grass gave way to the pebbled shore. She tossed them aside and continued toward the lake in her bare feet, nearly slipping twice on the slick stones. A wave rolled over the shore and splashed over the tops of her feet, causing her to laugh.

"It's freezing!" she gasped, clutching her skirt in one hand.

Her delight made Tamriel smile. The lake was beautiful, but after nearly eighteen years of living in the castle, it had become normal to him. Watching Marieve wade in a few more feet, laughing as the tide lapped at her ankles, made him feel like he was seeing it through new eyes.

She looked over her shoulder then and caught him staring. "What are you thinking?"

"That you are unlike any princess I have ever met."

She stepped out of the water and tugged on her flats, seeming not to care that the fine silk quickly grew wet. "I'm not a princess."

"Semantics."

They continued along the shore in comfortable silence. Although he should have been wary of her potential influence in his father's court, he found he did not mind her presence. Joking with her, teasing her, had lifted his spirits considerably.

After a few minutes, he said, "It's a terrible idea, you know."

"Hm?" She dragged her gaze from the lake and met his eyes. "Pardon me?"

"Granting the Cirisor Islands their freedom. Making them their own country. How could it *possibly* work?"

"It wouldn't be easy, but what other option do we have? Keep fighting until the other surrenders? That could take decades. Let us create a nation that will help both our countries. Use the funds that would have gone to fighting to rebuild the Islands. My uncle can arrange shipments of goods and—" She paused. "It could work."

"It won't. The advisors will never agree to it, and even if they did, the nobles could never be persuaded to help."

"Your father doesn't need their help."

Tamriel cocked his head. "Whose money do you think supplies the military? Whose sons march to war and do not return? Their blood has already been spilled—it cannot amount to nothing. If my father pulls the soldiers from the Islands, the nobles will turn their men against the crown."

Marieve turned, fixing him with her piercing gold-brown eyes. "If you really believe that, then your true enemies aren't the ones across the Abraxas Sea. They're the ones within your own walls."

26

"Lady Marieve!" Elvira called from across the grounds. She jogged over to them, her skirts bunched in a fist, and dropped into a low bow before Tamriel. "Your Highness, please excuse the interruption. My lady, the dressmaker must see you immediately if she is to complete your gown in time for Solari. I-I tried to explain to her that you are a very important client and would pay extra for the last-minute order, but she would have none of it."

Mercy glanced at Tamriel, and he nodded. "Go on," he said. "I may not have sisters, but I have spent plenty of time with noblewomen, and I know how dire fashion emergencies can be." He tried to say it seriously, but a hint of a smile tugged at the corners of his mouth.

"Thank you. I'll see you at the celebration tomorrow, Your Highness." Mercy curtsied and followed Elvira toward the front of the castle. Once they were well out of earshot, Mercy asked, "What's the problem? Why do we have to leave?"

"One of the guards *may have* spotted me snooping around the prince's chambers earlier," she said, biting her lip. "I didn't want them to recognize me as your handmaid and suspect you of anything, so I fled as quickly as I could. I don't think he was able to identify me."

"Good. And you've found a way for me to sneak into his bedroom?"

She held up an iron key strung on a length of ribbon. "Several of the cooks have them for delivering private meals. I visited Bron and pocketed this on the way."

Mercy tied the ends of the ribbon around her neck and tucked the key under the collar of her dress, grinning to herself as they passed through the gate and entered the city proper. "Excellent."

By the time Mercy and Elvira arrived at Myrellis Castle for the Solari celebration, the palace and its grounds had been transformed. Strands of white lanterns hung from tall stakes that lined either side of the carriageway, creating a canopy of light from the gate to the double staircases at the castle's entrance. The pieces of tinsel caught in the hedge mazes twinkled like stars under the flickering light of the flames.

"Wow," Mercy breathed, unable to keep the look of wonder from her face. While they had their own customs and celebrations in the Guild, nothing even compared to the grandeur of this night.

"Did you ever imagine it could look so resplendent?" Elvira asked, her voice full of awe.

Noblemen and women walked alongside them, carrying them in the current of eager revelers toward the castle entrance. A woman beside Mercy let out a soft laugh, clapping her hands in excitement. Elvira smiled at a boy who ran past her, dragging his little sister behind him.

Two slaves held the castle's front doors open. The nobility spilled into the great hall amid a sea of chatter. More slaves wearing stark white sashes wove between bodies, holding silver platters of food and drink high overhead. Panels of colorful fabrics lined the walls, and the flames from a brazier in the center of the room danced high in the air, bathing everything in warm golden light. A happy tune floated out from the throne room. Mercy had to dodge several dancing couples as she and Elvira made their way further inside.

Mercy tugged on her sleeve, her fingers brushing the hilt of the three-inch dagger concealed under the fabric. The plain blade had been easier to hide than her twin daggers, which Elvira currently wore sheathed under the layers of her skirt. Mercy's sheer gown left little to the imagination and few weapon-hiding places.

"My lady— My dear friend, happy Solari!"

Mercy tensed as an arm draped across her shoulders, but it was only Emrie. The serenna beamed at her with wine-flushed, dimpled cheeks. "Come with me. I'll show you where the real celebration is." She plucked a crystal wine goblet from a slave's tray and took a quick gulp before setting it down, grabbing Mercy's arm, and dragging her toward the throne room. Elvira hurried after them.

"Some of the richest and most powerful men in Beltharos are here, as well as some distant relatives of the Rivosi royal family," Emrie was saying as she led Mercy down the hall lined with paintings of past Myrellis monarchs. Beyond where Ghyslain and Elisora's painting had once hung, there were several feet of empty wall, places for the portraits of future kings and queens. Yet these spots were destined to remain empty.

The royal line would end tonight.

They passed through the double doors of the throne room, where throngs of people had already gathered to enjoy the revel. The sun blazed low in the west, partially visible through the wall of windows behind the throne, which was notably empty. Ghyslain stood on the dais a few feet away, speaking to Murray Bacha and a potbellied old courtier Mercy hadn't yet met. Prince Tamriel was somewhere in the chaos, and she needed to find him. Somehow, she had to get him somewhere private. The celebration would provide the perfect distraction for Mercy to kill the prince and slip out unnoticed.

"Do you see it? Right there, above the tallest boulder." Emrie pointed at the wall of windows, her fingers trembling with excitement.

Mercy followed her gaze. "The moon?"

"It's going to cross the sun, and I've heard it turns dark as night. Can you imagine?" Her eyes lifted to something over Mercy's shoulder, and her expression brightened. "Leon!"

Leon Nadra grinned as he shouldered past Elvira, who shot him a dirty look he didn't seem to notice. "You know what they say about Solari, don't you? About the moment the sun goes away?"

"If this is another one of your fanciful childhood tales, go find Maisie. I'm sure she'd love to hear."

He pressed a hand to his heart. "It's true as truth can be, I promise. They say when the sun disappears, the Creator can't see what's happening down here; he goes blind. They say for those few minutes, someone can commit the most heinous sin and the Creator will never know. At the end of our lives, he will welcome us all into the Beyond like we're his own kin, none the wiser."

Emrie nodded, an exaggeratedly grave look on her face. "Oh, I'm sure. What sort of heinous sin are you planning, then? Let's hear it."

He held up his hands in defense. "Just spreading a bit of Beltharan lore to the foreigner," he said, gesturing to Mercy. "I would never do anything so juvenile."

"I highly doubt that." Emrie propped her hands on her

hips, fighting back a smile. "What about night, then, genius? What happens when the sun goes down?"

"That's diff—"

"Is it? Oh! I think Narah would love to hear the fascinating tale you just told us, don't you? Narah, come here!" She rose onto her toes and waved to a girl across the room. Narah smiled, then saw Leon and blushed. She practically floated as she started toward them.

"Emrie, no!" Leon hissed, ducking his head. "I'm Elise's betrothed, remember? I haven't been able to face Narah since I made a fool of myself by the docks two weeks ago."

"Don't let Narah hear you mention Elise—she'll get jealous." Emrie cackled as Leon cringed and darted away, lost immediately in the crowd. When Narah reached them, Emrie pointed her in the direction Leon had gone, still giggling. "Sometimes I feel bad for teasing him, but he has been mostly insufferable since he was seven," Emrie confessed, looking pleased with herself.

"My lady, look," Elvira whispered. She'd been following and listening the whole time, but now her eyes focused on something at the front of the room.

Tamriel stood on the dais near the throne, turned slightly away from his father as Ghyslain listened to Cassius Bacha, whose wrinkled hands shook as he ran them through the few strands of wispy hair clinging to his shiny scalp. Cassius gestured first to the window, then to the people dancing and mingling throughout the room. Ghyslain placed a hand on his advisor's shoulder, saying something Mercy couldn't make out, and the tension immediately drained from Cassius's body.

Murray pushed her way through the crowd and gripped the collar of Cassius's shirt, her face flushed with embarrassment. She bowed to the king and prince before dragging her husband away. Tamriel watched them leave, frowning, then turned and murmured something to his father, who did not appear to respond. Ghyslain's eyes flicked to the mass of revelers, then he crossed the dais to speak with Master Oliver.

For a split second, Tamriel looked crestfallen at being so steadfastly ignored. He took a half step toward his father before he scowled, pivoted on his heel, and strode down the steps of the dais to join the celebration.

Mercy bade farewell to Emrie and kept her eyes trained on Tamriel's black hair as she wove through the crowd, determined not to lose sight of him in the sea of bodies. As she neared him, she snagged a goblet of wine from a slave's tray and drained it to the dregs, leaving only droplets visible through the crystal.

"Prince Tamriel," she said as she approached him. He was standing perfectly still at the edge of the crowd, watching one of the musicians pluck the strings of a lute. A shadow flitted across the prince's face, but it vanished by the time he turned to her and offered the ghost of a smile. "You don't seem in the best of moods." She swayed close to him as she spoke, hoping he would assume she'd drunk too much wine. "What's the problem?"

"Nothing of any concern right now."

She took her time scanning him up and down. Like before, he wasn't wearing armor; just a deep violet-and-gold brocade tunic and black trousers. His fine leather boots were so polished they shone like obsidian. "I see your servants chose not to dress you in a black velvet coat this time."

This time, his smile was genuine. "I *am* old enough to dress myself, you know."

Mercy shrugged and gracelessly tried to drain the last of the wine from her goblet, frowning when it came up empty. Then, for fear of being too subtle, she pretended to stumble.

Tamriel reached out to steady her. "How many of those have you consumed?"

"Not nearly enough." She stepped closer to the prince and met his dark eyes, asking in a soft voice, "What's bothering you?"

He glanced at the lute player, whose head was bent over his instrument, his eyes closed. "My mother used to play the lute," Tamriel admitted after a few beats of silence. "I've always wished I had been able to listen. I've been told she was quite talented."

At first, Mercy didn't know what to say. She hadn't expected that response, or the sliver of pain and grief that had slid into his voice. "Do you know much about her?"

"I know what others have told me about her, but it's not the same as knowing her. I don't care how fairly she ruled or how much she inspired the masses. Those are the actions of a queen, the things they write in history books. That's not my mother," he said, his expression turning bitter. He took a deep breath and turned to her. "I'm sorry. I'm afraid I'm not being a very good host. Perhaps I can make it up to you by telling you how nice you look tonight, my lady."

"Thank you, Your Highness. Now you see why I had to run off so suddenly yesterday." Mercy ran her hands over her skirt, relishing the feel of the lightweight fabric. The dress was floor-length and made of sheer champagne-colored silk, embroidered along the bust and sleeves with white lace, tiny crystals, and pearls. It resembled a robe, held closed with a line of satin laces from the center of the neckline to just below her hips, so a single tug on the string might send it fluttering away. Under it, she wore a long-sleeved gold leotard, which concealed both her dagger and her scars, but left her legs completely bare. As strange as it felt to wear something so soft, so ethereal, she could not deny its beauty.

Something shifted on Tamriel's face, but she could not

identify the emotion that passed through his eyes. "I do. You look—"

"It's starting!" a voice cried. Several people gasped. "Look! Look up there!"

There was a collective intake of breath as everyone turned to the wall of windows. The sun blazed over the lake, a tiny black shadow over its top right side. The music slowed to a low, mournful lullaby. Slaves ran from wall to wall extinguishing the torches until the room was bathed in shadow, the faint sunlight dimming as the moon crawled past one-quarter, one-half, three-quarters of the sun.

Beyond the windows, the sky grew darker, first blue, then violet. A line of pale pink divided the horizon, the outline of the Howling Mountains like sharp black teeth against the warmth of the light. The last note of the musicians' song was low, resonant, and held for what felt like an eternity as they watched the moon completely eclipse the sun. The sky turned dark as twilight. Stars twinkled in the distance. A ring of fire surrounded the moon like a halo, and Mercy could still see its outline when she looked away.

Glancing behind her, Mercy was shocked by the reactions of the revelers. Some of them stood in awed silence, their jaws slack and the plates of food in their hands forgotten. Some had their eyes closed, heads bowed, and were mouthing words of prayer. Others had opened their arms toward the sky, tears flowing freely down their faces.

Ghyslain was kneeling on one of the steps leading up to the dais, his head bent forward. He had removed his ceremonial diadem and now stared at it in his hands, mouthing the words of what Mercy assumed was a prayer. Hidden in the shadows along the far wall, Elvira sobbed into her hands. Mercy didn't doubt she was thinking of her husband and the night they'd met.

Beside her, Tamriel's eyes were locked on the reflection of

the sun on the lake's waves. His posture was rigid, his shoulders set in a tight line. After a moment, he looked away, blinking, and she thought he heard him breathe the word *Mother*.

Then, quietly—so quietly Mercy almost didn't hear—he whispered, "Forgive me."

A flare of sunlight burst from the upper right side of the sun as the moon continued its path, and a cheer rose up from the captivated crowd. It echoed throughout the city, a distant cry so loud Mercy could hear its rumble through the stone and glass of the castle. As the sun returned bit by bit, Ghyslain stood and placed his diadem on his head. He smiled as several young women—each dragging a dashing nobleman behind her—spread out across the floor and began to dance.

"What did you think?" Tamriel asked softly.

"It was— It was—" Mercy paused, searching for a word to do the experience justice. In the end, she settled for, "It was *incredible*." And it had been—she didn't need to believe in the Creator to know that this...this *thing* she'd witnessed was special. The hush that had fallen over the room had been so complete, so deferential, it was unlike anything she'd ever experienced.

But she had not come here for the celebration.

She grimaced and pressed a hand to her forehead, and Tamriel's expression shifted to concern. "Do you feel alright, my lady?" he asked.

Mercy frowned at the wine glass in her hand. "Perhaps I have had too much, after all. Could you show me to somewhere I could...lie down for a bit?"

"Of course." Tamriel took her hand and led her through the crowd. As they passed Elvira, Mercy grinned and winked at her behind the prince's back. She didn't miss the envious looks the noblewomen shot her when they noticed Tamriel's hand in hers. She felt like a cat toying with its prey as Tamriel escorted her out of the room and through the throngs of people mingling in the great hall.

Two hallways later, Mercy could still hear the waning notes of music from the throne room as the band finished its song. For a moment, it was Tamriel and her; the only sounds were their breaths and their soft footsteps against the red and gold rug, then the melody rose once more into a dizzying flourish.

Tamriel led her into a room slightly larger than her bedroom at Blackbriar, furnished simply with two expensive-looking velvet couches and a low wooden table between them. Without a word, Tamriel guided her to the couch and helped her lie down, then crossed to the window, setting his hands on the sill as he stared out at the land and lake beyond. As he watched the sun dip below the Howling Mountains, Mercy silently stood and walked over to the open double doors, easing them closed so Tamriel wouldn't hear the click of the latch.

Then she pulled the dagger out of her sleeve.

27

She stalked across the room, her eyes trained on Tamriel's jugular, just visible above the collar of his tunic. The prince was clearly absorbed in his thoughts. Mercy lifted the dagger as she lessened the gap between them by four feet, three feet, two, and—

A hand closed around her wrist, wrenching it so suddenly that the dagger slipped from her grasp. It hit the rug with a soft *whump*, and Mercy whirled, her heart leaping into her throat as she braced to meet her attacker.

No one stood there. She and Tamriel were alone.

She stooped to retrieve the dagger, but before her fingers could make contact, a woman's voice whispered a sharp *No*. Mercy straightened, shaken, and scanned the room with wide eyes. No one else was around—no one had even been in the hallway outside when Tamriel brought her here. By the window, the prince hadn't moved, hadn't given any indication that he'd noticed anything was amiss. As crazy as it sounded, the voice...it had spoken inside her *mind*.

She was still trying to figure out what exactly had

happened when Tamriel said, "My father was optimistic about the celebration tonight." He started to turn away from the window, and Mercy hastily kicked the dagger under the couch, out of sight. The prince shot her a strange look when he realized she was standing behind him—not lying on the couch as he'd left her—but he continued nonetheless: "He says it signals a change for all of us. The dawning of a new era."

"You don't share his excitement," Mercy responded, forcing her tone to remain nonchalant. "Why not?"

His expression soured. "I know what the nobles say about my father behind his back. I know what they say about me— the son of the mad king—but my critics tend to be slightly more forgiving. Still, the nobles, commoners, and advisors only support my claim to the throne because they think I'll turn out to be less crazy than my father. They're hedging their bets, biding their time until they can usurp me and stick some nobleman's son on the throne, some puppet who will bow to their every whim."

"You can't honestly think they would do that."

"Can't I? It's the curse of being royal. Tax the rich to feed the poor and they'll brand you a thief. Conscript men to strengthen the army and they'll complain about losing labor. Go to war for them and they'll curse you for their sons' deaths." He let out a quiet, humorless laugh. "And they say Solari years are blessed. Did you know that?"

"No," she said softly. She didn't know what to make of this prince, eyes wild and haunted, anger and bitterness in the twist of his lips. It was times like these she saw the way life in his mad father's court had affected him. He was a shadow of the prince who had strolled and laughed with her just one day before.

"Go home to Feyndara, Marieve," Tamriel said. "It's not

safe here. Every day you spend in the capital, you're less likely to make it home alive."

Mercy let a lazy smile spread across her lips, trying to mask her unease. "Don't be melodramatic, Your Highness," she teased. "It doesn't suit you."

"I'm being honest. Every elf you saw here today is a slave. They're nothing to the nobility, and I can assure you that they see you no differently."

Her smile faded. "I'm not a slave, nor will I ever be treated like one. I am Marieve Aasa, granddaughter to Queen Cerelia of Feyndara, and Creator help any man who dares to lay a hand on me."

For a moment, Tamriel looked almost impressed with her pronouncement. Then he shook his head. "You know what happened to Liselle. Do you really think your family name would protect you from the nobles' ire?"

"I can protect myself. What brought this on, Your Highness?" she challenged. Frustration rose within her—not at him, but at whatever had happened earlier, whatever had forced her to fail her attempt to kill him. Even now, she could feel that strange presence lurking nearby, watching with unseen eyes. The knowledge made her skin crawl.

"You don't care about elves," she pressed when Tamriel didn't answer. "None of you do. Why should my safety mean anything to you?"

And then she saw it: the guilt that flashed across his face. She remembered what he had muttered in the throne room —*Forgive me*—and realized he must have been thinking about Hero, about the way he had been forced to mutilate her. Even if he did not care about the slaves, he cared enough to warn *her* of the dangers of the court. He didn't trust her yet, but concern was better than apathy. She could work with concern.

"I'm sorry," she said softly, stepping closer to him. She

peered up at him through her lashes as she had watched so many Daughters do to the Strykers. "I've just been on edge lately. I've never been this far from home before."

That, at least, was true.

"There is no need to apologize, my lady."

Mercy placed a hand on his chest, and he went completely still. She could feel his heart beating out a strong pulse just below her fingertips, a cruel reminder of her failure. "Perhaps you could visit me in Feyndara sometime," she murmured, meeting his dark eyes. His hands curled into fists at his sides. "Then *you* would be the stranger in a foreign land."

"Perhaps," he choked out. She smiled, delighted at the way her words affected him. They stood face-to-face, nothing but a few inches between them, and she felt his pulse quicken beneath her fingers.

"I know what you're doing," he whispered. "I told you an alliance by marriage is out of the question."

"That's twice now you've brought up marrying me, Your Highness," she teased. "I think I could change your mind."

His gaze dropped to her lips, desire burning in his eyes, and she saw the moment his defenses crumbled. "You could certainly try."

She slid her hand up his chest and twined her fingers in his dark, silky hair. He reached for her, his hand cupping the curve of her waist, as she drew him closer. Her lips were almost to his when an ear-splitting scream rang out somewhere in the castle.

Tamriel jerked back, blinking with surprise. Before she could make sense of what was happening, he grabbed her hand and pulled her into the hall. "What's going on?" he called to the first slave they saw.

"I-I'm not sure, Your Highness. It sounded like it came from the throne room."

"Come on."

Together, they ran through the halls, their shoes slapping on the stone floors. They shoved their way through the crowd in the great hall and burst into the chaos of the throne room, breathing hard.

"Stay back!" Master Oliver was yelling from somewhere near the dais. His arms were out, herding people away from the steps, but the effort was unnecessary; terrified revelers tripped over themselves and one another in their haste to retreat. Several plates lay shattered on the floor, dropped in the panic. The porcelain crunched underfoot as Mercy and Tamriel made their way toward the throne.

A young woman clad in the flowing robes of the Church of the Creator stood on the dais steps, outlined by the fading light of the setting sun. The hood had fallen off her head, revealing the bright red rash and fluid-filled blisters marring one side of her face. She stumbled forward, her arms outstretched, and a nearby group of noblewomen recoiled, shrieking in fear. Oliver guided them away and turned to the priestess, speaking to her in a low voice she did not seem to hear. He glanced over his shoulder and spotted Tamriel and Mercy approaching.

"Don't go near her!" he called, genuine fear in his eyes. "She's sick, delirious!"

Every pair of eyes turned to them as they broke through the edge of the crowd. They crossed the half-circle of open space before the dais where, only moments before, people had been dancing and celebrating. The priestess trembled, whimpering in pain as she gazed down at them.

Now that they were closer, Mercy could see that the inflamed skin on the woman's face had begun to peel, and thick scabs pockmarked her cheeks and neck where the blisters had popped. One of her eyes was cloudy—blind, bloodshot, and swollen to the point of bulging out.

"Help them," she rasped. "Help them, please."

"Stay here," Tamriel whispered. He stepped forward, but before he made it more than two feet, Master Oliver caught him by the arm. Annoyance flashed across his face. "Unhand me."

"Absolutely not, Your Highness. She's mad, and she could hurt you or herself. Step aside while we await a healer."

"Help them, *please!*" the priestess begged.

"Tamriel!" Ghyslain barked. The king stood on the far side of the dais. His diadem was askew, his eyes full of pity as he regarded the woman. "There is nothing to be done."

"It's coming for you!" the priestess cried, and began sobbing into her hands.

Sympathy flooded Mercy. The woman's sickness was fatal —that much was obvious from her delirium and rail-thin form—but someone should have been comforting her, not gaping and gawking.

While Master Oliver and Tamriel glared at each other, neither willing to back down, Mercy darted past them. Oliver shouted and lunged for her, but she jerked out of his reach and ran to the woman, who let out a choked sob and swayed dangerously to one side. Mercy caught the priestess just as she was about to fall and eased her gently to the ground.

The woman sucked in a shuddering breath and knotted her fingers in Mercy's dress, pulling her close. Waves of feverish heat rolled off her body as her lids fluttered shut. "Help them, friend."

"What is happening to you? Help who?"

"In the end, he will come to you. Soon."

Soft footsteps approached them. Mercy looked up as Tamriel sank to his knees on the priestess's other side. He hesitated, then brushed the hair off the woman's face with a tender hand, being careful not to touch her skin. The whispers of the courtiers filled the room.

"What is your name, Sister?" Tamriel asked.

"P-Pilar."

"Pilar, who is going to come?"

Her swollen lids fell shut. When her chapped lips parted, her voice was deeper, rougher—a man's voice. "In that golden village I watched the Creator rise and craft the sun, the moon, the mountains, and the valleys from the flesh of the family he had butchered. Now *he* will watch as I destroy his dearest Creations, and he will weep as I build my dominion over the bones of his precious pets." Pilar rolled onto her side and drew her knees into her stomach. When she spoke again, her voice had returned to normal. "Stop him. Go north—northeast."

Mercy and Tamriel exchanged glances. "Pilar," Tamriel said quietly, "do you have the Sight?"

"Yes."

"Who spoke to you? Can you describe him?"

She shook her head and looked at Mercy. "Find the cure. Cure Fieldings' Plague." She coughed, a dry, rattling sound in her lungs.

Four elves carrying a stretcher pushed through the crowd. When they reached the dais, they stopped beside Pilar and lifted her onto the stretcher with gloved hands.

"Wait! Wait." Pilar reached out, blindly grasping the air until Mercy stepped forward and clasped her hand. Her palm was hot, moist where the blisters had popped. The bright red skin on the priestess's face stretched tight when she offered Mercy a pained smile. "Thank you, my friend."

"For what?"

"For what you're going to do."

The elves, handkerchiefs tied over their mouths and noses, lifted the stretcher and started toward the doors. They nobles recoiled as if burned, a few hissing with disgust.

Tamriel stood and held out his hand to Mercy. She

accepted, and he pulled her up, squeezing her hand once before letting go. "Thank you for calming her," he whispered.

"Get everyone out of here," Ghyslain said to Master Oliver. "Make sure every single person is off the property and safe. Answer no questions and instruct the slaves to do the same until we figure out what she meant by 'Fieldings' Plague'. We'll meet in the council chamber when you're finished."

"Yes, Your Majesty." Master Oliver pivoted on his heel and, arms stretched wide, began herding people toward the doors. He shouted orders to the guards stationed along the walls, and the throne room quickly filled with the confused and angry voices of the nobles as they were escorted outside.

Seren Pierce and Landers Nadra sidestepped Master Oliver, who let them pass without a second glance. "Your Majesty, allow me to help," Pierce said. "Elise and I will accompany the guards and ensure everyone makes it home safely."

"Very well. Landers, you and Leon head to the council room and prepare a strategy for containing this 'plague'. We don't want to incite a city-wide panic, especially on Solari."

While they spoke, Tamriel turned to Mercy. "Marieve, go home. Your handmaid, where is she?" He craned his neck and spotted Elvira across the room, fighting the current of bodies to reach them. "Go with her. I'll send a messenger when we know what's happening."

He started toward Elvira, but Mercy caught his arm. "Tamriel, wait. How serious is this? What was she talking about?"

The prince ran a hand down his face. "I-I don't know, but it seemed like she was looking for you. You might be important to whomever she was channeling with the Sight."

"What is the Sight?"

"It's a gift held by some old noble families and priestesses in the Church. The Creator sends them visions," he said impatiently, distracted by the panicked crowd slowly funneling out of the room.

"Come, my lady," Elvira called, pushing her way to the front of the room. She ran up the steps of the dais and grabbed Mercy's elbow, tugging her toward the great hall. "Forget our plans for tonight. We should return to Blackbriar."

Mercy glanced at Tamriel. She'd been so certain she would complete her contract this night. "But—"

"Do as your handmaid advises, my lady," the prince said. "Be safe, and I'll send word when I can." Without waiting for a response, he turned on his heel and crossed the dais, joining the discussion his father and Landers were having.

Mercy frowned, but followed Elvira from the throne room. When they reached the great hall, however, Elvira turned and led her down one of the castle's corridors, then into an empty meeting room. "Trade dresses with me," Elvira said, shucking off her slave sash and tossing it aside. "The guards are distracted. Now might be your only chance to sneak into Tamriel's chambers without anyone seeing."

They quickly changed. Mercy strapped her daggers' sheaths to her calves and straightened, the skirt of Elvira's simple floor-length dress falling over the bulk of the weapons. She slipped the slave sash over her head, then Elvira pressed a heavy iron key into her palm.

"I'll help you distract the guards, but after that, it's up to you. Once the prince is dead, return to Blackbriar and I'll see you safely out of the city."

Briefly, Mercy wondered whether she should tell Elvira about the strange voice that had whispered to her earlier that evening. She could still feel that iron grip close around her wrist, wrenching the blade from her grasp. She decided against it. Whatever had happened earlier, it wasn't going to keep her from completing her contract.

Come dawn, Tamriel would be dead.

28

When they were only one hall away from Tamriel's chambers, Elvira pointed to an empty dining room, and Mercy slipped inside. She pushed the door mostly closed and listened as Elvira ran back the way they'd come, shouting about more people infected with the plague.

"By the Creator—"

"More sick in the castle?"

A moment later, two royal guards ran past, their silver armor clanking with every step. As soon as they were out of earshot, Mercy pulled a dagger from its sheath and started toward Tamriel's room. She turned the last corner and was surprised to find Tamriel's door unguarded. The others had likely been called away to help clear the premises, which meant she only had a narrow window of time to slip in unseen. She slid the key into the lock and twisted, but it didn't move more than a quarter turn. She tried again to no avail.

"*Damn it,*" she hissed, pulling the key from the lock. Elvira must have grabbed the wrong one. She cursed under her breath and pulled a pin from her hair. Fortunately, all the Guild's apprentices were taught how to pick locks.

Soon enough, the latch released, and she crept silently into the room.

She locked the door behind her, then turned and surveyed the room. Prince Tamriel's bedchamber was bathed in heavy shadow, lit only by the sliver of moonlight cutting through the gap in the heavy curtains, illuminating part of the rug and massive, neatly-made bed. On the far wall, two doors stood open to a balcony. Several cushions surrounded a low table laden with a platter of wine, two empty goblets, and a vase containing a single rose. To her right, a wardrobe and an empty desk sat against a bare stone wall.

Wind whipped around Mercy as she stepped out onto the balcony, sending loose strands of hair flying around her face. She held them back with one hand and leaned over the railing, peering down at the lake's waves three stories below. They shimmered with the reflection of the stars, spray flying when they crashed against the large algae-covered boulders. Mercy ran her free hand along the smooth stone of the railing. It was not terribly high—not even waist-height. It wouldn't be difficult to lift a body over, and there was little chance of the prince being found in the lake, provided she could find something heavy enough to weigh him down.

Part of her mourned what she would do tonight. The prince seemed kind and honorable, and despite her efforts to remain aloof, Mercy liked him well enough. But it didn't matter. She'd come to the capital to complete her contract, and that's exactly what she would do. She'd waited seventeen years for this opportunity, and soon, she would prove her worth to everyone who had tormented her in the Guild.

Mercy returned to the bedroom. She perched on the edge of the mattress and set her daggers on her lap, trying and failing not to admire the downy texture of the pillows and the way the silk sheets slipped between her fingers. What would become of this room once Tamriel was dead? The answer seemed obvious: the fineries would be removed and sold, and the furniture would be hidden under dust cloths, like so many of the rooms she and Elvira had passed as they walked through the castle. Ghyslain would move on with his life, the threat to his rule gone, and Tamriel Myrellis would become nothing more than a name in a history book.

Thump.

Mercy seized her daggers and jumped to her feet. She crossed the room and pressed herself against the wall beside the door, waiting for the latch to release and Tamriel to stride in. Adrenaline coursed through her veins. She was still a little jumpy from her failed assassination attempt that evening.

The prince did not appear.

She peered at the door. The lock still held, and the line of light at the bottom was uninterrupted. No one stood outside.

When she turned back, her gaze caught on something shiny on the floor just beside the desk. It was a crystal paperweight, no larger than her fist. Mercy examined it, confused, as she approached. She bent down and picked it up, and as she straightened, she realized one of the drawers stood open a good five inches. It hadn't been open when she walked in; she was certain of it. She would have noticed it.

But inanimate objects didn't move on their own.

Unease settled in her stomach as she set her daggers and the paperweight on the desk, then knelt and pulled the drawer open. It was crammed with papers: legal documents, ledgers, and pages of financial reports from both Beltharan and Feyndaran banks. That struck Mercy as odd—what dealings would Tamriel have with Feyndara? Why would the prince have bank accounts in his enemy's country?

Mercy pulled the papers out of the drawer and sat back on her heels, her brows furrowed in confusion. The accounts weren't listed under the Myrellis name; they belonged to Drake Zendais, Queen Elisora's late elder brother. He'd been killed by Llorin shortly after Liselle's murder.

She flipped to the next page, and her breath caught.

The Guild's teardrop sigil was stamped at the top of the parchment, and lines of elegant cursive detailed the contract for the murder of—

Of Tamriel Myrellis.

Mercy dropped the paper and scrambled back, her pulse pounding in her ears. *He knows.*

She crawled forward, gathering the papers into her arms, and reread the contract twice more in the dim moonlight. Each time, she wished for another name, and each time, it remained the same: Tamriel Myrellis. At the bottom, in a slightly smudged, hurried hand, it was signed *His Majesty Ghyslain Myrellis.*

Where Tamriel found the contract didn't matter. He knew an Assassin was coming for him. He may not have realized the Assassin was Mercy, but it wouldn't take him long to figure it out. The possibility had to have crossed his mind. A royal visiting from an estranged and enemy country was hardly an everyday occurrence, and her arrival couldn't have been noted without a degree of suspicion. Why, then, had he talked and joked with her the day before, rather than reveal her identity to the guards? Why had he turned his back on her when they were alone earlier?

If he knows, why hasn't he done anything?

Men's voices in the hall outside startled her out of her thoughts. She shoved the papers into the drawer and pushed it closed, but it didn't move more than an inch before jamming. She muttered a curse and shoved it harder. It didn't budge.

Get out! a stranger's voice screamed in her head. *Now!*

"*Shit,*" she breathed as the door handle rattled. She gave

up on the drawer and grabbed her daggers, retreating to the corner of the room, where she would be concealed in shadow. Just as the lock released, she pulled off the slave sash and dropped it on the floor. Even in the dim moonlight, the stark white fabric seemed to glow. The last thing she needed was Tamriel spotting her and calling for his guards.

The door opened, and a man's silhouette stepped into the room. Tamriel shut the door, started toward the wardrobe, and paused when he noticed the open drawer. Mercy crept forward, her heart pounding so hard she was sure he could hear it. Now—she had to strike now, while his back was turned. She lifted the dagger in her right hand as he bent forward and opened the drawer. If she angled it correctly, the blade would slip through his ribs and pierce his heart before he even realized what had happened.

She drove the dagger toward his back, but before it could make contact, Tamriel pivoted out of its path, his arm swinging toward her. Mercy had just enough time to register the face that did not belong to the prince before the crystal paperweight cracked against her skull. She crumpled, black spots dancing in her vision. Something warm and wet spilled down the side of her head. *Get up!* her instincts screamed, *Get up now!* but her leaden limbs refused to obey.

Strands of bloody hair hung over her face, and through them, she saw him step over her and shuffle through the papers in the drawer. When he reached the contract, he clicked his tongue disapprovingly. The last thing Mercy heard before unconsciousness claimed her was, "Look what an awful mess you've made, love."

29

Something tickled Mercy's nose.

It was soft, the scent cloyingly sweet. A rose. Without opening her eyes, she scrunched her nose and turned her face away. The rose bumped her again, and when she reached up to swat it away, her arm only moved a few inches before the tether around her wrist pulled taut.

Her eyes snapped open. She lay spread-eagled on the bed, her wrists and ankles bound to the posts with strips of cloth torn from the sheets. Through the parted curtains, she could see the pale pink of dawn painting the sky. She'd been unconscious all night.

Calum smiled at her from where he sat on the edge of the mattress, the stem of the rose pinched between two fingers. "Good morning."

Mercy glared at him. "You'll have to give me more than flowers if you want me to forgive you for hitting me with a paperweight," she said, in far too much pain to put any bite behind the words. A raging tempest pounded within her skull, sending waves of agony through her.

Calum shook his head. "I'm afraid you're misinterpreting

my actions, love, but I'm not surprised. That was quite a hit you took last night—although, to be honest, I hadn't meant to hit you so hard. Since I'm woefully short on smelling salts, I figured this might work just as well." He brought the rose to his nose and inhaled deeply. "And let's not forget that *you* tried to stab me in the back."

"I thought you were the prince. Where's Tamriel?"

He dropped the flower on the bedside table. "I was just about to ask you the same question. Where is he?" Calum's voice was cold, edged with steel. "Because I can tell you where he's not, and that's rotting six feet underground, or bobbing along at the bottom of the lake, of whatever it is you had planned to do with his body. No, as far as I can tell, he's still very much alive."

Mercy frowned, trying to focus on their conversation through the pounding in her head. The man before her was so different from the Calum who'd helped her win the Trial. Where was the kind, funny blacksmith she'd met in the Keep? "Tying me up isn't going to kill him any quicker. What if he walked in right now? What do you think he would do if he found you holding me hostage in his bedroom?"

He barked a laugh. "You thought my room was his? A simple enough mistake, I guess, but I thought you were better than that, O Great Daughter of the Guild."

"What the hell do you mean, your room?"

Calum looked offended. "I'm the king's nephew. I've lived here for eighteen years, since my father was brutally murdered by one of your Sisters."

The name she'd seen on the bank accounts came back with startling clarity. "Drake Zendais. He was your father?"

He nodded. "I use my mother's maiden name when I travel. It's a little less conspicuous, don't you think?"

"...The contract is fake, isn't it?" she said, the pieces beginning to fall into place. "Ghyslain's signature is a forgery."

His expression didn't change, but Mercy knew she was right. Tamriel and Calum were cousins through Elisora's side, which meant Calum didn't have royal blood. Only a royal could buy a contract on another royal, so he had faked Ghyslain's signature.

Calum untied Mercy's wrists and ankles, then crossed the room and sprawled on one of the cushions around the low central table. He picked up the wine, pried it open with one of Mercy's daggers, and took a drink straight from the bottle. "I'll explain everything if you can make it all the way over here. If not, feel free to rest and build your strength back up. I won't hurt you."

"I find that extraordinarily hard to believe."

"Whether you believe it or not, it's true. I've invested in you. Why in the Creator's name would I do anything to compromise that?" He grabbed a goblet and filled it with wine, offering it to her with a raised brow. "You've already ruined my plans for the night—I might as well see this through."

When her doubtful expression didn't change, he let out an exasperated sigh. "I'm not going to kill you, Mercy. If I'd wanted to, I would have done it while you were unconscious."

He had a point. Mercy rose slowly, feeling the tendons in her neck strain as she lifted her head, then her back vertebra by vertebra. A thick bandage had been wrapped around her head to stop the bleeding, but it did nothing for the throbbing where Calum had struck her. The neckline and shoulder of Elvira's dress was crusted in dried blood, and it stuck to Mercy's skin as she shifted. Once she was fully upright, she swung her legs over the side of the mattress until her bare feet brushed the cold stone.

"That dress is ruined, so I had a slave bring you something from storage. You might want to wait until you're more steady to change, though," Calum said. "Don't worry about your cover, *Marieve*—I said I found you wandering the halls after drinking too much and offered you a place to spend the night."

"A true gentleman," she responded dryly. She pushed to her feet. When she took a step, the world seemed to slide out from under her. She clutched the nearest bedpost and let out an involuntary groan.

"Lie down, Mercy."

She shook her head. "When I make it over there, I am going to flay you alive."

A chuckle was his only response.

One slow step at a time, Mercy shuffled across the room and half sat, half fell onto the cushion opposite Calum. He offered her the goblet of wine and she drained the contents in a single gulp, not realizing until that moment how dry her throat had become. He refilled her goblet, then poured his own glass, and they drank in silence for a few minutes.

"Drake Zendais was my father," Calum finally said. He stared down at his goblet, absently swirling the dark liquid within. "When I was two, Ghyslain had him killed by one of Illynor's Assassins because of his involvement in Liselle's death. The Assassin who murdered him snuck into our house in the dead of night and stabbed him in the heart with a letter opener.

"My family wasn't nobility, but my father and grandfather supported the Myrellis line and had worked closely with King Alaric before his death. They were loyal and had grown wealthy trading art. That was part of the reason why the nobility supported Ghyslain and Elisora's betrothal."

Mercy crossed her arms. "I'm not in the mood for a history lesson. Skip to the part that has to do with *me*."

His dark eyes met hers. "How much do you know about your parents, Mercy?"

"You know exactly how much."

"My father's second wife was unable to have children, and he divorced his first wife before she could give him an heir to his fortune. So, to continue his bloodline, he raped one of his slaves so she could bear him a bastard he and his wife would pretend was legitimate. That slave was your mother, Mercy."

She froze. "No."

"Your mother and father had been slaves of my father for five years. They were married at the time. Drake Zendais raped her and she gave birth to me," he said calmly. "A few years later, she and your father had you. Your father was the one who found Llorin standing over Drake's body, and he gave you to the Guild so he and your mother could escape—"

"Don't lie to me, damn you!" she snarled. She jumped to her feet, staggering slightly as the world swayed. Calum reached out to steady her, and she recoiled.

"Mercy," he said. "A child between a human and an elf is born human. You know that. Affairs like those are not at all uncommon among the nobility. Make no mistake, I am not excusing my father's crime, but I can't change the circumstances of my birth—despicable as they may be."

"How could you possibly know all that? When you arrived at the Keep, how did you know that you and I... that we're...?" She couldn't force the word out—*half-siblings*.

"People talk. And several of my father's former slaves are still in the city. They'll tell anything for the right price."

Mercy clenched her fists as she searched Calum's face for...anything. Anything but the blatant honesty shining in his eyes. He didn't try to argue or convince her, he simply watched her process this revelation.

"I have no reason to believe a single word out of your mouth," she eventually said.

"You're right, you don't. But let me continue explaining, and it may start to make sense. Ghyslain took me in after my father's death—my so-called mother wanted nothing to do with me—and Tamriel and I were raised and tutored together. Last year, I joined the Strykers using our mother's maiden name and secretly collected the debts owed to my father while we traveled. I managed to amass a small fortune—enough to buy the contract.

"I want the prince dead, and I want the king to appear complicit. The nobles are already whispering about removing him from the throne, and they'll be clamoring to usurp him once I reveal that I found the contract he bought on his son's life. Without a Myrellis to rule, everyone will be vying for the crown. Now, my claim is only through marriage, but with my castle upbringing and royal education, I'm a better choice than some stuffy nobleman's son. The council will no doubt agree."

"The contract is void," Mercy said. Her head swam with everything he'd revealed, all the information he'd thrust at her. The wine turned sour in her stomach.

"The only people who know that are in this room, Sis." He shot her a crooked grin. "And you won't tell a soul, because you're going to go through with it."

"Oh, I am?"

"If you don't, you won't be a true Daughter. You won't be the Assassin who killed a prince on her very first contract. I know how much you hunger for Mother Illynor's approval. You reveal that the contract is fake and all the work you put in to compete in the Trial, everything you risked for the chance to swear your vows, is for nothing." His grin turned wicked. "Complete the contract, and no one's the wiser. I get my revenge on the king for having my father killed, and you become the Daughter who *murdered the prince*. Can you imagine the envy on Lylia's face when she learns of your success? And Faye might even forgive you for stealing her victory."

The possibility dangled before her, just out of reach. All

her life, she'd wanted nothing more than to become a full-fledged Daughter of the Guild. She'd come this far.

She remembered the terror she had felt as Tanni and Sienna walked her to what could have been her execution. She remembered Lylia's hand on her back as they stood atop the battlements in the middle of the night, and the cruel delight in Lylia's voice as she threatened to shove Mercy off the wall. She remembered the fury and betrayal on Faye's face when she went to say goodbye. This was her chance to prove that she—an elf whose own parents had bartered her life away—could become the greatest Assassin the Guild had ever trained.

"Yes," she said. "I'll do it."

30

Calum dismissed the guards in the hall outside his room before allowing her to leave. While he was outside, speaking to them, Mercy slipped into the dress he'd given her and found her shoes tucked under the bed. He had left her twin daggers on the low central table, perhaps in an effort to regain her trust. Even so, she couldn't resist imagining using them on *him* as she strapped the sheaths to her calves. She'd agreed to go through with the contract, but she was still furious with him for manipulating her.

When Calum returned, he leaned against the closed door and crossed his arms loosely over his chest. "I heard His Highness is on his way to the council room at this very moment. You'd better hurry, love."

She shot him a look. "What do you want me to do, stab him in front of all the advisors?"

"If I wanted to make a spectacle of his death, I wouldn't have gone to the trouble of hiring an Assassin," he retorted, rolling his eyes. "Something is happening with this so-called plague, and I'd like to hear what they plan to do about it, particularly because it could affect your ability to complete the contract."

"Go yourself, then. I have more important things to do—like icing my head where you hit me with that Creator-damned paperweight."

He plucked the bandage off her head. "I may be the king's nephew, but His Majesty doesn't want me on the council. He thinks the power would go to my head. Imagine that. Since you're a guest of the crown, it would be rude for Ghyslain to turn you away."

Mercy rubbed the sore spot on the side of her head, where a large, tender bump protruded. If Calum had hit her any harder, he could have killed her.

He frowned at her. "Don't worry about that. Your hair covers the bump. Now go." Calum placed a hand on her lower back and pushed her toward the door. As she stepped over the threshold, he said, "Don't keep me waiting, love," then shut the door on her heels.

Three feet separated her from the completion of her contract.

Prince Tamriel stood within the entrance of the council chamber, a sword at his hip and a cloak tumbling from a clasp at his throat. His clothes—the same ones he'd worn to the celebration—were rumpled. Mercy doubted he'd slept at all since the fest's abrupt end. For the fist time, he looked absolutely terrified.

"Three hundred," he breathed, and the quiet chatter filling the room went silent.

"What did you say?" Landers asked, the blood draining from his face.

"Three hundred infected, at least. We found two dozen

hiding in the Church in the market district. I have guards stationed there to make sure no one enters or exits until we have a plan to contain the disease. At minimum, there are two hundred infected in Beggars' End alone; the soldiers arrived to seal the gates before we could get a complete count. I don't know how many dead yet, but I saw several bodies in the End."

"They looked like Pilar?" Mercy asked, and Tamriel looked at her for the first time, only then seeming to notice her presence. "I was in the End two days ago, and I only saw—"

"You went *into Beggars' End?*" one of the advisors interrupted.

"*Voluntarily?*" another asked.

Seren Pierce, who'd been standing beside the king at the end of the table, slumped into the nearest chair. "No," he breathed, devastation plain on his face. "*Atlas.* My boy."

Ghyslain turned to Tamriel. "Did all the guards make it out of Beggars' End before the gates were sealed?"

The prince thought for a moment, then slowly shook his head. "I don't know. So much was happening, it's possible not everyone made it out in time."

"We'll do everything we can to keep your son and the other guards safe," Ghyslain said to Pierce. The seren merely muttered something under his breath, his skin turning deathly pale.

"Okay—Okay, so we set up healers' tents in the fields outside the city," Leon suggested, looking to his father for support. "They can hold the sick hiding in the Church and as many from the End as we can fit. The rest will have to remain in Beggars' End until we have more room for them—when the patients recover or, uh..." He cleared his throat awkwardly. "When there are empty cots for them."

"The chance of them infecting others during transport out of the city is too high. The End must remain in quarantine," Ghyslain said, rising and moving behind his seat at the head of the table. When he set his hands on the back of his chair, Mercy didn't fail to notice that they were trembling.

The king's eyes met hers, and the emotions she saw in them shocked her:

Agony.

Despair.

Acceptance.

Acceptance?

"Seize her," he said to the guards stationed at the doors. They sprang into action, but before they could grab her, he yelled, "Don't touch her skin!"

"Don't lay a hand on me." Mercy instinctively started to reach for her daggers, but forced herself to still. It was better not to let them know she was armed. She bristled as the guards grabbed her arms, being careful not to touch her bare skin. "What is the meaning of this?"

"Father!" Tamriel objected. "She is our *guest*."

"She touched the priestess's skin, which means she could be carrying the disease. She'll be quarantined in the infirmary while Alyss determines whether she has been infected. We shall soon see if she falls sick. Guards, escort her to the infirmary. Now."

One of the guards pushed her toward the door and chuckled under his breath when Mercy tripped over the skirts of her borrowed gown. His grip tightened on her arm, his fingers digging into her flesh hard enough to bruise. She shot him a glare over her shoulder as she straightened.

"Watch your step, elf," he murmured, eyes twinkling with mirth.

"Hold your tongue, Raiden," Tamriel snapped. "She is royalty."

The prince reached out and pulled Mercy out of the guards' grasp, drawing her close to him. "I will escort you to the infirmary, my lady, as some members of our guard have forgotten their manners. Raiden, touch her again and I'll break your nose."

The smirk fell from Raiden's lips. "Yes, Your Highness."

They walked down the hall, the doors to the council chamber swinging shut behind them. Tamriel led them around the corner and down the stairs to the main floor, the heels of his boots clicking on the stone floor. Every slave they encountered took one look at his stormy expression and scurried out of their path.

"Thank you for intervening on my behalf, Your Highness," Mercy said softly.

"No need to thank me."

With that, Tamriel turned on his heel and punched Raiden in the face. His fist connected with the guard's nose with a sickening crunch. The other guard drew Mercy close to his side as Raiden stumbled backward, his hands flying to his face. Blood gushed out of his nose and bubbled over his lips.

"What the hell!" he cried. "I didn't touch her!"

Tamriel shook out his hand. "Let that broken nose serve as a reminder to treat our guests with more respect next time. I suggest you apologize to Lady Marieve and get out of our sight."

Raiden stammered an apology, bowed, and ran back the way they had come. Tamriel sighed and turned to the other guard. "Go after him. Patch up his nose and tell him he's on duty guarding the northern gate of Beggars' End for the rest of the week, effective immediately. I don't want to see him within these walls anytime soon."

The guard bowed and ran after Raiden, leaving Mercy and Tamriel alone.

The prince flexed his hand and frowned at the faint bruises blossoming across his knuckles. "I forgot how much it hurts to punch someone. It's not as easy as people make it sound, is it?"

"I wouldn't know, Your Highness."

"Truly?" Tamriel offered her a faint smile. "I wouldn't be surprised. As I said before, you're unlike any other princess I've ever met."

"Not a princess."

He shrugged. "Anyhow, the guards should know better than to behave in such a barbaric manner to anyone in the castle. Perhaps I should have kept Raiden near. His face would serve as a warning to everyone in the barracks what would happen if they disrespected you." He shoved his bruised hand into his pocket. "To the infirmary, then. I have no doubt His Majesty is waiting for me in his study at this very moment, preparing to chastise me for speaking out of turn."

He continued down the hall at a quick pace, leaving her scrambling to catch up. His short temper didn't surprise her; after the events of the past day, he must have been exhausted.

"Your father—" Mercy began as they turned into a stairwell and began descending. "I think he knew something about the plague—hearing your report only confirmed what he'd already known. Didn't you see it on his face?"

Tamriel glanced back at her, his expression troubled. "I... It was nothing. He has a lot on his mind right now."

"You *did* see it!"

"Maybe there was something there. Maybe not. He's the mad king, remember? He prefers chasing ghosts to spending time with his own son. Hell, Master Oliver is more of a father to me than *His Majesty* has ever been."

She'd struck a nerve there. "...I'm sorry."

"He has an obligation to our people, and sometimes he lets his feelings for phantoms get in the way of that. What he fails to realize is that when he lost a wife, I lost *both* my parents." He let out a sharp, humorless laugh. "And Liselle. Perhaps if he hadn't spent so much time with her, he could have attended my mother better. She might have lived." Tamriel stopped at the bottom of the steps, his voice turning bitter, cold. "My mother was sentenced to bed rest for months, and while my father should have been at her bedside, he was off with another woman. How is that fair?"

"It's not, Your Highness," Mercy said softly, aching at the pain and sorrow on the prince's face. It was clear how deeply the queen's death had hurt him, how raw that old wound still was. Mercy couldn't care less about the woman who had given her up, but she knew Tamriel would give anything for the chance to know his mother.

On impulse, she reached up and cupped his cheek, his skin warm under her fingers. She was painfully aware of the fact that they were alone, that he wore no armor, that one thrust of her dagger could stop his heart forever. He would be dead before he could even open his mouth to call for the guards. She would complete her contract, and Calum would be free to pursue the throne.

But when the prince almost imperceptibly leaned into her touch, agony and grief flitting through his dark eyes, she faltered. She told herself it was because the timing was not right. There was no place to hide his body where it wouldn't be found; even if she managed to stash his body somewhere, she couldn't very well walk out of the castle covered in his blood.

A few days, she silently pledged. *Just until I'm released from the infirmary, and then I'll strike.* She knew better than to rush into completing her contract. One wrong step, and the court would have her head.

She could wait a few days.

"I don't want the throne," Tamriel murmured, "but if I

could, I would take it from him the day I turned eighteen. Beltharos deserves better than him."

"*You* deserve better than him."

He reached up and touched the hand she still held to his cheek, his lips twitching into the ghost of a smile. He gently lowered her hand to her side, giving her fingers a squeeze before letting go. "Let's get you to the infirmary."

Mercy let him lead her down the twisting halls, mentally cataloguing every detail. They were underground now, below the main floor of the castle, and many of the doorways had long since been filled in with stone bricks. Most of the doors that remained were so warped from the dank underground air Mercy was sure they were stuck.

She took note of every guard they passed, and it wasn't long before they arrived at the infirmary. Tamriel passed on his father's orders to the men standing watch outside, then left her with a promise that he would send word to Blackbriar informing Elvira of what had transpired. As soon as he disappeared around the corner, the guards opened the door, shoved her through, and slammed it shut.

31

The castle's infirmary was so different from the Guild's, it took Mercy a moment to gather her bearings. The infirmary at Kismoro Keep was dark and well-used, jars and bottles of medicine cluttering every available surface. The commercially-available tonics and tinctures Mother Illynor's contacts sometimes sent sat on the desk, rationed to the last drop. There were stains on the bed linens from blood that had not completely washed out, and always a bowl of needles and thread waiting for the next wound to stitch.

Myrellis Castle's infirmary was sparkling clean. A long line of floor-to-ceiling shelves stood in front of Mercy, each laden with a colorful concoction that shimmered under the light from the fire in the hearth. Something thudded against the opposite side of the shelves, and the jars and bottles rattled.

"Whoever ye are, don't just stand there! Get yer ass over here!" a woman called, her words lilted with a thick Rivosi accent.

Mercy rounded the shelves to find a short, stocky woman pinning Pilar—who'd been gagged—to one of the four cots.

The healer looked Mercy up and down, ignoring Pilar's wild bucking beneath her gloved hands. "Did they send ye to help? About time. Hold her down so I can do my work. Grab the gloves on the desk there."

Mercy didn't bother to tell her that she'd already come into contact with the so-called plague. She'd spent enough time in the infirmary with Mistress Sorin to know not to question a healer's orders. She quickly slipped the gloves on and approached the cot, pretending not to see the terror in the priestess's eyes as she fought to free herself.

The healer nodded. "Grab here an' here, an' be ready for her to put up a fight. They're stronger than they look when they're crazed like this."

The second the healer lifted her hands, Pilar jolted upright. Mercy scrambled to push her back onto the pillow as the healer ran to the desk. Even through the leather of the gloves, she could feel the heat rolling off the priestess's skin. She shoved Pilar down, gripping her shoulders tightly, and straddled her legs so she couldn't kick out.

Pilar squeezed her eyes shut and shouted something unintelligible, the words muffled by the gag. She squirmed, tossing her head from side to side, and several of the blisters on her face popped from the friction. Yellow-white pus oozed from the wounds, mixing with the tears spilling down her cheeks.

The healer jabbed a syringe into the priestess's arm, and Pilar's thrashing slowly eased. "Sleep now, Sister," she murmured softly.

Pilar's body went limp as the sedative took hold. Her head lolled, an unshed tear slipping through her lashes. Mercy clambered off the bed and tossed the gloves onto the bedside table, pushing away a strand of hair that had stuck to the sweat beading on her brow. "Was she like that all night?"

The healer shook her head. "She slept most of the time. Must've been a nightmare that woke her. All of a sudden, she just started screamin' bloody murder." She propped her hands on her hips and studied Mercy. Although the healer stood a head and a half shorter than Mercy, she still somehow managed to look down her nose at her, eyes narrowed. "Yer not a slave. Who are ye?"

"Lady Marieve of Feyndara."

She snorted. "Ye might be a lady in Feyndara, but I'm queen of this ward. Name's Alyss. Now, why are ye here?"

"The king thinks I might be infected, and he's ordered me to stay here in quarantine."

"Hm. Well, it seems they're not goin' to be sendin' any help my way, so I'm puttin' ye to work. Get the kettle off the fire and add some marroway leaves to the water. They're in the chest under the table. When she wakes up, the tea will keep her calm."

Mercy did as Alyss said, and once she'd finished, the healer ground a handful of dried mushrooms into powder and scraped them into the kettle with the edge of her knife, then poured in a splash of Ienna oil.

"She's not goin' to last long," Alyss said as she capped the bottle, the harsh lines of her face softening. "I'd like to give her some peace before she goes, but I'm not goin' to waste valuable medicine on someone who isn't goin' to get better. The best I can do is ease her pain for the little time she has left."

Mercy turned toward Pilar. Even in sleep, her eyelids fluttered, a crease between her brows. "She called it Fieldings' Plague. Have you ever heard of it?"

"No, never. Never seen a case of Fieldings' Blisters this bad, either. It's not uncommon for the common folk to come down with the blisters at the start of the summer, now that many of them are workin' outside day in and day out. But it's not usually more 'an skin deep. I've never seen it attack someone's vision."

Mercy stilled. "You mean her eye wasn't like that before? That her blindness happened recently?"

"I used to see her in the market when the shipments of herbs came in from Bluegrass Valley. Must've seen her not two weeks ago, healthy as an ox. Today, though..." The healer's expression turned uneasy. "She kept repeatin' things that made no sense to me or the slaves who brought her in. *Stop him. Find the cure.* The only way we could shut her up was with the gag. She would've screamed herself hoarse otherwise."

Alyss crossed the room and grabbed a mortar and pestle from the shelves. She placed it on the desk, then dumped a handful of colorful pills into the bowl. "Grind those down into a powder," she instructed, handing Mercy the pestle. "We'll mix them with the tea to lower her fever. I can't do much to help her, but I'll do what I can to keep her lucid while she's awake. Maybe ye'll be able to get somethin' meaningful outta her."

"Maybe," Mercy said doubtfully. She thought back to the night before, when Pilar had spoken with that stranger's deep, gravelly voice. Tamriel had seemed to think it had something to do with her Sight. "She said someone would come for us in the end. What could—"

The end.

The End.

She stopped, her eyes going wide as she remembered the map she'd seen in Seren Pierce's study. Cassius Bacha had painted the entirety of Beggars' End in blood red ink not even three days earlier. Dread and unease settled in the pit of her stomach as realization sank in. Cassius and Pilar had Seen the same thing: a plague originating in the End. Considering how terrified they were, it was going to get much, much worse.

"Beggars' End," Mercy breathed, hardly believing what she was about to say. Two weeks ago, she would have scoffed at the idea of visions and prophecies, but it seemed they were far more real than she would care to admit. "Pilar wasn't talking about a point in time, she was talking about the slums."

Fortunately, the king had already thought to close the gates to the End. That would limit the spread of disease, but there was no telling how many patrons and priestesses in the Church had unwittingly passed on the plague.

Alyss cursed under her breath. "We'd best get to work, then. Keep grinding those pills while I take inventory. If this truly is a plague, I'll need to get started working on a cure right away."

Mercy nodded and set to work. Soon, the only sounds were the scraping of the pestle against the granite bowl and the scratching of Alyss's pen against parchment. Every so often, Alyss paused her writing to rise onto her tiptoes and search one of the shelves.

They continued their tasks in silence, and eventually the pestle grew heavy in Mercy's hand. Her eyelids began to droop. The bumps on her head still throbbed, and the pounding only grew more painful the more tired she became. When Alyss stepped outside to give the guards a list of ingredients to purchase, Mercy folded her arms on the desk, rested her cheek on the smooth wood, and fell asleep.

32

"You don't have to worry about the contract anymore, Mercy," Calum said, his voice sharp as a blade on a whetstone. She lay atop his bed, her limbs once again bound to the bedpost, and could do nothing but glare at him as he loomed over her. "You failed me. Over and over again, you've failed me. But I've taken care of everything."

Her head still felt foggy from the wound she'd sustained when he hit her. Despite the throbbing in her temples, she tugged at the ropes tied around her wrists, trying desperately to free herself. Blood welled where the rough rope tore her skin, but the bonds didn't give. "What do you mean? This contract is mine."

"I thought it was. I gave you everything you needed. And still, you failed."

Something was on the floor behind Calum. She lifted her head to see what it was, but he shifted to block her view. A pile of cushions, perhaps? A rug?

Something wet
plop
plop
plopped

JACQUELINE PAWL

on the stone tiles.

Calum gazed down at her, his dark eyes like flecks of obsidian. "Go back to the Guild, where you belong. I don't need you anymore. I have a feeling Mother Illynor will not be kind when she learns how her prized Assassin fared on her first contract. Farewell, sister."

He reached forward to cup her face, and she recoiled when she saw that his hand was coated in blood. Fat red droplets plop, plop, plopped *on the sheet, then her pillow, as he traced her cheek with a light finger. One of the droplets caught on her lashes and trailed down the side of her face like a tear.*

Behind him, someone let out a choked sob. Mercy lifted her head again and realized with horror that what she'd thought was a pile of cushions was Prince Tamriel, lying in a heap on the floor. The red rug underneath him wasn't a rug at all, but a growing pool of blood.

Calum's mouth parted, but it was not his voice that said, "You can save them all."

Mercy awoke with a start. She was lying on one of the cots, and Pilar was kneeling on the side of the bed, her hand pressed to Mercy's cheek in the same place Calum's had been. Her palm was moist not from blood, but popped blisters.

"Save them," the priestess rasped, the gag hanging loose around her neck. She crawled toward the foot of Mercy's bed and sat with her knees close to her chest, then turned her face so her blind, bloodshot eye was out of Mercy's line of sight. "You have to save them."

Mercy slowly sat upright, wincing when pain shot through her skull. Alyss must have carried her from the desk when she realized she had fallen asleep, although how the four-foot-nothing woman managed to move her across the room without waking her remained a mystery. "Where is Alyss?"

Pilar flinched and lifted a finger to her lips. Her good eye darted to a curtained-off room on the far wall, from which Mercy could hear soft snoring. "She's asleep. The king gave her chambers up in the castle, but she likes to sleep in there when a patient might die. Sometimes the sound of someone coughing up blood or choking on vomit wakes her in time to save them. Other times, all she can do is call the guards to remove the body the next morning. People think she's harsh —she scared off her last two assistants—but when no one's around, she cries for the patients she cannot save. She cries for them all."

"How do you know all that? Did the Sight show you?"

She shook her head. "The Creator shows me only the good in this world. He shows me a girl falling in love for the first time, a married couple growing old together, watching their children build lives and families of their own. It is a fallacy—silk flowers given by an absent god. This is the work of Myrbellanar. He offers no comfort, no guiding hand, no light in this dark world. He offers only truth."

"What do you mean?" Mercy leaned forward, imploring her to explain. Although what she said sounded like nonsense, her good eye was clear and bright, no longer hazy with fever and delirium. "Who is Myrbellanar?"

"We once knew his real name, but it has since been lost to time. Myrbellanar is what they call him in the Islands. It's Cirisian for 'Fallen Father'. In their folk stories, they speak often of the last great battle between the Creator and the last of the Old Gods. Desperate to end the fighting, those who opposed the Creator sought to kidnap his beloved, Osha. They thought if the only person for whom he cared was in their grasp, he would be willing to listen to their pleas for peace, if only to save her. Myrbellanar was chosen to kidnap her, and he managed to steal her away in the dead of night.

"The Creator, blinded by love and rage, stormed into the Old Gods' camp and slew them one by one, until bodies littered the ground and the blood flowed ankle deep. Locked in her cage, Osha sobbed and pleaded for him to stop, but by the time he heard her, it was too late. All were dead—except one. Myrbellanar, his heart heavy with grief for his fallen brothers and sisters, released Osha from her prison and knelt before the Creator, begging his forgiveness," she whispered, her voice raw. "But the Creator's heart was black and full of fury. He condemned Myrbellanar for his crimes and disfigured him—carved his ears into points so he would be forever marked by his treachery. Then the Creator shattered his soul into millions of pieces, each of which he imprisoned in one of the elves he Created to serve his most treasured Creations —humans."

"That's not a story from the Book of the Creator," Mercy said, frowning. She had never believed in the Creator, but she knew the stories from her years at the Guild. "They—*you* —preach that the Creator treated all races as equals."

"It's a Cirisian tale. Those elves believe a piece of Myrbellanar's soul is freed every time an elf is slaughtered by a human, and when enough of his soul is restored, he will return to exact justice on those who have wronged his people." She lifted a bony shoulder in a shrug. "One of the priestesses in my Church is Cirisian. She came here after the fighting between Beltharos and Feyndara destroyed the island her clan called home. She doesn't speak much about her life there, but she often quotes that story. It may be nothing more than legend, but I can't help thinking it sounds more like a prophecy.

"I don't know what's causing this," Pilar continued, biting her lip, "but someone sent me to find you. And I keep seeing this...this *thing* in my head."

Mercy's blood ran cold as she thought back to the voice she had heard during Solari, and the objects in Calum's room that had moved of their own accord. There had been too many strange happenings lately for any of this to be coincidental. "Who sent you?"

"There's just...someone. I can't describe it. I can feel her nearby. She wanted me to find you. She can't speak to me, but sometimes she sends me visions—the same thing over and over. A flower, I think. Some sort of bud."

"I think I know what you're seeing." Mercy stood and fetched a piece of parchment and a pen from the desk, then quickly sketched the scaly flower bud Cassius had drawn. When she finished, she held up the piece of paper for Pilar to see. "Does it look like this? Scaly, with four leaves?"

The priestess peered at the drawing, then jerked back in surprise. "That's it! How did you know?"

"I saw it on a paper belonging to Seren Pierce. Does the word 'Niamh' mean anything to you? It was written beside the drawing."

"No. Maybe it's the name of the flower."

"I don't know. I have experience working in an infirmary, and I've never heard of it." She glanced at the books stacked on Alyss's desk. "But I'll have plenty of time to research while I'm stuck here. The king fears you've infected me."

"I didn't. I never would have come if that were a possibility. You're immune. The... The visions showed me. Myrbellanar and this plague are linked somehow. I can't explain it, but I knew I had to tell you." Tears filled Pilar's eyes, and she looked away, swiping at them angrily. "I thought the Creator might show me a way to stop the plague. He has shown me nothing. Meanwhile, th-this villain has been lurking in my head, showing me the most awful visions, and I am powerless to stop it!"

Pilar's voice rose to a tortured wail, and the sounds drifting from Alyss's room broke off mid-snore. After a thump and a muttered curse, Alyss shoved the curtains aside. She was dressed in a long tunic, her hair wild around her face, and she glowered at them as she rubbed her shin with a hand.

"Creator's mighty misery, you shoulda called me the moment she woke ye," she said, crossing the room and clamping her thick fingers around Pilar's arm. "Come now, Sister. Time to rest."

Short and stocky though she was, her strength was more than enough to overpower Pilar. The healer dragged her off the bed and across the room, laying her down on the farthest cot from Mercy. She placed a hand on Pilar's forehead and recoiled immediately. "By the Creator, yer burnin' up, woman!"

She moved to the desk and grabbed a syringe full of Ienna oil.

"Alyss, don't you dare!" Mercy blurted, jumping up. The sudden movement made her head throb, and the world swayed beneath her feet. She caught herself on the bedpost, regaining her balance just in time to see Alyss jab the needle into Pilar's arm and press the plunger. "She could have told us more about the plague."

Alyss pulled the blanket over Pilar, who mumbled something under her breath and curled up atop the mattress. "I said I'd try to keep her lucid for ye, but she's only hastening her own demise, workin' herself up like that. Now," she said, turning back to Mercy and lifting the syringe. "Do I need to drug ye too, or will ye be quiet and let me sleep?"

"You wouldn't dare."

Alyss raised a brow. "Wouldn't I?"

Mercy sank onto the bed, but she doubted she would be able to fall asleep anytime soon. The story Pilar had told her kept replaying in her mind. She didn't believe in all the talk of Old Gods, but perhaps there was something of meaning within Pilar's visions.

"Good girl." Alyss set the syringe on the desk, then moved to Mercy's bedside and began examining her arms. "How do ye feel? No rash? No blisters?"

"Nothing. I feel fine." *I'm immune,* she wanted to say, but she knew the healer would never believe her. In all honesty, she wasn't even sure if *she* believed it. How much of what Pilar said she'd Seen was nothing more than fever-induced hallucinations?

"What's that?" Alyss asked, nodding to the sketch of Cassius's flower.

"A plant that might be able to cure the plague. Do you know it?"

"Never seen anythin' like it. It certainly doesn't grow anywhere around here. I'll have to send word to the king to send men out to find it." She pressed a warm hand to Mercy's forehead. "Ye don't have a fever, which is promising. Wake me immediately if ye start to feel any different. Goodnight."

By the time Mercy awoke the next morning, all four cots had been filled. Apparently, two more priestesses had been brought in on stretchers while Mercy and Pilar slept, carried in by guards who had informed Alyss of the state of affairs outside the castle. Despite the short notice, Landers and Leon had succeeded in setting up healers' tents in the fields, and Ghyslain had ordered a company of guards to transport as many infected people out of the city as possible. Tamriel had accompanied them against his father's wishes and sent the two worst cases to the castle to be studied and treated by Alyss.

"He said I was the best healer in the capital," Alyss told Mercy as she prepared more marroway tea, pride in her voice. "By His Highness's own words, if anyone were to figure out the cure, it's me."

"I don't doubt it," she responded, but she wasn't so sure. After Alyss went to sleep, Mercy had spent half the night flipping through several of the medicinal tomes scattered about the room. Not one of them had mentioned a plant even remotely similar to Cassius's flower.

Alyss stuck her head into the hall and called for a wash basin and several buckets of warm water. Fifteen minutes later, the guards returned and set them before the hearth, each wearing gloves and handkerchiefs over their faces. Together, Alyss and Mercy stirred several handfuls of herbs into the steaming water, their earthy aromas quickly filling the room.

"Help me get Owl into the bath," Alyss said, referring to the youngest of the priestesses. The girl was less than half Mercy's age, and had neither moved nor spoken once since Mercy woke up. Alyss had taken to calling her Owl because of her large, unblinking hazel eyes. White scars crisscrossed her cheeks like the quills of feathers where she'd scratched the raw and peeling skin too deeply. Her knuckles, swollen to nearly twice their natural size, deformed her hands into claws.

Pilar had sobbed when she saw her.

Owl was huddled atop of one of the cots, staring at something in the distance with unfocused eyes. Mercy helped Alyss undress the girl, then threw her soiled clothes into the hearth. The second Alyss's arms closed around Owl, the girl came alive, bucking and squirming and flailing. She couldn't have weighed more than sixty pounds—her ribs were sharp and defined under her inflamed skin, and each of her vertebra protruded from her spine like a knot on a tree trunk—but she fought Alyss with every ounce of strength in her small body. She screamed, crawling backward on the bed until her back hit the wall, her feet tangling in the blanket. Alyss stepped forward and Owl's hand shot out, her fingernails scratching jagged lines into Alyss's cheek.

"Damn it!" Alyss cried, her patience reaching its end. She wiped at the blood welling on her cheek and gestured to the desk. "Grab those bandages and bind her hands with 'em. I was hired to heal, and by the Creator, I'm goin' to do my job."

Mercy did as she said, and as soon as she approached, Alyss snatched the bandages out of her hands. Mercy held Owl's wrists steady and watched as the healer wound the fabric around the young priestess's wrists so tightly her fingernails began to turn blue.

"The fabric will loosen in the water. Don't want her to slip out and hurt someone."

Mercy lifted Owl into her arms, and her chest tightened at how impossibly light the girl was. She could count every bone in Owl's body—could practically see through the sallow skin where the disease had not yet spread. Slowly, gently, she lowered the priestess into the bath. Owl's eyes went wide at the sudden warmth, and she relaxed against Mercy, the pain on her face replaced with relief.

"They always make it harder than it has to be," Alyss said with a snort.

Mercy let go of Owl, and the girl bobbed in the water for a moment before propping herself against the side of the basin. She stared at her pitted and mangled body in disgust, which slowly morphed into wonder as the heat and herbs soothed her pain. Mercy picked up a small brass pitcher and used it to pour some of the water over Owl's matted and tangled hair. The girl grinned, her eyelashes beaded with silver droplets, and gestured for Mercy to do it again. She did, and Owl closed her eyes and leaned back, sighing contentedly.

For what felt like the first time in ages, Mercy's lips parted into a genuine smile.

33

The peace lasted seven minutes.

Mercy was pouring more water into the bath when Alyss rounded the shelves with a jar of purple salt-like crystals in her hand. She stepped around Pilar, who had settled at the head of the basin, braiding flowers into Owl's long hair, and scowled.

"Those are for healin', not for ye to play with. I've half a mind to stick ye with another dose of that sleepin' oil if ye don't stay out of my stock."

Pilar's hands dropped to her sides. She glanced over at the other priestess, who had received a dose of her own, and scuttled toward the hearth, hugging her blister-covered arms around herself.

Alyss turned to Mercy. "This is a Rivosi housewife's secret weapon. We call it Pryyam salt. It helps to detox. Watch." She held a strip of leather up to Owl's lips. "Bite down on this."

Owl stiffened, but obeyed, gingerly taking the leather between her teeth.

Alyss grabbed a handful of salt and lifted Owl's arms out

of the water by their binding. "Hold her tight—she'll be slippery."

Mercy held Owl's wrists as Alyss began grinding the salt into the girl's skin. She screamed into the leather, her eyes filling with tears as she tried and failed to rip her arms free of Mercy's grasp. The crystal shredded the outer layer of flesh into ribbons. The blisters across her arms and shoulders broke, and the milky pus inside ran down her arms in little rivulets before dripping into the water. Tears streamed down Owl's face and her cries echoed throughout the room, loud enough to make Mercy's ears ring, but Alyss did not so much as flinch.

Alyss finished one arm and moved on to the next, never acknowledging Owl's agony. Mercy could see why: the salt was working. Little flakes of red, infected skin floated on the surface of the water and clung to Owl's wet arms, but through them, Mercy could see the pink, healthy flesh below.

"Don't put yer arm back in the water," Alyss instructed through the girl's screams, "or we'll have to do this again. Got it?" She waited for Owl to sniffle and nod before continuing, this time turning to Mercy. "Wrap her arms in fresh bandages while I work on her legs. Owl, I need ye to stand and move to the hearth so I can see better."

Owl nodded, whimpering, and Mercy and Alyss helped her step out of the bath. Goosebumps erupted across her raw skin. Pilar crawled out of the way, pity for the young priestess plain on her face, but Alyss pinned her with a stern look.

"Don't go too far. You're next."

Pilar trembled, but agreed, then settled on the corner of Mercy's cot to watch. Mercy wrapped Owl's arms in linen while Alyss worked the salt into one of her legs. Owl bit down so hard on the leather that the tendons strained in her neck. She tilted her head back and cried silent tears of misery, her long, flowered braid trailing down her bare back.

By the time they finished treating the last priestess—an older woman named Gwynn—Mercy was soaking wet, cold, and sore. The women had fought hard to try and escape the flesh-rending treatment, but none had been successful. Now, the three priestesses sat huddled on the other side of the shelves, whispering to one another, while Mercy and Alyss dumped the dirty bathwater into the drain in the middle of the floor. Two guards wearing handkerchiefs over their mouths and noses came in to carry the wash basin away. Once the door had swung shut behind them, Alyss turned to Mercy with an expectant stare.

"Strip."

"Excuse me?"

"Ye heard me. Yer turn. Strip."

Annoyance flared within Mercy. She held her arms out at her sides and made a show of spinning in a slow circle. "I'm fine, Alyss. I'm not sick. See?" When Alyss's expression didn't change, she dropped her arms and sighed. "You're not going to budge on this, are you?"

"Ye think I'm going to let ye waltz out of this infirmary without makin' absolutely certain yer not infected? Quit bein' so stubborn and let me do my job. Strip."

"Fine." Mercy tugged the dress Calum had given her over her head, then dropped the sopping fabric on the floor. Alyss raised her brows, and Mercy grudgingly removed her underclothes, as well. She made no attempt to cover herself, instead meeting the healer's appraising gaze with a glare of her own. After so many humiliations at the hands of the Guild's apprentices, she'd learned not to be bothered or ashamed by nakedness; the other girls would never have tired of tormenting her if she had continued to amuse them with shame and blushing whenever they stole her clothes while she bathed.

Mercy's thoughts drifted to the Keep as Alyss circled her, poking and prodding with her short, graceless fingers, frowning at her faded scars. What Calum had said in her dream still haunted her. He'd been wrong—she wouldn't fail her contract. All she had ever known was the Guild. It was her entire life; her world began and ended at the Forest's edge. Every bruise, every cut, every humiliation had molded her into the woman—the Assassin—she was. No matter that she had failed to kill Tamriel the night of Solari, or that she'd let him live when they'd stood in the hall together, completely alone. He had stood up for her, and she would repay that kindness by allowing him to live a few extra days. Soon, she would leave this infirmary, assassinate Tamriel, and begin her journey back to the Guild.

And yet, the discovery she'd made two nights before nagged at her. The contract was a forgery, and thus void. She knew if she returned to the Keep and told Mother Illynor the truth, she would be given another contract. It wouldn't make her any less of a Daughter, except in the eyes of the other Assassins. It didn't matter if she had proof that the contract was fake. They would only see her failure, and they would never let it go.

Tamriel did not have to die. Mother Illynor only allowed contracts to be taken out on royalty by other royals, otherwise ruling families all over the world would be murdered at the whims of every disgruntled commoner. She remembered the feel of the prince's hand on the curve of her waist, the desire in his eyes, the brush of his lips against hers...then promptly cast all thoughts of him from her mind. She was nothing more than a performer acting out her role, he an unwitting puppet dancing as she tugged on the strings.

No, she wouldn't back out of this contract, forgery or not.

It was a prestigious job, much more so than a newly-sworn Daughter deserved, and Mother Illynor had given it to *her*. She could have chosen anyone, and she'd given it to Mercy.

Alyss picked up Mercy's wet clothes and draped them over the back of the desk chair. "No sign of anythin' yet, but we can't be certain ye won't catch it. Another day, then ye have my blessin' to go back to yer partyin' and socializin'."

Mercy grinned at the healer as she slipped into the curtained-off room. "Is that all you think I do?"

"I don't pretend to know what goes on in the court, but it seemed a fair guess." Alyss returned and handed Mercy a simple threadbare tunic. "This is the only thing that might fit ye. Everything else'll be too small." She gestured to the scars crisscrossing Mercy's arms and legs. "Didn't think I'd ever see a royal with so many scars. They must not like you all that much over in Feyndara."

"My cousin and I liked to train with the soldiers when we were younger—much to my uncle's chagrin." She'd known revealing her scars to the healer would raise some questions, but arguing wouldn't have achieved anything beyond delaying the inevitable. The king would want Alyss's approval before allowing Mercy out of the infirmary, and the healer was too thorough to let her out without a full examination.

"Well, considering how many wounds ye got, doesn't look like yer any good," Alyss said. "Let me know the moment ye feel sickness comin' on, alright? Even if ye think yer only imaginin' it. Tell me right away."

"I will." Mercy slipped the tunic over her head and was surprised to find it long enough to fall to the middle of her thigh; it certainly didn't belong to Alyss. She tried not to imagine what terrible fate had befallen its previous owner, and instead narrowed her eyes at the thin sheen of perspiration across Alyss's upper lip. "How do *you* feel, Alyss?"

She waved Mercy's words away and started bustling

around the shelves, barely glancing at the jars and bottles as she gathered them into her arms. "Don't go askin' anythin' like that. I'm fine."

She raised a brow. "Really?"

"Don't be absurd." After a beat of silence, Alyss said over her shoulder in a softer voice, "It's been a rough couple of days, is all. It'll be nice when we can get back to our normal lives."

"Just...take care of yourself, alright? They need you." Mercy waved a hand to the shelves, behind which the priestesses were still huddled. Despite everything, the gruff healer had started to grow on her. "You're the best healer they could get."

For the briefest moment, Alyss's face lit up, brighter than Mercy had ever seen it. For a second, she thought the stubborn woman might even smile.

Instead, she turned on her heel and marched out of the infirmary.

The priestesses had been whispering for hours.

After recovering from the shock of the skin-shredding treatment, Pilar, Owl, and Gwynn had settled into a circle on the far side of the shelves, sitting cross-legged on the floor so closely that their knees touched. There they remained, quiet and unmoving.

Mercy stood at the end of the row of shelves, watching them. Pilar's eyes were closed, her face partially turned away so Owl couldn't see her blind, bulging eye. Owl sat ramrod straight, flinching whenever her tunic brushed against her raw skin. Now that she was clean, it was obvious the priestess was even younger than Mercy had first guessed—she couldn't have been older than seven. The priestesses' lips moved quickly as they mouthed words Mercy couldn't make out. She crept closer on silent feet and realized with a jolt of surprise that they were speaking a language she didn't recognize; it was all hissing *s*'s and soft vowels, nothing at all like the common tongue.

When Mercy was less than an arm's length away, the priestesses stopped their strange chanting and stared at her. Gwynn's eyes were glassy, not quite focused, but Pilar's functioning eye shot to Mercy's face and narrowed in hostility. She froze, startled by the unexpected hatred on the woman's face.

She took a step back. "What are you saying?"

"It's a holy passage," Owl said. "A prayer to ward off a malevolent spirit. It wishes to do you harm."

Gwynn nodded. "The Creator showed the spirit to Pilar while she slept, and it is nearby now. Something has been hiding in this castle, lurking in its halls. It seems to have... awoken when you arrived. It's looking for you."

She looked to Pilar, remembering the strange voice she'd heard the night of Solari. "Is it the same thing that sent you to me? The one who gave you those visions?"

Pilar shook her head sharply as if to clear it, and every trace of hostility disappeared from her face. "I can't tell. It feels like it has been corrupted somehow, twisted from its true nature. It seems to be at war with itself." She frowned. "Owl felt its presence this morning. Even Alyss felt it—that's why she left so suddenly. She cannot explain it, but she knows something feels very, very wrong. We're not going to survive much longer, Mercy, and we must protect you."

Her blood turned cold as ice. When she spoke, her voice came out a hoarse whisper. "What did you just call me?"

Pilar's brows furrowed. "What do you mean?"

Owl shrieked and ducked out of the way as Mercy stepped into the center of the circle and closed a hand around Pilar's throat. She hauled the priestess to her feet and pinned her against the wall.

"How do you know who I am?" Mercy snarled, panic sinking its claws into her. Pilar's fingers scratched at Mercy's as she struggled for breath, her eyes widening in terror. "Did Calum send you here to watch me? Is this another one of his clever tricks?"

"Stop!" Owl cried. "Let her go! She's protecting you!"

The girl's wail struck Mercy like a blow. She released Pilar and staggered back, clapping her hands to her mouth in horror. The priestess sank to her knees, clutching her throat as she sucked in ragged breath after ragged breath. A bruise was already forming around her pale neck.

"No," Mercy whispered, her knees beginning to tremble. The second she'd heard her name, all reason and logic had vanished. She'd acted purely on instinct. She'd acted like an animal.

Her cheeks burned with shame. "I'm sorry, Pilar. Please forgive me."

Owl stood in front of the shelves with Gwynn, the elder priestess's arms wrapped protectively around her. "She doesn't know anything about you," she offered meekly, not meeting Mercy's gaze. "Nothing beyond your name."

Still kneeling on the stone floor, Pilar nodded. "The Sight," she rasped. "Won't...tell anyone."

"I'm sorry," Mercy repeated, blood rushing to the tips of her ears. She turned on shaky legs and pulled the door to the infirmary open so hard it cracked against the wall. None of the priestesses tried to stop her as she bolted, slamming the door behind her.

34

The men guarding the infirmary let out surprised cries at her sudden appearance, but Mercy paid them no heed as she ran down the hall. Belatedly, one of the guards sputtered, "Y-You can't be out here! King's orders!"

Their footfalls pounded behind her as she climbed the stairs to the main floor and sprinted through the corridors, dodging surprised nobles and council members. A slave shouted and jumped out of the way as Mercy peeled around the corner, the tray of tea and pastries slipping from her grasp and tumbling to the floor. Several teacups shattered, and the shards crunched under the guards' boots moments later.

Mercy burst into the great hall and let out a sigh of relief when she saw the familiar silhouette standing in the open doors of the castle, backlit by the bright blue sky beyond. "Tamriel—" she choked out. She stepped forward, a hand outstretched, but froze when she realized who stood beside him.

Calum.

At her outburst, they stopped mid-conversation and stared at her, baffled by her sudden appearance. In the several seconds during which they took in her wild eyes and disheveled appearance, the guards caught up and clamped gloved hands around her arms.

"Apologies, Your Highness. She—"

"Release her," Tamriel said as he jogged over to them, his expression a mixture of fear and concern. His gaze swept over her from head to toe, searching for a sign of injury or sickness. "Marieve, what's wrong? Are you hurt?"

"No, I—" She stopped and shook her head, shame flooding her anew. Her cheeks grew hot as she remembered the terror in Pilar's eyes, the way the tendons in her neck had rippled beneath her fingers. For a few horrible seconds, she'd forgotten herself—forgotten the person she had to be in the capital. In the Keep, she had often needed to resort to violence to protect herself. In the Keep, she wouldn't have even hesitated. "I—I needed some fresh air. I was going mad being cooped up in the infirmary," she said, hearing how false the excuse rang even as she gave it.

A crease formed between his brows. "You look like you've seen a ghost."

A sharp laugh escaped her before she could stop it. After the last few days, she almost expected it. It certainly wouldn't be the strangest thing to happen to her in Sandori.

Tamriel and Calum exchanged looks of alarm.

"Might there be something I could help you with, my lady?" Calum asked, and Mercy's forced smile turned brittle.

"Do I know you? You look very familiar."

"My cousin," Tamriel explained, "although Calum has lived in the castle almost all his life. My father took him in after an unfortunate incident claimed his father's life."

"How kind of him," she responded, but her eyes did not

stray from Calum. Anger flared within her when he shot her a cocky, crooked grin. Her head still ached where he had hit her. "You two must have grown close after spending so much time together."

"He's like a brother to me," Calum said.

One of the guards shifted behind her. *Keep them talking.* She didn't want to return to the infirmary, didn't want to face what she had just done. "Then it's good that you're here to support His Highness. I've heard some of the members of the court can be rather two-faced. The prince is fortunate to have someone he can trust by his side."

Calum's smile took on a sharp edge. "I'm nothing if not loyal to my family."

"Let me speak to him! Let me speak to him, please!" A wail rose from the throne room, followed by muffled sobbing.

"Is that Elise?" Calum asked. He and Tamriel ran into the throne room, and Mercy hurried after them, the guards on her heels.

The first thing she saw when they passed through the double doors was Elise sobbing on the floor. There were streaks in her makeup, and she used a crumpled fistful of her skirt to wipe away her tears. Seren Pierce stood beside her, his skin more sallow, his wrinkles more pronounced than when she had last seen him. The only comfort he offered his daughter was a hand on her shoulder as he stared blankly at the floor, his face haggard and haunted.

When she saw Tamriel and Calum, Elise let out another hiccuping sob and reached for the prince. "Your Highness, he's locked inside! They've locked my brother— *You've* locked my brother inside Beggars' End!"

"Elise," Tamriel said in a low, sorrowful voice. "I'm sorry. Truly, I am, but the order to seal the End did not come from me." He knelt beside Elise and pried the wrinkled and stained fabric from her fist, then clasped her trembling hands in his.

"I know how much your brother means to you, but your anger is misdirected. No one ordered him to remain in Beggars' End. He chose to stay to keep the peace."

Her brows furrowed. "W-What?" She shook her head quickly, her curls bouncing. "No. That can't be right. He would never choose to stay in that—that *pit!* You ordered him to stay—you or Master Oliver or your father!"

"Elise, you know your brother. If he has the chance to help people who need him, he's going to choose that over his own safety, hands down. You know that, don't you?"

"Well, yes, but— We need him here; his family needs him!"

"Your Highness, please. There must be something we can do to get him out," Seren Pierce began in a shaky voice. "Imagine how your father would feel if you had stayed behind."

A sudden and inappropriate smirk crossed Tamriel's face, as if the thought was downright absurd. He squeezed Elise's hands and forced a frown. "In a couple days, when we have a better handle on the situation, I can arrange for you to send him a letter via the guards at the gate. I can't say whether it will sway his decision, but you are welcome to try."

"Oh, Your Highness, thank you!" Elise jumped to her feet and threw her arms around Tamriel's neck, choking on a relieved laugh.

Tamriel stood stiffly while she embraced him, his arms straight at his sides. After a pause, he patted her back awkwardly until Elise stepped back, blushing. "H-How inappropriate of me. I beg your forgiveness, Your Highness."

Mercy glanced at Calum, who still stood beside her. It surprised her to see sadness on his face as he watched them. When he noticed her looking at him, he quickly blinked it away.

"Of course." Tamriel nodded, looking relieved. "Go home

now and rest. I'll let you know when you can send him a letter."

"Yes, Your Highness. Thank you." She curtsied and ran from the room, shooting a sheepish look at Mercy and Calum as she passed. In the quiet following her exit, Seren Pierce stepped forward and rested a hand on Tamriel's shoulder. The prince stared at it.

"Thank you for your understanding and kind words, Your Highness. The situation with her brother has been hard on all of us, but it has hit her worst of all."

"Take care of your family, Seren. Make sure Elise returns home safely, then find Landers for your assignment. We need every pair of hands we have to contain this plague."

"Of course." The seren followed his daughter out of the room, calling her name as his footsteps faded into the hall. He didn't spare Mercy or Calum so much as a glance.

One of the guards grabbed Mercy's arm and pulled her back toward the doors. "Show's over, m'lady. Time to go back to the infirmary before you get someone sick."

She jerked out of his grasp. "I'm not sick." When she looked up at him, all she saw were Pilar's terrified eyes, her lips moving soundlessly as they turned a faint blue. She thought of the three priestesses waiting down in the infirmary, chanting in their strange language, and knew she could not yet face them. What she'd done was unforgivable.

"Please, Tamriel, don't let them send me down there again!" she pleaded, not too proud to resort to begging. She pushed past Calum and approached the prince. "I'm not sick, see?" She gestured to her bare legs, peeking out from under the tunic Alyss had given her, then at her arms. "Nothing. Don't let them take me back."

"Lady Marieve, you're hysterical—" Calum began, and she fixed him with an icy glare.

"He's right, Marieve," Tamriel said gently. "You need to calm down. Take deep breaths. It's only for another day or so."

She shook her head. "You're not listening to me—"

"Marieve." Tamriel cupped her cheeks with both hands, and she sucked in a breath at his sudden proximity. "I wish I could help you. I *do*," he breathed, sympathy shining in his eyes. "But I can't. Please don't make this harder than it needs to be."

Faint shadows hung under his eyes, Mercy realized, and she wondered how much rest he'd had since the Solari celebration. It had been almost a day and a half since Ghyslain ordered her quarantine, and Tamriel looked like he had been awake for every one of those thirty-six hours. He had changed into a clean shirt but missed one of the buttons. A stray strand of hair stuck out below his ear; he must have been running his hands through it as he thought.

She swallowed her shame and nodded. "Fine. One more day. But please, you must stay safe as well."

Until I'm able to complete my contract. No one—no plague—will steal it from me.

Mercy allowed the guards to lead her away, but before they passed through the doors, Calum called in a mockingly cheerful voice, "It was lovely to meet you, my lady! We should do this again sometime!"

The priestesses had returned to their prayers by the time the guards deposited Mercy in the infirmary, except this time, their mouths moved in silence. Mercy lingered just beyond the threshold as the door slammed shut behind her, waiting for the priestesses to shrink back in fear. None did. Pilar's and Gwynn's eyes remained closed. Owl watched her warily out of her periphery, but did not otherwise react to her return.

Mercy slunk past them and joined Alyss at the desk. When she tried to peer over the healer's shoulder to see what she was working on, Alyss grunted and moved to block her view. "At this rate, ye'll have infected half the city within the week."

"I haven't infected anyone." Mercy sank onto the corner of her cot, gingerly prodding the bump on her head. "Where did you go while you were out?"

"Spoke with a couple healers in the tents outside the city—inquired whether they had seen any disease like this so-called plague before. Fieldings' Blisters is close, but I've never seen it this severe."

"And?"

"Nothin'."

A glass vial slipped from her fingers and shattered on the floor. Alyss cursed as she fumbled for a pan to collect the pieces. Mercy rose to help her clean up the mess, but Alyss shooed her away. "It's alright. I'm too clumsy for my own good sometimes. Nothin' I haven't done a hundred times over the years." She set the pan on the desk and winced as she pulled a shard of glass from her finger. She dropped it among the others, where it shone with her blood. "Someone will be here to escort ye home in the mornin', once I clear ye to leave."

Mercy shook her head at the change in subject. "Alyss, you're clearly not well," she whispered, being careful to keep the priestesses from hearing their conversation. "Maybe you should rest."

"I'll rest when I'm dead," she snapped. "Don't be an idiot. It's just Pilar and the others. I don't like 'em whisperin' like that. Gives me the creeps."

"I know what you mean."

Alyss waved Mercy over to the desk. She seemed conflicted, drumming her fingernails on the desktop, but at last, she opened the lid of a small wooden box and pushed it toward Mercy. A sheer fabric bag full of dried black mushrooms was nestled inside. "Listen here. I want ye to promise me somethin'," she said in a low voice. "These mushrooms are the most poisonous in the world. If I fall sick, I want ye to use them. On me."

"I knew it! Alyss, you *are* sick, aren't you?"

"Shh! Look, I...I don't know yet. But if it turns out I have the disease—this Fieldings' Plague—I want ye to grind them up nice and fine and mix them into my food. I won't give up on them—I won't stop workin' on the cure—but I don't want to end up some husk of a person. I want to die while I'm still sane, while I'm still me. I'll give everythin' I have to these priestesses for as long as I can, but the minute I outlast my usefulness, put me out of my misery." She looked up at Mercy, pain, grief, and sorrow in her eyes. Her hand shook as she reached out and shut the lid of the box. "Don't leave me to waste away. If I'm to die, I want it to be on my terms."

Mercy studied her—the fear in her voice, the resolute set to her jaw. Alyss hadn't just gone to the healers to ask if they'd seen another disease like this plague. She'd gone to ask their advice, to see what they had learned from the patients they had tended...and the news hadn't been good. "You really want this?"

She nodded.

"Then I will. I give you my word."

The relief was plain on Alyss's face, and the tension left her body with one sharp exhale. "Well, I don't know what to say except thank ye. It's not worth much to a lady like yerself, but ye have my gratitude." She peered at Mercy, her gaze sweeping across Mercy's exposed skin, and nodded. "Ye were right about not bein' sick. Just help me take care of Pilar and the others today, and then yer free to go in the mornin'. Remember what ye've agreed to. Remember yer promise."

"Of course," Mercy vowed, her chest tightening. "I will."

35

Elvira was angry.

Not just angry—she was fuming.

Mercy lounged on the couch in Blackbriar's study, listening to Elvira slam the doors and drawers upstairs as she cleaned. Blackbriar's white stone walls and large windows were a welcome reprieve from the dark, dank infirmary. In accordance with the king's orders concerning the plague, the windows were closed, but not the shutters, and Mercy basked in the warmth of a sunbeam. She hadn't realized how much she had missed the sun, even for only a couple days.

"You could have killed him that night."

Elvira's voice startled Mercy, and she craned her neck to see the elf standing in the doorway, scowling. They'd hardly spoken since Elvira had met her at the front steps of the castle when she was released two hours ago.

"Solari. He was standing in the same room as you. You were *alone*. How hard would it have been?"

"Should I have killed him before or after the dying woman crashed the celebration?"

"Don't make light of this. You two snuck away from the party, and only you were supposed to return."

"Plans change," she said, not feeling the least bit inclined to explain everything that had happened to her over the past few days. First, the voices in her head, then the objects moving on their own, then the priestess's warnings... A chill snaked down her spine. Whatever was happening here, she'd had more than enough of it. All she wanted was to complete her contract and leave the capital far behind her. "I'm working on it. I'm looking for the right opportunity to strike."

"Look harder."

The bite in the usually subdued elf's voice grated on her nerves. She sat upright, her patience wearing thin. "What's your problem? What do you want me to do? Need I remind you I was locked up in the infirmary for two days?"

"I want you to *do your job!*" she shouted. It was so uncharacteristic of her, Mercy flinched. "I want you to do what you had planned to do three nights ago."

"You don't think I want the same? If I'd had the chance, I'd have taken it. There were other...circumstances...that I hadn't accounted for." She could have killed him that night, if only that strange voice had not interrupted her. She didn't try to explain it to Elvira, though. She didn't have an explanation herself. "Why are you taking it so personally?"

After a long, charged pause, something in Elvira shattered. She slumped onto the opposite end of the couch. "Kier and I had planned to sneak away that night. We were finally going to make a run for it. You were supposed to complete the contract, and then you wouldn't need me anymore. We were going to sneak out of the city in the chaos that would follow the discovery of the prince's body." She fidgeted with the hem of her shirt as she spoke. "But you didn't kill him, and now I'm terrified Kier is going to catch the plague before we can escape."

Elvira's hands closed into fists, and when she opened them again, her fingernails had imprinted little half-moons into her palms. She stood. "I'd appreciate it if you took your contract a little more seriously, Mercy. Your future is not the only one at stake."

"Elvi—"

She walked out of the room and, seconds later, the sound of the front door slamming shut echoed through the house.

Mercy let out a frustrated sigh and flopped back onto the couch. Had being in the capital softened her? Before, at the Keep, her mind had been consumed with thoughts of how to prove her worth to Mother Illynor and the others. She had spent every waking moment trying to impress the tutors—even Trytain, who had looked at her like she was scum stuck to the bottom of her shoe.

But if she was honest with herself, she couldn't deny wanting to extend the experience, to indulge the curiosity that seemed only to grow with each day she spent in the capital. She had never been surrounded by so much life and culture. She had never been in a place where no one knew her, where she didn't have to constantly look over her shoulder. Tamriel had warned her against the elf-hating members of the court, but compared to what Lylia and the others had done to her, they were ants. Could she be blamed for wanting to spend some time in the city? After all, she had been born here, to people she imagined had not been much different from Elvira.

For the first time, she let herself wonder what her life would have become had she never been given to the Guild. Would her parents have fled to the Cirisor Islands anyway? Would they have abandoned her on some porch, waiting for a random passerby to take pity on her? Would they have brought her with them?

Whomever Mercy would have become, the girl would have been unrecognizable to the woman she was now. Today Mercy would have sneered at her docility, her softness, her inability to ward off the punishing blows of her master. She would have been submissive, trapped in a life of slavery—if she had managed to survive into adulthood. Mercy shivered, marveling at how close she had come to that imagined life becoming reality; if her father had walked into Drake Zendais's study five minutes later, perhaps Llorin would have had enough time to flee. Perhaps her father would not have bartered her life for his.

Enough. She shook her head, clearing the thoughts from her mind. It was a waste of time to ponder the what-ifs. She rose and climbed the steps to her third-floor bedroom. Her daggers sat on the bed, having been tossed there by Elvira after Mercy had failed to return three nights ago. Mercy picked them up, smiling at their familiar weight, and began to practice her drills.

An hour later, Elvira still had not returned, so Mercy decided to head to the castle in search of the prince. She sheathed one of her daggers and tucked it into the waistband of her pants, allowing her loosely draped tunic to hide its bulk, then stepped out of the house. She paused for a few seconds, half-expecting Elvira to appear at the end of the block, back to her normal, quiet self. Of course, she didn't. In fact, the street was strangely empty; where it normally bustled with private carriages and workers pushing carts, today there was only a stray dog standing a few doors down, munching on food someone had dropped. When it saw Mercy, the dog yelped and bolted into an alley.

As she neared the street corner, the sound of stomping feet grew from somewhere to her right. She stopped just as a complement of a dozen guards rounded the corner and sprinted past her, their heavy mail armor jangling with every step. They were headed toward the market district. Curiosity drew her to follow them.

They wound through the narrow, twisting streets so quickly Mercy soon became disoriented. When they passed the market, the commander shouted an order and six of the soldiers broke off and turned down a side street. The rest continued heading straight, Mercy trailing behind as quickly as her delicate silk slippers allowed.

A sound like the crashing of waves built all around her, amplified and distorted by the stone façades of the buildings surrounding her. It puzzled her. The Alynthi River was on the other side of the city, and they were well away from the castle, where the choppy waves of Lake Myrella broke against the tall boulders. They shouldn't have been able to hear water from here.

Mercy turned a blind corner and nearly slammed into the back of one of the soldiers. She caught herself just in time, one hand automatically reaching back to make sure she hadn't dropped her dagger, but froze when she saw what lay before her:

More people than she'd ever seen at once were gathered outside the eastern gate to Beggars' End; the waves she'd heard were actually the roar of their voices, overlapping and distorting. There had to be at least a couple thousand people here, all crammed into the narrow streets. The crowd in front of her was packed so tightly with bodies that she couldn't see more than two rows in front of her. Above her, people hung out of the broken second-story windows of a derelict house, shouting and gesturing wildly. The guards in front of her began to shove their way toward the wall surrounding the slums.

Go, something whispered in her mind, and an unseen force propelled her forward.

She darted into the crowd and elbowed people out of her way, fighting for every inch of space, fighting to remain in the wake of the soldiers slowly advancing. The intersection wasn't very large, but with so many bodies around her, she might as well have been wading through quicksand.

Finally, she burst into open air, gasping for breath after escaping the stifling heat of the crowd. Her tunic was soaked through with sweat. She had emerged in the intersection before the gate, where royal guards had managed to secure some space between the mob and the wall. Behind them, a group of nobles stood arguing. The men Mercy had been following quickly fell into formation beside the other guards. One noticed her and moved to shove her back, but Leon, who had been pacing the width of the clearing, spotted her and ran over.

"Leon, what the hell is happening?" she asked, yelling to be heard over the shouts of the crowd. As she spoke, a pebble pinged off one of the guards' helmets. To their left, two guards used their shields to shove a crazed-looking man back into the mob.

"Well, uh, we have our first confirmed death by Fieldings' Plague. Apparently, someone wandered into the market this morning and started ranting about the Creator. He'd been deathly sick already, but he worked himself up so much his heart gave out. Terrified a whole bunch of people. Word has gotten out that the plague originated in Beggars' End, and now they want to purge the district."

"Purge the district? Are they mad? They can't do that!"

"They've given it a damned good try so far. Normally, the

guards would be able to quash this immediately, but we only have so many on retainer right now. Most are on patrol in the other parts of the city or stationed in the fields with the healers' tents." Leon tried to keep his voice steady, but his eyes—and the constant drumming of his fingers against his thigh—betrayed his fear. "If we don't come up with a plan soon, they're going to stop playing nice."

"You call this 'playing nice'?"

"They haven't set any fires yet, and no one has been drawn and quartered, so overall, we're faring pretty well."

Mercy searched his face, but his expression didn't give any hint as to whether he was joking. She glanced at the nobles, who continued to argue amongst themselves. "Please tell me you have a plan...or some *semblance* of a plan, at least."

"Not one we can agree on. If you have any suggestions, I'm all ears." He placed a hand on her lower back and steered her toward the nobles. "You haven't met these members of the court yet, have you? Allow me to introduce Porter Anders, Edwin Fioni, and Tanner Morris. You remember Cassius Bacha."

"I told you this would happen!" Cassius was shouting. He gripped the sides of his head with trembling hands, his knuckles as white as the wisps of hair clinging to his scalp. "Who told you to reinforce the walls, to set double the guards, to treat this situation with the utmost urgency? But no—no one listens to an old man's paranoia!"

"They were dreams, Bacha! How did you expect us to take them seriously?" Edwin snapped. "Pouting isn't going to achieve anything now. We're stuck here until we figure out what to do!"

"Taking your head out of your ass seems like a good start, Fioni—"

"Gentlemen!" Porter stepped between them, placing a hand on each man's chest. "Arguing hasn't gotten us anywhere, and it's not going to change the past. Calm down. Let's examine our options."

"Don't take too long, Porter," Tanner said nervously. "This crowd is becoming rowdier by the minute."

Porter shoved Cassius and Edwin apart, then wiped his forehead with a handkerchief and straightened his lapel. "You're right. We can't delay this any longer. Leon, how many guards are at our disposal?"

"Twenty-nine, plus Commander Willis."

"Commander, could the soldiers press outward in one wave, push the people out of the intersection and into the side streets?" Porter called to a man standing near the guards, towering and muscular. "If we split up the main group, they'll become more complacent, easier to manage."

Mercy bit her lip, eyeing the angry faces surrounding them. Thirty of the king's men were nothing compared to the thousands here, but Porter was right—they had to use the city to their advantage. What other option did they have?

"It's possible, sir, but as angry as they are, they may mistake it for an attack and respond violently. They outnumber us more than I care to consider."

"Wonderful," Porter muttered under his breath, rubbing his temples.

"There is another option," Edwin began. "We could—Bacha, don't bite my head off for saying this—but we could give them what they want."

"Let them *in?* Are you insane, or just plain stupid?" Cassius snapped, glaring at him.

"Who lives here, Cassius? Truly? Slaves, bastards, orphans, beggars, cripples—what good are they to us? Hm? We have an obligation to the masses—to these people!" He flung a hand toward the crowd. Their voices had grown raucous and they pushed against the guards, testing the strength of their defenses.

"You know there are more poor in this city than anyone else, Edwin. You really want to cater to the masses, protect them!"

"You open that gate," Leon interjected, "you won't be able to close it again. They'll swarm the second you give them the chance."

"We aren't really entertaining this idea, are we?" Cassius asked, horrified. "It'll be a slaughter!"

"No, we're not," Porter said, shooting a stern look at Edwin. "You don't have to like the elves, but I won't stand idly by while you allow a genocide. We serve the people of this city—that means the people on this side of the wall *and* that side." He fixed Edwin with a glare. "And you will remember who has the higher rank here, Fioni."

That set off their argument all over again. Edwin said something rude to Tanner, who responded with an insult of his own. Porter looked ready to punch someone. Leon began to pace again. "We're going to die here," he murmured. He repeated it twice more before Mercy couldn't stand it any longer.

She crossed the clearing and stepped in front of Commander Willis. "Prepare your men to push outward. We're going to split the crowd like Porter said. They want a fight, we'll fight them for every inch."

Leon stopped and stared at her. "Lady Marieve, what are you doing?"

"What none of them have been able to do," she said, jerking her chin to the nobles. "I'm making a decision. Commander, tell your men not to hold back. They have swords, and if the people do not retreat, they will be forced to use them."

"Marieve, stop. You don't have the authority to make this decision."

"The people who do can't stop bickering long enough to come up with a real plan. Commander, give the order."

"I'm sorry, my lady. I cannot take orders from foreign nobility. I must hear it from one of them."

"This mob isn't going to wait patiently while they deliberate. Sooner or later, they're going to come for us. Give the order." When he ignored her again, she turned to Leon. "Give the order. He'll listen to you."

Leon wavered, glancing from Mercy to the crowd. Just when she thought he wouldn't listen, he pressed his lips into a tight line and nodded to the commander.

Willis turned to his men and shouted to advance. The guards moved closer, forming a blockade with their shields. At the commander's next order, they began to press forward and outward in a half-circle, forcing the mob backward. The crowd pushed back. A few of the people hanging out of the upstairs windows of the surrounding buildings shouted obscenities and tossed pieces of wood, broken bottles, and stones into the crowd, hitting both guards and civilians.

The nobles watched the chaos unfold, their argument forgotten.

"What have you done?" Porter's face was a mask of shock.

"Someone had to decide what to do, so I did," Mercy snapped. "You're welcome. Look, it's working."

"She's right," Leon said. "They're moving back."

The guards had unsheathed their swords, and several men and women were scrambling away, the fire dimming in their eyes. The shouts shifted from those of anger to those of confusion, and the crowd slowly began to retreat.

Suddenly, a speeding carriage careened around the corner behind the crowd, several guards on horseback riding alongside it. One of them carried a banner emblazoned with the royal crest.

People dove out of the way as the carriage continued

toward the edge of the crowd. The guards on horseback moved to the front and acted as a wedge, driving the citizens backward, away from the center of the street. The carriage stopped in the middle of the road, but the men and women on horseback continued herding people out of the way until they reached Mercy and the nobles, clearing a makeshift aisle from the gate to the end of the street.

For a few seconds, it was completely silent.

Then the door to the carriage flew open and out stepped Ghyslain, fury and betrayal blazing in his eyes. He was resplendent in his finest clothing: a dark purple doublet, fitted black trousers and boots, an ermine-lined cloak tumbling from a ruby clasp at his throat. At his hip he wore a sheathed sword, and his crown sat atop his immaculately combed hair.

"You have disappointed me greatly," he said, his voice booming over the hushed street, his heavy gaze sweeping over his people. He approached the commander. "I came as soon as I could. Has anyone been seriously injured?"

"No, Your Majesty. A few minor cuts and bruises, but there was little open fighting. Hardly any damage had been done to the gate when we arrived. It will hold, should anything like this happen again."

"It won't. Not while I sit the throne. Now arrest the ringleaders of this attack—enough to send a message. Have your men transport them to the castle immediately."

"Yes, Your Majesty." The commander shouted the order to his men, pointing out a handful of people from the crowd as he did. Half of the guards broke from the line and dragged the leaders out into the street.

"Porter and Tanner, accompany them," Ghyslain said, and the two noblemen hurried to obey. They passed Tamriel, who had climbed out of the carriage and now stood beside the horses, resting a hand on one's neck. He caught Mercy's eye and shook his head.

"I'm terribly ashamed of you," Ghyslain shouted over the whispers of the remaining subjects. "The people on the other side of that wall are no different than you, and all are under my protection for as long as I am king. The safety of my subjects is of the utmost importance, and anyone who compromises that safety will be swiftly and severely punished. I expect you all to be in front of the castle gate in one hour. There, you shall see how sincere I am."

He waited one long, charged moment, as if daring someone to challenge him. When no one did, he smiled and started back the way he'd come. As his father approached, Tamriel straightened and bowed stiffly, while the slave who had driven the carriage opened the door for the king. The carriage dipped slightly under his weight as he settled onto the bench. Tamriel moved to follow him, but a snicker in the crowd halted him mid-step.

"Defender of the damned and the destitute," someone called, just loudly enough to ensure Tamriel heard. "The elven whore turned the king soft."

"He's brought his bastard prince along with him, trying to rub our noses in it," another jeered. "No elven-blooded prince is going to rule over us."

Tamriel's foot hovered an inch above the carriage's step. The backs of his ears and neck flushed red with anger, and he closed a hand around the grip of the sword at his side. Sensing her gaze on him, Tamriel glanced back and his eyes met Mercy's, his scowl softening. He let go of his sword, straightened his jacket, and climbed into the carriage without a word.

36

After the royal carriage rounded the corner and disappeared from view, the rest of the crowd began to disperse. Mercy, Leon, and the other nobles lingered by the gate for another half hour, until the street emptied of everything save for its usual traffic. It was eerie how quickly the people fell back into their usual routines, promptly forgetting that they had threatened the lives of thousands of their fellow citizens less than an hour ago. Ghyslain had done well diverting their anger, but Mercy knew they wouldn't remain complacent for long. She could only hope the punishment Ghyslain had planned for the leaders would be enough to keep the people from rebeling until Alyss and the other healers developed a cure for the plague.

"Commander, remain here with your men. Send a few guards to check on the other gates, as well—make sure they're still secure," Cassius instructed.

"Yes, my lord."

"Lady Marieve, His Majesty will expect to see us at the castle," Leon said, offering her his arm. "Would you be so kind as to walk with me?"

"Of course." She slipped her hand into the crook of his elbow, and they started in the direction of the castle. For a block and a half, neither of them said much, each consumed with thoughts of what they'd just witnessed. The anger on those people's faces, the terror... They'd been ready to destroy the people of the End, they were *that* afraid of the plague.

"Elise's brother is still inside the End," Mercy said, remembering the sight of Elise sobbing on the throne room floor, tears leaving pink streaks across her fair cheeks. "Do you know how he's faring? Or she, for that matter? She and Seren Pierce took the news hard."

Leon shook his head, pain flashing across his face. "I wish she would talk to me. I've tried to speak with her, reassure her, but she just brushes me off every time. Always makes excuses about having to go about her duties or the like. I just want to tell her that everything will be okay. It kills me to see her so sad."

"You really love her, don't you?"

"I do. By the Creator, I've loved her from the moment I laid eyes on her." A small, sheepish smile tugged at his lips. "She was seven—this short, skinny thing—but I'd have sworn she was royalty by the way she carried herself. There was always this mischievous sparkle in her eyes, like she knew something no one else did, and the way she spoke would have made anyone stop and listen.

"The day I met her, my father had dragged me and my sister to a dozen useless meetings, and we were bored out of our wits. While our father was occupied, we snuck out of the council chambers and crept down to the shore of the lake, where Maisie bet me her dinner I wouldn't jump into the frigid water. Naturally, I had to prove her wrong—"

"*Naturally*," Mercy agreed, grinning as she recalled her walk along the shore with Tamriel. Even in the middle of summer, the water had been cool and crisp, a welcome reprieve from the heat of the sun.

"—and I nearly froze to death. Meanwhile, Elise had been watching from the upstairs window and took it upon herself to discipline us 'heathens'. Half the castle heard her scolding, and you can bet our father whipped us into shape that night. I think she only did it to impress her father and the other nobles, though, because the next time our father trusted us enough to bring us to the castle, she managed to convince the prince, his cousin, and some of the other advisors' children to jump into the lake as well. We stood atop the tallest boulder and amused ourselves for hours, jumping and splashing and play fighting. Later that night, I begged my father to arrange our betrothal, and he did." He smiled at the memory, but it quickly faded. "But now that we've grown...I fear she loves someone else."

"Who?"

His cheeks turned a faint pink. "Forget it, it's foolish."

"More foolish than jumping into a frozen lake?"

"I think she's in love with the prince," he blurted, his blush growing. "It's ridiculous. She's not of high enough rank to marry him. But...I mean, all her spare time is spent in the castle, even when she's not tending to her duties. When we were younger, she and the prince and his cousin...they were practically inseparable."

Mercy tried to hide her surprise. Elise in love with the prince? Now *that* was interesting information. She hadn't gotten the impression that there was anything more than friendship between them, but what young noblewoman wouldn't want to marry a handsome prince?

"I'm paranoid, right? She accepted our betrothal. She likes to tease me and torture me sometimes, but she knows how I feel about her. Plus, my family are Nadra. It's more than a step up from Serenna." He paused for a moment, then added,

"But I don't want her to settle for me. I don't want to be a consolation prize."

"If that's how she sees you, I think you're the one settling." *Just call me matchmaker*, Mercy thought with a wry twist of her lips.

"I know she cares for me. I'm just afraid she still sees me as that stupid eight-year-old from so long ago." Leon cleared his throat. "I appreciate you listening, Marieve. It's good advice, it's just...I don't know if I'm ready to accept it yet. But, ah, speaking of the castle—" He trailed off as the walls surrounding the castle came into view before them. A significantly smaller crowd stood in a semicircle around the intersection just outside the gate, where a large wooden stake had been planted in the cobbled street.

Ghyslain stood beside the gate, the very same one upon which Liselle's body had once been strung. It was obvious he was making an effort not to look at it. Even so, he glanced at it out of the corner of his eye every few seconds, his face slightly green.

Mercy and Leon joined the crowd just as Tamriel strode out of the castle grounds, leading the guards and six offenders forward. The guards forced the leaders of the mob to their knees in the center of the intersection, each shirtless and bound at the wrists. The woman kneeling in the middle of the line shrank away from the crowd's eyes and attempted to cover herself with her arms.

Master Oliver stepped forward, a whip coiled in one hand.

"You are guilty of threatening the peace and inciting a riot," Ghyslain said, "with the intent to murder civilians. Have you anything to say in your defense?"

None of the offenders made a sound. They merely glared up at Ghyslain, eyes like burning embers.

"Very well. I hereby sentence you to twenty lashes each."

Master Oliver pulled the first offender to his feet and

dragged him to the stake, securing the rope around the man's wrists to a hook that stuck out near the top. Without a word, without a flicker of emotion, he backed up, cocked his arm, and sent the whip cracking.

The leather snapped against the man's back, wrenching a cry from his lips. A thin red line blossomed across his bare skin. Master Oliver let the whip fly again, and again, and again, no expression on his face. The speed and power behind the lashes never changed, never faltered. Halfway through the twenty lashes, the man's legs gave out, and he hung from his wrists alone.

On the fifteenth strike, the whip landed in the same place the first one had, causing the skin to split and leak bright red blood. Mercy's stomach turned.

After the final lash, a guard stepped forward to collect the man, and they disappeared through the castle gate. The next offender was tied to the stake, but this time, he did not make a sound as the whip tore his flesh to ribbons. He stood there, silent tears running down his face, and glared daggers at Ghyslain.

The third offender was an elven woman, her body soft and undefined. Her pale skin split after the fifth lash. By the twelfth, her back and the waistband of her pants were soaked in blood. When Master Oliver swung his arm back for the next lash, she yelped in fear and twisted to one side, attempting to protect herself. The leather struck her side and the curve of one breast, tearing the tender skin like tissue. The blood shone under the sunlight as she let out a choked sob and sucked in quick, shallow breaths, her ribs visible as they expanded and contracted. Several women in the crowd turned away or watched through their fingers. Across the intersection, Tamriel's throat bobbed, his face turning pale despite his efforts to remain emotionless.

"Enough, Oliver," Ghyslain called. "That's enough."

"That's only thirteen, Your Majesty."

"Look at her. She's learned her lesson. Take her away."

A guard unhooked her arms. He slipped an arm around her waist, being careful not to touch her broken skin, and slowly walked her toward the gate. Halfway through, she went unconscious. Without pausing, the guard lifted her into his arms and continued to the castle.

While the other three were punished, Mercy averted her gaze, focusing on the dirt-coated tips of her fine silk slippers. Her throat tightened with every agonized scream, and Leon shot her a concerned look. She'd bet her precious Stryker-made daggers that her face was as pale as his.

Once all six people had been escorted into the castle grounds, Master Oliver wiped the sweat from his forehead and coiled the bloodied whip in one hand. He tossed it aside and pulled the wooden stake from the ground, then carried it toward the castle with the help of a guard. Another stepped forward and returned the cobble to the street where the stake had been planted.

Ghyslain rubbed a weary hand across his brow, knocking his diadem askew, then stepped forward and opened his mouth. The crowd hushed, waiting for him to address them. For a moment, his jaw worked, but no sound came out. His eyes searched the intersection until they found his son, who stood across the clearing, watching him with an impassive expression. His face was still white from having watched the lashings. Without a word, Ghyslain turned sharply on his heel and bolted through the gate.

Tamriel's mouth parted in surprise. He stepped forward and gestured to the nearest guard. "Emerick, send these people home, and have someone clean up this mess."

"Yes, Your Highness."

Tamriel nodded and strode across the intersection, his boots leaving dark prints across the bloodied cobblestones.

The bottom of his cloak dragged behind him and left a thin line of blood which followed him through the gate and into the castle grounds.

"Take them to the castle to be tended. Don't put them in the infirmary, put them...somewhere else. Put them—well, you know the castle. Find somewhere they'll be comfortable. Send for a healer, too. Not Alyss—she has enough to do already and she's been working with the plague-infected priestesses. Send for someone in the market, someone who won't be too queasy at the sight of all the blood. See that they're well enough to make it home, then turn them out."

"Yes, Your Majesty."

Ghyslain paced on the grass just within the castle grounds, his fingers rubbing small, agitated circles on both temples. As the guards led the battered and beaten offenders up the gravel carriageway to the castle, Ghyslain stopped and stared after them, swaying slightly, as if he'd just stepped onto land after a month at sea. He pressed a hand to the wall to support himself, his eyes fluttering shut.

"I'm not cruel," he murmured. "I did what I had to do to keep them safe. To buy time. They won't try again—not yet."

"Do you think he realizes we're here?" Leon whispered. They stood awkwardly a few yards away, watching as the king removed his diadem and stared down at the large central ruby as though it held all the answers. Leon shuffled his feet, digging the toe of his shoe into the grass.

Mercy elbowed him. "He will if you don't shut your mouth."

Across the gardens, Tamriel said a quick goodbye to the guard to whom he'd been speaking and jogged over. "You're not leaving yet, are you? I need you to save me."

"What?"

He shook his head, gazing at his father with an unreadable expression. "He's inconsolable when he's like this. In about five seconds, he'll stop talking to himself and start talking to the ghosts that live in his head, and I promise you, you don't want to see that. *I* don't want to see that. So please, help me escape somewhere he'll never look."

Without waiting for their response, he started toward the castle. Mercy and Leon exchanged confused looks and hurried after him. She would have rather gone with the prince on her own—perhaps wherever Tamriel wanted to go would give her the chance to kill him and complete her contract—but it would be easy enough to get the prince to dismiss Leon if she played her cards right.

"He's been like this for as long as I can remember," Tamriel said, looking back at Mercy over his shoulder. "He blames himself for the crimes of his people and calls himself a failure of a king. Usually, he holds it together long enough to return to his study."

"Would he prefer you stay with him, Your Highness?" Leon asked. "He looks like he might need the company—or something to distract him, at least."

"The only people whose company he enjoys have been dead for years. Follow me."

Tamriel climbed the castle steps two at a time and pushed the main doors open wide. They trailed him through the great hall and down the staircase she and Tamriel had taken to the infirmary. The prince turned right at the fork in the hall, and Mercy nearly slammed into his back when she made to follow. Leon caught her arm, steadying her, and frowned at the cobweb-covered door before which they stood. The prince turned the handle, and the door swung open with a low groan. "Welcome," he said, "to my mother's tomb."

37

Leon let out a nervous, strangled sound that was almost a laugh. "Uh, not her *actual* tomb, right?"

"After her death, her body was buried at her grandparents' estate in Redscale Down, so no, it's not her actual tomb," Tamriel said, rolling his eyes. "My father had many of her personal effects placed into this room so he wouldn't be reminded of her every day. These objects held enough of *her* in them that he couldn't even bear the sight of them. He still can't. I don't think he has ever set foot in this room."

"Are we allowed to be in here?"

He shrugged and led them inside. "My father's not going to come searching."

The room was packed from wall to wall with bookshelves, sculptures, paintings, gowns, bolts of fabric, and various baubles. On a dust-coated vanity was a silver tray of hairbrushes and combs, several jars of makeup, and pearl hair clips. A gemstone-encrusted box sat open beside the metal mirror, spilling necklaces of rubies, sapphires, and diamonds, along with strands of gold and tarnished silver. While Mercy and Leon moved further into the room, working their way around pieces of cloth-covered furniture, Tamriel left and returned with two torches from the hall. Their warm glow illuminated the dust motes suspended in the stagnant air.

"Here." He handed one to Leon. "Have you taken a look at that bookshelf over there? There are a few books I think would interest you. My mother loved classical literature, or so I've been told."

"Really? You'd let me...?"

"Sure. Right over there. You too, Marieve."

She followed Leon to the bookshelf. He picked up and read the titles of a few of the leather-bound tomes, coughing when dust flew up from the covers. After a few minutes, he wandered around to the other side of the bookshelf. When the light from his torch faded, leaving her in darkness, she realized Tamriel hadn't joined them. Mercy glanced back and spotted him sitting cross-legged on the floor on the other side of the room, partially hidden by the arm of an enormous settee.

He didn't move at all as Mercy approached, and only looked up at her when she stopped beside him. The flickering light of the torch reflected in his dark eyes, laying bare the grief in their depths. For the first time, Prince Tamriel Myrellis looked *vulnerable*.

She tore her gaze away and focused on the painting leaning against the wall opposite him. In the large gold-framed canvas, King Ghyslain and Queen Elisora stood on a balcony overlooking Lake Myrella, their hands clasped between them. The Ghyslain in the painting was dressed in a dark blue doublet and black trousers, and Elisora was draped in a gold gown that clung to the curve of her round stomach, heavy with child. The king and queen gazed lovingly into each other's eyes, a smile tugging at Ghyslain's lips.

"It's beautiful," Mercy whispered.

"It was painted right before she was bedridden with... complications," Tamriel responded, his voice tight. "I've seen other paintings of her, but this one is my favorite. They look so happy. I've never seen my father smile like that."

"Never?"

He shook his head. "You've seen the paintings outside the throne room, haven't you? The ones of my ancestors? According to tradition, they're supposed to be portraits of the king alone. Instead, my father was so excited for my arrival that he commissioned a family portrait, and had it hung on the wall for all to see. He was so proud of it." Tamriel didn't look at Mercy as he spoke, just kept staring at the painting as the light of the torch flickered and danced across its surface. "Tell me, does that sound like the king you saw outside?"

"No, not at all."

"This painting hung in that hall for years after her death. The advisors had thought the subjects should have a space to dedicate to her memory, since she wasn't buried in the city, and this painting became an unofficial shrine to her. People used to leave coins, jewelry, flowers, letters—they cared for her so much, my father had had no choice but to leave it there, no matter how much it killed him to see it.

"One night, when I was five, I awoke to a crashing sound downstairs, and a howling of such despair it made the hair on the back of my neck stand on end. I climbed out of bed and followed the sound downstairs, and when I reached that hall, I found my father on his knees, the flowers and vases in pieces around him. His knees were bleeding from the shards of porcelain and glass, but there he remained, sobbing into his hands."

Tamriel swallowed tightly. "It terrified me. I called out to him and he froze. He simply froze. Then his face turned bright red and he started shouting, screaming at me. He chased me up the stairs and told me to never, ever spy on him again. The next morning, the painting was gone, and he had blunted a letter opener scratching her name off the inscription."

The sorrow in the prince's voice made Mercy ache. She sank to her knees beside him and placed a hand on his shoulder. He leaned into her touch. "You can't blame yourself for her death, Tamriel, or the way your father responded to it."

He was quiet for a few seconds, then he said, "It's just— It's ridiculous, isn't it? How can you mourn someone you've never met? Everything I know about her, I've learned from other people. When my father looks at me, all he sees is her ghost. And I don't— I don't understand it. How could he have loved her so much and still fallen for Liselle? How could he have betrayed her like that?"

"Have you tried asking him?"

Tamriel choked on a bitter laugh. "You don't know us very well if you think he'd be willing to talk about that. He can hardly say either of their names without falling apart."

Mercy nodded, unsure how to respond, and sat down beside him.

"I want you to know that I appreciate all the help you've given us since your arrival. We've been so busy since Solari the negotiations have fallen to the wayside, but you've still helped in the infirmary, and you didn't have to. None of what is happening is your responsibility. You could have left for Feyndara at the first sign of a problem, but you didn't." He glanced over at Leon, who was still lost somewhere in the bookshelves far out of earshot, and said, "That's why, when I challenge my father's rule on my eighteenth birthday and ascend the throne, I will ensure you are granted everything your country is owed—namely, a peace treaty over the Islands."

She gaped at him. "You're going to challenge your father?"

Tamriel nodded. "I hadn't seriously considered it until this morning, when I saw how unhinged he has become. He's getting worse—more distracted, more deranged. He told me he sees Liselle... He—He talks to her. How can I in good conscience allow him to keep the throne? I have a responsibility to my people.

"There are several nobles whose loyalty to my father is questionable, at best. I believe that if I meet with them, they'll support my claim to the throne. They'll help me remove my father from power, and then I will be able to negotiate with you for the Islands." A spark of excitement grew in his eyes. He leaned closer, his knee brushing hers, and hesitated before adding, "And if you should still desire it... I will need a queen to rule beside me."

Her mouth dropped open. "I thought you said marriage was out of the question."

"It's not ideal, I know, but it would benefit our countries greatly. This animosity between Beltharos and Feyndara cannot continue. You said it yourself—what better way to form an alliance than through marriage?"

"I, uh, I did say that."

He reached forward and cupped her cheek, his thumb gliding lightly over her skin. "So, what do you think?"

Mercy swallowed painfully, her mouth suddenly dry. She might have laughed in his face if not for the way he was watching her. His eyes were trained on hers, the firelight flickering mesmerizingly in their depths, and his lips parted into a small, sheepish smile.

Creator damn her, she couldn't deny that he was beautiful.

She had a role to play. She was Lady Marieve Aasa of Feyndara. She opened her mouth and silently cursed herself for what she was about to say.

"Yes."

38

Late that night, Mercy was training with her daggers in her bedroom when a series of quick, short taps on the front door interrupted her. She frowned and wiped the sheen of perspiration off her brow, then twisted the pommels of the daggers together and slipped them under the mattress. The tapping came again as Mercy descended the stairs. She padded down the hall, opened the door, and found herself staring into Owl's wide hazel eyes.

"Thank the Creator I found you," she breathed, clasping Mercy's hand in her gloved one. Every inch of the girl's skin was covered save for her face, from the silken scarf wound around her head to the too-large cloak that pooled around her feet. "Come, we must return to the infirmary immediately."

"Why? Owl, what are you talking about?"

"It's Pilar—she doesn't have much time. Alyss doesn't think she'll last the night. Now let's go, and I'll explain on the way."

Mercy tugged on the slippers she'd left by the door and followed Owl to the street. The young priestess grabbed her hand and led her toward the castle. When they passed a house and the light bleeding out of the window hit Owl, Mercy saw that three-quarters of her face—which had been clear, healthy skin after Alyss's Pryyam salt treatment—was now covered in pitted, crusty scabs.

Owl noticed Mercy's shock and quickly turned away, quickening their pace until they were once again hidden by the shadows. "Alyss's treatment didn't work," she said in a quiet voice, pulling the scarf closer around her face.

Hearing the pain in the girl's voice, Mercy decided not to pry further. "How did you manage to leave the infirmary without the guards stopping you? Aren't they still guarding the door?"

"Yes, but they can't do their jobs nearly as well if they're unconscious. Alyss drugged them so I could come get you. Pilar kept asking for you—she's half delirious, spouting all these things about visions, and she wouldn't quiet down until Alyss agreed to send for you."

Together, they made their way through the castle gate, across the lawn, and around the side of the castle. A wooden door was nestled between two vine-covered trellises, nearly hidden from sight unless one stood directly in front of it. On its surface were a series of metal latches and switches, which Owl unlocked with quick, dextrous fingers. The door swung open. "Alyss taught me the combination," Owl said in response to Mercy's questioning look. They stepped inside and pulled the door shut behind them.

The servants' entrance was only a few short hallways from the infirmary, and when they turned the last corner, Mercy suppressed a snicker at the sight of the two guards slumped against the wall, one dangerously close to falling off the stool on which he sat. Owl rapped on the door and Gwynn let them in, a grave expression on the elder priestess's face.

Owl darted around the shelves and Mercy followed close

on her heels. Alyss was leaning over Pilar's bed, tightening ropes around the priestess's wrists. The bed frame groaned as Pilar fought to get free, a moan slipping from her lips.

"Pilar, look who we brought," Owl murmured, slipping past Mercy to kneel beside Pilar's cot.

"Mer—"

"*Lady Marieve,*" the girl corrected sharply.

Satisfied with her work, Alyss straightened and turned to Mercy. She slipped her hands into her pockets, but not before Mercy noticed how hard they were trembling. "She's hangin' in there, and I've done what I can, but I'm afraid her pain's not goin' away. I've given her as much medicine as I safely can."

Pilar looked over at Mercy, and it took every ounce of self control within her not to let out a gasp of shock. The priestess's face was scabbed and scarred, just like Owl's and Gwynn's, but her blind eye was no longer white—it had turned a dark red, almost black, and the skin around it was crisscrossed with tiny scratches. Her good eye, now slightly cloudy, tracked Mercy as she approached and sank to her knees beside Owl.

"Sh-She was havin' delusions," Alyss said in a soft, shaky voice. "She says she no longer feels the Creator's presence in her visions—all she sees are death and destruction. Last night, I found her tryin' to scratch her eyes out to make the visions stop."

Behind them, Gwynn let out a sob and began muttering a prayer under her breath.

Pilar reached for Mercy, but the rope around her wrist pulled taut. She growled in frustration.

Mercy rested a comforting hand on her arm, then looked up at Alyss. "May we have a moment in private?"

Alyss nodded and led Owl toward the hearth, next to where Gwynn was still whispering. After a moment of hesitation, Owl and Alyss bent their heads and joined the prayer.

Mercy rested a hand on Pilar's cheek, waiting for the priestess's cloudy eyes to focus on her before asking, "How do you feel?"

"I'm scared," she whispered, a shudder wracking her body. "I'm not ready to go to the Beyond. I want to stay here. I want to help."

Mercy's heart broke. As ruthless and cruel as she had always been in the Keep, she couldn't bear to watch Pilar's suffering. Her time in the infirmary with Sorin had instilled in her that much empathy, at least. She forced a small, reassuring smile. "You are helping. You're the one who warned us about Fieldings' Plague. Because of you, Alyss and the other healers in the city are working to find a cure."

"The cure isn't going to stop it—not completely. To end it, you must defeat it...defeat *him*."

"Who?"

"The one who preys on the Islands. Myrbellanar."

"The Old God from the legend?"

"I thought it was a legend—I used to. But my visions... Something more than a plague is at play here." Her gaze drifted to the ceiling, her face turning ashen under the red, bloody scratches marring her skin. Her voice was little more than a hoarse whisper when she said, "He has shown me such terrible things, Mercy. Things that would destroy the toughest Daughter. You mustn't let him win."

"How do I do that?" Mercy asked softly. What Pilar expected her to do, she had no idea. Her time in the capital would end once Tamriel was dead.

Pilar didn't say a word. Tears glistened in her eyes, and she began to mumble under her breath. Every few seconds, her eyelids drifted shut, and each time stretched a little longer before she opened them again.

"Pilar? Pilar, don't go yet, okay? Stay here. Stay with me." Mercy shook Pilar's arm gently until the priestess's eyelids fluttered open once more. "Stay with me."

"I'm here. I'm here. For a little bit longer..." She gritted her teeth, shifting her legs under the blanket. "It... It hurts."

"Alyss, is there something you can give her to ease the pain?"

"No, don't!" Pilar blurted before Alyss could respond. "The pain is something to hold on to. I don't want to slip away. Not yet."

Mercy took one of her hands as Gwynn and Owl walked over and settled on the ground on the opposite side of Pilar's cot. Alyss silently moved to the foot of the bed and bowed her head in grief. Owl braided a small section of Pilar's hair, humming under her breath. Mercy recognized the melody as an old folk song some of the Guild apprentices sang while doing their chores. Sorrow sent a pang through her chest. She had never meant to become entangled in these people's lives, but now that she had, she didn't regret it. She tightened her grip on Pilar's hand, and the four of them stood vigil over Pilar long after the priestess's eyes drifted shut for the final time.

They sat around Pilar's bed for so long, Owl fell asleep leaning on the mattress, her arms folded under her head like a pillow. Her eyes were swollen, her cheeks stained pink by the trails of her tears. Without a word, Gwynn stood, grimacing at the cramps in her legs, and gently lifted the girl into her arms. She set Owl down on the farthest cot and tucked the blankets around her small body, then curled up beside her.

Alyss stared at Pilar, her face carefully neutral. "We should move her out now," she whispered, her voice tight with pain. "I don't want her here when they wake up."

Mercy nodded and stood. Together, they peeled the blankets off the bed and untied the ropes around Pilar's wrists, throwing both into the fire. Alyss placed Pilar's left arm at her side, then reached over to move her right. As she did, the collar of her shirt slipped forward enough for Mercy to glimpse the bright red rash streaking across her shoulder and chest.

"Alyss!" Mercy gasped. The healer's eyes followed hers down to her torso, then she yanked up the collar of her tunic, hiding her diseased skin. "I *knew* you were sick."

"Don't say a word to anyone!" Alyss hissed, anger flaring in her eyes. Only...it wasn't just anger, Mercy realized as she gaped at Alyss. It was terror. Alyss's hands had begun to shake. She occupied them by pulling up the sides of the sheet on Pilar's cot. "We'll wrap her up in this, then we can take her outside. Better we move her than expose the guards to the plague."

"Don't change the topic. You're sick. You shouldn't be going outside at all. What if you spread it?"

"It's— It's only in the early stages, okay? I'll be careful. I'll cover up. It's transferred through touch, as far as I can tell, so I won't touch anyone. I'll help ye carry her out of here, then we'll come back. No contact with anyone, no spreadin' of the disease. When we get back, ye can scold me as much as ye like."

Mercy sighed, crossing her arms. "Fine, but I don't like this."

"It's not up to ye. I'm not puttin' two guards at risk of catchin' it. Now, ye can either help me, or ye can go."

Mercy relented, and they wrapped Pilar's body in the sheet and carried her to the door, Alyss at her head and Mercy at her feet. Alyss pounded on the door with her heel, and it swung open a moment later to a very confused and groggy guard. He rubbed his eyes and frowned down at the bulk in their arms. When he realized what it had to be, he jerked back, a hand coming up to cover his mouth.

"Send for a carriage," Alyss said, her tone brooking no argument. The guard ran off, and Alyss turned to the other man, who was blinking up at them blearily. "Go open the servants' entrance."

He pushed to his feet and jogged down the hallway ahead of them. When Mercy and Alyss arrived at the servants' door, breathing hard from carrying Pilar's limp weight, the guard recoiled and shut it behind them as soon as they crossed the threshold. Slowly, painfully, they made their way along the side of the castle and found the other guard already waiting with a carriage, his expression grave. Alyss scowled when the driver tried to help them place Pilar's body on the floor. "We can manage her just fine. Ye'd be wise to stay well away."

He lifted his hands in surrender as Mercy and Alyss climbed inside, each taking a bench. Alyss closed the door behind her, stuck her head out, and called, "To the Church, please."

The driver paused halfway up to his seat. "You... You do know there's barely anyone left, don't you? Most of the priestesses have fallen ill or left the city."

"She should be returned to her family. Take us to the Church."

"...Very well." The carriage dipped under his weight as he climbed up to the front. He snapped the reins and the horses lurched forward, their hooves crunching on the gravel of the narrow path leading to the gates.

Mercy leaned forward. "You can't hide this, Alyss. You're sick, and if you go out again, you risk spreading it to more people. You should tell Tamriel or the king so you can be moved to the infirmary tents to be treated."

"Pft. So I can rot in some putrid tent out in the fields? No, not while I'm able to work. I can find a cure for this—I know I can. I just need more time."

"*You don't have more time!*" Mercy hissed, imploring her to understand. "You don't have to be the one to figure out a cure. There are other healers in the city. You can't hide this."

"The hell I can't! I will keep workin' as long as I am able, 'cause I swore an oath to serve the royal family and the people of Sandori, and Creator damn ye if ye think I'll turn my back on that for a measly rash! Ye saw what this disease did to her," she said, nodding to Pilar. "Ye saw how it corrupted her and poisoned her mind. If this plague kills me, so be it, but I will not sit idly by and wallow in self-pity waitin' for it to claim me. I will spend what little time I have left exactly where I belong—tendin' those in my care and workin' to find a cure. If I fail, another healer will pick up where I leave off, and there will be no need for any more people to suffer." Alyss's voice broke on the last word, and she turned to swipe angrily at the tears welling in her eyes.

For a few long moments, they sat in heavy, thick silence. Mercy pushed the curtain away from the window and watched the dark houses pass.

After composing herself, Alyss added quietly, "I will not hear another word on the matter."

Mercy nodded—not because she thought it was the right choice, but because she knew arguing wouldn't change the healer's decision. Mistress Sorin would have done the same.

"When it comes time for me to die, ye must remember yer promise."

"I will."

"Good."

Alyss offered her a small, grateful smile before turning to the window. Neither of them spoke again for the remainder of the ride.

39

When the carriage rolled to a stop in front of the church, the driver climbed down from his seat and pulled the door open, then backed away to watch them shift Pilar's body into their arms. Together, they carried her up the steps and knocked on the tall doors, the sound jarring in the nighttime quiet. A moment later, the door swung open to reveal a surprised priestess clutching the front of her dressing gown. In the moonlight, Mercy could just make out the frizzy halo of hair around her face, the intricate tattoos coiling across her forehead and cheeks. The priestess was a Cirisian elf.

"How may I— Oh," she said, her gaze dropping to the body in their arms. "Who— Who is that?"

"Pilar," Alyss said.

Her face fell, and she stepped aside, opening the door wider. "Please, come in."

She led them through the center of the Church, past rows upon rows of pews set before a dais and a bowl-shaped altar. The vaulted ceiling stretched high overhead, amplifying and echoing the sounds of their footsteps on the stone tile. They followed her through a curtained archway and down a hall. The few bedrooms they passed were notably empty despite the late hour, the mattresses stripped of sheets, the bedside tables bare save for well-worn copes of the Book of the Creator.

Most of the priestesses have fallen ill or left the city, the carriage driver had said.

The rooms belonged to ghosts now.

"You can put her in here," the priestess said as they approached a door near the end of the hall. She opened it and gestured to the marble table in the center of the room. "This used to be the High Priestess's room, but...she has since returned to the Creator's embrace. Please, place her there. Rosalba will give her the last rites before she is laid to rest."

They did as the priestess instructed. Mercy felt a weight lift from her chest when she set Pilar on the table. The grief that had settled in her heart was unfamiliar—unwelcome—to her. She backed away immediately, letting out a sharp breath. No one in the Guild spoke of this side of death: the grief, the sorrow, the mourning. She turned her back to the table. She was an Assassin. She did not mourn the dead.

"I wouldn't do that if I were ye," Alyss said, and Mercy turned to find that the priestess had removed the sheet from Pilar's face and reached out as if to touch the woman's cheek.

"Do not worry about me." She ran a light finger along the soft line of Pilar's jaw. "There are only a few of us left, but we who remain are immune to the plague."

"How do ye know for sure?"

"The others are either dead or in the tents in the fields. Some left, but I and four others did not. We have a duty to serve the terrified people of this city. We will stay as long as necessary."

"Who was the first infected?"

"The High Priestess, then it spread through the ranks."

The priestess lowered her hand to her side. She bit her lip, seeming to weigh some internal debate, then said, "It didn't behave like a normal sickness. It's strange to think about, but...it felt like it was targeting specific people—those with the Sight. Pilar insisted on going to the king for aid, but the High Priestess refused. She didn't want to frighten anyone until she knew more about the sickness. She thought the others would recover. When it claimed her life... Well, Pilar snuck out of the church to find help and never returned. Until now, we hadn't seen her since Solari."

She shook her head and gestured to the door through which they had entered. "You have two more of our priestesses, do you not?" the priestess asked as she led them into the main room. She motioned for Mercy and Alyss to sit on the first pew, then picked up a candle and a handful of herbs from a table near the wall. "I am eager to hear how Gwynn and Mavi fare."

"Mavi, that's her name!" Alyss said. "She never did tell us."

"It's not unlike her. A few years ago, her village was destroyed in a fire and she fled to the nearest church for shelter. She's been shuffled about ever since, and it has made her wary of strangers. Mavi is the only name the High Priestess was able to coax out of her."

As she spoke, the priestess sprinkled herbs into the bowl-shaped brazier and lowered the tip of the candle to them. They ignited immediately, burning with an impossibly bright light, and illuminated the strange tattoos on the priestess's face. Mercy had only ever read about them. The dark brown ink stretched in curling, coiling vines across her forehead and down the bridge of her nose, then continued over her lips and disappeared under the collar of her robe. When she moved her hands, Mercy spotted more tattoos on her arms, looping around her wrists like bracelets before slinking down the backs of her hands and twining around her fingers.

"Yes," Alyss said hesitantly, fear flashing in and out of her eyes as the priestess descended from the dais and perched on the pew next to Mercy. "Well, Gwynn and Ow—Mavi, I mean—are doin' alright, but I won't lie to ye: they'll die if we don't find a cure soon. I'm doin' everythin' I can to keep their conditions stable, but even that is failin'."

"I see." The priestess frowned, sorrow tugging at features only a few years older than Mercy's. "Nevertheless, I am grateful for your help, and for returning Pilar to us. Sometimes easing the suffering of others is all we are able to do in times of crisis."

Alyss frowned. "That's not enough. Not for me."

"Then do not give up." The priestess started to stand, then paused, her lips twitching into a sad smile. "There is no need to fear me because I am Cirisian, you know."

Alyss looked away, color rising on her cheeks. "I don't fear ye."

"You don't have to lie. I understand. My people seldom leave the islands on which they are born, and even fewer choose to leave for good. I'm afraid you will see more and more of us in the years to come, however, if the ceaseless fighting between Beltharos and Feyndara does not come to a peaceful resolution."

"Then let's hope the war ends soon," Alyss said. She stood and gave Mercy a meaningful look. "We'd best be returnin' to the infirmary now, though. I don't want to leave Gwynn and Mavi there alone for long."

"Must we?" Mercy objected, ignoring the pleading look on Alyss's face. She felt like an unwelcome stranger in the dark church, the flames in the brazier casting long shadows on the walls and high, arched ceiling, but she found herself not wanting to leave. The priestess studied her with curiosity, her eyes unguarded and kind, and it was hard for Mercy to resist the urge to pepper her with questions. Growing up, she'd read every book the Kismoro Keep had on the Cirisian elves, who worshipped strange gods and lived in tribes along the archipelago between Beltharos and Feyndara. She'd been fascinated by them.

The first—and only—time Mercy ran away from the Guild, she had been trying to go to Cirisor.

"No, your friend is right. I've occupied too much of your time already," the priestess said, standing with the fabled grace of the Cirisian elves. She smiled warmly, seeing Alyss's discomfort—which only succeeded in making Alyss more uncomfortable. "Thank you for returning our sister to us. For what it's worth, you have my gratitude. Should you have need of me, I am Lethandris."

"You kept your Cirisian name?" Mercy asked.

Lethandris blinked at her. "Of course. To many people in Beltharos, my culture is strange and primitive, but it is not something of which to be ashamed. My upbringing shaped me, as everyone's does, and I will not pretend otherwise." She grinned and gestured to the tattoos on her face. "I can't hide it, anyway."

Lethandris led them down the narrow aisle and to the front doors, one of which she held open for them. "Your driver is a good man. He waited for you. My apologies for keeping you so long."

"No apology necessary." Alyss slipped past her, being careful not to brush against the priestess's skin, despite her assurance of her immunity. "Come on, Marieve."

As Mercy made to follow, Lethandris reached out a hand to stop her. "When we send Pilar back to the Creator, would you like me to send you a message? Would you like to attend her funeral?"

"No," Mercy blurted, too quickly. She couldn't help remembering the weight of Pilar's limp body in her hands, the way the heat had seeped out of her and left a stranger's cold corpse in its place. Her heart ached to think of Pilar lying dead on that stone table. "I hardly knew her."

"But—"

"I'm sorry." Mercy jogged down the steps before the priestess could say anything more, then slipped into the carriage after Alyss. The driver closed the door behind her, but not before she saw Lethandris standing in the doorway, gazing after her sadly. The driver snapped the reins, and Mercy looked away as Lethandris closed the tall front door of the church.

40

"See? There was no reason for ye to worry," Alyss whispered as they stepped into the infirmary. "I didn't touch anyone."

Across the room, Gwynn whimpered quietly in her sleep. Alyss rushed over, tugging off a glove and pressing a hand to the side of her face. "She's burnin' up." She rounded the cot to check on Owl, leaning in close to listen to the girl's breathing. "They only have a few days left, I'm afraid. A week, at the most. Thankfully, it's spreading more slowly than it did with Pi—Pilar," she whispered to Mercy, her voice catching on the name. "My treatments are helping."

Mercy crossed the room to join her. "It's only been a few days since Solari. Do you have any idea why it affected her so strongly?"

"No. She might've had a weaker immune system, or she may have been infected for longer than we realized. Or...it may have had somethin' to do with her Sight."

"You believe what Lethandris said about the disease *choosing* people to infect?" Mercy gaped at her, incredulous. "That's not possible."

"I'm not wont to believe anythin' those Old God-worshippin' elves claim, but ye heard what she said—the High Priestess and the others with the Sight were the first infected. They share the church, the common rooms, they're a family. Two dozen people in such close quarters means any sickness, no matter how severe, is goin' to spread like wildfire. So why would only those people be infected first? They must have all been exposed around the same time, but the disease worked faster in the priestesses in higher positions of power." Her voice, initially kept low to avoid waking Gwynn and Owl, became faster and higher as she continued, her eyes widening in panic. "So, yes, I believe the plague is *somehow* choosing people."

"Alyss, listen to what you're saying," Mercy snapped, seizing the woman's shoulders and dragging her over to the desk, away from Owl and Gwynn. "A disease is not capable of choosing its victims. It is *impossible*."

"Pilar said—"

"Yesterday you said Pilar was raving mad."

"I changed my mind!" Alyss retorted, her fear giving way to anger. "Yer not a healer, Marieve—just another silly court lady. Shouldn't ye be up in the throne room, wearin' yer pretty gowns and dancin' with all the dashin' noblemen? Or perhaps ye have yer eye on a better prize." She tapped her temple with a finger. "I've heard the prince is quite taken with ye."

Frustration rose within Mercy, and she was filled with the sudden urge to wipe the smug, knowing grin off the woman's face. She took a few steps toward Alyss, dark thoughts coursing through her mind, then jerked to a stop and forced herself to take a deep breath.

"Alyss, listen to yourself," she whispered, anger turning to pity at the sight of the feverish glint in the healer's eyes. "You're acting paranoid, just like Pilar the night of Solari. You remember, don't you? That's why Lethandris made you so nervous, why you're so convinced the disease is hunting people. It's not you, Alyss, it's the sickness. You're worse than you think."

Shock, denial, and a flicker of fear flashed across Alyss's face. For a few seconds, she didn't say anything, considering the possibility that what Mercy had said was true. Then her expression darkened. "Get out of my infirmary," she said in an icy voice. "I don't want to see ye around here anymore. Take yer pity and yer reprimands and go to hell, princess—and forget about yer Creator-damned promise!"

"You want me to leave? Fine." Mercy glanced over to the far cot, where Gwynn and Owl were sitting upright in petrified silence. She didn't know how long they'd been listening, but they'd heard enough. She offered them a curt nod, then pivoted on her heel and walked out of the infirmary. Just as she closed the door, she heard Alyss burst into tears.

She didn't look back.

The council room looks a lot larger when it's not full of bickering nobles.

The thought ran through Mercy's head as she sat alone at the center of the long rectangular table, her fingers drumming idly on the arms of her chair. Across from her, the tall doors engraved with the Myrellis family crest swung open, and King Ghyslain entered, his tunic rumpled and untucked as if he'd just risen from a fitful sleep—which was more than likely. It wasn't yet dawn. Despite his disheveled appearance, his dark eyes were awake and alert when they met hers. Behind him, his guards took up positions on either side of the doorway in the hall outside. The council room doors swung shut, leaving Mercy and the king alone.

"Your healer is infected," Mercy said without preamble. She didn't bother to stand and bow, but Ghyslain either didn't notice or didn't care. He merely went still.

"How much longer does she have?"

"I'm hardly a healer, but given what I've seen so far, I'd say a week. Maybe two."

He frowned. "I see." He pulled the chair across from her back, its legs scratching across the stone floor, then sat and rested his elbows on the table. "And what of the three priestesses?"

Mercy shook her head and held up two fingers. "As of this morning."

His face fell and he looked away, a muscle working in his jaw. "So why did you demand this audience?"

Mercy opened her mouth, then closed it. She wasn't entirely certain why she had asked to meet with him—only that after everything she'd witnessed since coming to Sandori, it had felt almost...right. She'd been struck by a strange desire to learn more about Ghyslain and Tamriel, about the people whose lives she'd come here to ruin. Now, knowing the king was not the one who had bought the contract on Tamriel, Mercy felt something akin to pity for him for what she was planning to do to his only child. "Your son," she blurted. "Do you think he will be a good king?"

He glanced at her sharply. "Why would you ask such a thing?"

She shrugged.

"I think Tam will make a fine king."

"You're not a great liar, Your Majesty."

His lips twitched into a sad smile. "He's his mother's son. If there was ever a person more fit for the throne than she, I have not met her. I'm sure the boy has many of the same qualities."

"Is that why you continue to push Tamriel away? He reminds you too much of her? Are you that much of a coward?"

"I loved my wife," he responded, ignoring her insult. "Can you blame me for mourning her death?"

"People die every day."

He shook his head. "Not like her. The day she died, it was like the Creator had reached inside of me and ripped the heart out of my chest. Do you know what it's like to lose someone whose mere presence lit up the room when she entered? Do you know what it's like to hold your newborn son in your arms as you listen to the healer explain why the bedsheets are soaked in blood and your wife's heart no longer beats?" He was looking straight at Mercy, but his eyes were unfocused, staring through her as the words tumbled from his lips. "When he told me, it was all I could do not to drop the baby. I didn't feel anything at all. I was just numb.

"Seeing her face in his, I resented him for it," he continued, shame flashing across his face. "I resented him for killing her. I know it's unfair, but I couldn't control it. He was a constant reminder—he had lived and she had not. By the time I realized how wrong I was, Tamriel was almost grown and I had long been unworthy of calling myself his father."

"It doesn't have to be that way anymore," Mercy said, recalling the sorrowful, agonized look in Tamriel's eyes anytime he spoke of his parents. Once Mercy completed her contract, how would Ghyslain react to the murder of his son? They seemed to hardly know each other. Would a small part of him be relieved, knowing he would no longer have to live with the constant reminder of his wife? Would he regret not spending time with Tamriel while he had the chance? "He's still here. He grieves for a father who still lives. You can change this."

"No, I don't think I can. The boy needs his mother."

"His mother isn't here. You are."

"The die has been cast; the damage done. The boy carries a wound that won't easily be healed. At least in that way, he takes after me." Ghyslain's voice was thick with self-loathing. He met her gaze, his eyes focused once more on her face. In the candlelight, Mercy noticed a faint shadow of a beard across his jaw, and she was suddenly struck with the wish that he would grow it out. Then he wouldn't look so much like Tamriel. As much as the prince hated to admit it, he and his father had a lot more in common than looks—from their manner of speech to their stances, to the way they watched her with the same mixture of amusement, curiosity, and wariness. "But what was your initial question? Whether he will make a good king?"

She nodded.

"What do you think?"

"I think if you want him to become a great king, he shouldn't be running around completing meaningless tasks and pointless errands. He should be at your side, learning how to run a kingdom."

He chuckled humorlessly. "And you believe I could teach him that? The mad king? His presence is good for the public. He has their hearts, much more than I ever have. In due time, he will learn how to rule." The king stood and pushed his chair back under the table. "Now, if we've nothing more to discuss, I'm sure this can wait until *after* the sun rises, don't you think?"

Without waiting for a response, he turned and started toward the door.

"I know about the cure."

He paused, his hand hovering over the door handle. "What do you think you know about it?"

"There isn't one."

Silence.

"How long have you known?" she asked. "How did you find out?"

No response.

"When are you going to tell your subjects?"

In the blink of an eye, he crossed the room and splayed his hands on the table, the candlelight casting long, sinister shadows across his face as he loomed over her. "Lady Marieve, you have not hesitated to insert yourself into every problem you've managed to find since your arrival in my city. Now I'll admit I haven't a clue how foreign royalty is treated in Feyndara—your grandmother made certain of that—but I am not so much a fool that I would willingly overlook the actions of someone as influential as yourself without a degree of suspicion, particularly when it concerns my son. This, at least, I can do for him. So, again, I'll put to you the question I asked when you first arrived: why are you really here?"

She stood, staring back at him unflinchingly. "I am here for nothing more than the Islands."

He let out a sharp laugh, and the sudden whoosh of breath caused the candles' flames to sputter and dim, obscuring them in darkness for a few seconds. When they swelled again, his head hung forward, his shoulders shaking with quiet laughter. "You know I can't give you that. Your grandmother should have known that before she sent you."

"I'm an optimist."

He smirked. "Very well." He turned and opened the doors, waving one of his guards over. "Until you choose to reveal your true motivation for being here, Ser Morrison will escort you to and from the castle, and on any other promenades around the city, as well—for your own protection, of course."

Mercy's answering smile was razor-sharp. "Thank you for your concern, Your Majesty."

"My pleasure." He offered her a small bow—more out of courtesy than sincerity—and left the room. As the double doors swung shut behind him, he said, "Ser Morrison, see her out."

41

The next morning, a curious sight greeted Mercy when she rounded the rear of the castle: a dozen slaves were crowded in a circle a few yards from the lake's edge, two royal guards hovering nearby with worried expressions. The ring of steel on steel echoed off the castle's stone façade, and a sudden *Oof!* elicited a burst of excited cries from the onlookers. As Mercy approached, Elvira and Ser Morrison in tow, a man flew from the circle, crashing through the crowd and landing hard on his back at Mercy's feet. The point of his sword quivered in the air, still clenched in one fist. Mercy frowned down at him, his head mere inches from the toes of her flats.

Calum grinned at her. "Hi."

"Hi."

"Lovely morning, isn't it?"

"Quite."

Tamriel stepped out of the circle and lowered the point of his sword to his cousin's throat. He was dressed in a lightweight tunic and trousers, a sheen of sweat beading on his brow. "The goal is to stay *inside* the ring. You know that, don't you?"

"Of course. I just thought I'd give you a few easy wins before I start trying. Wouldn't want to embarrass you in front of all your admirers."

Tamriel smirked. "Brave words from the man on the wrong side of the sword." He glanced up at Mercy and smiled. "Hello, Marieve."

Calum knocked Tamriel's blade aside and rolled to his feet, immediately slashing at Tamriel, who parried his swing with ease. They exchanged several blows, their swords clashing loudly amidst the chatter of the onlookers. An elven woman across from Mercy watched with awe, clapping excitedly as the two men shuffled back into the center of the circle, their gazes locked.

"Dear Creator," Elvira gasped quietly, hovering behind Mercy. "You'd think they wouldn't use real swords for sparring."

"They've been doing this since they learned to hold a sword," Ser Morrison said. "Don't worry. They've had the finest tutors in Beltharos." His voice was even, but Mercy saw his throat bob as Tamriel narrowly avoided a nasty gash in the arm.

The prince lunged, his blade aimed at Calum's chest. Calum deflected it, and the sword glanced to the side, slicing into his shoulder. The slave next to Mercy tittered with worry as the sleeve of Calum's shirt darkened with blood, but he didn't seem to notice the wound. The cousins' teasing smiles had vanished, giving way to frowns of concentration, eyes narrowed against the sunlight reflected off the lake's waves.

Mercy couldn't help but smirk as she watched, imagining them facing off against a Daughter of the Guild. Tamriel and Calum had undoubtedly been well taught, but they fought with manners and sportsmanship; it wasn't the biting, raking, dirty fighting style Mistress Trytain had taught her apprentices. Tamriel and Calum wouldn't stand a chance against them.

Their swords locked. With his free hand, Calum pulled a dagger from his waistband and slashed out with it, catching Tamriel across the face. The prince recoiled—more out of surprise than pain—and his hand flew up to the narrow gash above his eyebrow. A shadow passed through his eyes. He swung at Calum with both hands on the grip of his sword, allowing his cousin only enough time to lift his blade and absorb the brunt of the strike before Tamriel slammed into him, knocking him backward. Calum stumbled and dropped the dagger, and Tamriel quickly scooped it up, leveling both his sword and dagger at his cousin's throat.

Calum smiled and lowered his sword. "An excellent fight, Your Highness."

"You've been neglecting your training. You're a bit rusty." Tamriel dropped his weapons and clapped his cousin on his uninjured shoulder. "But I must admit you landed a few good hits there." He swiped at the trail of blood dripping from the gash above his brow, accidentally streaking some of it across his forehead.

"You as well." Calum fingered the hole in his shirt, dark with blood. "Nothing a few stitches can't fix." He grinned and turned to the slaves gathered around them, offering a flourishing, theatrical bow. Several clapped excitedly, while others wandered off to complete their duties.

Mercy glanced at Ser Morrison—still hovering two feet behind her—then walked over to where Tamriel stood, watching Calum with an amused and bewildered expression.

"Has he always been like this?" Mercy asked, rolling her eyes when Calum stooped to kiss the hand of a pretty slave.

"Overly dramatic and starved for attention? Yes."

"And, fortunately, not yet hard of hearing," Calum added,

turning back to them. "But what is life without a bit of showmanship?"

Mercy ignored him and gestured to the weapons. "Friendly skirmish or settling an argument?"

"Neither," Tamriel responded. "We simply hadn't practiced in a while, what with Calum traveling these past several months."

"You traveled?" Mercy asked Calum, feigning surprise. As far as Tamriel knew, she and Calum had only met a few days ago. "Where did you go?"

He shrugged. "Here and there. Blacksmithing has always interested me, so I traveled with the Strykers for a while, learning the craft. Call it a hobby."

"The Strykers? I've heard a lot about them recently. Weren't they planning to go to Feyndara? It's a shame you had to return here rather than go with them." *I'm still angry at you for hitting me with a paperweight, you bastard,* she thought.

"I would have liked to see your country, my lady. Perhaps someday. For now, my place is here, at His Highness's side." He slung an arm around Tamriel's shoulders, mischief sparkling in his eyes. "Until such time as I am no longer needed, my duty is to the people of this kingdom."

Mercy offered him a saccharine smile. "They're lucky you value your loyalty so highly."

"As are we," Tamriel said, oblivious to the dark look Calum shot Mercy. He shrugged off his cousin's arm. "But I won't have you standing around, bleeding on everything. Go inside and get one of Master Oliver's men to patch you up."

"Of course." Calum bent down to pick up his sword, then reached for his dagger, but Mercy scooped it up before he could.

"Here you go," she said cheerily. Then, their heads bent close together, she whispered, "The guard standing behind me—I need you to get rid of him. Have him reassigned or something." She could have killed him, but she didn't need a body to worry about besides Tamriel's.

"Done." He straightened and smiled at her, tucking the dagger into his waistband. "I must return to work, unfortunately, but I'll see you soon, Your Highness. My lady." He bowed to them and walked away, whistling as he rounded the side of the castle, seemingly unperturbed by his still-bleeding arm.

When Mercy turned back to the prince, he was studying her with a strange expression on his face. It vanished in the blink of an eye, replaced by a concerned frown. "Have you heard the news? My father put the infirmary on lockdown this morning." He paused, then added, "Alyss has the plague, and Pilar... She's dead."

"I know. I was there."

"You were—? Oh. How did... How did she look?"

She grimaced, her stomach tightening at the memory of Pilar's scabbed flesh, her bulging bloodshot eyes, the feel of her limp weight in Mercy's arms. "You don't want to know."

"Oh." His face fell. "I don't know what we're going to do, Marieve. We've—"

Tamriel stopped and glanced at Elvira and Ser Morrison, then took Mercy by the elbow and led her several paces away, out of their earshot. Mercy tried not to focus on the warmth of his hand on her arm, or the fact that he didn't let go as he spoke. "We've already transported two dozen people from the castle to the tents outside the city. It just— It makes no sense. I've had the guard-commanders check every day for signs of infection among the castle staff, and it's been fine. But two days ago, it came out of nowhere. *Two dozen people.* We should have been able to root it out before it spread that much." Tamriel dropped Mercy's arm and rubbed a weary hand across his forehead, hissing in pain when one of his fingers brushed the cut. He lowered his hand, staring at the blood on his fingertips as if he'd forgotten about it.

"Allow me," Mercy said, then pulled her sleeve over her hand and dabbed gently at the blood streaked across his skin. The cut was long, but not deep. "You won't need stitches. Just make sure you keep it clean."

He smiled. "Thank you, Healer Marieve."

She made a face and pulled her hand back, ignoring the fluttering in her stomach. "About the plague... Is there anything...odd about the way it infects people?"

"Odd?"

"I mean, is it random, or does it seem like it's, um, choosing people?" she asked, fully aware of how absurd the notion sounded. When he did nothing but stare blankly at her, she explained what Lethandris had said about the disease preying on people, and Alyss's certainty that the priestess was correct. "It's ridiculous, I know, but...it's starting to sound like they might be right. The priestesses, Beggars' End, and now the castle? It keeps popping up out of nowhere."

"You...may have a point," Tamriel said slowly, the blood draining from his face. "The castle and the Church are the two most powerful institutions in the city, and Beggars' End... Well, it's not powerful, but it's one of the most highly populated areas in the city." He trailed off, considering what she'd said, then shook his head. "But that's impossible. A disease can't pick and choose."

"However it works, there's something more to it. It's not a normal plague." Out of the corner of her eye, she saw Ser Morrison shift his weight, looking impatient. Clearly, her time with Tamriel was nearing an end. "You should speak to your father. He knows something, I'm sure."

"Then let's ask him now." He grabbed Mercy's hand and led her toward the castle, Elvira and Ser Morrison dutifully falling into step behind them. As they walked along the side of the castle, passing slaves tending to the grounds, Tamriel asked in a low voice, "You don't care much for Calum, do you?"

Mercy started. Apparently, he hadn't been as oblivious to her dislike for Calum as she'd thought. The memory of their slashing swords filled her mind. She recalled her dream from several nights before of Tamriel lying on the floor, a pool of blood growing beneath him. *You failed me,* Calum had whispered. *Over and over again, you've failed me. But I've taken care of everything.*

He was losing patience. If she didn't act soon, he would find a way to kill the prince himself, damn the risks. She would not allow him to steal her contract.

"It's just... Do you trust him?"

Tamriel shrugged. "As much as I trust any member of the court. He's my cousin—we grew up almost as brothers—but I know he sometimes resents the fact that I am of royal blood and he is not. When we were younger, while I was being praised and paraded around all my father's social events, he sulked in the background, ignored by most of the nobility. Whenever someone did pay attention to him, he took it as pity," he said. "But that was a long time ago. I think he's grown up and realized that few people have the privilege of going home to a castle every night."

Mercy frowned at the levity in his tone. "Well, you know him better than I do, Your Highness. But if I were you, I'd keep an eye on him. Something about him gives me a bad feeling."

"Says the woman currently being tailed by one of my father's guards. Perhaps I should watch myself around you." He squeezed her hand, a grin tugging at his lips. "You don't have to worry about me. I think I proved I can handle myself in a fight."

"What, in that sparring match?"

"You're not impressed?"

Mercy raised a brow. "Was it meant to impress me?"

"Not necessarily, but it wouldn't be an unwelcome side effect."

She let go of his hand and walked ahead of him, lifting her chin. "I've seen better."

"You've seen better," Tamriel repeated skeptically. "Where?"

"You wouldn't believe me if I told you. Now, do you want to speak to your father, or not?"

"You're cruel," Tamriel said, then laughed and jogged after her.

42
TAMRIEL

"There isn't a cure for the plague, and you've known it all along. When were you going to tell someone?"

Tamriel stood before his father's desk, his arms crossed over his chest. The king sat with his eyes trained on the fire roaring in the hearth, his clothing rumpled, his hair hanging in loose waves around his face. He looked like he'd barely slept, but Tamriel didn't care. On the way to his father's study, Marieve had explained everything she'd witnessed during her time in the infirmary. The way she'd spoken about Pilar's visions had left a bone-deep chill within him. Something was preying on his people, and he had no idea how to stop it.

"What have we been doing all this time? What was the point of setting up those tents outside the city if not to save our subjects? Is it all just for show?"

Ghyslain ran a hand through his hair. "I'm doing my best, Tam."

"It's not enough. It never is." His voice turned cold. "What else are you not saying? What are you hiding?"

"Whose idea was it to ask me that? Yours or Marieve's?"

Trying to change the subject, as always. "Mine."

"I see." His father sat back in his chair, folding his hands in front of him. His eyes met Tamriel's. "And was it on your order that she asked for an audience with me this morning, as well?"

"That she— What?"

"She didn't tell you? I'm surprised, considering how much time you've been spending with her lately." He sighed. "Why, Tam? Why do you trust her? She's from Feyndara, in case you've forgotten—a country with which we are at war! You cannot allow her into your confidence."

Tamriel shook his head. He'd known all along that his father distrusted Marieve—Tamriel himself had distrusted her at first—but he'd since seen the sort of person she was. She wasn't like anyone else in the court. He'd seen the way Pilar's suffering had affected her the night of the Solari celebration. Few people would care so much for a stranger's well-being, and fewer still would put her life at risk to offer that stranger a modicum of comfort. Marieve had. "She has done everything you asked and been nothing but helpful to us. We owe her, Father."

"*I* do not owe her anything. Whatever foolish promises you've made to her are yours alone." The king rose, and although he stood a head taller than Tamriel, he didn't back down. "Someday, when you take the throne, you will make these decisions. You can meet with the Queen of Feyndara and negotiate for the Islands. You can give away all of Beltharos if it pleases you, as you seem so enthralled by the Feyndarans already."

"Don't be ridiculous."

"Ridiculous? It's not Marieve, then, who is standing outside, eavesdropping?"

He didn't blink, didn't turn to look at the closed double

doors. He merely narrowed his eyes. "Seeing ghosts again, Father? Who is it this time—Mother or the elven slut?"

Ghyslain jumped to his feet, knocking over the candelabra and sending a splatter of hot wax across the desk. The flames guttered out as it fell, thin ribbons of smoke rising from the blackened wicks. "Don't ever call her that, you ungrateful child. You have no idea what it was like, losing her—losing them both—"

"You're right!" Tamriel shouted, throwing his hands in the air. "I have no idea what it was like because you refuse to speak about it. You refuse to speak about anything remotely related to them. My entire life, all you've ever done is sulk and shout and push me away. I used to beg your advisors to tell me stories about Mother, because you've never told me anything! You think it was hard losing her? I never *knew* her!"

"Then you're lucky! You didn't grieve for her like I did!"

"You think I didn't *grieve?*" Tamriel asked, bewildered. "You think I don't ask myself every day why she had to die? That I never wondered why my father could barely stand the sight of me? It killed me to know you blamed me for her death. I blame *myself* for her death!"

Ghyslain went still. "Y-You do?"

Tamriel froze, more startled by the emotion in his father's voice than when he'd shouted. "How could I not?" he said quietly. "I read it on your face every time you looked at me. I've never been your son, not to you. You only see me as your wife's killer. It wasn't hard to start seeing myself the same way."

"Tamriel—" Ghyslain choked out, and the word held so much anguish it struck Tamriel like a blow to the gut.

He took a step back and closed his hands into fists. "Forget it. Just answer my question: what are you hiding about the plague?"

"Son—"

"You have no right to call me that."

They stared at each other, the tense silence between them becoming more and more charged by the second. Tamriel's chest tightened, anger and hurt churning within him. How could his father be surprised by his admission? Their relationship had long been broken, tainted forever by the events that had brought him into this world.

Ghyslain's sorrowful expression gave way to resignation. "There...may be a cure," he said slowly. "A flower native to the Cirisor Islands—Cassius Bacha saw it in a dream. But, Tamriel, you must not search for it. Promise me."

The cure isn't going to stop it—not completely, Pilar had told Marieve. *To end it, you must defeat the one who preys on the Islands. Myrbellanar.* Tamriel wasn't sure he trusted the half-delirious woman's ramblings, but he wouldn't ignore an opportunity to save his people, no matter how remote it seemed. He couldn't. Perhaps one of his father's men would figure out why Pilar had mentioned the Old God during his journey to the Islands.

"Promise you?" Tamriel asked, his brows rising. "Have you not sent men to retrieve the flower? You're willing to let our people suffer—to let them die. Why?"

"No, and I forbid you from searching for it on your own. It will only bring you and the rest of Beltharos harm. There's nothing you or I can do to stop it. I suggest you forget I even mentioned it, and put on a brave face before the court. That is all we can do. Trust me, Tamriel."

He gaped at his father, betrayal burning within him. How could he stand to do nothing? How could he let their people suffer? Ghyslain had never been a good king, but this was the final straw. His subjects needed him, and he had abandoned them. Tamriel would not do the same.

Ghyslain must have seen the minute change in his expression. The king rounded the desk and reached for Tamriel, but he backpedaled before his father could touch him. Ghyslain's face fell. He stopped mid-step, his hands falling to his sides. "Please," he whispered. "I can't lose you, too."

"You're mad."

"You must not go searching for the cure," Ghyslain said again, pleading. "It's too dangerous. I won't lose another person I love. Please, *please* promise me."

"Fine. I promise," Tamriel snapped.

Ghyslain's shoulders slumped with relief. "Thank you, Tam. Thank—"

Tamriel turned on his heel and walked out of the room, slamming the door behind him. Marieve, Ser Morrison, and the elven handmaid were waiting in the hall outside, and it was obvious from their expressions that they'd heard every word Tamriel and his father had spoken. He didn't care. He was too angry, tired, and hurt to care. Letting out a long breath, he leaned against the door, trying to regain his composure.

After a beat, he looked at Ser Morrison, who'd been steadfastly against allowing Marieve and her handmaid to listen in on his conversation with Ghyslain. "You heard my father. He's known about a potential cure all this time, and he's done nothing to help our people. Do you still think Marieve is the untrustworthy one here?"

The guard's gaze flicked from Marieve to the closed study doors. "I... I'm not sure, Your Highness."

"You are. She cannot hurt this kingdom any more than my father already has."

Without waiting for a response, he straightened and started down the hall, a cool mask of composure slipping over his features. His father could not be allowed to sit on the throne any longer. He'd done enough damage to Beltharos and its people.

Marieve fell into step beside him. "Are you alright?" she

asked softly, too quiet for the others to hear as they trailed behind.

No.

"I'm fine," he said.

He and Ghyslain had never spoken to each other that openly, that truthfully, before. Ghyslain had only ever been a stranger to him—the monster of his childhood, the broken husk who had haunted the castle corridors all Tamriel's life. He'd only intended to confront his father about the plague. But once he'd mentioned his mother, all his hurt and frustration had boiled over. It was long past the time they should have talked about her.

And Marieve had heard everything.

"...Do you really blame yourself for her death?" she whispered.

Every day.

He quickened his pace, eager to leave this conversation behind him, to forget what a fool he'd made of himself. "I have to speak to Master Oliver about sending some men to look for the flower. Ser Morrison will see you back home."

"Tamriel." She hurried after him and grasped his arm, pulling him around so he was forced to meet her eyes. She stepped close to him and studied him with her brows furrowed, the soft, clean scent of her perfume wrapping around him. "Please don't shut me out."

He glanced at Ser Morrison and the elf—who had stopped several yards back to allow them to speak in private—then down at her, feeling an ache grow within him. Tired. He was so damn tired of being alone in this cold, empty castle day in and day out. "Meet me in the library tonight. We'll speak then."

"Master Oliver!"

Tamriel ran through the soldiers' barracks, tripping over books and piles of clothing, until he spotted Master Oliver standing in the doorway of his office, speaking with several senior guard-commanders. He stopped mid-sentence and pushed the commanders out of his way as Tamriel approached, breathing hard.

"Creator's mercy, Your Highness. What's wrong?"

"We— We must speak in private. Your office?"

Master Oliver nodded and led Tamriel into the adjoining room, rounding his desk and shuffling the mess of papers and reports into a haphazard pile. At the sound of the door's bolt latching, he paused. "Your Highness?"

"Do you trust everyone in your command?"

"Of course," he responded without hesitation. "Why do you ask?"

"My father cannot know about this. I need you to send a company of guards to Cassius Bacha's house to inquire about a flower he dreamt of—"

"A flower?"

"He'll describe it to them. They must depart immediately for the Cirisor Islands, find it, and bring back as many as they can. Make sure they tell no one what they are doing." He sank into one of the armchairs before Oliver's desk and offered the Master of the Guard a weary, relieved smile. "We may have found the key to the plague's cure."

"And why do you not want your father to know?"

"Oh, he's known about the flower for a while—he just wasn't planning to tell anyone. He made me promise not to search for it, which is why you have to help me do it behind his back."

Master Oliver frowned. "Your Highness... I've known your father a long time. I've been in his service since before you were born. You're asking me to betray decades of trust and friendship to help you." He sat and rested his arms on the desk, hands folded before him. "Listen, son, the things your father does... He may be unpredictable at times, but if he made you promise not to pursue this, he must have a reason. He cares for you—"

Tamriel snorted, and Oliver fixed him with a look.

"You know he does."

"You've been more of a father to me than he ever was." Tamriel shook his head, toying with a loose thread on the arm of the chair. "I don't understand why he's not exhausting every opportunity to prevent our people's suffering. On good days, he's cautious—on bad, he's paranoid. But he's never selfish. Has he said anything about the cure to you?"

"Not a word."

"I thought not. Will you help me?"

The Master of the Guard hesitated, then nodded. "I'll have Leitha Cain visit Cassius right away, then gather a small company and start for the Islands today. A half-dozen men should be sufficient to travel there and back without drawing much attention."

"Six men? What if they encounter Feyndaran forces?"

"Leitha is one of our highest-ranking commanders—trained well, and resourceful, too. If she and her men find themselves in a jam, she'll get them out alright."

"No one will question her absence?"

"She often travels to gather recruits for the army and oversee training. No one will question it."

Tamriel stood, the weight on his chest marginally lessened. "Thank you." He started toward the door, but Master Oliver's voice halted him before he could reach for the handle.

"Your High— Tamriel."

"Yes?"

"Don't be so hard on him. Your father raised you the best

he could, while grieving and ruling the country, no less. Don't forget, you weren't exactly a saint as a child, either," he said, a wistful smile on his face. "Each of you carries blame and each of you is responsible for pushing the other away. I'm not saying it has to be now, but you know if you ever want to find peace, you have to forgive him."

Tamriel was quiet for several moments. "I'm trying," he finally said, then he walked out of the room.

43

That evening, Mercy opened Blackbriar's front door to find Ser Morrison sitting on the grass just beside the doorway, his head lolling to one side, legs stretched out before him. He was snoring quietly. To passersby, it would appear he was only slumbering, but Mercy could see the small dart sticking out of his neck just above his collar. She hadn't been sure how Calum would free her from Ser Morrison's watchful eyes, but he was resourceful, and she hadn't doubted that he would find a way. She bent down and picked it up, a small bead of blood welling where it had struck the guard. A scrap of paper had been wrapped around the shaft. She unfolded it and read the note scrawled in loose cursive:

You have about three hours before he wakes up and finds you missing—don't waste a second, love.

—C

Mercy crumpled the note and tucked it into her pocket,

smiling to herself. She wore fitted trousers and a loose, flowing tunic of crimson silk under a heavy woolen cloak—the garb was far from the finery she'd grown accustomed to in the court, but it was luxurious enough to fit in at the castle, and dark enough to blend into the night once she fled the city. Her sheathed daggers were tucked into the waistband of her pants. Tonight, her contract would be complete. She hadn't planned on Tamriel inviting her to meet him in the library, but she took what opportunities she was given.

"It's almost dark." Elvira stood in the doorway behind her, gazing up at the deep violet streaks painting the twilight sky. She passed Mercy a small coin purse, a slave sash and the Guild token Aelis had given her tucked within. "There's not much traffic going in and out of the city due to the plague, but they haven't closed off the gates, so you shouldn't have much trouble getting out. There are stables outside the city walls where you can secure a horse."

"Thank you."

"Good luck."

Mercy pulled her cloak tighter around herself as she started toward the castle. The hour wasn't terribly late, and the roads still bustled with pedestrians, carriages, and wagons carting last-minute shipments. No one paid her any heed as she walked through the castle gate and across the grounds. Guards roamed the gardens, but they didn't spare her more than a cursory glance as she rounded the side of the castle and approached the vine-covered trellises that disguised the servants' entrance. With the low light and the distance, she could have been any one of the castle slaves. Only a member of the staff would know of the entrance, anyway.

She found the door and unlatched the complicated locks as Owl had done the other night. It sprung open to a dark corridor, a far-off point of light flickering where the hall to the infirmary intersected the one ahead of her. Mercy pushed away thoughts of Alyss and the priestesses as she closed the door and started down the hall. She couldn't help them. She was an Assassin, nothing more.

Two flights of stairs later, she emerged in front of the library doors. They swung open with a whisper of well-oiled hinges, and a rush of warm air swept over Mercy. A fire crackled somewhere within.

"Tamriel?" she called softly as she wandered down the aisle between the floor-to-ceiling bookshelves. Iron ladders leaned against the shelves at regular intervals, the sides shiny where countless hands had rubbed the metal smooth. Oversized velvet settees overflowing with satin pillows and soft throw blankets were clustered around low tables along the center of the room. Heavy shadows draped across the high ceiling, dancing and shifting with the flickering candlelight from the sconces on the ends of the shelves.

At the rear of the library rose a huge black fireplace, a latticed iron gate protecting the ornate rug from the sparks flying from the crackling logs. Mercy's silent footsteps slowed as she approached, then untied the laces of her cloak and draped it over the back of the nearest settee. The prince was nowhere in sight. *Is this a trap?* Could he have somehow figured out that she wasn't who she'd claimed to be? She reached under the hem of her tunic, her fingers brushing the grip of one of her daggers, and—

She saw him.

Tamriel was sitting on the floor near the end of an aisle, his back against one of the bookshelves and a candelabra on the floor at his side. One of his legs was stretched before him, the other bent to prop up the spine of the book he was reading, and he was leaning into it as if wishing he could step into the pages and transport himself into another world.

Mercy had never seen him more at peace.

She let her fingers drop from the dagger and simply

stood there, watching him. His head was bent forward, a shock of hair falling into his face, a small crease between his brows as his eyes moved across the page. He bit his lip, his fingers curling tighter around the book's cover. Two more books were stacked beside him, as if he had decided to stay and read all night if that was how long it would take her to arrive.

She leaned against the shelf and crossed her arms loosely over her chest. "I can come back later, if you're busy."

Tamriel started and looked up, his lips spreading into a smile so bright it put the stars to shame. "Too busy for you?" He closed the book and placed it on the stack beside him, then stood. "Never."

"How did—"

Before she could say anything more, Tamriel closed the distance between them, cupped her face in his hands, and kissed her.

For a moment, Mercy stood frozen in shock. Her hands were pressed against his chest, curled in the soft fabric of his shirt, and she could feel the pounding of his heartbeat under her fingertips—the heartbeat she was supposed to be *ending* tonight. Yet as his mouth moved against hers, his teeth grazing her lower lip, every thought left her head.

Every thought except *I want this*.

She wrapped her arms around Tamriel's neck and rose onto her toes, smiling against his lips when he let out a soft chuckle. His hand slipped under the hem of her tunic and grazed her bare skin, leaving trails of heat over the curve of her hip, the dip of her waist.

Too soon, he pulled back, breathless, and rested his forehead against hers. "You have no idea how long I've wanted to do that," he whispered, his eyes still closed. When he leaned in to kiss her again, she turned her face away, guilt rising in a thick, choking wave within her.

What are you thinking? she wanted to scream at herself. *What the hell is wrong with you?*

She sucked in a shaky breath. "Have you spoken with the nobles about supporting your claim to the throne?"

He frowned at the sudden change of subject and released her. "I have. Unfortunately, they're all convinced it's a plot my father and I concocted to test their loyalties. I'm going to speak with them again tomorrow night and see if I can convince them to trust me."

"I'm sorry."

"Don't be. They listened, which means they'll at least consider supporting me. After the day we've had, this feels like a step in the right direction."

Mercy's brows rose. "Is that optimism? From *you?*" If he noticed the quiver in her voice, the shakiness of her hands, he had the grace not to show it.

"The guards Master Oliver dispatched spoke to Cassius Bacha and left for the Islands a couple hours ago. With luck, they'll send word of their progress by my birthday. Then I can reveal the truth of the cure—and my father's inaction—to the nobility, and hopefully that will persuade them to support my claim to the throne." He rubbed the back of his neck with a hand, frowning at the ground. After a moment, he looked up, troubled. "You heard my father earlier. Whatever he thinks is coming terrifies him."

She nodded. "So much so that he put the lives of everyone in this city at risk."

Tamriel bent down, picked up the candelabra, and set it atop the mantle of the fireplace. His fingers hovered an inch away after he released it, then he straightened. "No."

"No?"

"I won't dwell on this any longer. I'm done wracking my brain trying to make up excuses for that pitiful, broken man. All I can do is try to fix his mistakes." He stared into the fire, the light from the flames turning his olive skin copper. "You're not here to listen to my troubles. That's not why I asked you to come."

Tamriel turned toward her, his gaze dropping to her mouth. "Everything we've accomplished thus far, we've accomplished because of you. On Solari, Pilar came looking for you—her visions had led her to you. You suggested we seal off Beggars' End just days before a mob tried to raze the neighborhood. *You* figured out my father was hiding the cure." His smile widened. "Because of you, we will save thousands of lives."

Mercy stood frozen. Her heart thudded within her chest, the taste of his lips lingering on hers. *Remember your vow. Remember how Lylia tortured you all those years. Remember Calum.* Yet how could she focus on anything but the way Tamriel was watching her, a crooked grin tugging at his lips? This sullen, brooding, honorable, *beautiful* boy standing before her... "I wouldn't give myself that much credit."

He shook his head, his voice softening. "You're extraordinary, Marieve."

Tamriel placed his fingertips under her chin and tilted her head up until their gazes met. His eyes searched hers with an unspoken question, and he read the answer on her face. She swallowed painfully as he cupped her cheek, his thumb gliding over her skin.

Traitor! a voice within her screamed.

Tamriel leaned forward. She lifted her face in response, her fingers tracing the light stubble along his jaw. When their lips were only an inch apart, she closed her eyes and whispered, "We shouldn't do this."

He smiled. "What are you afraid of?"

So much.

A jolt rushed through her when their lips met again. She pulled him back until she was pressed against the bookshelf, her spine arching with pleasure. The shelf dug into her back, but she didn't care, hardly noticed as his hands slipped down her sides, exploring the curves of her body and leaving trails of heat in their wake.

Then he shifted, and his fingers brushed her back just above the handles of her daggers. Mercy stiffened, reality crashing down like a rush of ice-water, and pushed Tamriel away. She darted around him and picked up her cloak, trying not to look at the prince as she swept it around herself and clutched the fabric tightly in her fists.

"What's wrong?" Tamriel didn't move closer, didn't reach for her—just watched with a mixture of sadness and hurt on his face.

Mercy took a deep breath, raking her fingers through her hair to banish the memory of his touch. She felt unsteady, uprooted. The world had fallen off-kilter. She'd promised to marry him that day in his mother's tomb, but that had been Marieve speaking. She'd been playing her part. Tonight, she was just Mercy. He was so closed-off and cold around the court, but when they were alone, he let his armor fall. Somehow, he'd stripped her of hers, as well. The realization terrified her.

"I told you we shouldn't have done this," she said.

And then she bolted.

44
CALUM

"I told you we shouldn't have done this."

Mercy's words hardly registered in Calum's ears; it took a few moments for the impact of what he'd just witnessed to sink in, and he drew back into the shadows of the bookshelves just as her dark silhouette flew past the aisle in which he crouched. She didn't notice him, but it was still instinct to duck out of view after years of nobles kicking him out of every important state function he'd tried to attend as a child. The double doors swung shut behind her without a sound, and just like that, she was gone. Like a ghost—as if she'd never been.

And Tamriel was still alive.

Across the library, the prince let out a frustrated bellow, and something thumped loudly against one of the bookshelves. Calum jumped, then stood and peered around the edge of the shelves. Tamriel sat slouched on the settee before the fire, his head in his hands, the flames limning him in golden light.

She didn't kill him, he thought in disgust. *Even after everything I did for her, she couldn't do it.*

Calum pulled his dagger from the sheath on his belt, stepping out of his hiding spot and into the center of the library. His fingers tightened on the smooth leather grip of the dagger. So much for Mercy's bravado. She was a coward. Where was the vicious, heartless assassin he'd met in the Forest of Flames? Where was the girl who had risked death to cheat the Trial?

A black wave of rage flooded him.

After all these years, I should've known better than to rely on anyone else.

Calum crept forward, his footsteps silent on the ornate rug. He'd come tonight for this exact reason. He'd seen the way she and the prince looked at each other. He had known it was more than an act. Still, he had hoped he wouldn't have to be the one to end his cousin's life.

He stepped over the books splayed on the floor—Tamriel must have thrown them in his frustration—and stalked closer to the prince. On the settee, Tamriel lay on his side with his head propped on his arm like a pillow, his eyes shut and legs tucked in close to accommodate their length. His face was calm and relaxed, no trace of its usual sharpness. His breathing was even. Calum had no idea how much sleep Tamriel had been getting since they learned of the plague, but it certainly wasn't enough. Even now, in the soft light of the fire, he could see the shadows hanging under the prince's eyes. He shifted his grip on the dagger in his hand, the handle growing slick in his palm.

One slice, right across his throat.
Now, before he wakes.

Just as Calum made to lift his blade to Tamriel's throat, his cousin shifted, his hand falling limply over the side of the settee. A memory struck Calum at the sight, the sound of shattering ice ringing in his ears.

Calum hadn't recognized the sound at first. It was subtle—a faint crackle, like the scrape of autumn leaves against cobbles—and he'd thought it only the sound of their boots crunching on the snow. They didn't have winter in Sandori, not really. The nights grew cold and the lake gray and chilly, but it was nothing like the flat expanse of solid white surrounding them. The king had wanted them to remain in the castle where they'd taken lodging, hosted by some noble or other on their tour of the country, but Tamriel had insisted on exploring. Neither he nor Calum had seen snow before.

Which was why neither boy had realized that the ice over Bluegrass Valley's frozen lake was too thin to cross.

The little prince's laughter broke off into a shriek of terror as the ice shattered beneath him, a dark hole opening like the maw of a great beast and swallowing him whole.

Calum screamed, running, stumbling over the snowdrift and past the young boys standing petrified by the shore. One grabbed Calum's wrist, but he shoved him off without slowing, his eyes locked on his six-year-old cousin's hand as it bobbed once above the water and disappeared. Heedless of the danger, he broke into a sprint, his feet pounding on the ice. Tamriel surfaced again, his face pale and eyes wide.

"Calum!" he screamed, choking on the black water. "Help!"

He'd lost one of his gloves. His fingers scratched at the ice but couldn't find a hold, and he screamed again as his body was pulled under by the weight of his surcoat.

"Tam!" Calum cried. He dove onto his stomach as he neared the hole, nearly sliding in himself as he plunged his hands into the frigid water. His skin prickled as though stung by a thousand needles, and he cried out at the agony.

No no no no no

Please, Creator, please—

He reached as far as he could into the water, scrabbling for a hold on something familiar—Tamriel's hand, maybe, or the hood of his coat. Anything. The water numbed his fingers, but he could still feel enough to tell when something twined between them. Tamriel's hair? Calum pulled at it but came up with nothing but a handful of algae. He tossed it aside, a choked sob escaping his frozen lips, and plunged his hands back into the water.

Someone had run out after him. They tugged at his boot, shouting at him to come back, that it wasn't safe, that he wouldn't find the prince. Calum grunted in response and kicked at the hand wrapped around his ankle. He reached in further, the water up to his shoulders.

Creator, please don't let him die, Creator—

His arm struck something solid. Calum let out a cry of victory as he recognized the thick fur trim of Tamriel's surcoat. He closed his hand around his cousin's forearm and dragged him up to the surface. The second he broke through, Tamriel began to cough and sputter, his lips a terrifying shade of blue. He struggled against Calum's grasp, caught in the claws of panic, and Calum's heart stuttered when he nearly lost his grip on Tamriel's arm. Grunting with the effort, he wrapped his arms around Tamriel's chest and yanked him up, not letting go until he'd pulled his cousin back to the safety of the shore.

Calum peeled off his cousin's soaked coat, tossing it aside and wrapping his own around the younger boy's shoulders. The other boys had run back to the castle for help, and Calum could see the king, the noble, and several guards running toward the lake, struggling through the thick snow. Tamriel curled up on his side and vomited dark lake water onto the snow as, beside him, Calum sobbed. After he'd expelled more water than Calum had thought possible, Tamriel rolled over and clasped Calum's hand in a vice grip, his hand small and trembling, but strong.

The little prince attempted a smile. "I really don't like winter."

Calum stumbled away from the couch, the clarity of the memory making him weak in the knees. "Damn it," he whispered, sheathing his dagger. His fingers shook when he let go, and he clenched them into a fist. He couldn't do it. Not tonight, at least. Biting back a string of curses, he turned and left the library, easing the door shut behind him without a sound.

In the hallway, he made it three steps before stopping and turning back, reaching for the door handle.

Just one slice, and it'll be done.

"Coward," he cursed himself. "Go back inside and—"

He tugged at his hair. Tamriel was innocent—innocent and as close to a brother as Calum had ever had. He'd forged the contract on the prince's life to get revenge on the king, but did it have to be this way? Ghyslain was the one who had hired the Assassins to kill his father, the man who'd orchestrated the plot to murder Liselle. Drake had done nothing more than his duty, protecting Beltharos when the king was too blind with love to see the threat Liselle posed to the kingdom. Did his father not deserve to be avenged? For all the pain the king had caused Calum's family, losing his son and his throne seemed a fitting punishment.

And yet, could Calum betray the man who had brought him into his home, who had raised him, to avenge the father he'd never known?

Calum took a deep breath. He pivoted on his heel and returned to the great hall, then mumbled, "The prince is asleep in the library. Make sure he doesn't burn the place down," to the first guard he saw. She nodded and began to run, her footfalls echoing through the empty hall as Calum opened the double doors and walked out into the night.

45
ELISE

Something pinged on the window.
Elise looked up from her painting, her brows furrowing in confusion. A second later, the sound came again, and she sighed and placed her palette and brush on the stool beside her. Her soft skirts swished quietly over the stone tile as she crossed to the window and cupped her hands against the glass, peering out into the night. A dark, familiar figure stood in the alley below.

"Creator help me," she breathed. She stepped into the hall, pausing at the sound of her parents' voices drifting from her father's study. If she was quiet, they wouldn't hear the whisper of her slippers on the staircase. Liri had already gone home after serving dinner, and Aelyn would be busy cleaning up the kitchen at this hour. Biting her lip, Elise tiptoed down the stairs and hurried to the front door.

"Elise?"

She cringed and turned. Aelyn stood in the archway to the kitchen, wiping her hands with a towel. "Everything alright?"

"Of course. I just need some air." Upstairs, her mother laughed, and Elise's gaze darted to the front door. After her outburst the night Marieve had come for dinner, her parents had been watching her with eyes like a hawk. They'd convinced themselves she would try to find a way into Beggars' End to see Atlas and end up catching the plague. She hoped Aelyn hadn't been commanded to keep her under watch.

The elf nodded. "Just be careful out there—don't go near anyone who could be sick. I'll be in the kitchen if you need me. Would you like some tea when you return?"

"That would be lovely,"

"Okay, it'll be ready in a few minutes." She smiled and turned to leave, then stopped and looked back over her shoulder. "Do you think Calum would like some, too?"

Elise nearly choked. "*Aelyn!*"

She held up a hand. "I won't tell them he's here, but you must get rid of him. Your father won't take kindly to him lurking outside. He needs to accept the fact that you're betrothed to someone else."

Relief swept over her. "I know. Thank you."

Satisfied, Aelyn returned to her work in the kitchen. Elise slipped outside and pulled the front door closed behind her, then rounded the side of the house. Calum stood just below the window to her studio, one hand full of pebbles and the other poised to throw. Annoyance rushed over Elise.

"What are you doing here? You're not supposed to—" Elise hissed, but Calum's kiss cut her off. She lifted a hand to push him away, but before she could, he pulled back, frowning.

"She didn't do it."

"She didn't—*what?* Mercy didn't kill him? Why?"

He shook his head. "I tried to do it, to get it over with, but... Elise, he's my cousin. He's the only real family I have."

She frowned. "Your father was your family."

"I know, but I can't be the one to kill Ta—" He glanced

around, then lowered his voice. The words came out a broken rasp, laced with misery and self-loathing. "I can't be the one to kill Tamriel. I just...can't do it."

She sighed and laced her fingers through his, stroking little circles with her thumb. "I know. I don't want to hurt Tamriel either, but this was your idea, remember? I love you, but I'm betrothed to someone else."

"Leon." Calum spat his name like a curse.

"Yes, and you know I have to marry him—"

"You don't."

"Yes," she said, tightening her grip on his hand. "I do, because no matter what my brother does, they'll never give him the title of Cain—not after they found him with Julian. Now he's locked in Beggars' End, surrounded by people who are sick and dying and would kill for a single coin, and it's only a matter of time before he—"

Her voice broke, and Calum wrapped her in his arms. Creator, she'd missed him during his year-long journey with the Strykers. She fought the tears welling in her eyes, the crushing hopelessness that had threatened to tear her apart since she'd learned of Atlas's fate. Once she had regained her composure, she stepped out of Calum's embrace, wishing she didn't have to. Wishing things were different. "It's my responsibility to care for my family, and I can do that by marrying Leon and becoming a Nadra. I can't marry you, Calum—not if you're a commoner."

He hung his head. "I know."

"I have to go before my father notices I'm not in my studio." Elise waited a moment, expecting him to object and beg for a moment longer. They'd gone through this ritual a thousand times before. It never became any easier.

When he said nothing, she turned and began to walk away, hating the tears that prickled in her eyes.

"Wait—" he blurted, and she stopped in her tracks, her heart lifting.

"Yes?"

"I have an idea. Tomorrow night, I need you to go to Blackbriar and escort Mercy to Tamriel's meeting with the nobles an hour early. I'll speak to that skittish handmaid of hers and have her send a letter back to the Guild saying Mercy's in trouble. With any luck, they'll send someone to collect her and complete the contract before Tamriel's birthday next week. We won't have to do a thing. If not..." He trailed off, looking uncomfortable.

"It'll be up to us," Elise finished.

He nodded grimly.

"I understand. Goodnight, Calum."

"Goodnight, my love."

46
TAMRIEL

Tamriel's eyes flew open, and he sat up abruptly. "Marieve?" he called hopefully, turning around to search the dark library for her, but no response came. He was alone. Strange. He thought he'd heard someone moving behind him, but he must have imagined it. He hadn't been sleeping nearly enough since Solari.

He groaned and ran his hands through his hair. *Look what you've done, you idiot. Not for the first time today, you've gone and made a fool of yourself.* He remembered with a flush of embarrassment the look of surprise on Marieve's face when he had kissed her, the way she'd tensed when his lips met hers. For a moment, he'd been seized with panic when she hadn't immediately kissed him back, but it had all vanished a second later when she melted in his arms. Creator, he hadn't wanted that kiss to end.

Yet everything—the fear, the nerves—had come crashing back when she'd backed out of his embrace and fled from the room.

She hadn't looked back.

Tamriel shoved the memory away. He stood and piled the

books he'd thrown on the low table beside the settee, then blew out the flames of the candelabra. His fingers drummed against his thigh as he walked the length of the library and stepped into the hall, nearly colliding with a guard who had just turned the corner.

"Forgive me, Your Highness," she said breathlessly, a flush rising on her cheeks. "Your cousin said you were sleeping in the library, and he didn't want you left alone."

Calum must have come to speak with him about something; he was the person Tamriel had heard moving in the library. "He does know I'm a grown man, doesn't he? I can take care of myself."

"Rightly so, Your Highness. Shall I escort you to your bedchamber?"

"No, thank you." He started in the direction of his room, then paused, remembering a conversation between advisors he'd overheard. "The healers in the infirmary tents have been working on cures, haven't they? And they've sent samples here for Alyss to test?"

"Yes, but she hasn't come to collect them in several days. Rumor has it she's been infected, too."

"Can you take me to where they are being stored?"

The guard nodded and led him through several corridors, then into a long-unused meeting room someone had converted for storing the potential cures. The central table was laden from end to end with small glass vials, the mixtures inside illuminated by the moonlight pouring in through the open drapes. There had to be hundreds here. Tamriel's heart sank at the sight. So much hope bottled up in those little vials, so much time spent researching and mixing and testing, and not a one could save the thousands of sick people languishing throughout the city. His only consolation was that while they wouldn't cure the plague, they'd been crafted by skilled healers with the symptoms of the disease in mind.

They wouldn't cure anyone—not without the flower from the Cirisor Islands—but perhaps they could temporarily alleviate a patient's pain.

He picked up one of the vials and rolled the cool glass between his fingers, watching the pale pink liquid slosh against the sides. "What is your name?" he asked, turning back to the guard, still waiting in the doorway.

"Vela, Your Highness."

"Please fetch me a bag and gloves, Vela—and call for a carriage."

She obeyed, and when she returned, he carefully placed as many of the wax-sealed vials into the soft canvas bag as he could fit, then slung it over his shoulder and followed Vela to where the carriage waited at the base of the castle's front steps. As they walked, he tugged on the supple leather gloves she had brought him, much too fine for what he was planning.

"Shall I accompany you, Your Highness?"

Tamriel glanced up at the castle's tall, imposing structure, the gilded towers and flecks of obsidian reflecting fragments of the starry night sky. He imagined his father inside, doing Creator-knew-what while his people suffered beyond the castle walls. "Come with me if you wish—I won't order you. I'm going to Beggars' End."

Her throat bobbed, but she nodded. She called their destination to the driver before clambering into the carriage behind Tamriel, her mouth set in a tight line.

"I know it's dangerous," Tamriel said. "You don't have to risk your life for this."

"I am sworn to protect you, Your Highness. My place is at your side."

When they reached the outer wall surrounding Beggars' End, they found three guards standing watch over the gate. It wasn't the same one the mob had tried to break through only days ago, but Master Oliver had posted more guards all around the slums in case they tried again. Usually, the gates were unmanned. That's why Tamriel had been able to work with Hero and Ketojan these past few years. The three young men bowed as Tamriel and Vela approached.

"Let us through the gate, please," Tamriel said to Dorian, the eldest of the trio. When the guard straightened, his brows furrowed in confusion, Tamriel added in a tone that brooked no argument, "That's a command, not a request."

"Of course, Your Highness." He lifted the large ring of keys at his hip and unlocked the heavy padlock. The iron gate creaked as it swung open, and the three guards exchanged concerned looks as Tamriel and Vela stepped through. The clang of the gate closing behind them echoed in the silence of the night. Vela rested a cautious hand on the grip of the sword sheathed at her side.

Together, they walked along the narrow streets, skirting potholes and pools of what Tamriel hoped was merely foul-smelling water. They passed shops with broken shutters and peeling paint, sagging houses reeking of filth and rot, and, occasionally, small groups of people huddled in the alleys, who peered out at them with sunken, feverish eyes. Vela stuck close by his side, the jingling of her chainmail and the quiet clinking of the glass vials the only sounds. Finally, a large warehouse came into sight before them, one of the few still standing in the slums. As they approached, a familiar figure pushed off the wall and started toward them.

"No one's supposed to be out this late," Atlas called, lifting a lantern and peering out into the darkness. "By decree of the king."

"At ease, friend," Tamriel said, and Atlas's brows shot up at the sound of his voice.

"Your Highness?"

"The one and only." They met in the middle of the block,

the lantern's flame temporarily blinding Tamriel after the long trek through the End. Once his eyes had adjusted, he reached into his pocket and pulled out a small envelope Elise had given him the day before. Atlas's eyes widened when he recognized her perfect, elegant cursive. "This is for you."

"Your Highness, please tell me you didn't venture all the way out here to deliver a letter."

"I promised your sister that she could write to you. She made quite a fuss when she found out you were stuck here."

"Sounds like her." He choked on a laugh and accepted the letter, slipping it into his pocket to read later. "Will you let her know I'm okay? The other guards and I are watching out for one another. We'll be alright."

"Is that true?"

Atlas looked away. "We...lost Willard and Geoff to the plague two days ago." Tamriel didn't recognize the names, but his chest tightened at the grief in Atlas's voice. "Please don't tell her that, Your Highness. Tell her I'll see her when this is all over. Soon."

Tamriel placed a hand on the guard's shoulder. "I'll tell her," he promised. "I trust all has been quiet since the district was put under quarantine."

"In some ways. In others, not so much. When people are trapped in a place—unable to work, unable to do much of anything—they grow restless, and restlessness can be dangerous. Just within the first few hours of lockdown, violence between humans and elves here tripled. People panicked when the gates were locked. But, uh, as more people fall sick, the streets grow more empty by the day."

Tamriel started toward the warehouse, the guards falling into step beside him. The light from Atlas's lantern bobbed as they walked, the small orange flame reflecting in the shards of glass hanging in the windows where the wooden boards had rotted away. Even after almost twenty years, streaks of soot marred the gray stone, scars from a blaze that had claimed over a dozen buildings and taken the city's firemen two days to extinguish.

"I've brought what medicine I could," Tamriel said, gesturing to his canvas bag. "They haven't been tested because our healer is...indisposed...at the moment."

When they reached the door, Atlas set the lantern at his feet and pulled three handkerchiefs from his pocket. He handed one to Tamriel, who tied it over his mouth and nose, then turned to Vela. He stopped Atlas before he could hand her one. "You two are waiting out here."

They objected in unison.

"But—"

"Your Highness—"

Tamriel huffed. "If one more guard questions my orders tonight, I'll have the lot of you thrown into Lake Myrella."

They closed their mouths.

"Atlas, your family has served mine for generations. I owe too much to your father and sister to allow you to put yourself more in harm's way. You shouldn't have been locked in here in the first place. Vela, wait out here until I return. I *will* return," he said with a wry smile at her stricken look. *It's hardly my first visit to Beggars' End*, he thought, but he didn't dare voice it.

"Take the lantern," Atlas said. "The moonlight's enough for us to see by."

He accepted it, then turned to the front door of the warehouse. The whoosh of air that greeted Tamriel when he stepped into the building was thick and stale, putrid with the odor of unwashed bodies. The lantern's flame sputtered and flickered, illuminating the vague shapes of people huddled in blankets against the walls, strung up on stained hammocks between large stone pillars, or lying on the bare ground. It was nearly impossible to tell which were dead and which were merely sleeping. All was silent save for the quiet rasp of labored breaths.

"Here," Tamriel whispered as he knelt beside an elderly woman with raw, inflamed skin. He broke the wax seal on the vial and poured the contents into the woman's half-open mouth, catching a droplet that dribbled down her chin with a gloved fingertip. "Rest now. The medicine will ease your pain."

The woman nodded once, weakly, and her eyes fluttered shut.

Tamriel worked quickly across the massive room, rationing the medicine as much as possible. He sidestepped more corpses than he cared to count, stopping only to close their eyelids and send a prayer to the Creator for their passage into the Beyond. No priestess would pray for the lives lost in the End. There were simply too many.

By the time he climbed the steps to the second floor, three-quarters of the vials were empty, and Tamriel's heart was heavy with grief. Nestled in among the dying and the dead, he'd found an elven woman clutching her dead child to her breast, stroking her babe's round, colorless cheeks as silent sobs wracked her body. She hadn't said a word to Tamriel, only holding her child closer and shaking her head vehemently every time Tamriel had offered her medicine. Her eyes had been as hollow and lifeless as the bodies scattered around her.

He was pulling an empty vial from a sick man's lips when soft footsteps sounded behind him. "I knew I'd find you here," Tamriel said quietly.

"Where else would I be when my people need me?" Ketojan asked, his voice a deep rumble. He crossed the room and stopped beside Tamriel, cocking his head. "Are you sure it's wise of you to be here?"

"No," Tamriel admitted. He stood and shifted the bag, the empty vials clinking. "Is she here?"

"Upstairs." Ketojan plucked the lantern out of Tamriel's hand and led him up the stairs on the far wall. Like most of the warehouse, the stone was soot-stained and chipped from age and wear, a few steps slanted dangerously to one side. "Your father made a bold show outside the castle, I'm told. Whipping the mob leaders outside the gate where Liselle was killed? One might think he cares about us poor wretches."

"Half of Sandori knows he is sympathetic to the elves." As always, Liselle's name set his teeth on edge. While he understood her desire to see the slaves freed, she would forever be the woman who had torn his family apart.

"Half of Sandori *thinks* he is sympathetic to the elves. Whispers without proof are just that, son. *Whispers*. Nothing more. And what of you? What do the people make of their prince?"

"I'd like to think I'm better at hiding my allegiances than my father."

"If you keep visiting like this, someone will put two and two together eventually."

"Then I'll just have to hope I have the power of the throne behind me when they do."

"And with your growing feelings for a certain Feyndaran lady come to light..."

Tamriel was glad Ketojan was in front of him on the stairs; he couldn't see his face flush. "How do you know so much about the goings-on outside of this place?"

"You aren't the only one who works in secrecy, Your Highness."

"Hm." It didn't surprise him. Ketojan and Hero had been working together to free elves from their human masters for decades, long before the name *Liselle* meant anything to anyone. Tamriel was merely a piece of their operation—a rather important piece, but still. There was only so much information they trusted to him.

Ketojan left the lantern on the floor when they reached the top of the stairs. Half of the roof had collapsed after the fire and never been repaired, and through the gap, the stars twinkled brightly against the nighttime sky. Bathed in their silver light were a dozen bodies wrapped in stained and patched sheets. A woman was kneeling over the farthest one, her head bowed and lips moving as she murmured a prayer for the dead. One of her arms was in a sling, her shoulder swollen and bruised beneath the rags she wore. When she looked up at Tamriel, his heart broke.

"Hero," he croaked. "I'm so—" He couldn't force out the word *sorry*; it felt too small, too feeble, too flimsy after what he'd done to her.

She rose and walked to him, resting her good hand on his arm. The light, gentle touch caused a lump to form in his throat. In her eyes was none of the malice or contempt she had shown the king, and somehow, that made it worse. Ketojan crossed the room and leaned against the wall, crossing his arms loosely over his chest as he stared out into the night, providing them a moment of privacy. His white hair practically glowed in the moonlight.

"You could have told him it was me," Tamriel breathed. "By the Creator, Hero, you—you should have told my father and the court that I was the one helping you. They wouldn't have hurt you... *I* wouldn't have hurt you. I'm so..." This time, he did manage to say it, but he had to look away to stomach his shame. "I'm so sorry."

Hero moved her hand from his arm to his cheek, turning him so he was facing her. She made a sound that might have been *I forgive you*, but Tamriel didn't dare to hope.

"Our Hero is tough," Ketojan said, his voice soft with affection. "That wasn't the first time she'd been threatened or tortured"—Tamriel flinched at the word—"and it will hardly be the last. Even so, the reward far outweighs the risk."

Hero nodded. She took Tamriel's hand and led him to Ketojan, gesturing to the elf. He hesitated, then pulled a sheaf of papers out of his tattered jacket. He handed them to Tamriel. "The noble Davron Eddas. You know him?" When Tamriel nodded, he continued, "Apparently he's a less than desirable owner—if such a one exists. Three elves have contacted us from outside the End wishing to flee to the Islands. They've scraped together enough money for food and supplies, but need help sneaking past the guards now that Hero's tunnel out of the End has been filled."

Tamriel turned to her. "You're sure you want to continue this? The price you've already paid—"

Hero's eyes shone with fierce protectiveness as she nodded, and Tamriel knew there was no talking her out of it. As long as there were elves in need, she would be there to help them.

He handed the papers back to Ketojan. "Then consider it done. The next guard schedule goes out in three days. I'll find a way to intercept it and apprise you of the gaps." He glanced from Ketojan to Hero, their faces tight and grim. "Tell me how else I can help."

47

Mercy leaned against the well in the center of the market as dawn broke over the city, turning the Guild coin over and over between her fingers. She grimaced when the early morning sunlight reflected off the shiny teardrop embossed in the center and into her tired eyes. It would be so easily to let go, to watch it fall through the air and hear the *plink* of the coin breaking the water's still surface, swallowed forever in its inky depths.

She ran the edge of her thumb over her lips, feeling the ghost of Tamriel's kiss, and sighed. She'd wandered through the city all night, too restless to return to Blackbriar, too certain Elvira would read the truth of her failure on her face. The muscles in her legs ached, her silk slippers pinching at her toes.

A child's laugh sounded across the square and Mercy looked up, closing her fist around the Guild token. A woman stepped out of a shop and closed the door behind her, a bucket in one hand, her daughter following close at her heels. The girl giggled as she hopped from one cobblestone to the next, her copper ringlets bouncing.

As they neared the well, the girl stopped, her smile giving way to a scowl. "Mama," she said, "why is the knife-ear staring at us?"

The woman shot Mercy a dark look. "I don't know. It should mind its business if it doesn't want us to report it for not wearing its slave sash. It should know better than to slink around like a dog without its tags."

Anger flared within Mercy, but she merely pocketed the coin and walked away without a word.

She turned the corner out of the market and rubbed her tired eyes with the heels of her palms. *Where did everything go wrong?* she wondered for the millionth time. A shiver trailed down her spine at the memory of the prince's hands roving over her hips, exploring the dip of her waist, before she shoved thoughts of him aside. The daggers tucked in her waistband felt cold against her flesh, much too cold, and the Guild coin was heavy in her pocket. They felt like betrayal.

A while later, she found herself standing in front of Blackbriar, not entirely sure how she had walked all the way back without realizing it. Although whatever drug Calum had given him had long worn off, Ser Morrison was still slumped beside the front door, snoozing. Elvira had been kind enough to drape a blanket over him. Mercy didn't want to risk waking him, so she slipped around to the back of the house and tapped on one of the study windows as loudly as she dared.

"Come on, Elvira," she murmured. A few minutes later, the sleepy, frizzy-haired elf appeared in the doorway, clad in a rumpled nightgown. Her mouth dropped open when she saw Mercy. She pushed the window open and grabbed Mercy's elbow to help her through. "I hadn't expected to see you again. The prince is still alive, then?"

Mercy nodded once, in no mood to explain what had happened. "For now."

Mercy woke late that evening, still in the clothes she'd worn the night before, and ignored the rumbling in her stomach as she crossed to the wardrobe against the far wall. Behind the extravagant silks and fine brocades hung the threadbare tunics and trousers she'd brought with her from the Keep. Her leather boots sat on the bottom of the wardrobe, atop the small bag that had carried her belongings. She pulled them all out and laid them on the bed, tucking her worn Guild clothes into the bag, then changed into a simple black tunic and tucked her sheathed daggers into the waistband of her pants. Her usual silk slippers she traded for her old leather boots. The woolen cloak she'd worn the night before hung from one of the bedposts, and she grabbed that as well, draping it across her shoulders.

Once everything was packed away, she slung the bag over her shoulder, expecting it to be heavier than it was. Was that all her life amounted to? A couple pieces of ratty clothing and two daggers? As much as she might pretend otherwise, she would miss the luxuries to which she'd grown accustomed in the capital—the fine food, the downy mattress and silken sheets, even the gowns. Compared to Blackbriar, her gray, sparse bedroom in the Keep was no better than a cell.

Mercy pushed the thought from her mind and went down to the kitchen, where Elvira was busy cleaning dishes. Last night had been a mistake, and she was going to right it. She'd mourn for Tamriel, but she would complete her contract. She'd worked for this moment all her life.

"I thought it best to let you sleep, since you're going to be riding most of the night. Here," Elvira said, nodding to a plate of chicken with roasted vegetables. Mercy's stomach rumbled again at the sight. As she ate, Elvira wrapped bread, nuts, cheese, and several pieces of dried meat into a small bundle and set it beside her. "So you won't have to stop somewhere on the road. Should last you a day or two, and by then, you'll be well enough away from the city to stop in a tavern somewhere for rest and a real meal. Considering the animosity between Beltharos and Feyndara, the guards likely won't realize you're from the Guild, and will assume that the murder was politically motivated. They'll be searching the eastern roads for Lady Marieve, not the southern for an Assassin."

Mercy nodded, swallowing the last bite of chicken. "Thank you. For everything."

"You're welcome."

A comfortable silence settled over them as Mercy washed her plate and tucked the bundle of food into her bag. She wasn't sure whether she'd be able to return to Blackbriar before fleeing Sandori, so she would stash it somewhere with easy access in the city before heading to the castle to find Tamriel.

And this time, she wouldn't falter.

"You and your husband are going to make a run for the Islands once my contract is complete, aren't you?" Mercy asked as she picked up her bag. When Elvira nodded, she said, "Good luck."

"And to you, Daughter."

Mercy crossed the length of the hall and reached for the front door. Just before her fingers made contact with the handle, a loud knock sounded on the other side, surprising her. She set her bag on the floor, out of sight, and opened the door to find Elise standing there, her fist still hovering in the air. The serenna took one look at her outfit and raised a brow. "Going somewhere?"

"Depends. Do you need something?"

"I don't, but Tamriel asked for you." Her gaze flicked to back to the street, then she leaned in and whispered, "It's about his meeting with the nobles—he wants you to attend. Hearing about the potential for peace between our countries might persuade more nobles to support him."

"Very well." That wasn't what she'd expected, but she'd find an opportunity to kill the prince at some point this evening. In fact, it might even work in her favor. Once news got out that the prince had met with members of the court to plan how he was going to usurp his father's throne, suspicion would be placed on every noble in attendance that night. In the chaos, no one would notice that she'd fled until it was too late.

She stepped outside and pulled the door closed behind her, noting with a mixture of surprise and happiness that Ser Morrison was nowhere to be seen. "What happened to the guard?"

"He *may* have been called away to deal with a plague outbreak across the city," she said with a sly grin. "Shall we?"

Mercy reached into her pocket and closed her fingers around the Guild coin, the metal warm from the heat of her body. "Let's go."

48
ELVIRA

Elvira watched from one of Blackbriar's front windows as Mercy trailed after the serenna, her clothes drab and gray compared to the blonde girl's rich emerald gown and sparkling jewelry. It felt odd to see the Assassin in clothes like those she'd worn the day she arrived in the city. The girl had changed. She'd walked into the castle a living weapon, but her time among the court had softened her. Her time with the *prince* had softened her. Oh, she was still deadlier than most people could ever hope to be, but she'd begun to let the life she'd led as Lady Marieve tempt her. She'd lowered her guard. Elvira had seen it happen to many of the younger Daughters over her years in Mother Illynor's service.

She wondered idly if Mercy would be strong enough to kill the prince tonight, or whether she would fail again. She'd have to kill him eventually. Allowing him to live would be a death sentence for them both. Mother Illynor had contacts all around the world, and sooner or later, Mercy would be found and killed. Another Daughter would be sent to complete the contract on the prince's life, and that would be the end of it. Mercy knew that. A bit of hesitation wasn't unusual for a Daughter's first contract, but she would get over it. There was no other choice.

Elvira flipped a heavy envelope over and over in her hands. It bore no name, no address, no marking at all save for the teardrop pressed into the top corner of the paper. The prince's cousin had arrived unannounced earlier that afternoon and explained what had happened between Mercy and the prince the day before. Mercy had been soundly asleep two floors above, oblivious to the fact that anyone else knew of the kisses she'd shared with the prince. Elvira had tried to persuade Calum to be patient, to give Mercy another chance, but he'd been adamant that she send the letter to Mother Illynor. He didn't trust her to complete the contract—which he'd reluctantly revealed was a forgery. Elvira didn't care. All she wanted was to find Kier and escape to the Islands. The petty squabbles and power grabs of the courtiers didn't concern her in the slightest.

The letter Calum had written claimed that Tamriel had discovered Mercy's identity and was holding her in the dungeon for execution. Mother Illynor would send Daughters to collect her and complete the contract; she would never let an investment like Mercy rot in a cell for long.

Elvira ran her thumb over the Guild's teardrop sigil. She'd never been certain whether it was meant to represent the blood of the Guild's victims or the tears of those who'd lost loved ones to Illynor's ruthless Assassins.

One more chance, Mercy, she thought as she slipped the envelope into her pocket. If the prince was alive by sunrise, she would send it.

49
CALUM

Calum crouched in the shadow of the castle's outer wall, his eyes trained on the front door of the late queen's house. Gifted to her by the king, the house had once been one of the largest and most opulent in the city, tall columns supporting the second-floor balcony that looked out over the street and across to the imposing façade of the castle. The flower boxes on the large bay windows had once overflowed with colorful blossoms. Now, its crumbling form slumped like a decaying corpse in the center of the block, its white limestone grayed and weathered, its pillars cracked and covered in ivy. Shards of glass hung from the window frames like jagged teeth.

Calum crossed the street and slipped through the gap between the queen's manor and the neighboring one until he emerged at the rear of the house. What had originally been intended as a private garden now overflowed with brambles, some of the weeds higher than Calum's waist. He clambered over the low stone wall surrounding the property and trudged through them toward the back door. They caught and tugged on his clothes, and he tried not to think of all the insects, mice, and other vermin that undoubtedly lived in this mess. *Look at all I do for you, Father,* he thought sullenly. *Just look at what I'm willing to do.*

One of the rear windows had been shattered. He pulled the hem of his shirt over his hand and swept the bits of broken glass off the sill and into the grass. He glanced at the door a few paces away and sighed. One of the hinges had rusted away completely but, even if he could open it without alerting the entire block to his presence, the wood had warped out of its original shape. He hoisted himself over the sill and, as he did, a sharp pain sliced through his shoulder. A fat, warm drop of blood rolled down his arm as he dropped to the ground and spotted the shard of glass he hadn't seen, sticking out just a few inches from the frame. He reached up and felt the wound. It wasn't deep; he'd bandage it later when he returned to the castle.

Outside, the moonlight had helped him to see, but here, heavy velvet curtains reeking of mildew covered each of the intact windows, blocking out nearly every modicum of light. Once his eyes adjusted, he could vaguely make out the shapes of furniture and tarp-covered canvases scattered around the room. Most of Elisora's art collection had been locked away in the castle after her death, but the less expensive stuff had been thrown here and forgotten.

The sharp sound of metal snapping echoed from the front of the house, and Calum froze. Tamriel was here. He must have broken the aged lock which had held the front door closed. He was early, so he wouldn't think anything of the fact that none of the nobles were here to speak with him. Calum had never bothered to invite them to this meeting. They were too unpredictable, and he didn't want any surprises tonight.

Calum slowly made his way into the hall, carefully skirting the piles of animal droppings on the floor. He pulled his dagger from its sheath and crept forward silently, peering into the foyer through the open doorway.

Tamriel had taken off his cloak and tossed it aside, revealing the shining armor he wore over his finery. He wasn't foolish enough to meet in secret with the courtiers without it, but unfortunately for him, it wouldn't make a difference in the end. Calum could see that the prince was nervous. When a gust of wind blew outside, whistling through the broken windowpanes somewhere upstairs, he jumped. His hand moved to the sword sheathed at his hip as if to remind himself it was there.

Calum moved out of the doorway and into the room, flipping the dagger's grip in his hand. *I will not be weak. I will not give in to affection like I did in the library.* Tamriel, not hearing Calum's approach, took a step toward the window, his hand rising to pull the curtain aside. Calum lifted the dagger and swung. The pommel connected with Tamriel's skull with a sickening *thunk*, and the prince crumpled to the ground at Calum's feet, a low moan escaping his lips as he lost consciousness.

50

"This is where he's meeting them."

Mercy frowned up at the derelict manor, crinkling her nose in disgust. "I understand he needs to work in secrecy, and it's his mother's house, but why would Tamriel want to meet with the nobles in there? I can practically smell the shit from here."

"Hiding in plain sight. Only the lowliest of beggars deign to sleep here."

Elise led her up to the front of the house and knocked on the door. Nerves danced within Mercy. She didn't know what to expect of this meeting with the nobles, but she would play her part, and once they'd left, she would kill Tamriel.

No one came to answer the door.

Elise glanced at her, then knocked again. This time, the door swung open a couple inches on its own; someone had snapped the lock. She pushed the door fully open and shrieked at something Mercy couldn't see over her shoulder. The serenna picked up her skirt and rushed inside, Mercy on her heels. When she saw what had caused Elise to scream, she stopped in her tracks, her heart stopping in her chest.

Tamriel lay on the floor, dead.

Mercy fell to her knees beside the prince and laid her hands upon his chest. Whoever had attacked him had removed his breastplate and tossed it aside. She let out a choked gasp of relief when she felt his ribs expand and contract under her palms. He was breathing, but it was slow and shallow.

"Creator preserve us," Elise whispered. She was trembling from head to toe, her face stark white.

"He's alive," Mercy said, "but he may not be for long. Go find help. *Go!*"

Elise let out a sob and nodded, stumbling outside.

The prince's hair was sticky with blood. It pooled in the curve of his ear, pouring from a wide gash behind his temple, and Mercy ripped a long strip of fabric from the hem in her shirt and pressed it to the cut. The other side of his head bore a large bump from where it had hit the ground when he fell.

That was when she saw the pool of blood.

It was seeping out from under him, a puddle on the stone below his shoulder. Her hands shaking, she grabbed his shirt in one hand and his belt in the other, and used them to roll him onto his side. Her breath caught in her throat when she saw the large gash carving a crescent moon across his back. His shirt was soaked through with blood. He would have bled out if Mercy and Elise had arrived just five minutes later.

Leave him, Mother Illynor's voice whispered in her mind. *Let him die, and come back home with your contract complete. Be the Assassin you were raised to become.*

But now, seeing the ashen tint to his skin, the blood pouring out of the gaping wound in his back, Mercy knew she couldn't. She couldn't kill the boy who had welcomed her into his city, who had walked with her along the lake's edge and laughed at her awe, who had so much love for the people of his kingdom. She couldn't let him die. She pressed her hands to the wound, trying to stanch the blood.

I know how much you hunger for Mother Illynor's approval, Calum had said. *You reveal that the contract is fake and all the work you put in to compete in the Trial, everything you risked for the chance to swear your vows, is for nothing.*

Calum was wrong about her. Mother Illynor would understand once Mercy explained to her everything she'd learned about the forged contract. The headmistress wouldn't be happy about it, but she would understand. Mercy didn't care if the apprentices and Daughters teased her about failing her first contract, not if it meant Tamriel would survive. She would have to return to the Keep—she might never see Tamriel again—but it would be worth it to know he was alive.

For the first time in her life, she bent her head and prayed. *Creator, if you exist, please don't let him die.*

Something crashed in the back of the house. Mercy jumped to her feet, her pulse pounding in her ears, and pulled her daggers from their sheaths. The blood coating her hands made her grip on the weapons slick.

She ran through the hallways and into the back room, letting out a string of expletives when she realized it was empty. A breeze swept in from the broken window, which offered a glimpse into an overgrown garden, brambles climbing up the legs of a statue nearly lost amidst the weeds. The gaping hole was large enough for someone to climb through. As Mercy neared, she spotted blood on the edge of a piece of glass hanging from the window frame. It looked as if it had only just dried.

Run, said a voice in her mind—the same voice that had spoken on Solari, when she'd nearly killed Tamriel.

Footsteps and voices sounded in the foyer, and Mercy returned to find Elise hovering over a healer, who had knelt to tend to the prince's wounds. Royal guards flanked them on either side.

Mercy, RUN!

"That's her!" Elise yelled. "She tried to assassinate the prince!"

"What—" was all Mercy managed to get out before the guards swarmed her. Two grabbed her wrists and twisted her arms behind her back hard enough to make her cry out in pain, her eyes watering. She tried to fight them, but they wrenched her arms to the verge of snapping, forcing her to drop her daggers. They clattered to the ground and another guard scooped them up. Someone locked shackles around her wrists, and another clamped them around her ankles.

"Elise, what the hell are you doing?" Mercy shouted, anger and fear rushing over her. She bucked against the guards holding her in place, but their grips didn't waver.

Elise didn't respond, all her attention focused on the dying prince. She wrung her hands as the healer opened his case and pulled out bandages and a needle and thread. Her worried expression gave way to relief as the man began to work on the wound. Tamriel was starting to regain consciousness; his eyes were still closed, but his lids fluttered, and a moan escaped him when the healer pierced his flesh with the needle.

"You'll be alright, son," the healer whispered. "We'll get you fixed up."

"Let's go, filth," one of the guards hissed into Mercy's ear. He and the others dragged her toward the front door, and she fought them every step of the way.

"What are you doing?" she yelled when they passed Elise. "You know I didn't attack him."

"I found you standing over him with your daggers out and his blood on your hands. How can there be any doubt of your guilt?"

Realization struck her like an arrow to the chest as the guards hauled her out of the house. Elise *knew*. She knew of Calum's plot to have Tamriel murdered. For whatever reason, they'd planned this attack to frame her for the attempt on Tamriel's life. She opened her mouth to tell the guards, then closed it. They wouldn't take the word of a Feyndaran noble over the daughter of a council member. Calum and Elise would try to kill Tamriel again—of that, she had no doubt—but in the immediate aftermath of the attempt on his life, Tamriel would be taken to the castle and surrounded by guards at all times. For now, he would be safe. She just had to find a way to keep him that way.

Her knees cracked against the stone tile, and she twisted just in time to avoid falling face-first onto the grimy dungeon floor. Mercy pushed herself up, her chains jangling, and glared over her shoulder at the guards standing at the doorway of the cell into which they'd thrown her. Her hands were still shackled behind her back, useless.

"I didn't touch him," she growled. "I found him like that."

"Shut up."

"Whoever attacked him left through the back window. There's blood on one of the shards of glass hanging from the frame. Look at me—I don't have a scratch on me."

"Your hands are coated in His Highness's blood. You obviously put it there."

"I didn't!" she insisted, her eyes widening. "Let me speak to the king, I'll—"

"You're lucky you're not swinging from the gallows," the leader snarled, slamming the cell door shut. The lock snapped into place with a sharp clank, the sound echoing with finality. "But that'll come soon enough."

"No!" she yelled as they began to file out of the dungeon, her frustration boiling over. "The attacker is still out there! He's going to try again! He—"

The senior guard shut the door, plunging her into darkness, and Mercy spat a curse. She moved blindly to the rear of the cell and braced herself against the wall, lifting her butt off the ground high enough to bring her wrists—and the chain connecting them—from behind her, under her, to her front. She gritted her teeth when the heavy cuffs dug into her wrists and pinched the skin, then let out a sigh of relief when she finished working her feet around the chain. Her arms were free—well, not *free*, but at least her shoulders no longer ached from being stuck behind her back.

She pushed to her feet and paced the length of the small cell, trying not to picture the gaping wound in Tamriel's back. Worry for him gnawed at her. She could have been wrong about the timing. He could have bled out too much. He could be a few floors above her right now, lying cold and dead on his bed as a priestess read the last rites for his burial. The second Mercy thought it, the floor seemed to slide out from under her.

No. He will *make it. He* will *survive.* She glared up at the ceiling. *Creator, if you take him, I'll come up there and kick your ass myself.*

If he survived, what would they tell him when he woke up? What would he remember? He'd been attacked from behind, that much was certain, so chances were he never saw his would-be assassin. Would he believe Elise's claim that Mercy had attacked him? Would he think of their kisses in the library and assume it was all just part of an elaborate game she'd played with him?

Mercy sat against the wall. The stone floor was filthy, emanating a wet-cold that seeped through her clothes and chilled her to the bone. She closed her eyes and sucked in a shaky breath.

Calum would try to kill him again. She wasn't surprised he had taken matters into his own hands, but the way he had done it was odd. Why go through the effort of taking off the prince's breastplate only to leave him to bleed out, rather than stabbing him in the heart?

"...Oh," Mercy breathed, suddenly understanding. Calum couldn't do it. He couldn't stand there and plunge his dagger into his cousin's chest, couldn't watch the life bleed from his body. Instead, like a coward, he had left him there, alone. He had been planning on Mercy finding him, but hadn't been sure of the timing. For him, either result would have been positive: Mercy could have found Tamriel and been executed for attempted murder, leaving Calum or another Daughter to strike once everyone had let down their guard, or Tamriel would have died and Mercy been executed for murder. One way or another, he would have gotten what he wanted: revenge, and the throne.

The king would keep Tamriel safe. Mercy had to trust in that. Ghyslain hadn't been a good father to Tamriel, but he was terrified of losing another person he loved. He would keep a careful eye on his son until he was back on his feet. And soon, someone would come down to question her.

All she could do was wait.

Male voices woke her some time later. Mercy rose and moved to the front of her cell, her fingers curling around the iron bars, Tamriel's blood crusted around her fingernails. She'd tried to clean it off, but there had simply been too much.

The door opened and someone walked in carrying a torch, the bright flame blinding Mercy. *Finally.* They'd come to question her. She lifted a hand, her chains clanking, and watched through her fingers as a guard opened one of the cells on the opposite wall.

"Haul her in," the woman called, ignoring Mercy completely. Two guards strode into the dungeon, each with a hand clamped around one of Elvira's arms. Her dress was sleeveless, and Mercy could see an inky bruise forming on her shoulder. Her face, although pale, was strangely devoid of emotion. She didn't look Mercy's way as the guards threw her into the open cell.

The door clanged shut, the lock snapping into place. The commander pocketed the keys and nodded to her men, and the three of them left without a word, taking the torch with them. Pitch blackness swept over the dungeon once more. Heavy silence settled over the room. Mercy was surprised Elvira wasn't crying; considering how nervous and flighty she'd been when Mercy first arrived at Blackbriar, she would have expected the woman to be a blubbering mess.

"Are you alright?" Mercy asked.

For a long time, Elvira didn't answer. Then, she said in a flat voice, "You should have killed the prince when you went to meet him in the library."

Mercy's hands tightened around the iron bars. "I know."

Elvira wore no chains, so it was only by the swishing of her dress against the stone that Mercy could tell when she moved to the rear of her cell and sat. Mercy did the same, curling up on her side. She closed her eyes, but this time, sleep refused to come.

51
TAMRIEL

Tamriel awoke lying on his stomach, his head throbbing distantly behind a haze of cotton. Out of one eye, he could see over the swell of the monstrous downy pillow on which his head rested to the balcony, stars twinkling in the sky beyond. The doors stood open and bumped against the wall with each cool gust of wind off the lake, the curtains dancing in the draft.

Slowly, he became aware that he lay atop the blankets in nothing but his underclothes. Thick, scratchy bandages had been wrapped around his bare torso. When a breeze drifted in and sent goosebumps rippling across his skin, he frowned and began to push off the bed, until a flash of white-hot agony shot through his back. He cried out in pain and fell back onto the pillow, trembling, a sheen of perspiration beading on his brow.

"Try not to move. You've lost a lot of blood, and you'll only make it worse."

Tamriel went rigid. He was facing away from the man sitting beside his bed—it was too painful to turn his head—but he knew that voice, even thick with sleep. "What happened?" He fought to keep his voice steady, to conceal his fear. "Who did this to me?"

Ghyslain crossed the room and closed the balcony doors, then moved to Tamriel's side, peering down at him with concern. "Do you remember nothing?"

"I was...inside Mother's house," he said hesitantly, trying to wade through the haze of pain medicine in his system. No doubt his father was going to have plenty of questions about that later, but from the look on the king's face, it was the furthest thing from his mind right now. "Someone struck me from behind. I never saw him."

Ghyslain sucked in a shuddering breath. "Some... Someone tried to kill you, Tam." His pale face was terrifyingly grave, his eyes more somber and lucid than Tamriel had ever seen them. "If Serenna Elise hadn't found you when she did, you wouldn't be alive. Thankfully, she caught the would-be killer red-handed."

Tamriel lifted his head from the pillow, gritting his teeth against the pain. "Who? Who did this to me?"

The king seemed to wrestle with something internally, a shadow passing across his haggard face. He looked away. "You can't possibly imagine what it was like to watch them carry you in here, Tam. Your face was so pale... I thought you weren't going to last the hour, let alone the night."

Surprise shot through him. "Have you been sitting here this whole time?"

"You're all I have left. What else am I supposed to do when the person I love most in the world is on his deathbed?"

Tamriel wanted to laugh at that. *Love.* What a strange way to describe their relationship. "Father. Who did this to me?"

Did he look...*guilty?*

"Lady Marieve," he finally said.

The world stilled. Tamriel stared at his father, waiting for him to take the words back. When he didn't, Tamriel said, "You're lying."

"I wish I were."

"It wasn't her. It couldn't have been her."

"She's in the dungeon right now. You can see for yourself when you're healed."

"Why would Queen Cerelia send her granddaughter here to murder me?" Tamriel scoffed. As he spoke, his father began rifling through his pockets. "Why send her all the way from—"

He bit off the rest of the question. Pinched between Ghyslain's fingers was a gold coin—a very *distinctive* gold coin—with a teardrop in its center.

"You recognize this, don't you?" his father asked in a soft, sorrowful voice.

Tamriel merely stared.

Of course he recognized it.

"She's an Assassin. A Daughter of the Guild. This fell out of her pocket when the guards arrested her." Although his warnings about trusting Marieve—whatever her real name was—were right, Ghyslain didn't look smug or victorious. There was nothing but sympathy on his face.

Tamriel closed his eyes, an icy wave of hatred filling his veins. "She's still alive?"

"For now."

"Keep her that way. I want to speak to her. I want to see her punished."

"Are you sure? You don't have to be there—"

"I'm certain. Now please leave."

Ghyslain hesitated. "I don't think I should leave you alone—"

"Leave! Now!" Tamriel shouted. His father fell back a step, shocked. After a second, he nodded and left, murmuring something about waiting in the hall outside. The door latched shut behind him.

Tamriel let out a long breath, then inhaled so deeply his stitches pulled. Could it be true? All this time, had he really failed to see Marieve's true intentions? After so many years in his father's court, he had thought himself a good judge of character, so how... How had he failed to predict this?

He remembered the way her eyes sparkled whenever she teased him, the joy she'd taken from rendering him speechless. She had always spoken to him bluntly and without remorse—so refreshing compared to the forced politeness of his father's courtiers and advisors. He had dismissed it as her being Feyndaran, but now he recalled the tales of the infamous Assassins' Guild from his mother's storybooks. The Daughters were ruthless, emotionless, vicious to the core, but they were also exceptionally skilled liars.

Creator, Tamriel thought as the memory of the night before returned to him. She had taken his breath away when he saw her in the library, her skin glowing gold in the firelight, the tips of her ears peeking out from her beautiful black curls. He remembered pulling her into his arms, her hands tracing the line of his jaw, the way she had moaned against his lips.

We shouldn't have done this.

She could have killed him that night. Why had she spared him then, only to change her mind the very next day? Why, why, why. A thousand questions filled his mind, a thousand conversations, a thousand moments she could've taken his life. But one stood out among the rest:

Why—*why*—had he allowed himself to fall for her?

"Your Highness! I'm glad to see you're well!"

Calum's voice preceded him into the throne room, and a moment later, he stepped through the double doors, a charming smile on his face as he strode toward the dais. Tamriel and Ghyslain looked up from the documents they'd been reviewing, Tamriel rubbing his weary eyes with the back of his hand.

Over the past five days, Tamriel's back had healed well enough that he was cleared from bedrest and given permission to move freely about the castle. As aching and medicated as he was, however, that movement had been limited to walking from his room to the council chambers or king's study, then working with his father until the pain in his back demanded respite. Today, though, bored of the monotony and eager for a change of scenery, Tamriel had walked all the way to the throne room, where he'd been sitting with his father for the past few hours.

Since the attack, Ghyslain had refused to let Tamriel out of his sight. On the rare occasion state matters demanded his attention, the king left at least two soldiers to guard him, and three while he slept. In his almost eighteen years, that was the most time they'd ever spent together. Fitting that it would take an attempt on Tamriel's life to make his father see what he'd been missing all his these years.

Calum didn't acknowledge the guards flanking the throne as he bounded up the steps and stopped before Tamriel, his gaze sweeping over the prince from head to toe. "How do you feel?"

"About as well as you'd imagine," Tamriel responded. "But I'm alive, which is not a blessing I take lightly."

Yet another troubling issue—since the castle infirmary had been locked up and quarantined a week ago, no one had been brave enough to check on Alyss or the priestesses. The sounds of life the guards had heard through the door were enough to convince them there was no need to intervene yet, beyond delivering food and emptying chamber pots. They were clinging desperately to life, and Tamriel had no idea how much longer they would last.

Calum sat on the top step. "Have you gone to see her yet? The Assassin?"

Ghyslain's head snapped up. "Calum..."

Tamriel ignored his father's warning tone. "Not yet. I want to, but I could hardly manage walking all the way down here. I don't know if I could make it to the dungeon on my own."

"I'll go with you, if you wish."

"I don't think that's a good idea." Ghyslain turned to Tamriel. "You're not well enough, and I would advise against speaking with her at all. As loathe as you may be to believe it, she tried to murder you, Tam. Elise and all the guards found her standing over you with her daggers unsheathed, your blood dripping from her fingers. Now that you're better, I shall arrange her execution immediately."

"Without giving her a chance to speak on her own behalf?"

"We know she's guilty, Tamriel," Calum said softly. "You care for her—that much is plain to see—but the woman you know as Marieve doesn't exist. I know it's hard to hear, but it's the truth. Everything she said was a lie. You don't owe her a second of your time." He shook his head, stretching his legs out in front of him. "I say execute her and be done with it. Have her escorted to the gardens tonight—allow enough time for word to spread among the court—and execute her then, in front of everyone. Show them the consequences of hurting you."

Tamriel looked away, gripping the arms of his chair until his knuckles turned white. Everything Calum had said was true. He had no idea who sat in that dungeon cell, but it wasn't Marieve. It wasn't the woman who had kissed him in the library, who had shared so many smiles and teasing laughs with him, who had talked with him when the grief for his mother had been almost too much to bear. And yet...he couldn't help but be skeptical. Sometimes, he could have sworn the mask slipped. Sometimes, she hadn't been Lady Marieve of Feyndara.

But perhaps she truly was that good. Perhaps it had all been part of her game.

Tamriel nodded, his heart turning to stone. "Okay," he finally said, "but not today. Two days from now, have her brought in during my birthday feast. I want all the nobility to see the price this assassination attempt has cost her."

He stood, and the sudden movement caused the world to tilt beneath his feet. He swayed for a second, feeling the blood rush from his face, and caught his balance on the back of his chair, waving away the steadying hands Ghyslain and Calum proffered. He straightened, bracing himself for pain. "But I am going to speak with her now. I won't sentence her to execution without at least hearing her out."

He descended the steps of the dais, then turned back to Calum. "Are you coming, or not?"

Calum sighed and pushed to his feet. "I'll come, but when she starts making doe eyes at you and tugging at your heartstrings, just remember this was *your* idea."

52

Mercy's stomach ached, a yawning chasm within her. The guard hadn't yet arrived with the daily cup of water and meager scraps she and Elvira had been allowed during their imprisonment. Hunger was a constant companion, along with the ceaseless chill which had seeped into her bones. Sleep came infrequently, as did the meals—if a cup of water and meager scraps could be called *meals*—so she had no way to gauge how long she'd been in the dungeon. Nor did she know how much longer they'd wait to execute her. It had quickly become apparent they had no intention to question her about the events of the night she'd found Tamriel lying in a pool of blood. Not that she could really blame them. If she'd been in their place, she would have done the same. Still, it killed her that she had no idea whether the prince was alive or dead.

Please, Creator, let him be alive.

"They're going to kill us," Elvira said, speaking for the first time in ages.

"Undoubtedly."

"We wouldn't be in this situation if you had killed the

prince when you'd had the chance. Solari. The night you went to meet him in the castle. Why did you wait so long?"

Mercy closed her eyes. She didn't have an answer—not one that she could give Elvira, anyway.

After a few beats of silence, Elvira scoffed. "I haven't the slightest clue how you became a Daughter."

Her jaw clenched. "I worked hard, and I earned my place."

"Sorin told me you cheated your way into the Trial."

"I fought, and I won. I do not regret it, nor will I apologize for it."

"Apologize for this, then," she snarled. "The king will soon tire of keeping us locked in here. Any minute now, the guards will come in and haul us out to the Plaza to execute us in front of everyone. It's not enough that my husband has lived in chains longer than he's been without them—now he must be made a widower, as well. And all for what? For you to forget your sacred vow the second a boy looks twice at you?"

Mercy opened her mouth to respond, but at that moment, the door creaked open, light flooding the room. Mercy and Elvira clambered to their feet and moved to the doors of their cells, their shared thought hanging in the air as if they'd spoken aloud: *Food?*

The two men who entered were not guards. One leaned against the other, their heads bent together so Mercy couldn't make out their faces, but their fine clothing betrayed their identities.

"Tamriel?" Mercy breathed, hardly believing what she was seeing. He was *alive*. *Thank you, Creator*.

He lifted his head and met her gaze. Devastation passed across his face, but it was gone in the blink of an eye, so quickly Mercy wasn't sure whether she'd imagined it. Icy hatred took its place. "I didn't believe it when he told me," Tamriel said, his words clipped and precise. "I couldn't believe that you'd been the one to try to kill me, but my father showed me your coin. I know you're from the Assassins' Guild."

At his side, there was nothing but concern on Calum's face as he looked from Mercy to his cousin, leaning against him with his arm slung across Calum's shoulders. *What a good actor,* Mercy thought, loathing rising like a tide within her. *It's almost like he cares.*

But he hadn't tried to kill Tamriel again, so she would take the small victory.

She focused on the prince again. "I am from the Guild, but I wasn't the one who attacked you. I swear it."

Tamriel frowned, and it was agony to see the ice in his eyes as he glared at her. They had done it. They had turned him against her. Yet...he *had* come to see her. Did that mean a part of him doubted what they'd told him about that night? "If you weren't the one who attacked me, who did?"

She fought the urge to look pointedly at Calum. He hadn't tried to kill the prince yet, which meant either Ghyslain was keeping Tamriel well under guard or Calum hadn't gathered the courage to try again. But if she told the prince the truth, there was no doubt in her mind that Calum would find a way. He wouldn't let Tamriel live with the knowledge that *he'd* been the one to buy the contract on his life. She had to hold her tongue—for now.

Mercy gripped the bars tightly, imploring him to believe her. "I don't know, but Tamriel, listen to me. It's true that I'm an Assassin, but that night in the library, I couldn't do it. I couldn't kill you. If I'd been the one to attack you in your mother's house, you wouldn't have survived. Daughters of the Guild don't leave their marks to bleed out. That was your attacker's mistake. Elise and I found you in that house, unconscious, and I tried to stop the bleeding while she called for the guards. That's why there was blood on my hands when they found me."

"Coming down here was a mistake, Tam," Calum said. "She'll say anything to save her own skin."

"Why would Elise lie?" Tamriel asked, ignoring his cousin. "Why claim that you attacked me?"

"Perhaps she's working with whoever wants you dead."

Calum's glare sharpened, and Mercy tensed. If she said anything more, Calum would surely kill the prince. She could imagine it now—him running into the throne room with Tamriel in his arms, claiming Mercy had attacked him after he stepped too close to the bars. There was no guarantee she could save her own life, but she could at least protect Tamriel for as much time as she had left.

"Who bought the contract?"

Mercy met Elvira's eyes through the bars of the cell doors, silently begging her to keep quiet. She would find a way to get them both out of this alive. She just needed time.

"I don't know. Mother Illynor works with clients. I just went where I was told."

He shook his head in disgust. "You shall be executed in two days' time. You"—he turned to Elvira—"will have your hearing the next day, where you may protest your innocence." He glanced at Calum. "Let's go."

Calum nodded, and they turned to leave. Just as Tamriel was about to cross over the threshold, Mercy called, "Don't you want to know my real name?"

The prince paused, but didn't look back.

"It's Mercy."

53
CALUM

The next day, Calum stood at the window in Blackbriar's study, absently running his thumb along his lower lip. All day long, slaves and advisors had been bustling in and out of the castle in preparation for the prince's birthday celebration, draping the great hall in panels of shimmering, diaphanous silks, stringing colorful tassels across the hedge mazes, preparing platter upon platter of delicacies. And, of course, arranging Mercy's execution.

"Was it everything you'd hoped for?" Calum had asked as Tamriel sagged against the wall outside the dungeon the day before, closing his eyes and letting out a long sigh. Adrenaline still coursed through his veins—his heart had been hammering in his chest since Mercy began to speak. He'd been waiting for the moment she revealed who was truly behind the contract...but she hadn't. Good girl. He didn't want to be the one to shove the blade into his cousin's heart, but he would if it meant saving his own skin, if it meant getting the revenge his father deserved. It was one thing to buy a contract on someone's life, and a very different one to be the person wielding the blade.

"It wasn't exactly the reunion I'd wanted, no. I'd... A foolish part of me had been hoping they were wrong. I'd wanted her to be innocent. Am I mad?"

"...You really care for her, don't you?"

"I do. Or, I did. I don't know anymore."

The squeal of hinges drew him from his reverie, and he turned as three young women filed into the room. Although Calum could see no weapons on their persons, there was no doubt who they were. Assassins. They moved silently as phantoms, sharp eyes taking his measure in seconds, and all three were stunningly, *painfully* beautiful. One sat on the settee, one lingered by the door, and another took up a position at the bookshelves. Even now, even here, they were prepared for an attack.

"You were almost too late. The prince turns eighteen tomorrow," Calum said, sending a silent thanks to Elvira for sending Mother Illynor the message he'd given her. He gestured to the papers on the low table before the settee. "There's a map of the castle. I've marked where the guards will be stationed tomorrow, and the combination for the lock on the servants' entrance is on the bottom." He reached into his pocket and pulled out a heavy iron key, which he handed to the eldest Daughter. "That's for Tamriel's chambers."

She nodded and slipped it into her pocket. "What's this?" she asked, eyeing the pile of aurums next to the map.

"From the king, for your trouble."

As he spoke, the Daughter pulled out a pouch and dropped in the money. Calum flinched at every clink of the coins—*his* coins. His father had been a rich man, but Drake's wife—the woman who had masqueraded as Calum's mother—had taken everything in his Beltharan accounts after his death. The rest were secured in accounts across the Abraxas Sea. All Calum had to his name was the money he'd earned during his year with the Strykers. After all this nonsense with the Guild, it was running dangerously low. *Look what I do for you, Father,* he thought once again.

"You must leave the capital by tomorrow night," he continued. "The guards will be on high alert, but you should be able to blend in among the revelers coming and going from the celebration."

The Daughter leaned forward and tore a long strip from the bottom of the map, the piece bearing the combination code. "Destroy that," she said, nodding to the remains of the paper.

"You...don't need it?"

"We're going to the castle tonight. Tell your king that the prince will be dead by daybreak."

He swallowed the twinge of guilt that rose within him. "Tonight. Very well."

"You seem surprised." The Assassin at the bookshelf bared her teeth in a smug, cruel grin, and it was only then that Calum recognized her: Lylia. The apprentice who had tortured and tormented Mercy all her life. "You don't have to worry about us. We're not all as inept as Mercy."

He nodded. "Her daggers are on the counter in the kitchen."

The Daughters left as swiftly and silently as they had come. Calum sank onto the corner of the settee, rubbing his hands down his face. In a matter of hours, it would be done. Tamriel would be dead. Ghyslain would be condemned for the murder. Calum groaned, fighting the guilt threatening to overwhelm him. This was the revenge his father deserved.

Soon, it would all be over.

54

Mercy looked up at the sound of running footsteps pounding down the hallway.

"Are the guards coming for us already?" Elvira asked, her voice thin and trembling.

In the corridor, someone cried out in surprise, but the sound broke off with a muffled gurgle. Something thumped hard against the wooden door, and a second later, a shard of light cut through the darkness of the dungeon as it swung open. But the person who stepped over the threshold, a ring of keys in hand, wasn't a guard. Mercy scrambled to her feet, nearly tripping over the chains binding her ankles as she ran to the front of her cell.

"Faye?"

"Mercy!" Faye ran to the cell door and fumbled with the keys until she found the correct one. She pulled the door open, then knelt and began working on the shackles around Mercy's ankles. No hint of the hatred she'd borne for Mercy after the Trial lingered on her face, thank the Creator.

The shackles on her ankles fell away, then those on her wrists. Mercy sighed with relief and gingerly rubbed the places where the heavy iron had cut into her flesh. "How did you know I was here?"

"Elvira sent a letter that you were in trouble."

Mercy glared at Elvira. "And you couldn't be bothered telling me this? You let me think I was going to be executed all this time?"

"I wasn't sure they'd make it in time, and I wasn't much inclined to offer you comfort after *you* got us into this mess."

Mercy opened her mouth to snarl a response, but Faye shot her a look. "There'll be time for bickering later," she said as she unlocked Elvira's cell. She dragged the body of the guard she'd killed into the dungeon, then led them into the hall and pulled Mercy's precious daggers from a small pack slung over her shoulder. "Feels good to see these again, huh?"

"More than you know. How did you find them? The guards confiscated them when the brought me in," she said as she slid the sheaths onto a belt Faye handed her, then looped it around her hips. "Ah—Calum. Of course."

The next time she saw him, she would flay him alive. That was the least he deserved for everything he'd done to her and Tamriel.

They crept through the halls on silent feet, listening for guards on patrol. After a while, Mercy couldn't help but whisper, "Why are you here?"

Although Faye's back was to her, she could sense her old friend's eye roll. "To save you."

"I meant, you're still an apprentice."

"I came with Aelis. Mother Illynor promised to make Lylia and me full-fledged Daughters if we were successful tonight. I think she feels bad about the botched Trial."

"So...you're not angry at me?" Mercy asked, remembering the way Faye had shouted and screamed at her the day she'd left the Keep.

"Of course, I'm angry. But you're a Daughter of the Guild, and I won't abandon you to rot in a cell."

They ran through the twisting, labyrinthine corridors, blades at the ready, ears straining for the sounds of patrols. When they passed the stairs up to the main floor of the castle, Elvira slowed to a stop. "Wait," she said in a tight voice. "My husband."

"Come on," Mercy responded. "If the guards see you out of your cell, they won't stop to ask questions. They know you've been working with the Guild."

"If I leave tonight, I'll never be able to return to the castle. I'm not leaving without Kier."

"You're wasting time, and—more importantly—you're putting all our lives at stake by delaying us." Faye approached the woman and set a hand on her shoulder, looking into her eyes. "We leave now. If you go back, I cannot offer you my protection." The meaning behind her words was clear: *Escape now, or search for him on your own.* "Make your choice."

Elvira lifted her chin. "I made my choice when I married him."

"Very well. Should you change your mind, we have horses waiting in a stable near the southern city gate."

Faye continued down the hall, leaving Mercy and Elvira alone. They stared at each other, neither knowing what—if anything—there was left to say. After a moment, Elvira offered Mercy a firm nod, then turned and ran up the stairs.

Together, Mercy and Faye crept through the dark hallway until the faint outline of the servants' entrance appeared at the end of the corridor. Faye pulled out a scrap of paper and, after consulting it in the light of a torch, she moved to the door, her fingers flying over the complex set of dials and latches until the door clicked. She pushed it open. "Freedom," she said as she emerged onto the castle grounds. The moon hung low in the sky, obscured by a thick blanket of clouds. "How does it feel?"

Mercy didn't respond, guilt rising within her. The infirmary. Alyss. She wasn't sure exactly how long she'd spent in the dungeon, but she knew it had been days. Had Alyss succumbed to the plague yet? Right now, was she lying in a cot beside Gwynn and Owl, her mind and body too disease-ridden to do anything except lie in misery until Mercy came to deliver the poison she'd promised? How long had it taken before she had given up on finding a cure? Or was she still feverishly working, determined to toil away until her heart stopped?

It's not too late to turn around. The infirmary was only guarded by two men. She and Faye could take them down in the blink of an eye.

But one look at Faye, at the cold, focused expression on her face and the bloody dagger in her hand, and Mercy knew the woman standing before her was not her old friend. The woman standing before her was an Assassin—ruthless, heartless, pitiless. The girl who had regaled Mercy with tales of the world beyond the Forest of Flames, who had raced her through the tall redwood trees, who had stood with her against Lylia and her minions, did not exist here in the capital.

She followed Faye along the side of the castle, their black clothing rendering them nearly invisible in the night. When they reached the corner, Faye paused and peered around to the front gardens. "Four guards in all, but they're scattered across the grounds," she whispered. "Sheathe your blades, and when the closest one passes, we'll start walking slowly to the gate. At best, they'll mistake us for servants. At worst...well, you have your daggers for a reason."

As she waited for Faye's signal, Mercy glanced up at the dark silhouette of the castle looming above them, its towers soaring high over the city, their gilded peaks shining faintly in the weak moonlight. Tamriel was somewhere inside. The betrayal she'd seen on his face the last time they'd spoken, when he'd sentenced her to execution, haunted her. He hated her. No, he *despised* her, and he was right to. She hadn't buried a dagger in his back, but she'd lied to him, manipulated him, and plotted to murder him. She would never be able to go back to the way things were that night in the library. But she could live with that—she could live with knowing she would never speak to him again, never hear his laugh or feel his lips on hers—if it meant he would live. She just needed to get back to the Keep and tell Mother Illynor about the forged contract.

I came with Aelis, Faye had said. *Mother Illynor promised to make Lylia and me full-fledged Daughters if we were successful tonight.*

"No," Mercy breathed, understanding washing over her. Mother Illynor had sent Aelis and Lylia to complete the contract in Mercy's stead. Tamriel wouldn't survive the night.

She grabbed Faye's shoulder. "We need to go back inside. I have to complete my contract."

"Mercy, there are countless guards between us and the prince. We're skilled killers, but we're not miracle workers. Leave it to Aelis and Lylia."

"I can't return to the Guild a failure, Faye. If we leave now, I'll return a laughingstock, as I always have been. The girl who cheated her Trial. The girl who couldn't complete her contract. I know you hate me for what I did, but if you ever cared at all for me, help me. We can be the Assassins who slew a prince."

Faye hesitated, warily eyeing the castle.

Mercy tightened her grip on her old friend's arm, letting the ruthless, cruel apprentice she'd been take over. She had trained all her life for her first contract. She'd been born to become an Assassin. Tonight, she would prove that. "Help me, Faye."

"Shit. Very well. But when it's all over, you'll give me your daggers. It's the least I deserve."

"Deal."

Faye smiled wickedly, drawing a throwing knife from the sheath at her hip. "Then let's go."

55

The door to Tamriel's chambers stood ajar, the ring of steel on steel reverberating from within. Two dead guards were slumped against the wall outside, their eyes open and unseeing, faces contorted in surprise and pain. One was still clutching the entrails pouring out of the gaping hole in his side. The sight made Mercy's stomach turn, but she pushed her disgust away as she and Faye burst into the prince's bedchamber, the door flying open with a resounding *crack*.

Lylia was a blur in the center of the room, slashing and hacking at the six guards surrounding her. She held a sword in her right hand—taken from one of the dead guards lying at her feet—and a dagger in her left. As Mercy watched, she caught a guard's blade with her dagger, then plunged her sword through the gap under his breastplate. Blood sprayed from the man's lips. He went down, gurgling, as Lylia ripped out the blade and turned to face her next opponent. Before he could so much as raise his weapon, one of Faye's throwing knives buried itself in his eye socket. He howled, the sound more animal than human, and Lylia deftly slit his throat.

Two guards down. Two more bodies joining those already sprawled across the floor. Distantly, Mercy could hear people shouting in far-off corridors of the castle, trying to make sense of what was happening, but they would be too late.

Where the hell is Tamriel? Mercy thought, her heart hammering against her ribs. She couldn't see him amidst the chaos, the armored bodies and slashing swords and spraying blood. She leapt onto Tamriel's bed and surveyed the carnage. When she finally spotted the prince, her breath caught.

He'd been backed into a corner, he and two royal guards forced into a defensive position by Aelis's lightning-fast, vicious attacks. His sword was in his hand, but he wore no armor; his loose tunic and pants were rumpled from sleep. The guards kept trying to position themselves between Aelis and their prince, but they were no match for the Daughter's training. Already, Tamriel bore several superficial cuts along his arms and torso, blood staining his linen tunic crimson.

Mercy jumped off the bed and ran for them, stumbling over the bodies and overturned furniture littering the floor. She paid no heed to the guards fighting Lylia and Faye—only three left now, each bleeding heavily—as Aelis lunged, her teeth bared in a snarl. A guard leapt forward to meet her, but she feinted right and twisted left, ducking under the arc of his sword and plunging her blade into the back of his thigh. He cried out in agony as his leg gave out. Tamriel roared and made to charge her, but the other guard shoved him out of the way and swung at the Daughter.

Aelis pulled her sword out of the man's leg and knocked the guard's attack aside, then buried her blade in his chest. He crumpled, dead before he hit the ground. Mercy watched, ducking blades and dodging blows, as Aelis turned to the man she'd downed. Despite his wound, he lifted his sword and struggled to his feet, pain contorting his features. He only made it halfway before falling back to his knees. Aelis offered him a predatory grin and swung her sword.

His head thumped to the floor.

His body followed.

Tamriel stood alone—cornered, without guards, without armor—before the Daughter. Even so, he rushed at Aelis, fury on his blood-splattered face.

NO!

Mercy threw herself between them, lifting her dagger to catch Tamriel's sword. Their blades met with a clash of steel, the force of the blow sending a jolt down Mercy's arm, and she shoved him backward with all her strength. He stumbled over a dead guard and caught his balance on the wall, his hand leaving a bloody streak on the stone. Mercy didn't miss the fact that it was trembling.

He lifted his head, his eyes widening when he realized who stood before him. A storm of emotions passed across his face—surprise, disbelief, anger, fear, loathing...

"End it now, Mercy," Aelis said. "Kill him."

...and utter devastation.

The world stilled. She could do it. Every day of her life, she'd been preparing for this moment. Every scar she bore, every foul name they had called her, every moment of torture and torment she had endured—it had all been for this. To prove that she was the greatest Assassin the Guild had ever trained.

You may be skilled with a bow, knife-ear, but that's never going to make you one of us, Lylia's voice whispered in her mind. *Elves were only meant to be two things in this world: slaves and savages.*

Mercy had belonged to the Guild since the moment Llorin carried her through the Keep's gate at one week old. Her parents had abandoned her, handed her over to be enslaved or killed by the Guildmother, and yet Mother Illynor had given her a place among the apprentices. Until leaving for Sandori, her world had begun and ended at the Forest's edge. She had been waiting for the opportunity to complete her first contract all her life.

All it would take was one slice across the prince's throat. One dagger to his heart. One blade to the gut.

Do it, the bloodthirsty apprentice within her urged. *Kill him and prove them all wrong.*

Mercy's fingers tightened around the grips of her daggers, the leather slick under her calloused hands, stained with the blood of the guards she and Faye had encountered on the way to Tamriel's chambers. She stepped forward until only two feet remained between her and the prince. Two feet between her and the completion of her contract.

Tamriel halfheartedly lifted his sword, agony on his face. Mercy wasn't wearing any armor. If he wanted to, he could plunge his blade straight through her heart—and she could do the same to him. Yet neither moved. The sharp point of his sword quivered in the air between them, reflecting the moonlight bleeding in through the open curtains. Across the room, the last guard cried out, his lifeless body thumping to the ground.

"Mari— Mercy," Tamriel breathed.

I want you to understand that my regret isn't that I tried to drown you. It's that I failed. Because you, Mercy, Trytain had said, her voice cool and emotionless, *you will be the ruination of the Guild.*

"Kill him," Aelis snapped, her patience wearing thin. "Or I'll do it myself."

So be it.

Mercy lifted her dagger, then turned and plunged it into Aelis's stomach.

The Daughter's lightweight leather armor split like silk before the Stryker-made blade. Her mouth dropped open, but the only sound that escaped was a low, agonized groan as

Mercy twisted the dagger and pulled it out, causing blood to gush from the gaping wound. She swayed for a moment, hatred burning in her eyes, before crumpling to the ground.

Mercy glanced at the prince, whose face was white with shock. When his gaze met hers, she smiled weakly. "You're welcome."

"TRAITOR!" Lylia roared.

She launched herself at Mercy, knocking her off her feet and sending her tumbling across the hard stone tile, her daggers flying from her grasp. Mercy's back cracked against an overturned table. She coughed and sputtered, a hand going to her ribs. They were almost certainly bruised, if not broken. Spots of darkness danced in her vision as she pushed herself onto all fours.

"I should have killed you when I had the chance," Lylia snarled, stooping to pick up Mercy's daggers. She stalked forward slowly, a wicked grin on her face. Behind her, Faye hovered by Aelis's body, looking uneasy. "Drowned you in the river, poisoned your dinner, buried an arrow in your heart. The only thing that stopped me was Mother Illynor's rule against killing another apprentice. But now that you've forsaken your vows, you're no longer under her protection."

Tamriel stepped between them, his sword unsheathed. "Do not touch her."

Mercy looked up at him, and her stomach dropped. The back of his tunic was soaked through with blood; he'd pulled his stitches while fighting the Daughters. He had to be in agony, yet his face betrayed no emotion as he reached down and helped Mercy to her feet, never once taking his eyes off Lylia. He edged in front of Mercy, lifting his sword higher. "Do not take one step closer."

"Aw, you're protecting her now? How sweet."

Lylia lunged, blades whistling as they cleaved the air. Even though she was unarmed, Mercy leapt forward on instinct, no thought in her mind but to protect Tamriel. He couldn't die tonight. He *wouldn't*.

Yet Lylia never reached them.

A crack like thunder filled the air, loud enough to make Mercy's ears ring, and Lylia and Faye flew across the room like straw dummies. Lylia's head struck one of the windows with a sickening crack, causing a spiderweb of fissures to bloom across the glass. Faye hit the far wall and fell still. Mercy ran over and pressed her fingers to Faye's throat, feeling for a pulse.

"She's alive," she breathed, relief rushing over her. She may have betrayed the Guild, but she didn't want to see the only friend she'd ever had die. "Just unconscious."

Tamriel didn't respond. He was too busy gaping at the woman standing in the middle of the room.

Her body looked as if it was made of gray smoke—opaque enough to have form, but translucent enough that Mercy could see the silhouettes of the overturned furniture through her. The stranger looked from Mercy to Tamriel, her long, pointed ears peeking through her curls.

"You must leave the castle now," she said, and Mercy's blood ran cold. This woman's voice was the one that had been whispering in her ear all this time. "The soldiers are coming, and when they see you both covered in blood, they won't stop to ask questions. This time, you won't have to wait for an execution, Mercy."

"How do you know my name? Who are you?"

The woman picked up Mercy's daggers and crossed the room to hand them to her. As she reached up to take them, Mercy looked into the woman's face for the first time, stifling a gasp. She was strikingly beautiful, from her heart-shaped face to her full lips, dark, wavy hair framing her face. There was something strangely familiar about her.

The woman smiled. "Hello, sister. My name is Liselle."

Tamriel let out a choked sound, his face pale. "How—"

"No time," she said, extending a hand to Mercy. After a moment's hesitation, she accepted. Strangely, Liselle's hand was as solid as hers, soft and warm, as if she were still alive. As soon as Mercy was back on her feet, Liselle pushed her toward Tamriel, who caught her in his arms. They exchanged bewildered looks as Liselle continued, "I've risked too much to find you and I've stayed too long already. You both must leave the castle and go northeast, to the Islands. The things Pilar saw... The danger brewing in the Islands—it's real. Myrbellanar, the disease. It's all connected. You must stop it. You remember the flower Cassius drew?"

Mercy nodded.

"Find it." She looked at Tamriel. "The soldiers Master Oliver sent to the Islands are gone. If you value your people's lives, you must leave tonight. Do not let your father dissuade you."

Tamriel slowly nodded, his fingers tightening on Mercy's arms. Somewhere in the halls outside, a man shouted, and the stomping of heavy boots thundered behind him—more guards, drawn by the sounds of fighting. Mercy stiffened. When they found her, they would kill her.

"I kept the guards away as long as I could," Liselle said. "You needed to make your choice, Mercy: the prince or the Guild. Now, Tamriel, it is your turn. Cast Mercy out and let the guards kill her for her crimes, or protect her and save your people."

The prince released Mercy and raked a hand through his hair. Sorrow and anger warred on his face as he surveyed the carnage throughout his room: the broken furniture, the blood pooling on the tiles, the bodies sprawled limply across the floor. All this destruction—all these lives lost—because of Mercy and the Guild.

"Choose," Mercy whispered to Tamriel, her pulse thumping in her ears.

"Quickly," Liselle urged.

The prince closed his eyes and let out a long breath. Then he seized Mercy's hand, and together, they ran out of the room.

56

He dragged her into the hallway, pausing at the sight of the slain guards slumped on either side of his bedchamber door. A ragged, broken sound escaped him, and Mercy wondered how well the prince had known them. They could have been watching over him all his life. And tonight, they had died trying to protect him.

The hall extended to their right and left. From their left, Mercy could hear the pounding of guards' footsteps, racing toward them at breakneck speed. To their right, it would only be a few corridors to the stairs that led down to the main floor and out of the castle. Tamriel wavered, glancing from one side to the other. Mercy tried to swallow her fear. Would the prince trust Liselle, or hand Mercy over to the guards for what she and the Daughters had done?

Tamriel made his decision.

They raced through hall after hall, then down the spiral staircase to the castle's main floor. Tamriel's hand was wrapped around hers, slick with perspiration and blood, and Mercy gripped it like a lifeline. The guards were drawing nearer: the clattering of their plate mail echoed on the stone walls of the stairwell above Mercy and Tamriel's heads. As they stepped off the last stair, Tamriel pulled her to his side with a sharp tug, but not before one caught a glimpse of her from above.

"The Assassin's there! She's with the prince!"

"Stand down!" Tamriel yelled, but they didn't heed his order. They probably thought she was holding a blade to his throat in an attempt to escape the castle unscathed.

"Hurry," she urged him.

"This way."

They burst into the great hall and stopped in their tracks when they saw the dozen guards in full armor standing before the castle's main doors, blades unsheathed. Master Oliver was among them. Tamriel released Mercy's hand and lifted his chin, his chest rising and falling rapidly. Although he was trying to appear strong and regal, it was obvious he needed to be seen by a healer soon; the blood darkening his linen tunic was still spreading. "Stand down, guards."

None of them moved.

Behind Mercy, the guards who had been pursuing them rushed into the room, flanking them. There was nowhere left to run. She lifted her daggers, bracing herself for another fight. By the Creator, how many more people would lose their lives this night?

"Move away from the Assassin, Your Highness," Master Oliver called, taking a careful step forward. His eyes narrowed at Mercy. "Whatever your plan was, it's over. You're surrounded. Lay down your weapons and surrender."

"Stay away from her," Tamriel said. "That's an order."

"That is not an order."

Tamriel started at the voice, then turned to face his father, standing in the doorway to the throne room. The king held up a hand, and the guards lowered their swords, but did not sheathe them.

"Tamriel," Ghyslain said, slowly and cautiously. "Step away from her."

"She saved my life."

"She's the reason you almost *died* the other night. I don't know what game she and the other Assassins are playing, but do not make the mistake of trusting her again."

Mercy stepped forward, opening her mouth to say—

"Not one more inch," Ghyslain snapped. His eyes were dark as obsidian, full of rage. "Do not go any closer to my son, or I swear to the Creator I'll have your head right here, right now."

"I haven't done anything except protect him when your guards failed. If not for me, he would be dead."

"Stop!" Tamriel commanded. He crossed the great hall and glared at the king, anger pouring off him in waves. "This ends tonight. She and I are leaving for the Islands, and we will return with the cure for the plague—the cure that you are too cowardly to search for. How many people have died so far, Father? A thousand? Two thousand? Do you even know? Do you even *care?*"

Ghyslain's hand flew out and struck Tamriel across the face. The prince staggered back, a hand to his cheek, and the anger on Ghyslain's face bled away to horror. "Tam, I-I didn't mean to—"

"Don't." Tamriel lowered his hand and squared his shoulders, slipping on the emotionless mask he wore so often around his father and the court. When he spoke, his voice came out icy. "Enjoy the rest of your time on the throne, because it ends when I return."

"It's not that simple. There are things you don't know—things you must learn before you decide whether you are going to leave."

"I'm listening."

"Come with me into the throne room. We must speak in private."

"No. Anything you have to say, say it now."

A muscle worked in Ghyslain's jaw. "If that is how you wish it to be, so be it." He turned to Master Oliver. "Seize them. Escort the prince to my chambers and have the Assassin returned to her cell to await her execution."

A handful of guards rushed forward, but Tamriel jerked out of their reach, pushing Mercy behind him. "Fine," he spat. "I'll listen to what you have to say, but it's not going to change my mind. And Mercy stays here."

The king nodded and gestured for the guards to return to their places. He turned on his heel and strode into the throne room, not bothering to check if his son was following. Tamriel shook his head and started to trail after him, but Mercy caught his arm. "Be careful."

He didn't even spare her a glance as he shrugged off her grip and followed his father into the throne room.

Mercy strained her ears, but all she could hear was the low murmur of their voices drifting from the other room. She sighed softly and sheathed her daggers at her hips, painfully aware of the guards surrounding her, the blood splattered across her clothes. Her chest was tight, adrenaline coursing through her veins. She had killed a Daughter tonight. Now, the Assassins would never stop hunting her.

Whatever Liselle had done to Lylia and Faye hadn't disabled them for long. After the prince and his father left to speak in the throne room, Master Oliver had sent some men to arrest the Assassins. The guards had returned ten minutes later and reported that they'd found the room empty save for the dead. Mercy wasn't sure whether they had holed up in some unused room of the castle or fled to lick their wounds, but she wasn't planning to wait and find out. She and Tamriel needed to leave for the Islands as soon as possible. It wouldn't keep Lylia and Faye off their trail for long, but it would buy them some time. Somehow, she would have to prove to Mother Illynor that the contract was forged, and therefore void—if Illynor would even care, after all the effort she'd gone through to see this contract completed. If Mercy tried to return to the Keep, they'd kill her before she even set foot beyond the gate.

The castle doors swung open, and Calum rushed inside, his huge crossbow in one hand. He pushed through the guards standing watch at the doors and stopped dead when he saw Mercy, his face paling when he saw the blood on her hands and clothes. The crossbow slipped from his grasp, clattering loudly on the stone.

"I'm too late, aren't I?" he whispered, his voice a hoarse rasp. "It's done."

Mercy narrowed her eyes. *What game is he playing now?*

Across the great hall, Tamriel walked out of the throne room. His expression was troubled, lost in thought, but it shifted to shock when Calum tackled him in a hug. "Thank the Creator," Calum said, choking on a relieved laugh. He pulled back and stared in horror at the blood on his palms, then turned Tamriel around to gape at the back of his soaked tunic. "Tam, you must see a healer." He glared at the guards, then at Master Oliver. "Has no one sent for Healer Tabris? Go. Go now!"

Two guards rushed out of the room.

"No, I don't have time for that," Tamriel said. "I have to leave."

"Leave? And go where?"

Ghyslain trailed in from the other room, regarding his son sorrowfully. "If you still insist on going, I cannot stand in your way. You know the risks, but it is your choice to make. No one will stop you." He nodded to Master Oliver, who gestured for his men to stand down. They bowed their heads in respect and withdrew to the sides of the room. "However, I insist that you wait until Healer Tabris arrives and tends to your wounds. In the meantime, Master Oliver will see to it that you have all the supplies you will need for your journey."

Tamriel frowned.

"Humor me. I need to know you won't be leaving here only to bleed out on the road."

The prince clenched his jaw. "I'm fine."

"Don't even try it," Calum snapped.

"Very well. One hour, and not a minute longer."

Ghyslain nodded, and he and Calum left to speak with Master Oliver about gathering provisions for the road. Mercy caught a flicker of movement out of the corner of her eye, and she moved to Tamriel's side, lightly resting her hand on his arm. "Tamriel, look," she said softly, nodding toward the hall that led to the throne room.

His breath caught when he saw Liselle peering out from behind the archway, her slate gray skin nearly blending into the stone wall behind her. Mercy might have mistaken her for a shadow if she hadn't known better. Liselle watched the king sadly, the ghost of a smile on her full lips, then her gaze found Tamriel's. She offered him a single nod before disappearing.

Protect each other, she whispered in Mercy's mind, and she could tell by the way Tamriel stiffened that he had heard her, too. *And trust no one.*

57

Mercy stood in the middle of Tamriel's bedroom, taking in the sight before her. In the fighting, several end tables and ottomans had been knocked aside, the candles splattering wax when they had fallen. Books lay splayed on the floor, their old and yellowed pages now soggy with blood, the ink smeared and illegible. The blankets on Tamriel's bed were crumpled in a pile on the floor, thrown off in haste.

And, of course, there were bodies.

Eight guards lay sprawled across the room, their blood pooling into one big puddle that stuck to the soles of Mercy's boots as she carefully stepped around them. She had come back to check for survivors, but that had only been wishful thinking. The Daughters were trained too well. Every body she had examined was undeniably, irrefutably dead.

Faye and Lylia were nowhere to be found. There wasn't a trace of them in the room. Even Aelis's body was gone.

Two guards were moving about Tamriel's room in silence, picking up their fallen comrades and carrying them out to be prepared for burial. Mercy pretended not to see their tears, and they pretended not to hate her for being associated with the monsters who had slaughtered their friends.

"Ready to go?" Calum asked. She turned to find him standing in the doorway, a rucksack slung over his shoulder beside his massive crossbow. He edged aside to let the guards carry out another body, then carefully picked his way over to where she stood.

She glared at him. "I don't know what you're doing here, but don't think for a second you're fooling me into believing you're actually grateful Tamriel is still alive. You'll stab him in the back the first chance you get."

Calum shook his head. "He's like a brother to me. This—all of this—was a mistake. I don't want him harmed for a crime his father committed. Ghyslain is the one who is responsible for my father's death. I'll find a way to avenge him without hurting Tamriel."

"But you were fine with having me executed?"

"You were never in any danger. The Daughters were already on their way, and I knew Tamriel wouldn't have you executed immediately. Somehow, you managed to put him under your spell. He cares about you a lot."

Mercy scoffed. In the aftermath of the Daughters' attack, Tamriel had barely looked at her. He hadn't said a word to her before leaving to have his wounds tended by Healer Tabris. The message was clear enough: he may have convinced his father not to have her executed, he may have allowed her to accompany him to the Islands, but she had lost his trust. As much as it hurt, she would gladly bear that pain a thousand times over if it meant he was alive.

"Look," he said. "I know you don't trust me, but I owe you for saving Tamriel's life. Should you choose to accompany him on this foolhardy journey of his, you have my aid. But," he murmured, his voice dropping to a whisper when the guards returned for another body, "if you breathe a word of what I've done to anyone, I will put a bolt through your skull."

Mercy glared at him, but she couldn't keep the memory of the crossbow bolt pulverizing the brick in the Keep's wall from surfacing in her mind. "You had a partner in all this," she responded. "Elise."

"Do not touch her."

She savored the fear that flashed across his face—the first genuine emotion she'd seen from him. Whatever was between them, it was more than a mere business arrangement. She ran her fingers lightly over the pommels of her daggers. "I believe we've come to an understanding, then."

"So it seems," he said through clenched teeth.

"It was her calligraphy, wasn't it? She forged the signature for you." As a serenna, Elise had access to countless documents bearing Ghyslain's signature—perfect for practicing forgeries. Mercy suddenly remembered the huge canvas in Elise's gallery, the painting of the strangely familiar boy, and realization struck her. It was Calum. Her father was one of Ghyslain's right-hand men, and she had practically grown up in the castle alongside Tamriel and Calum. They'd fallen in love and concocted this plot together. "You offered her a solution to her arranged marriage *and* a chance for the throne. How could she have resisted?"

A guard hesitantly approached, sensing the tension. "We've moved the last of the bodies, sir," he said to Calum.

"Thank you, Aksel. I'm...sorry for your loss."

"They gave their lives for the prince, and he is alive today because of it. That is the most any royal guard can hope for." The guard gave a shallow bow. "But we should return to the throne room—the prince is waiting. My men will clean all this up. The slaves are terrified enough already."

Calum nodded, then turned to Mercy, adjusting the bag on his shoulder. "Shall we?"

"You go. I have something I have to do first."

"Oh-ho, not so fast. You think I'm going to let you go anywhere alone?"

"You think *I'm* the untrustworthy one here?" Mercy crossed her arms. "Come with me, then."

He frowned.

"It'll only take a minute. I made a promise to someone."

"A promise! And you're going to follow through? Is this a first for you?" He widened his eyes, staggering back as though struck.

She punched his arm, much harder than strictly necessary.

"Damn. Fine. Let's go," he said, rubbing his bicep. "I'm trusting you not to pull a knife on me, though."

Mercy rolled her eyes and left the room. *If only I could.*

When Calum realized where she was leading him, he stopped and caught the back of her shirt. "No. Nope. Not going in there." He nodded toward the infirmary door, raising his brows. "Are you mad?"

"I didn't say you're going in. I am."

"Because you think you're immune?" he asked skeptically.

"I spent days in there and wasn't affected." Mercy batted her lashes at him. "Oh, Calum, are you worried about me? I didn't think you capable."

He released her, making a sound of disgust. "Just do what you have to do. Get in and get out."

Calum followed her down the hall, and when they reached the two guards standing in front of the infirmary, he ordered them to step aside.

They glanced at each other uneasily. "Sir, we can't let anyone inside. It's not safe, and it's against orders."

"This order comes directly from the king." When they

didn't move, Calum let out a long-suffering sigh. "What, do you wish me to fetch him? His Majesty doesn't have enough to deal with after the Assassins attacked and nearly killed his son—now he must be dragged down here to personally deliver orders to two imbecilic guards, does he?"

"No, of course not. Just be careful." One of the guards unlocked the door and held it open for Mercy. She stepped through, and he practically slammed it on her heels in his haste to close it.

"Alyss?" she whispered.

She crept forward, trying to peer through the shelves of ingredients and medical tomes, but the light on the other side of the room was so dim she couldn't make out anything more than the silhouettes of the four cots—three of which appeared empty. A slumbering form lay huddled on the one closest to the fire, as if Alyss had stumbled to it one night after working at the desk and hadn't had enough strength to make it to her bed. Judging by the stench, she'd been lying there a while.

"Alyss, are you awake?"

The Rivosi woman shifted, and Mercy fell to her knees at her bedside. On the nightstand was a candle burned down to about a half inch, the pool of hot wax surrounding it threatening to overtake the weak flame. Beside it was a pile of half-eaten food, most of it now rotten.

The healer's eyes fluttered open, hazy with fever. A sheen of perspiration sparkled across her brow, and the entire left side of her face was covered in boils, some crusted with scabs. A lump formed in Mercy's throat.

"I'm sorry I didn't make it here sooner. How long have you... Did Owl...?"

Alyss stared straight at her, but her gaze was distant, unseeing. She made no indication of having heard Mercy—or of being alive at all, save for the shallow, rasping sound coming from her throat. The neckline of her tunic was damp with sweat. Below it, the rash had grown and spread across her collarbone, red and angry.

Mercy stood and moved to the desk, shuffling around until she found another candle. She lit it and began searching for the poisonous mushrooms Alyss had shown her, digging through papers scribbled with possible cure recipes, each more illegible than the last. Scattered across the desk's surface were more glass vials than Mercy had ever seen. Each was filled with a strange mixture, and several of them had tipped over and leaked onto the wood. There, at the back, was the small wooden box Alyss had shown her. She opened it and—

Nothing.

It was empty.

Mercy set down the candle and shuffled through the papers on the desk again. She shoved the vials aside, and several fell to the floor and shattered, bleeding their foul-smelling contents. The dried mushrooms had been in a sheer bag inside the box. It had to be somewhere nearby.

Behind her, Alyss fell into a coughing fit so violent Mercy flinched. She rushed over to Alyss's side.

"I can't find them," she cried. "Where are they? Please, speak!"

The healer shut her eyes tightly, a few tears slipping out of the corners of her eyes. As Mercy watched, Alyss reached out a trembling hand and dropped a soft cloth bag into Mercy's cupped palms. The fabric was moist from her sweat, the mushrooms reduced to little more than dust from the strength of her grip.

She'd had been holding onto it in case Mercy hadn't kept her promise.

"Oh, Alyss..."

At that, Alyss looked up, her eyes meeting Mercy's. She nodded.

Do it.

After searching the shelves, she found a chipped mug and filled it with water, mixing in the mushrooms until the water turned a muddy gray. She returned to Alyss's side and lifted it to the healer's lips. Alyss drank eagerly, some of the water spilling out of the corner of her mouth and dribbling down her chin. When she'd finished, Alyss lay back on her pillow and sighed, a peaceful expression coming over her face.

Her eyelids drifted shut slowly, and her last breath came out one long sigh. If Mercy didn't know any better, she'd have thought Alyss was sleeping, as the healer had intended.

58

When Mercy and Calum returned to the great hall, they were surprised to find it empty, the tall doors open to the outside. As Calum jogged to the throne room in search of the prince, Mercy ran her hands over her new clothes, savoring the feeling of the clean fabric on her skin. They were nothing elaborate—just a simple tunic and riding pants retrieved for her by a slave—but the clothes she'd worn in the dungeon had been rank after wearing them for so long. A wool cloak tumbled from a clasp at her throat, and her daggers were strapped to her belt, freshly cleaned.

While Calum was distracted in the other room, Liselle appeared next to Mercy, causing her to jump. "Stop doing that!"

"*What?*" Calum called.

"Nothing!" She lowered her voice and glowered at Liselle. "I don't know what you are or how you're here, but I suggest you explain all of this right now."

"There's no time. The prince is waiting for you."

"Then I'd suggest you explain quickly."

She huffed. "Everything will become clear soon. You must go—"

"To the Islands. Yes, I know that part."

"You will understand when you arrive. Just know that I am here to help you. I have done nothing but aid and protect you since you arrived. If it is in my power, I will continue to do so."

"You stopped me from killing Tamriel on Solari," Mercy said, recalling the hand she'd felt grip her wrist that night. "And the contract? The paperweight, the drawer—"

"I couldn't let you kill the son of the man I love." Liselle shot a dark look toward the throne room. "I never liked Calum. Do not trust him."

"Believe me, I won't be making that mistake anytime soon." She hesitated, then asked, "Are you really my sister?"

Liselle gave her a knowing smile. She had only been a couple years older than Mercy when she was killed. Her features were regal and beautiful, soft and feminine where Mercy's were sharp, but there could be no doubt they were related.

She blinked, and Liselle vanished. Calum's footsteps tapped on the stone tile as he approached, frowning. "Were you speaking to someone?"

"Just telling a guard about how you tried to have Tamriel killed."

His expression darkened, and he gestured to the castle doors. "Very funny. Tamriel and the king are outside."

She followed him out of the castle and down the steps, where they found Tamriel, Ghyslain, and a handful of guards standing on the gravel carriageway. Someone had fetched horses from the royal stables, and the huge beasts had already been saddled and loaded with packs of provisions. Tamriel approached Mercy and Calum with quick, clipped steps, his stony expression masking whatever true emotions he was feeling about the journey that lay ahead. He had changed from his ruined sleep clothes to his shining silver armor, a sword sheathed at his hip. A midnight blue cloak trailed from the clasps at the shoulders.

"Are you ready?"

"I suppose," Mercy responded, hating the cool, flat way he was looking at her. "Did the guards find Faye and Lylia?"

"They've disappeared. No one's seen or heard a thing."

"And Elvira? She was going to look for her husband. He's a slave here in the castle."

He shook his head. "I don't know. They likely escaped in the chaos."

Calum swung up onto his horse and grinned down at them. "Well, let's be off, then. Your adventure awaits, Your Highness."

Tamriel turned to his father, who had been overseeing the journey's preparations with an unreadable expression. Without a word, the king crossed the carriageway and pulled his son into a tight hug. Tamriel grunted in pain, awkwardly patting his father's back, and shot Mercy a *Help me* look.

"You don't have to do this," Ghyslain whispered to Tamriel. He pulled away and gripped his son's shoulders. "Remain here. You know the cost this choice will demand of you. You don't have to pay it."

Annoyance flashed across the prince's face. "If that is what I must do to save my people from the plague, I will gladly pay it."

The king frowned, but nodded. "Master Oliver and the guards are waiting for you outside the eastern gate. Oliver has a map to our outpost on the Islands, where you will be able to rest and resupply."

"Thank you, Father."

Ghyslain trailed behind them as Mercy and Tamriel mounted their horses. Tamriel started to turn his stallion toward the castle gate, but the king caught his hand, stilling him. "You are an excellent prince, Tamriel. Our people deserved better than I for a king...and you deserved better than I for a father."

Tamriel wavered, clearly uncertain how to respond. After a moment, he straightened in his saddle, his armor gleaming in the predawn light. Mercy marveled at how regal and beautiful he looked, armored and armed, midnight blue cloak draped gracefully behind him. "Take care of our people, Father. Farewell."

With that, he turned and rode his horse through the castle gate, Mercy and Calum following close behind.

59
TAMRIEL

They met Master Oliver and the rest of the guards outside the city walls, and it didn't take long before they'd ridden halfway around Lake Myrella, the Howling Mountains steadily growing on the horizon. The mountains were enormous even from this distance, the yawning mouths of the caves dark with shadow. The few explorers who dared to enter the karsts did not often return; most perished after losing their way in the labyrinthine caves formed by the dissolution of the limestone.

That was where they were headed.

Master Oliver insisted that they would remain in the outermost caves only, and solely for rest. They would ride from sunup to sundown, then make camp in the caves on the way to the Cirisor Islands each night. That way, they would be able to avoid the myriad bridges and rivers that ran throughout the eastern sector of the country.

Even so, Tamriel would be lying if he claimed the thought of setting foot in the Howling Mountains didn't make him uneasy. Too many people had gone missing within them.

An entire race had gone missing within them.

He glanced back at Mercy and Calum, riding side by side near the rear of their small company. Calum was leaning close to her, a crooked smile on his lips as he spoke, but Mercy's gaze was trained straight ahead. They were far enough behind that Tamriel couldn't make out the individual words, but whatever Calum was saying seemed to touch a nerve. She turned and snapped something at him, hands curling into fists around her mare's reins. Instead of shrinking back, however, Calum merely grinned at her.

Tamriel watched Mercy, the now-familiar knot in his stomach returning at the sight of her. After everything that had happened the previous night, he hadn't had a chance to stop and consider what he'd learned about her and the Guild. She was an Assassin, and hadn't denied the fact that she had been sent to the capital to kill him. She had been planning to kill him the night he had asked her to meet him in the library...and yet, she hadn't done it. She'd had countless chances to kill him, and she had spared him. She had betrayed the Guild and killed a Daughter to save his life.

Don't you want to know my real name?
It's Mercy.
How fitting.

That night in the library... He could still feel her hands curled in the fabric of his tunic, her small, yet strong frame folded in his arms. He could still feel her fingertips running through his hair, her lips moving against his, a soft sigh of pleasure escaping her. She'd been lying to him for so long, but that night... That night had felt *real*. Despite everything, Tamriel longed to kiss her again, and that fact alone made him wish she had killed him.

Finally, she looked up and met his gaze, her expression softening. Tamriel turned away, focusing on the first rays of sunlight peeking out over the eastern horizon. The dawn was beautiful, the sky streaked with pinks and oranges and purples, stars still twinkling faintly over the city at their backs. The lake's waves lapped gently at the pebbled shore along which they rode, and in the distance, tall-masted ships with large sails floated on the water.

He pretended not to notice when Mercy spurred her horse forward, slowing when she reached his side. For a few minutes, she didn't say anything, just rode beside him. When he finally looked at her, she offered him a sad smile. The hood of her cloak was up, concealing all but a few strands of hair that had fallen forward to frame her lovely face.

"Happy birthday," she whispered, startling him. Was it really *today?* "When we return to the capital, you'll be able to claim your father's throne."

Tamriel nodded.

"You're going to make a wonderful king, Tamriel."

He nodded again, his gaze fixed on the dark silhouette of the mountains in the distance. She may have saved his life, but his guards were dead because of her. He did not owe her anything. There was nothing left to say between them.

Mercy seemed to know this already. She offered him a curt nod, the smile fading from her lips, and tugged on her horse's reins until it slowed enough for her to fall back to Calum's side. Tamriel tried to ignore the ache that shot through him at the sight of the pain in her eyes.

All she would ever be to him was an Assassin.

He didn't trust himself enough to let her become anything more.

ABOUT THE AUTHOR

Jacqueline Pawl spent her teen years trapped between the pages of books—exploring Hogwarts, journeying across countless fantasy worlds, and pulling heists with Kaz Brekker and his Crows.

But, because no dashing prince or handsome Fae has come to sweep her off to a strange new world (yet), she writes epic fantasy novels full of cutthroat courtiers, ruthless assassins, unforgettable plot twists, and epic battles. She is a Slytherin, and it shows in her books.

She currently resides in Scotland, where she can be found chasing will-o'-the-wisps, riding unicorns, and hunting haggis in the Highlands.

For news about upcoming books, visit her website at:
www.authorjpawl.com

- instagram.com/authorjpawl
- amazon.com/author/jacquelinepawl
- bookbub.com/profile/jacqueline-pawl
- goodreads.com/Jacqueline_Pawl

ALSO BY JACQUELINE PAWL

Defying Vesuvius

A BORN ASSASSIN SERIES

Helpless (prequel novella)

Nameless (prequel novella)

Merciless

Heartless

Ruthless

Fearless

Limitless

HEARTLESS

A Born Assassin, Book 2

Turn the page to read a sneak peek of *Heartless*, book two of the Born Assassin series.

I
MERCY

The ghosts tormented Mercy at night.

In the monotony of the constant riding, Calum and the soldiers found ways to entertain one another on the road to the Islands, filling the time trading stories of travel, brawls, and gossip. Mercy tried to lose herself in the melody of their voices and the beauty of the lush, vibrant landscape surrounding them. During the day, it worked. At night, however, when the only sounds were the chirping of crickets and the low rumbles of the men snoring, she couldn't escape the onslaught of memories that flooded back:

The screams of the castle guards as the Daughters slaughtered them. Tamriel's face, contorted in horror, as Mercy stood before him, the point of his sword quivering between them. The moment of hesitation when Mercy had been forced to choose—Tamriel or the Guild.

Then, the shocked gasp Aelis had made when Mercy plunged the dagger into her Sister's stomach.

For seventeen years, Mercy had devoted her life to the Guild. Every night, she had trained in the solitude of her room, lit only by the moonlight streaming through the crooked and cracked shutters. She had practiced longer, trained harder, than any of the other girls. When she knelt and spoke the sacred vows of the Guild, she had meant every word.

It had taken just one decision to shatter it.

Now, the Daughters would never stop hunting her.

Shaking off her thoughts, Mercy rose from her bedroll and tugged her heavy wool cloak around herself, then glanced at her slumbering companions. All but one slept; Tamriel leaned against a tree trunk in the sparse patch of woods where they'd camped for the night, his back to her as he kept watch. She stalked silently over the soft grass in the opposite direction, being careful not to alert him to her movement, and continued until the light from the dying embers of their campfire faded behind her.

After a few minutes, the hairs on her arms stood on end. Mercy looked to her right and frowned at the woman walking beside her. *This* ghost was a much more immediate problem.

"So now you return. *Days* after we leave the capital. Are you planning to explain all this anytime soon?" she asked Liselle, gesturing to the woods around them, the camp behind them, the wide dirt road barely visible through the trees. They had been riding and camping along this road for two days, counting down the hours to their arrival at the city of Cyrna. "Why are you here? What do you want from me? Why did you call me your *sister?*"

"Because that's who you are. You were only a few days old when the nobles killed me, but I still remember you. I recognized you the first time I saw you in the castle." Liselle smiled, but the gesture was fleeting. Her gaze dropped to her smoke-colored feet. "As for why I'm here...I have no idea. Something pulled me from the Beyond about a month ago, I think—it's hard to keep track of time when one isn't affected by it." Her brows furrowed in thought. "The priestesses in the infirmary could sense my presence, but there was something else there, too. Something kept pushing me back whenever I tried to help you. It took all of my energy to appear to you the night you and Tamriel fled. I hadn't had the strength to manifest until now."

"So you had been wandering aimlessly around the castle until you recognized me? And now you're telling me—after whispering to me for weeks, ruining my contract, and sending us on a wild goose chase for a cure that may not exist—that you're not sure why?"

Liselle huffed in frustration. "When I saw you in the castle, I knew you were my baby sister. After I followed you and realized what had happened to you after my death—that you had been sent to live in that terrible Keep—I figured the Creator had brought me back to protect you. That's what I've been trying to do all this time, so you wouldn't end up like our siblings—"

"Siblings?" Mercy stopped midstep. "What are you talking about?"

Surprise flashed across Liselle's face. "The Guild didn't tell you anything about our family?"

Mercy shot her a look. "What do you think?"

"Our parents had five children: me, Ino, Cassia, Matthias, and you. I was killed, you were given to the Guild, and...I don't know what happened to the others. I don't even know if they're still alive."

"Oh," was all Mercy could say. After being alone for so many years, the thought of having siblings—*living* ones—was too much to consider. She shook her head. *Not important.* "Liselle, listen. You know the truth about the contract on Tamriel, don't you? How it was Calum who—"

"Yes, I know."

"He hasn't seen you, has he?"

"No, I've been careful. The only people who know I'm here are you and the prince."

"Good. You must promise me you will not say a word about the contract to Tamriel. Leave that to me."

"But—"

"No. I don't care that Calum has supposedly changed his mind about the contract. I don't trust him, and I value Tamriel's safety too much to put him at risk. I don't know what Calum will do if Tamriel learns the truth, but he certainly won't allow word of his treachery to make it back to Sandori."

"The prince must be told at some point. You can't protect him forever."

"I know. Calum will pay for what he has done, but not until we've returned to the castle with the cure. In the meantime, I'll keep an eye on him."

Somewhere in the distance, a twig snapped. Liselle gasped and disappeared. Mercy whirled around, raising her fists. Master Oliver had confiscated her daggers the second they left Sandori, and she hadn't yet become accustomed to the feeling of vulnerability that accompanied being unarmed. Even so, knowing she was more dangerous with her fists than most people were with a blade bolstered her confidence.

Tamriel stepped into the clearing, scowling. Mercy lowered her fists, but her body remained tense as the prince strode up to her, anger and mistrust contorting his handsome face.

"What did she tell you?"

"Who?"

He rolled his eyes. "Don't play dumb. Liselle. What did she say?"

"Nothing important."

Tamriel sighed in exasperation. They had hardly spoken since leaving the castle, exchanging nothing more than snapped orders and the occasional clipped conversation. She could feel Tamriel drawing further from her each day. Whenever he looked at her, the betrayal in his eyes burned like a brand.

"You shouldn't sneak away from camp."

"I wasn't *sneaking*—"

"That's *exactly* what you were doing."

Mercy crossed her arms. "I wasn't running away. You think I'd leave without my daggers? They're worth more than anything I've ever owned. I *earned* them. Besides, *you* shouldn't have left your watch."

"I woke Calum. He's standing guard until I return."

"I... Fine."

Mercy shuffled her feet, longing to reach out to him, as an uneasy silence settled over them. Tamriel had been sleeping even worse than she had, now that the shock of everything that had happened in Sandori had worn off. It killed her every time she lay awake on her bedroll, listening to him toss and turn. Much to Master Oliver's frustration, Tamriel insisted on taking more nighttime watches than any of the guards—a vain attempt to stave off the nightmares of the Daughters' brutal attack. Oliver's concerned looks and whispered advice had met blind eyes and deaf ears thus far, but Tamriel wouldn't be able to ward off sleep forever.

"Are you okay?" she finally murmured, aching to speak to him with the ease she had once enjoyed.

He barked a harsh, humorless laugh. "Am I okay? Are you really asking me that? You betrayed my trust, played me for a fool, and now the woman who destroyed my family—" A pebble flew out of the woods and hit Tamriel in the back of the head. He spun around, rubbing the place where the stone had struck, and glared into the trees. "Fine. *Liselle*, who has been *dead* for eighteen years, has somehow returned from the Beyond and is now following us. That's after a group of Assassins broke into my bedchambers and slaughtered my guards. That's perfectly normal. Why could I possibly be upset?"

When he turned back, Mercy scowled at him, her temper flaring. How *dare* he speak to her this way, after all she had given up for him? "Liselle is helping us find the cure for the plague *and* she saved our lives from Lylia and Faye. I killed a Daughter—I risked my life to protect you—and now the Guild won't rest until I'm dead. I turned my back on everyone I know for you."

His eyes narrowed. "You attacked me in my mother's house."

"No, that was someone else, I swear. Please, Tamriel, you must believe me—"

"After you lied to me and everyone else? No, I don't have to believe a single word out of your mouth. Everything you did was to get close to me—it was all a part of the plan to kill me, wasn't it? It was all a ruse, and that night we kissed in the library meant *nothing*." He stopped and took a deep breath, hurt flashing across his face. His hands clenched into fists. "I always knew you were different from the court. I'm ashamed it took me so long to realize just *how* different."

He stormed back toward camp, but Mercy's voice halted him at the edge of the clearing.

"You're right," she said, and she was filled with self-loathing when she heard the tremble in her voice. Damn him for having this effect on her. Damn him for making her weak. "I am different. Would you like to know why?

"My father gave me to the Guild when I was one week old. He bartered my life away—like it was worth no more than *a sack of grain*—so he and my mother could live. Do you have any idea what it's like to grow up in the Guild? When I was five, I was handed a dagger and told to attack the other apprentices. When I was nine, my tutor cut a gash into my arm and forced me to sew myself up. When I was eleven, I sat on the back of a Daughter's horse as she ran down a woman who was trying to escape to the man she loved. The Guild was my entire life. I had never even left the Forest of Flames until I went to the capital," Mercy said. She lifted her chin and forced her voice to steady. "So you will believe me when I tell you that until a week ago, I would have done anything to prove my devotion to the Guild, but I threw it all away for you. The Daughters have contacts all around the world and no matter where I go, they won't stop hunting me until I'm dead."

Tamriel flinched and slowly turned to her, his face slack with shock. For one foolish, desperate moment, Mercy allowed herself to hope that he would forgive her.

Then his expression hardened. "While I am grateful for your sacrifice, that choice was yours to make. Pilar believed you will play a part in discovering the cure, so you have my protection while we are together...but once this plague is defeated, I want you gone. I don't care where you go, so long as you never show your face in my city again."

He squared his shoulders and marched back to camp, leaving Mercy alone and miserable. When she finally summoned her courage and returned to camp, she spotted Calum sitting at the base of a tree, peering out into the woods. He acknowledged her with a nod and a wink, the dying fire reflecting off the blade of the dagger twirling between his fingers. Tamriel lay on his bedroll on the opposite side of the camp, his back to her.

Despite the exhaustion tugging at her, when Mercy stretched out on her cloak and closed her eyes, sleep eluded her for hours.

"Trouble in paradise, princess?"

Calum grinned at Mercy from atop his black stallion. His shirt was unbuttoned, billowing gently in the wind that provided only momentary relief from the heat. The farther northeast they traveled, the more summer sunk its claws into the land. Fields of long grass swayed as far as Mercy could see, patches of vibrant wildflowers and small copses of trees occasionally interrupting the verdure of the plains. Despite the breeze, the air was humid and sticky.

The people tending the fields and fishing the narrow channels paused in their work when the prince and his company rode past, staring with a mix of curiosity and wariness at the strangers surrounding His Highness. It wasn't often they saw their prince with their own eyes, Mercy knew. She doubted they had ever expected to see him at all, let alone in the company of nine guards, one elf, and one unarmored human.

Mercy dragged her sleeve across the sweat beading on her brow and scowled at Calum. She lowered her voice so the guards wouldn't hear as she hissed, "Don't call me that. And stop grinning, you idiot. In case you don't recall, you're the reason we're in this mess with the Guild."

He guided his horse closer and leaned over so far she was amazed he didn't fall out of his saddle. "Really? Because I seem to recall a certain Daughter failing to complete her contract." He straightened and shot her another infuriating grin. "*Idiot.* Is that any way to speak to family?"

Mercy snorted. Three weeks ago, she'd had no one. Now, she had a pain-in-the-ass half-brother and the ghost of a sister who'd been murdered eighteen years ago. It wasn't exactly the family reunion for which she had once longed.

She glanced at the front of the group, where Tamriel rode tall and proud beside Master Oliver. A week ago, she had tasted his lips, had smiled and laughed with him. Later, she had counted every agonizing minute she had endured in the pitch-black castle dungeon, not knowing whether he had survived the attack for which Calum and Elise had framed her.

"Brave words from a man who paid to have his cousin murdered," she murmured. Satisfaction filled her when he flinched.

"I couldn't go through with it. I thank the Creator every day that you stopped the Daughters before they could kill him. If you hadn't gone back, he'd be dead. I know you don't trust me, but I swear I will do everything in my power to protect Tamriel. I will give my life for him, if necessary."

"What about getting revenge for your father?"

Calum hesitated, confirming her suspicions. He still wanted to avenge his father's death.

"My father has been dead for a long time," he said. "Nothing I do will change that."

Liar. Instead, she said, "I'm glad you see it that way, because if you ever lay a hand on Tamriel again, I'll rip off your arm and beat you to death with it."

Calum laughed. "I'm beginning to suspect one of your favorite pastimes is thinking up colorful ways to kill me."

"I've started a list. That was only the fifth most gruesome death I imagined for you."

"Fifth? Hm. I think I could come up with a few that would knock it out of the top ten."

Mercy rolled her eyes and spurred her mare; not wishing their conversation to be overheard, they had begun to fall behind. Calum's easygoing charm had fooled her before, and she wouldn't allow it to happen again. Hunger for revenge didn't fade to remorse in a week. Vengeance didn't give way to devotion.

But you can so easily turn your back on the people who raised you? a doubting voice in her head asked. *Where is your loyalty to the Guild?*

Mercy's gaze drifted to the prince once again. He had traded his finery for the light clothing favored by the people of the fishing sector, and the bandages wrapped around his torso were visible through his linen shirt. The memory of the bloodstained tunic he'd been wearing the night of the Daughters' attack flashed through Mercy's mind. She had seen far too much of his blood spilled. Tamriel pretended that the wound was nothing, but she could tell by the careful way he moved that it still caused him pain. Calum had carved a deep, curving gash across his back, and although the damaged muscles would heal with time, Tamriel would bear the scar for the rest of his life.

"You know I don't approve of this," Calum called, gesturing between her and Tamriel. "You and him. But I don't suppose you and Tam could quit arguing for the sake of making this journey more enjoyable for the rest of us. At least until we return to Sandori. After that, rip each other to shreds or rip each other's clothes off, I couldn't care less."

"I have told him what truth I can afford, and the prince has made his opinion of me abundantly clear."

Calum raised a brow. "You're not giving up, though."

"Of course not."

He scoffed. "You two are like a damn tragedy. He has never looked at anyone the way he looks at you."

"Calum?"

"What?"

She fixed him with a flat look. "Shut the hell up."

Heartless will be out on October 22nd, 2021. To receive new release alerts, follow Jacqueline Pawl on Amazon or join her newsletter at www.authorjpawl.com